SHE WHO WOULD BE KING

SHE WHO WOULD BE KING

KIM PRITEKEL

SAPPHIRE BOOKS

SALINAS, CALIFORNIA

by Kim Pritekel

Stand Alone

1049 Club

After Shadow

Blinded

Connection

Damaged

The Plan

The Gift

Shadow Box

She Who Would be King

Wild

Zero

Dance with Me Series

Curtain Call

Swann Song

Encore Performace

The Traveler Series

The Traveler - The Hunted

The Traveler - The Hunter

The Wynter Series

Finding Faith

Justice Won

by Kim Pritekel con't

The Wynter Series
Taking Liberty
Keeping Hope

Dedication

To She.

Note to reader:

Cateline's name is pronounced: cat-ay-lene. It's the
French version of the name, Catherine.

Chapter One

France, 1365

Cateline was quiet as she and her father roamed around the gardens she had personally planted and taken care of over the last fifteen years. It had begun with her mother teaching her, showing her the beauty in plants, herbs, and the wonder of what her mother had called "shapable nature."

They walked the paths in silence around the *Motte Baussay*, the small castle bestowed upon her father, the Baron Tumas Aubert, twenty years ago by King Philip VI. Though the property in Les Trois-Moutiers, two hundred or so miles from Paris, had been a hotly contested area during the Edwardian War, that had finally cooled. It had been a scary time for the Auberts and for many in the area.

The twenty-one-year-old's mind raced at the news she was just given. Suddenly, the flowers lost their color, lost their fragrance, the sun stopped shining, and the gentle breeze against her face felt more like a chilled slap.

"Is this a punishment for Sophie and I?" she asked softly, reaching up to brush a few curly strands of auburn hair out of her face.

"No, of course not," her father insisted. "Young girls like you and your friend have each other for your silly emotional needs while you're still so young. But," he added, directing her toward the path back to the castle with a little nudge to her arm. "When you become a woman, as you have, that's when you get a husband that can guide you and lead you from the frivolous pursuits. Give you a purpose in taking care of his needs and happiness. His children."

Cateline chewed on her bottom lip for a moment, not liking what he had to say at all. "But, what about *my* happiness, Papa?"

He looked at her, heavy eyebrows drawn. "What of it?"

She looked down at her hands, which fidgeted against the front bib of the tunic she wore over her underdress. "Nothing, Papa," she murmured.

He let out a heavy sigh, sounding annoyed as if he knew he'd hurt his daughter with such a blunt assessment. "Listen, Daughter," he explained. "The mistake I made with you is I allowed you to learn to read and write." He clasped his hands behind his back as they continued. "You think too much of yourself, Cateline. Perhaps a husband to bring you down to your proper place isn't a bad thing."

The comment stung, as many a night she and her father had sat by the fire as she read to him, her father not very proficient at it. They both enjoyed Greek and Norse mythology as well as Greek tragedies, particularly *Oedipus*.

"Who is he?" she finally asked, not entirely sure why. Did it matter?

"You met him once." Her father opened a wrought iron gate for them to step through into a small stone courtyard. "He is Prince Fergus, son of King Carthac of Sursha."

She looked at him with wide eyes. "The Gaels?" she asked. "They're...they're *barbarians!*"

"They are not," he exclaimed loudly, voice firmed. "They are a proud and noble people, warriors. If it weren't for their help, our king wouldn't have been able to control the *routiers*, put them back in the bottle. You wish to speak of barbarians, those militia men are such."

She felt sick to her stomach at this news. How could it be so?

"You look quite displeased," he said, sitting back on a stone bench, where she joined him.

She took several deep breaths so as not to get sick in her father's lap. "We have nothing in common with those people, Papa," she whispered, true fear gripping her heart. "What have I done so wrong for you to do this?"

The baron pushed up from the bench and began to pace, looking irritated at her voiced concerns. "You must do this for your family, Cateline," he said, heavy brows drawn as he looked down at her. "An alliance with the Gaels is good for our standing, Daughter. Our survival."

"I don't even speak their language," she murmured, feeling close to tears but knew she dare not cry in front of her father. He'd get angrier at her.

"You will learn," her barked, legendary temper building. "This is my decision, Cateline. Preparations begin tomorrow." He reached down and gripped her chin between his fingers, forcing her to look up at him. "You will be ready for your husband." With that, he stormed off, his booted steps echoing in the stone space.

Left alone, Cateline buried her face in her

hands, taking a deep breath before she let it out, slow and shaky. Dropping her hands back to her lap, she blinked back her first tear.

⁂

Later that night, the young noblewoman lay in her bed in her unique octagon-shaped room. Not a large room, but a place she'd spent many hours dreaming, wondering what her future would hold for her. Now she knew. She was terrified. And confused.

For her two older sisters, young hopefuls had paraded through the castle, courting their father more than the young sisters. Eventually the baron had chosen one for each sister. Sadly, one sister was lost three years before during childbirth, and the other, the one Cateline had been closest to, hadn't been heard from in more than a year, busy with her life in Spain. They sent letters, but it took many months for them to arrive.

Why had Cateline not been given many to look at, ponder, speak to her father about? She stared up at the ceiling, a tear slipping from her left eye. She let it slide down into her ear, a shiver passing through her at the feel. Was she worth so little? Or, she thought, perhaps she was given to the highest bidder, like a horse or a sow?

How badly must her father hate her to send her off with a bunch of butchers? The Surshans weren't any better than the stories of the raiders and looters up north, famous for their longboats and brutality that Cateline had read about.

Would she be chained in a room? She'd heard such horror stories. She turned from her back to her side, bringing her legs up beneath the covers, her thighs nearly touching her chest, feeling incredibly vulnerable. The tears continued to roll silently down her cheeks until she fell asleep.

⁂

The springtime was a flurry of activity and excitement—for some—as the castle and grounds were readied for the upcoming nuptials. They would be taking place in the small cathedral on the grounds of the estate.

Cateline stood still in her bedroom, her lady-in-waiting Marie working feverishly to measure her body just perfectly for her wedding dress. She stood there feeling like Jesus on the cross with her arms held out and body stiff, bare feet together.

She felt hands on her hips and warmth behind her. She knew it was Sophie, the daughter of the castle's head seamstress and special friend to Cateline. She and her mother had arrived a few months after Cateline's first sister had been married off, and Sophie had been a wonderful distraction from the sadness.

At the time, the young noblewoman had been only twelve years old, and the addition of the fourteen-year-old had been a gift. The two had bonded and Cateline, against what she knew would be her father's wishes, had taught the young servant how to read and write. After that, they'd begun passing notes, making each other giggle, and eventually, making each other burn as feelings began to change and grow in a more confusing direction.

A light squeeze to her hip let her know that Sophie wanted to talk to her. They'd not spoken in nearly two months, since the announcement of the upcoming marriage. There had been no time, as Sophie and the rest of the servants had been breaking their backs to get everything perfect one more time as the last of the three Aubert daughters were married off.

"Okay, I think this will work," Marie said, taking a step back, looking Cateline up and down.

Cateline met the older woman's gaze. A widow and nearly thirty years older than her charge, Marie had been with Cateline since the age of six and, to Cateline's relief, would be going with her on her new journey. She was a trusted member of Cateline's tiny inner circle, which effectively amounted to the seamstress, her still-living sister, her tutor, who had opened up entire worlds for her through books, and Sophie.

She could see in the brown depths of Marie's eyes that she, too, was worried about the young noblewoman, which not only helped to comfort Cateline, knowing she wasn't alone in this, but also concerned her.

"Will it look okay?" she asked softly, unsure.

"It will," Marie said with a nod. She reached out and touched the long strands of Cateline's long, curly auburn hair. "We'll put this up in a twist," she said, the wheels in her head already turning as Cateline knew they would. She was already envisioning the updo she'd create for Cateline's "mane of hair," as the older woman called it.

"We can put flowers in it," Sophie added quietly.

Marie nodded. "Agreed. Would be a nice touch."

Cateline stood there silently, listening as, yet again, others discussed her future. There was no need to add her thoughts or opinions as she knew Marie would get irritated with her. A lifelong servant, she had little control or say in her own life, so control over the personal aspect of Cateline's life was *her* place.

The two women finished up with the final measurements for the dress that had already been started, and began to clean up their mess of material, needles, pins, lucets, and other such tools of the trade. Before Sophie slipped out of the room, she tucked a note into Cateline's hand.

⁂

It was dangerous, and she knew it, but she had little time before she would leave for her new life. The moon was full and it was a warm summer night. She made her way to the small pond where she often stopped to let her horse drink when out on a ride. She saw the silhouetted figure sitting on a large rock, dipping her fingers into the moon-reflecting pool.

"Hello, Sophie," she said, knowing they were far enough away from the manor to not be heard, though they'd still need to keep it down to not draw any unwanted attention from anyone who might be in the woods.

The slightly older young woman glanced up at her, though her lovely face was still in shadow. "Hello. Thanks for coming."

"Of course." Cateline lowered herself to sit on a large rock close to Sophie's. She rested her hands in her lap, looking out over the gently rippling water, reaching up to brush back the ever-present tendril of auburn hair that seemed to always escape its bonds.

"When are they coming?" Sophie asked.

"The Gaels?" Cateline asked, unable to keep the bitterness out of her tone.

"Yes. Your husband." Sophie lowered her chin so it rested on her pulled-up knees. "I can't believe you're leaving." She was quiet for a long moment before saying, "You know, we could run away together. Just the two of us."

Cateline glanced over at her, eyes adjusting enough in the dimness to make out the two sad-looking green eyes staring back at her. She was surprised at the suggestion and at the pain she heard in the other woman's voice. She did not love Sophie; that much she knew. But, she did cherish her friendship, the ability to be close to her emotionally, which was not a privilege she possessed with anyone else, including her father.

"It's not that simple, Sophie," she said.

"Because of your father?" the young servant asked.

"Yes," Cateline said with a heavy sigh. "Because of him and other things. Obligations."

Sophie said nothing for a long time, simply stared out over the water. "I had a dream the other night," she began softly. "You and I were lying in your bed, naked."

A little nervous thrill raced through Cateline at the imagery that brought to mind. The two young women had never been naked together, had done nothing more but share that one, very small and very brief kiss when they were caught by her father.

"What were we doing?" Cateline asked, her voice a bit breathless from surprise.

"We were kissing," Sophie said. "And..." She turned away for a moment before saying, "And, you were letting me touch your breasts."

A small gasp left Cateline's mouth, her hand fluttering up to the very body part in question. She rested her palm on her upper chest, which was heaving slightly with her increased breathing.

"Cateline," Sophie whispered, turning on the rock so she was facing the young noblewoman.

"Yes?" Cateline whispered back, hardly able to catch her breath, her heart pounding so hard.

Sophie's fingers seemed hesitant as they touched Cateline's jaw. "I want to do those things," she said. "I've wanted to for so long, but now we're just about out of time."

Cateline nodded, knowing the wedding party was due on the morrow. She could feel the warm breath of the woman she sat so close to, brushing her face. She wanted it too. In that moment, she wanted to feel free to be who she was, even though she wasn't entirely certain who that was. The first touch of Sophie's lips against her own was magical, soft. It made her want to go back for a second feel, which Sophie obliged her on. The servant's lips were even softer the second time, their kiss lingering for a long moment.

Sophie's hand moved from Cateline's face to the back of her head, holding the younger woman still as she deepened the kiss. Cateline was confused and startled when she felt the brief touch of Sophie's tongue against her own.

"Shh," Sophie said, caressing Cateline's cheek. "It's okay."

The young bride-to-be relaxed and allowed the intimate touch, though hesitant, returning the action. When the kiss deepened fully, Cateline sighed softly as it felt wonderful. She'd never felt such a connection to another human before, let alone a woman.

A small whimper managed to escape Cateline's mouth as Sophie's hand gently cupped one of her breasts over her dress. There was a lot of material between that hand and the fullness of her breast, but the pressure was there, the shock of being touched there. Her body was warming up in her nether regions in a way that nothing she'd ever felt from Sophie's notes could compare to.

Sophie pulled away, her breathing as heavy as Cateline's. "Can we go back to the castle?" she asked. "Marie would never know," she added, noting the lady-in-waiting had a small bedchamber just off Cateline's.

She had no idea what Sophie was asking of her or what she wanted to do, but she knew she wanted more of what they'd already done. Nodding, she got to her feet and reached for Sophie's hand, pulling her to her feet. Hand in hand, the two young women ran across the open field toward the dark, looming castle.

Suddenly, a loud rumble passed through the night, the ground beginning to shake under their feet. Eyes wide, Cateline tugged Sophie with her to hide behind a stand of trees. Huddled together, they watched.

The mist settled over the hillside, turned silver by the moonlight above. The rumble grew louder, making Cateline's bones vibrate. Through the silvery fog appeared the silhouettes of one, two, five, fifteen, thirty men on horseback. One of the men flew the flag of Sursha.

"I think your husband has arrived," Sophie whispered.

Chapter Two

The morning brought loud, boorish voices to the great hall. Cateline, who had managed to sneak back to her room unseen, made her way to the small antechamber that butted up to the large banquet room. The small room was used to temporarily house the entertainment for a large gathering, be it minstrel or dancer or poet, but this morning it simply housed a fretting bride-to-be.

As a child she'd discovered the room and its peephole, used by the performers to watch and wait for their cue to enter and entertain. As a precocious young girl who was supposed to be tucked in bed, Cateline had watched her father's raucous parties and soirees that used to leave her often blushing and confused.

Now, she watched the gathering of the men who had arrived in the middle of the night. She wasn't allowed to just waltz in there and introduce herself, as there were official rules and ways of introductions to be made. In other words, formal introductions would be made at the altar. Even still, she felt she had a right to at least get an idea of what she was in for.

There were about twenty seated around the table eating, servants buzzing around the long table to make sure everyone had what he needed. She realized that the additional men they'd seen last night riding with the group must have been her father's own personal guard dispatched to ensure their safe arrival.

Her father sat in his place at the head of the table, and the man to his left she vaguely recognized, meeting him a year or so before. His name was Fergus, Prince of Sursha and eldest son of King Carthac, whom she did not see. Fergus looked older than she was by several years, his hair long, like all of the men there, though his was pulled back from a pale face by braids. His hair was dark, as were his eyes. He wore his beard thick and heavy, nearly covering his mouth when he wasn't speaking or laughing.

He was dressed in what she imagined was considered finery for his people, though it was nothing even close to the finery her father would wear to such an event, or what he was currently wearing. The baron wore materials and fabrics the commoners could never even fathom draped upon their bodies, let alone run their fingers across: rich silks and velvets. The clothing of the average commoner was made of flax or hemp, inexpensive and easy to obtain.

Prince Fergus was dressed better than any other of the Gaels, but even still, he was dressed primarily in leather trousers and not the hose the men of her country wore. The gathered group did wear tunics, like the Frenchmen did, and they were long, belted with sword belts at the hips.

Of the twenty in the party, fourteen of them were dressed similarly, clearly the Elite Guard unit sent to protect the prince and ultimately his wife upon the return trip to Sursha. They all had long hair to varying degrees, though many of them had their sides shaved and only a long braid flowing down the back of their head. They were all clean shaven, surprisingly, as the six in the party of royals all wore beards.

Ironically, the royals looked slovenly and unkempt while the Elite Guard were tidy and well put together. There was one of that group that caught Cateline's eyes. He was sitting at the opposite end of the table from the prince. He wasn't speaking to anyone, and as he ate, he was clearly observing everyone and everything.

She thought he might be the head of the Guard, as the shirtsleeves protruding from beneath the otherwise uniform tunic were a rich blue color, singling him out. His hair, a very dark brown, was long, past his shoulders with warrior braids trailing down along either side of his deeply tanned face. He had a proud jaw, extremely handsome, so much so that he could almost be called beautiful.

It wasn't the studded leather straps that criss crossed over his chest to hold the double blades whose grips and pummels were visible over his shoulders that made him stand out, Cateline thought. It was his eyes. From such a distance it was hard to tell their color, but the intensity of their gaze was very clear.

The leader took in everything, and Cateline was just positive he was looking directly into her soul as his visual sweep crossed path with her. Gasping softly, she backed away from the peephole. She knew there was no way he could know she was there, but she felt the strike of his observation all the same.

Deciding she'd seen enough, she turned and hurried from the chamber.

※ ※ ※ ※

Feeling like the eyes of the country were on her, which wasn't terribly far from the truth, Cateline made her way down the aisle of the cathedral with her father at her side. She'd been told she looked beautiful, but she didn't feel beautiful. She didn't feel much of anything. Even as she looked through the sheerness of the veil covering her hair and face, it was almost as though she were looking outside of herself. She felt numb, cold, simply going through the motions.

Once they reached the man she was essentially being sold to, she said what she was supposed to say, her Latin perfect. She did what she was supposed to do. She always did.

Finally, everything was done, the pronouncement made, and she belonged to Prince Fergus of Sursha. Life as she knew it was now officially, legally over. As though walking through a bad dream that never ended, the ceremony came to a close and she was ushered to a reception in the great hall for the royalty and nobility and finally got to meet her husband.

Her father's firm hand on her back, she was led over to where Prince Fergus stood with some of his men, including the one with the intense eyes. Up close, Cateline got a better look at her husband. He looked to be about ten years her senior. He was taller than her father but a larger man, clearly well fed in Sursha.

His eyes were dark, and as he looked her over, they made her feel very uncomfortable. Her father cleared his throat. "Good evening, gentlemen," he said. "We're overjoyed that you're here."

Fergus stared at Tumas, blinking before looking to the man standing next to him, who was a bit shorter than the prince himself. He once again had his double blades strapped to his back. It was a bit intimidating, Cateline thought, but somehow comforting.

The man looked to the groom who stood to his right, the two sharing a look before he turned back to Tumas and his daughter. "We are glad to be here for such a joyous day," he said, his French perfect. Fergus said something in their native tongue of Gaelic then looked at the other man as though waiting for him to translate. "His Highness Prince Fergus is humbled by your hand in marriage and—" He glanced over at the prince as he spoke again. The look the French-speaking man gave him was one of surprise before he turned back to Cateline and her father. "And," he said, looking at the bride. "He says you look beautiful."

Cateline wasn't sure what to think as the warrior before her looked distinctly uncomfortable, He brought his hands up to grip the leather belts across his chest which secured his blades. The leather bracers he wore extended from just above his wrists to nearly his elbows. Cateline had the random question sift through her brain of just how many blows had those bracers stopped from landing their mark.

"You are very kind," the baron said. "Isn't he, Daughter?" He turned to her, a slight hardening of his voice letting her know she needed to respond.

"Yes," she said, bowing her head a bit in appreciation of the compliment. "You are kind, sir." Her gaze flicked to the other man. "And you are?" she asked, surprising herself. From the sharp pinch to her lower back, she gathered her father didn't approve.

"I am Fallon, milady," the man said, giving her a deep bow of respect. "I am in charge of His Highness's personal guard, here to assure the safe return to Sursha."

She met his gaze and realized that the warrior had the most unusual color of eyes she'd ever encountered. They were a deep violet. She'd never seen anything like it. There was so much depth to those eyes, intelligence and yet, somehow kindness. No doubt this Fallon had seen many horrible things in his life, if the long scar on his face was any indication. It ran through his right eyebrow, a ghost line across his eye and continuing under the eye a short way.

"Thank you," she said softly.

He nodded. "My pleasure, milady."

Later that night, Cateline sat in one of the two chairs before the fire that had been started in the large fireplace in her bedroom. The rain was coming down in torrents outside. They were supposed to have left a week before, but the weather had been too severe to head out. The journey back to Sursha would be over land before they would reach the ship and finally set sail.

She heard the soft scraping against the wall outside her door. She glanced over at the closed door to her bedchamber. She knew he was out there, standing guard, just like he did every night. Well, after his rounds, of course. Tonight, hearing the rumble of the thunder beyond the secure walls of the castle, she felt bad.

Not entirely sure why, she pushed up from the chair and walked over to the door, the robe she wore over her sleeping gown flowing out behind her. She was about to pull open the heavy wooden door when she heard a thunderous sneeze in the hallway beyond.

Quickly pulling open the door, as expected, she saw Fallon standing dutifully outside. His long, dark hair hung in wet strands in his face as he was blowing his nose with a kerchief. She immediately felt guilty.

"Come, please," she said, stepping back and opening the door wider in invitation. "Dry by the fire."

Those mysterious purple eyes looked up at her through the long hair in his face. Sniffling, he shook his head, lowering the kerchief and bringing up a hand to brush the hair back from his face. "No, milady," he said. "Thank you."

"Oh, come, now," she said, taking another stop back into the room. "It's because of me that you're out there in this awful weather. What better way to protect me than to sit two feet from me?" she added with a small smile.

He stared at her for a long moment before a small smile graced full lips. "Valid point, milady."

Cateline hurried over to her armoire and grabbed some loose fabric as Fallon entered the room, the soft closing of the door behind him barely heard. She closed the door to the wardrobe and walked over to the warrior standing near the fire. "Here," she said, handing him the material. "Dry off."

"Aye," he said, taking it from her. "Thank you, milady."

Cateline retook her seat, watching as the strange man wiped down his face and hair. She noticed yet again the double blades he always carried. "Why two?" she asked, pointing at the short swords.

He met her gaze. "Does it bother you, milady?" he asked. "I can step out—"

"No, not at all. Just curious. Most warriors, knights, and the like I see carry one at their hip. A longsword. Why two short ones?"

"Well," he said, lightly placing the cloth on the chair seat before reaching behind him and gently pulling one of the blades free from its scabbard. "When I was younger, a long sword was a bit too much for me to handle, so I began learning with a short sword," he explained. "I was quick, much faster than my peers, so even as I grew bigger and stronger, my preference remained with this." He pumped the blade in the air a bit for emphasis.

"How does it work?" she asked, fascinated.

Fallon reached behind him and unsheathed the second blade. Looking around him, he moved away from the chairs and anything nearby. With a flourish of twirls and movements, he used one blade to block an incoming strike while whipping around to slice his imaginary opponent at the midsection, effectively gutting them.

Eyes wide, Cateline gasped at the grace yet ferocity of the tactical move. "My goodness!" Hand to her heart, she watched as both blades sheathed. "That is something to watch, Sir Fallon."

He met her gaze as he strategically placed the material upon the seat of the chair before sitting down, his tunic and leather trousers still damp from the rain. "Just Fallon, milady," he corrected softly.

"Fallon," Cateline said with a nod of understanding. She realized that she found his presence and voice rather comforting. His energy was calm like a still lake, though anyone who understood water knew that at any moment, it could be deadly. His voice was low, not deep like Fergus or some of the other men, but still low, and soothing. "Very impressive, as is your grasp of the French language. Lucky for Prince Fergus you could speak for him."

The warrior looked away and into the fire before he finally cleared his throat. "I've always had a keen interest in languages and have studied them since I was a child."

"Can you teach me Gaelic?" she asked. "I have a feeling I'll need it."

He gave her a small smile and nod. "Of course, milady."

Cateline nodded, pleased. She studied the dancing flames for a long moment before asking what was truly on her mind. "Why are you guarding me in my father's home?" She gave him a rueful smile. "Have I become a prisoner before I even leave?"

"No, milady," he said, shaking his head. "In Sursha, there are certain customs and bylaws that must be observed."

"Such as?" she asked, part curious and part irritated at the whole situation.

"When a member of the royal family marries, especially marries a foreigner, she or he must be presented to the nation immediately upon the completion of the marriage or return to the country from marriage in the foreign country."

"Such as this," she said, indicating the building around them.

"Aye," he said with a small nod. "After the person is presented, consummation of the marriage must occur, and proof shown to select members of the Court. But," he added. "With any act of intercourse, including consummation of a marriage, pregnancy can occur, and an heir must be conceived within the boundaries of Sursha."

Cateline's stomach roiled at the understanding of what it would take to consummate the marriage, let alone conceive a child. She swallowed, feeling nauseous. "So," she said, her voice a bit shakier than she'd prefer. She swallowed again and took a weak stab at humor. "You're guarding me to protect the prince?"

He met her gaze, the unusual violet unwavering. "No, milady."

She met his gaze for a long moment before looking away, understanding hitting her between the eyes. "Oh," was all she could say.

The air suddenly became heavy and filled with tension. Fallon cleared his throat again and slapped his hands on brown leather-clad thighs. "Thank you, milady," he said, pushing to his feet. He gathered up the cloth and handed it to her. "Grateful for the warmth, but I must get back to my post."

"Of course," she said, cradling the damp material.

"If the weather holds, we may leave upon the morrow," he said, then, with a deep bow, left the room.

Left alone, Cateline stared at the closed door for a long moment before returning her attention to the cloth in her arms. She needed to hang it up so it would dry but strangely wanted to hold on to it for a moment. In a very strange, sudden, and frightening situation, Fallon was a source of comfort in a small way. She found that she trusted him, though knew him not but for their handful of exchanged words.

Finally, she decided to hang the cloth and get some sleep. If Fallon was indeed right and they began their journey the following day, she'd need rest. She was grateful that her father was allowing her to take her horse, a beautiful dappled gray with a dark mane and tail. Her name was Liberté—freedom—as that's what she gave Cateline. She would have been heartbroken had she had to leave her behind.

Walking over to a large trunk that sat near the armoire and was already packed for the journey, she spread the cloth over it so it could dry. Finished with that and nothing else to do, she went to the bed. Shedding her robe, she let it pool at her feet before climbing into bed, tugging the covers up to her chin.

Lying there, listening to the rain outside, which seemed to be slowing down, she heard a distant sneeze, muffled by the thickness of her door. Looking over in that direction, she felt guilty yet again. She knew that Fallon was simply doing his duty, and that's how he seemed to see it as well, but she wasn't worth all of this.

Staring up at the ceiling, she watched the strange shadows dance and jump with the flames in the fireplace. It reminded her of a bunch of wild dancers cavorting beneath the moon. Perhaps they were Druids, the ancient ancestors of the Gaels, welcoming her into the fold?

With visions of such in her mind, she closed her eyes and drifted off to sleep.

Chapter Three

It had been a terribly long day—well, six terribly long days, actually—and Cateline was tired and sore. Her back and her tailbone felt like they'd become dislodged as the days dragged on. She and Marie were housed in one carriage pulled by Liberté and another horse. A second carriage was pulled by another team and filled with personal belongings of the new princess and her lady.

Now, they were in the tent that had been set up for the two ladies every night wherever the group saw fit to slumber before another day of travel to the sea. It was remarkable to Cateline how Fallon and his men so quickly assembled the little tent city for the night. In under an hour three tents were set up, one for Cateline and Marie, one for Prince Fergus, and a third for the other nobles, forced to cram in together.

Fallon, his men, and Baron Aubert's soldiers, who were accompanying to the water's edge, all bunked under the stars if not on guard duty. The soldier picked to hunt had done his duty, and Cateline and Marie finished up their dinner of a simple rabbit stew.

Now, the two sat alone, the tent containing only two narrow bed pallets for them to sleep on and one trunk filled with the absolute necessities to get them through the night and reading material for the following day. Marie sat on her pallet knitting while

Cateline attempted to read by the single candle they were allowed for light. The guards explained anything more and they feared a fire.

In truth, she'd never had such limitations and felt like she was in prison. It humbled her a bit as Marie explained to her that this was how so many lived every single day, minus the safety of dozens of soldiers.

As the women sat in silence, some muted discussion drifting in from outside the thin walls of their tent. Suddenly, they heard the sound of somebody plucking at a lyre. Cateline looked toward the direction of the sound. An unusual instrument for a woman to be taught, she'd been playing the small stringed instrument her entire life.

"We should go out there," Marie said quietly.

Cateline glanced over at her lady-in-waiting and shyly shook her head. "No. It's not appropriate."

"Says who?" the older woman challenged.

"My father," Cateline said, her gaze returning to her book.

"Forgive me, *ma fille*," Marie said. "But your papa is not here. You must try your boundaries in this new life before you become boxed in." She raised an eyebrow. "You are a princess now, one day to be queen. They are your people out there."

Cateline thought about what her trusted servant and friend had said, chewing on her bottom lip as she stared at the closed flap of the tent and hearing the strumming begin to morph into a song. With a deep breath for courage, she slapped her book shut and set it aside. Without a further word on the subject, she got to her feet and headed to the flap, Marie not far behind her.

A handful of Fallon's men were gathered around

the main fire in the small temporary compound, the man with the lyre seated on a felled log. He was strumming a song that was clearly a well-known Gaelic tune as his comrades were tapping fingers on thighs, bobbing heads, and tapping toes.

As Cateline and Marie neared, the music stopped immediately upon notice and all the men knelt to one knee, their head bowed to her presence. She was stunned by this behavior, but then remembered who she'd become in their world. It made her infinitely uncomfortable.

"No," she said, waving her hands. "Please, stand." Some of the men glanced up at her, but none rose. Remembering none spoke her language, she felt a bit frustrated. She used her hands to indicate they should rise. "Stand, please."

"*Ar do chosa!*"

At the command, all the men instantly stood, stiff and still, the musician holding his lyre close to his chest. Cateline glanced around to see the source of the words and saw Fallon just outside the circle of the light from the fire. He stood by a tree, shoulder resting against the trunk. He sent out a second, longer demand in their language and the men relaxed, retaking their previous positions though they looked a bit uncertain as they eyed the two women.

Right then and there Cateline decided as soon as she was settled in Sursha, she'd seek out someone to teach her the language of the Gaels. She stored that thought away and walked toward the men. No doubt she'd be interacting with them often, as they seemed to be part of the royal guard, so she wanted to have a good relationship with them.

"Please," she said, indicating the man with

the lyre. "Continue." She pretended to play to give him the idea, which he misunderstood and held the instrument out to her. "Oh, no, I—"

"Take it," Marie said, meeting Cateline's gaze when the younger woman looked at her. "Show them what you can do." She gently urged the young royal toward the man. "Endear yourself to them. Will help you."

She gave him a shy smile. "*Merci*," she said softly before taking the instrument.

Feeling a little shy and unsure as a couple dozen pairs of eyes stared at her, now including some of her father's men and the prince himself, Cateline took a seat on the fallen log offered her. She glanced over at Marie, needing her support and comfort in that very uncomfortable moment. A small smile from the older woman and Cateline cleared her throat.

She began to play a song that she remembered her mother singing to her when she was little, one of the few memories she had of her before she died. Her fingers took immediately to the seven strings of the instrument. Her playing was clean and clear, and she certainly hoped her voice would be too. She sang to herself all the time while she spent the many hours alone at her father's estate but rarely ever sang for others. Marie or Sophie were among the few.

She closed her eyes and allowed herself to get lost in the lullaby about a mother swan and her one baby, the little cygnet nearly getting lost by not following behind closely. Her voice floated over the still evening, the men around her, those gathered nearby, and those farther in the woods on guard duty or patrol not making a sound.

As the final note rang out from her lips and the

final string was strummed, Cateline sat there, eyes still closed and absolute silence surrounding her, save for the pop of the campfire close by. Her eyes slowly opened to see everyone staring at her, many with their eyes wide and mouths opened.

She swallowed and looked away, feeling shy and unsure. As if a spell were broken, the men around her, and some deeper in the woods, began to applaud loudly. The shyness really hit her now, her cheeks burning. She figured her face and neck must be as dark red as her curly hair.

She glanced up and saw Fallon still leaning against the tree, a soft smile on his lips, also clapping for her performance. She sent a small nod his way before her attention was grabbed by the man whose lyre she was using. He'd pulled out a wooden flute. He put it to his lips, tapping his fingers as though playing it while nodding at her and the lyre.

Understanding, she brought the instrument back to her lap, looking at him. She knew it was beyond doubtful that they knew any of the same songs, but she didn't know if he wanted to begin or was leaving it to her. At another nod from him as if to say, "You," she began, strumming a general tune that would be easy for him to pick up on and add to.

Music being the universal language, made the same way no matter what language one spoke, soon enough the warrior picked up on the rhythm she'd created and added to it. Once the two had become synced, they both began to add little extras here and there.

As the music got faster, those gathered began to clap their hands and tap their toes, including Fallon, even as he stood there looking rather stoic. To Cateline's surprise, one of the men jumped to his feet and reached for Marie's hand, pulling her up so he could sweep her around the area by the fire, the other men moving out of their way.

Cateline's smile was large as she watched her closest friend laugh and giggle along with the man who dragged her around almost like a rag doll in his enthusiasm to move to the music. Marie, like Cateline, had little fun or excitement in her life, so it was beautiful to watch.

Finally, with a boisterous *Whoop!* from her music partner, the rousing song came to an end. She and the flute player shared a grin; there was nothing like the bond of an impromptu session with another musician. She did notice, however, not everyone was thrilled.

Standing at the open flap of his tent was Prince Fergus. His face was nothing more than pockets of shadow from the dancing firelight. His deep-set eyes were hidden beneath a heavy brow, but she could feel their dark stain upon her.

❧❧❧❧

Cateline's eyes opened, startled. Blinking a few times, she looked around but could see nothing in the inky blackness. Glancing over to where she knew Marie slept, she heard nothing. She was about to close her eyes again, wanting to get some more sleep as she knew morning would come soon enough, when she heard something.

Whispering. She heard whispering. It was French, though it was so quiet it was hard for her to understand. It could be her father's men. Most, as she'd come to learn over the long trip to the sea, made camp farther out to form a layered defense, so she was surprised any would be in the inner camp in the middle of the night.

She wanted to feel better, but something felt wrong. She was about to reach over to wake up Marie, but something told her to stay still. She did, however, move her hand slowly and as quietly as she could toward the small dagger Marie had been using to cut yarn for her knitting.

Relief washed through her when the cool grip met her fingers, which she wrapped around it. She knew the long, slender blade would defend them. Well, she hoped, anyway. Dagger in hand, she slowly sat up on the pallet, eyes wide as she desperately tried to adjust to the darkness.

Suddenly, there was yelling and the clang of metal against metal, blade against blade. Clearly either the baron's men or Fallon's men had caught the intruders. Cateline's heart was racing, fear trickling down in beads of sweat between her breasts. She gripped the dagger tighter.

"What is it?" Marie hissed from the darkness to Cateline's left.

"Fighting," Cateline whispered. "I think somebody got into camp."

Marie gasped. "Oh God."

"Shh," Cateline hissed, listening as the fighting intensified. More men were involved, grunting, yelling, more clashing of swords.

"We must get out of here," Marie said, her hand on Cateline's arm.

"And go where?" Cateline asked, looking in the direction of her lady-in-waiting. "The only way out takes us right into the fight."

Nowhere to go and feeling like sitting ducks, the two women clung onto each other, Cateline praying it would soon end. It was to be their last night, reaching the Gaels' ship to take them the rest of the way. Maybe.

She gasped as the fighting got closer to their tent, Cateline just barely able to make out two silhouettes battling each other through the material of the tent wall. She backed up a bit toward the back wall in case one or both of the fighters fell or were thrown through the front of their tent.

"What was that?" Maria whispered, panic in her voice.

"What was what?" Cateline asked, just in time to hear it too.

Behind them, the sound of ripping material. She cried out when she saw a dagger blade thrust through the material, slicing the tent wall as it slid downward. She had just enough time to gasp before the material was yanked open and she was grabbed from behind.

"Marie, run!" she screamed as she was yanked out of the tent and into the night beyond.

She was dragged back into the trees, anything she tried to do to fight against the man a moot point as he was incredibly strong and clearly determined. She tried to scream for help, Fallon's name on her lips, but the arm around her neck tightened against her throat as she was forced to her feet and against the large body behind her.

Desperately looking around as she tried in vain to get the arm loosened so she could breathe, she saw that they were totally alone, even as she could still hear the battle behind them in the camp.

Panic was setting in as the edges of her vision

dimmed from lack of air as the arm around her throat tightened; they were on the move again. As though a reminder from up above, she suddenly felt the handle of the dagger in her hand, hot like it was burning her skin. With every ounce of strength she could muster, she aimed for whatever part of her captor she could reach and buried the blade as deep as she could.

The man grunted and she felt his hold on her falter as, she thought, she'd stabbed him in the thigh. She took the opportunity to struggle out of his hold, which sent her falling to the ground, crying out in pain as she landed on a splinted branch that tore into her arm. As she looked up, something caught her eye.

Stepping out from behind a tree was Fallon, one of his blades already in hand. The look on his face was pure rage as he sent that blade flying through the air, end over end until the deadly sharp tip pierced the man's throat, the rest of the blade embedding itself there, pinning him to the tree behind.

A small cry of frightened shock escaped Cateline's throat as she covered her mouth with her hand. She popped up to her feet, anxious to get away from the man's body as he was obviously dead.

"Here," Fallon said softly, hurrying over to her and gathering her in his arms. "Don't look," he murmured.

Cateline buried her face in his neck, one of his hands cradling the back of her head to hold her there as it sounded like he pulled the blade out of the man's throat, the body falling to the forest floor with a sickening thud.

Understanding that it was over, relief washed over her and the tears began. She clung to him, able to feel a well-developed chest against her, even as distantly in her mind she wondered why it was so hard. It didn't matter in that moment as Fallon held her as she cried. Finally, she began to calm, taking several deep breaths to bring herself under control.

"Okay?" Fallon asked gently as she pulled away.

"Who are these people?" Cateline asked, using the sleeve of her sleeping dress to dry her eyes and face.

"*Routiers*," he explained.

She'd heard the term before, in conversations with her father and between others that she wasn't supposed to hear, but she had no idea what they were. Her expression must have shown as much as Fallon explained.

"Before your king, Charles V, created an army, paid and supplied, local men would gather in militias—*routiers*—to act in defense of the country." He shrugged, looking out into the dark woods beyond where they stood. "Now, they have no work, rudderless, desperate, and angry, so they have become a scourge across your land. Many times, people like your father have hired us to help with these wolves."

Cateline looked down at the dead body slumped against the tree, and though it was upsetting, she gained a better grasp on just how real the danger was. She looked to Fallon again and nodded, profound understanding seeping into her heart. "Thank you, Fallon. Truly. Thank you."

Fallon reached down and, with a small grunt, pulled out the dagger from the man's thigh. He wiped it on the man's clothing before holding it out to Cateline with a smile. "You helped."

Together they walked back to camp where the fight was over, a half dozen men lying dead on the ground. They were dressed in everyday clothing, which to Cateline indicated they were likely with the man who had taken her.

Fallon's men were helping each other up, as well as beginning to bind bad slashes on their hands. One man had a terrible abrasion on his head. She was relieved to see Marie helping them, unscathed. She was tearing off long strips from the skirt of her sleeping gown to make tourniquets to stop the bleeding on some of the men.

Marie glanced up from the young man she was helping, and she and Cateline locked eyes. A cry of emotion erupted from Marie as she jumped to her feet and ran over to Cateline, the two women embracing.

"You are okay?" Marie asked like a mother, taking her young charge's face between her hands and looking her over.

Cateline nodded. "Yes." They embraced again, this time in joy. Cateline pulled out of the hug when she heard some ruckus behind them, her guard instantly raised after what she'd just been through.

One of Fallon's men was stumbling out of Fergus's tent, losing his balance and falling to one knee outside as the prince himself appeared. He looked enraged with red face and bulging veins in his thick neck. He turned and looked behind him into the tent before briefly disappearing, another of Fallon's men being shoved through the flap, landing next to his peer in the dirt.

Fergus appeared once more and began to bellow, his voice deep and booming across the night. Cateline couldn't understand a word he was saying, but by the way his eyes were daggers directed at her, she felt like she was added to the diatribe.

Fallon hurried into the situation, hands pressed against Fergus's massive chest as the taller man began to charge in Cateline's direction. The head of the Elite Guard was trying to reason with the bullish prince in low, but firm tones.

The two men were in an all-out argument, Fergus's rage turning to the smaller man, fingers pointing, including at Cateline. Finally, Fallon bellowed, "Enough! She did nothing wrong!"

Cateline was shocked to hear the burst of French, and even more shocked when Fergus seemed to not only understand but backed down. Not looking at anyone, the prince turned and slammed back into his tent.

Fallon looked at everyone in camp who was staring back at him. He met Cateline's gaze for a brief moment before giving her a brief bow of respect and disappearing into the darkness.

Chapter Four

The cabin was small, with only one bunk, though one of the bed pallets had been brought in for Marie. It was only one night, so they'd be happy with whatever they were given. The same trunk that had accompanied them every night in the tent was placed on the floor, squeezed between the pallet and the wall.

Cateline removed her mantle, tossing the garment to the bunk as she reached up to tuck a few strands of her hair that had come loose from the updo Marie had fixed for her best she could earlier in the carriage. Her attention went to the narrow, closed door to the cabin when somebody knocked on it from the other side.

Marie pulled it open to reveal Fallon standing out in the narrow corridor. He nodded at her in acknowledgment. "Milady."

"Good eve, milord," she said, pulling the door open wider for the warrior to step inside.

"Milady," he said again, giving a bow of respect to Cateline. "Wanted to make sure you ladies have everything you need for the night." He gave them a sheepish smile. "I know it's tight, but we should be to Sursha by midmorning." He looked at Cateline. "You should get some good rest, milady. Tomorrow will be a busy day for you."

The princess nodded. "All right, thank you."

He turned to leave but she stopped him with a hand placed on his bracer-clad forearm. "Milady?"

"I wanted to thank you again, Fallon," she said quietly, feeling almost unworthy to be speaking with him after seeing what he was capable of, what he did for her. "You saved my life," She gazed down at the floor.

"Milady," he said softly, using two fingers to lift her chin so she was looking up at him. "You are very welcome, but you should be proud of what you did." He gave her an encouraging smile. "You were brave, so very brave."

Cateline looked into those unusual violet eyes which were filled with so much depth, intelligence, and caring. She'd not seen anything like it in a man before. "Thank you. I guess we worked together."

He nodded. "Indeed." One more smile and he turned away.

Not wanting him to go and she wasn't sure why, she called for him again. He turned back to look at her. "Was it my fault?" she asked. "As Fergus seems to think."

Fallon tucked in a full bottom lip for a moment before letting it back out again and saying, "His Highness doesn't do well in situations where he feels he's not in complete control." He looked away for a moment before looking at her again. "I'm afraid this marriage hasn't been easy on anyone," he added softly. With a final smile, he bowed and walked away.

❧❧❧❧

Cateline and Marie had headed upstairs when they'd heard commotion from up top. They stayed out of the way as the sailors scurried around the decks to bring the ship home. It was fascinating to the princess, as she'd never been on any sort of floating device of any kind in her entire life.

She saw a man up in the crow's nest waving his sword in the air. Confused, she looked around to see what or who he was getting the attention of. She saw two massive wheels on shore that had spokes protruding off them that looked to be half a man's height. Three men on each wheel, they used those spokes to turn the massive wheels. It took a moment, but she heard something behind the ship that alerted her to what the men were doing.

Several yards behind the ship, at the mouth of the natural harbor, a wooden gate began to rise out of the water like magic, walling off any enemy ships. The cove was shaped like a crescent, the two rocky ends circling around to form the harbor. The land mass itself was sloped from the high back down to the beach. A rocky edge all around the island gave natural protection from the opposite side of the island, almost forming a wall of stone, which was amplified by the actual wall of stone built by the Gaels.

From what she could see as they moved in slowly to dock, the lower part of the island was a string of market stalls, though she couldn't tell what was being peddled. Winding roads leading up to higher areas of the island showed scattered villages and pockets of round and oval stone houses with thatched roofs.

Up toward the higher part of the island was the castle, large and intimidating, and what she assumed would be her home. Outside the curtain wall of the castle made from stone and built-up earth behind serving as an outer layer of protection for the fortress, was an expanse of wooded land. Dotting the expanse were some manor houses, which no doubt housed the nobility.

The ship pulled up to the dock, men grabbing the giant ropes that were tossed down from the sailors on board and wrapped around the mooring anchor affixed to the dock. Like a well-oiled machine, men on board scurried around, some carrying things from down below while others quickly lowered the gangway so everyone could disembark.

Two of Fallon's men escorted Cateline and Marie down the long, slick ramp, assuring they didn't fall. Once they were on the dock, they were ushered off to a carriage that was waiting for them, then whisked off toward the castle up the long, windy roads.

The two women were pressed to the widows, taking everything in. It was so green and lush! Cateline was left speechless at how beautiful everything was. People were milling about, working, talking, and some even waving. All bowed as the carriage passed them.

"Your people," Marie said, sparing a glance at her charge.

Cateline nodded, letting out a slow, nervous breath at that realization. Knowing something and seeing it with her own eyes were two very different things. She saw a field of sheep and a man walking out of the trees with a bow and quiver of arrows slung across his back, the day's hunt laid across his shoulders.

She smiled when she saw a little girl, no more than two or three years old, standing at the side of the road, long blond hair hanging in her face and a finger tugging at her bottom lip. She lifted a hand and gave the carriage a finger wave.

Cateline waved back, overjoyed to see life. People living their every day, working, playing, real people. *Her* people. She'd never seen anything like it, as she'd been cooped up in her father's estate her entire life. Over the course of twenty-one years there had been endless parties, guests, and privilege. But she'd never been able to see what regular people did. What were their fears and worries?

She hoped she'd be allowed to meet them, to travel to the town and see what their homes looked like. She hoped she'd be able to go to the market and buy something frivolous, paying twice as much as the asking price simply to help the person. Perhaps even give away what she'd bought to someone who needed it more than she?

"*Ma chérie,*" Marie said, tapping Cateline's arm to get her attention.

Cateline moved to look out Marie's side of the carriage and saw what the older woman was looking at. A group of children were clustered together, gathered in a circle and singing and dancing, smiling and giggling.

A smile fell across the princess's lips, wondering what it would be like to be surrounded by children as a child. What would it be like to play such games? Near the children was a garden, a young girl of perhaps fifteen or sixteen on her hands and knees tending to it. Her long, dark hair was pulled back into a thick braid that fell over one shoulder. She paid no mind to the carriage, so intent on her task.

The villages were set farther apart as they neared the castle. The wheels of the carriage and horses' hooves clopped across the wooden drawbridge that gave them safe passage over a wide, dark moat filled with water that was an ungodly color. They traveled through the gatehouse, a massive iron gate lifted for their entry through what amounted to a stone tunnel and into the open again in the outer bailey.

In the large courtyard were many buildings she was familiar with, such as the stables, where her mare would now be housed, workshops, barracks for Fallon's men and the rest of the king's army, as well as the larger hall, which would hold celebrations for commoners, and kitchens where food was prepared for the military and non-royals who lived or worked on property.

People who worked for the king went to and fro, large baskets in arms as well as a driver with an ass pulling a wagon filled with cut logs, headed to the stone building with multiple chimneys, smoke spewing from their tops. She figured that was the main kitchen. It was located nearest the long, stone building that she knew was the hall, where most meals and entertainment would be taken, much like at her father's estate, though this hall was within the keep.

The keep was a large, round stone tower that was placed on a motte, a huge built-up mound of earth to raise it high above the level of the bailey grounds for the protection of the royal family that it housed. The carriage drove on the road that wound its way up the steep earthen mound to the structure at the top. The keep's individual towers and turrets made for an imposing skyline.

At the top of the winding path was a portcullis, which was a tall, arched entryway for a rider or carriage to deliver the person safely to the small bailey inside. A latticed iron gate lifted to allow entry, closing behind them only for a second to draw up, the horses' hooves echoing in the stone corridor until they reached the open air again.

The carriage pulled to a stop and the driver jumped down, opening the door as three servants hurried from the massive building. The bailey was closed in on all four sides, three of which were massive stone walls and the fourth the structure itself.

One servant ushered the women inside while the other two began to unload the trunks. The double arched doors, wood ribbed with iron, were very thick and looked extremely heavy.

They entered the keep, an enormous room with thick stone columns spaced on either side. The stone wall to the left had a massive fireplace at its center, the size large enough for four five men to easily stand side by side in its depths. The wall on the opposite side was an outer wall and had huge, beautiful stained-glass windows at the top of the room, near the thirty-foot ceilings.

Expert stone masons had created stone veins of support throughout the groined vault ceilings, like spiderwebs in every direction. There was a stone staircase along the back wall that led to upper floors, but also a huge balcony where guests could mingle and look down upon the happenings in the hall below.

The hall within the keep was for more intimate gatherings, special occasions with only the royal family and foreign guests, or, as Cateline had been told during the voyage, the wedding celebrations that would be happening the following day for her and Fergus.

They were met by a woman at the top of a staircase. She was a very short woman, her dress appropriate yet dark in color. Her dark hair was pulled back into a harsh updo, revealing features that were sharp, eagle-like. Intelligent, dark eyes looked at them from a pale face. She said something in Gaelic to the servant man who had been leading them, the man bowing deeply before hurrying away, leaving Cateline and Marie with the woman.

"*Bonjour,*" the small woman said. her lips thin and tight. "I am Collette, and I run this house. I tend to all who live within the walls, and the king." She met both women's gazes, her own hard and penetrating. "So, follow."

Cateline looked over at Marie to see her already looking her way. They said nothing, simply followed the smaller woman. The princess was relieved that this strange woman spoke French. By her accent, she seemed to speak Belgian French, which was common in the northern part of the country.

The women were led up to the third floor. The second, as explained by Collette, housed the elite warriors—Fallon's men. It was also where the other servants' quarters were who worked solely in the castle. They walked past a few small bedchambers clearly meant for other royals or those seen in higher standing than simply a military man or servant.

"Your Highness," Collette said, indicating the closed door of one of the rooms. "Your husband, Prince Fergus, resides in here. He has since he was a boy. He will remain here until he takes the throne."

Cateline nodded, wondering about the condition of the room beyond. From the other two she'd seen, they were small, though larger than a knight's quarters to be certain, and contained a bed and a press made of oak with shelves for the storage of clothing and other such belongings.

There was a single garderobe shared by the occupants of the three bedchambers. It was a small, stone room on the outer wall with one tall, narrow, glassless window at the back. A stone step the width of the narrow room served as a resting place for the user's feet while he took a seat upon the thick wooden plank atop another stone stoop. A hole was at the center of the wooden plank for the user's bodily business to drop down through a special space that jutted out from the wall, landing in the moat far below.

They continued their ascent. At the top floor of the fortress, Cateline and Marie were led to the queen's chambers, a massive room with a four-poster bed. Purple velvet curtains were tied back currently but could be released to form a warm cocoon on a cold night. Ornate furnishings decorated the large space, including two luxurious armchairs set before the massive stone fireplace.

Strategically placed windows would allow in the most sunlight possible without giving an enemy combatant a good target to aim for. Cateline could easily imagine her books and the wonderful reading space she'd make for herself.

"In here," Collette said, pushing open one of the three doors in the room. "Is your boudoir," she explained. "Where you will bathe and ready yourself for your obligations."

Cateline looked around, eyes wide. She'd never had such a thing. There was also storage space for her personal belongings kind clothing. "Why am I being put in the queen's chamber?" she asked. "I'm not the queen."

"Indeed." The older woman agreed with the obvious. "The queen died many years ago," she explained.

"Why I am doing this and not she."

"Oh," Cateline said, feeling stupid. "Forgive me."

"In here," Collette continued, leading them back to the bedchamber and through the second door, which proved to be her own private garderobe. The third door opened to a small bedroom for Marie.

Filled with the bare-bone basics—narrow bed, a press, a clay chamber pot as well as a small table with a clay pitcher and wash basin—the room was still nicely appointed. An arrow-slit window allowed in some sunlight, but a candle or fire in the small fireplace would be necessary for any real light. The room also had a door to the hallway beyond so the lady-in-waiting wouldn't have to bother her mistress in order to leave the room and go about her business.

Back in Cateline's chamber, Collette looked Marie up and down, hand on her hip. "You are old to be a lady-in-waiting."

Cateline was surprised by the very blunt nature of this woman but got the feeling she'd better get used to it, as she had no doubt she'd see a lot of her.

"I've been with Cateline since she was a young child," Marie explained. "After her mother died, the baron thought it would be best I retain my position as a trusted friend and guide for her as she grew older. You know as well as I how difficult it is for women in this life."

Collette studied the other woman for a long moment, Cateline guessing they weren't terribly far apart in age. Finally, she nodded. "*Oui.*" With the swish of her skirts, they were off again. "We go to meet the king, now," she explained as she headed for the door. "He's awaiting your introduction in the Solar, Your

Highness."

The Solar was the king's chambers, which was a much larger version than that of the queen. His bed was tucked into a far corner in the space, the massive room filled with furnishing for a large group of people to meet, be it his advisers, his family or simply trusted friends.

The space was meant to be a retreat away from a noisy, bustling castle, time for a country's ruler to relax and breathe. The fireplace was aglow, and a man with a full head of gray hair sat at a table with quill and parchment. Though dressed in finery befitting his position, he wasn't flashy.

Looking up, the man smiled at the three women entering the space. His mustache and goatee were nearly all white, while full eyebrows still sported the salt-and-pepper hues of his long hair, which was braided at the sides, coming together down the back of his head and trailing down to his upper back.

Placing the quill down on the desk, he got to his feet, a bit of a grunt with the effort. He walked over to them, all three women instantly falling to a knee in respect to his station. He said something in Gaelic that got Collette to her feet, a touch to Cateline's arm letting her know she needed to rise, as well.

"He said he is deeply pleased to meet you," Collette said, translating for the man.

Cateline gave the handsome older man a shy smile. "The pleasure is all mine, Sire."

He gave her a kind smile, taking her much smaller hands in both of his. His eyes were dark like Fergus's, but there was a kindness there, a softness that was familiar to her somehow, though she couldn't place why. He shook his head.

"Athair," he said softly.

Cateline tasted the word on her tongue, one she'd heard spoken among Fallon's men in conversation with each other. *Ah-her*, it was pronounced, and she'd taken it to mean father or some such paternal term. She nodded. "Athair."

His smile was broad as he nodded. Suddenly, she felt a little bit better about her situation.

Chapter Five

It was a beautiful morning, though the clouds seemed to be churning overhead, threatening storms later in the day. It was the day for Cateline to be presented to the people of Sursha. The previous night had been spent getting her belongings unpacked and organized under the direction of Collette and the help of Marie and three other young castle servant girls.

Now, dressed in one of her finest gowns with her long hair braided and wound tightly atop her head, she had a slight headache. The updo had to allow her small crown to fit snugly. She'd never worn any such thing before, and it was heavy and felt strange, but it was part of her new role during a public appearance.

She sat next to Fergus, the moment they'd climbed into the carriage at the castle the first time she'd seen him since they'd boarded the ship on the final leg of their journey to Sursha. He hadn't said a word to her as they'd loaded into the carriage, which made its way down to the Surshan people nearest the sea. The carriage was flanked by guards on horseback, Fallon at the head of the entourage.

The journey back down toward the docks was long, the carriage driver taking it slow with the horse team at times as the slant was significant in places. Finally, they reached the village closest to the harbor. It was near where Cateline had seen the fish market and other shops and peddler wagons the previous day.

As the carriage got closer to their destination, Cateline was surprised to see a festive atmosphere with the villagers gathered, awaiting their arrival. She looked to Fergus to see if he was as surprised and excited as she was, but he was looking the other direction, his body language reading bored and almost recalcitrant.

A bit disappointed as she'd like to at least share this with her new husband, Cateline looked away, turning back to those who were racing toward the market area, the excitement growing in the air. Despite the brooding negativity in the carriage that oozed from Fergus, Cateline could feel her heart becoming lighter, her own excitement growing.

The carriage came to a stop, Fallon dismounting before heading back to the carriage, just outside of Cateline's door. Their gazes met for a brief moment before the warrior leader looked away, opening the carriage door for her.

"Milady," Fallon said, the usual soft, low timbre of his voice so calming to her.

"Thank you," she murmured, allowing herself to be helped down from the carriage, the wide skirts of her dress a bit of an impediment anywhere she dared go, let alone through the limited space of a carriage doorway.

Fergus, dressed in his finery, bejeweled and flashing, met them on Cateline's side of the carriage. He took her hand roughly in his, placing it at the crook of his arm before he began walking toward the gathered crowd. Like the change of the ocean, he was all smiles and greetings.

Cateline had no idea what he was saying, but

from the smiles and reactions of the villagers, she assumed it was greetings and pleasantries. As Fergus and Cateline neared the gathering, the people, one by one, fell to a knee, heads bowed as they passed. Cateline was growing a bit more accustomed to it, though no more comfortable with it.

A little girl with long, flowing golden hair ran up to her, the long, tunic-like *léine* she wore covering her entire little body, save for little leather shoes poking out. She looked to be about four or five. She held a bouquet of wildflowers in her little hand and looked up at Cateline with big, blue eyes.

Cateline smiled. "*Bonjour, petite*," she said. The little girl said nothing, simply held up the flowers to the princess. Cateline turned to Fallon, who stood nearby. "What is the proper response in your language?" she asked, not wanting to seem so scary to the young girl, who looked a bit uncertain at the French princess's greeting.

"*Go raibh maith agat*," Fallon said softly.

No clue what she was about to say, Cateline nodded and smiled down at the girl, repeating the strange words of a familiar tongue to the little one who smiled up at her. Cateline returned the smile and cradled the flowers against her chest. She reached out a hand and lightly touched the young girl's cheek in affection before the little one scampered away.

She watched her go before glancing over at Fallon to catch a smile on his face before he looked away. The two royals continued on, Fallon to Cateline's right, another of the elite squad to Fergus's left, and a third bringing up the rear. The rest of the men stayed back with the carriage. Collette had told Cateline that morning that other men in the army had infiltrated the commoners throughout the villages to ensure the peace was kept.

They reached the center of the village, near the very fragrant fish market, where they stopped, the armed guards pushing people back so a good circle of space was given to the couple.

Fallon walked to the center, just in front of the couple. His voice boomed over the crowd, bold and forceful. Though Cateline couldn't understand Fallon's words, it was strange for her to hear his voice so loud and commanding. His usual manner was so quiet and only seeming to speak when necessary, the change left her a bit unsettled.

She figured he must be introducing them, as she understood Fergus's name, then he indicated her. "Cateline *Banphrionsa*!"

The crowd cheered, then individual flowers and small carved wooden crafts resembling horses, flowers, and boats began to land at the feet of the couple, the crowd throwing what Cateline assumed were offerings of goodwill to the new couple.

"Can we collect these?" she asked Fallon, hope in her voice.

"You want them?" the warrior leader asked. At Cateline's nod, he got the attention of one of the other guards. In short, quick sentences, he got his message across. The guardsman looked at two little girls near him and bent down to a knee, speaking softly to them. He handed them both a coin and the two little girls immediately hurried to the gifts and carefully gathered them up.

Cateline smiled, touched. The day moved on in the same fashion, the couple spending a limited amount of time in each village as they came to them, the carriage taking them farther into the island. If it were up to Cateline, she would spend hours with each village, meeting the people and understanding their lives and their needs, but she knew it wasn't logical or feasible. Also, Fergus seemed to be getting less and less enchanted by each village as they went.

By late afternoon, they were making their way back to the castle where a dinner would be thrown that night in the great hall for the wealthier Surshans—merchants, ship captains, and other such people who had a loud voice in society.

The list had been personally compiled by Fergus and his advisers, and it was to be quite the celebration, as Cateline understood it. She dreaded it.

Back in her chambers, Cateline was deciding on what to wear for the night's festivities. She would be bathed soon, her second in as many days. It surprised and confused her. Some believed it was bad for a person to bathe often as it washed away beneficial germs. What she'd come to understand about the Surshan people, the majority of whom had survived the Black Death due to their hygiene habits, was that they were a clean people. It made her think of her studies of older cultures like the Greeks, Romans, and Egyptians centuries ago.

It didn't seem they were a Christian people, which was a bit shocking to Cateline, as the Church was everything to those in France, England, and Spain. The Surshans seemed to be more a spiritual people, reaching back to their pagan roots.

Once the presentations and parties were over and she was able to get to a normal, daily routine, she hoped to be able to speak to someone about the culture, to better understand her new home.

A knock on the door pulled Cateline from her thoughts. She walked across the expanse of the room and pulled open the heavy door by the iron ring that was mounted for that purpose. On the other side stood Fallon.

"Good eve," she greeted him.

The warrior bowed at the waist before presenting her with the burlap sack he held. "From today's presentations, milady."

Cateline took the bag, noticing its heft. "My goodness," she said softly.

"May I?" Fallon asked, reaching for the bag again. "My apologies."

"Of course." Cateline allowed him to take the bag back, stepping aside as he carried it across the room to a table. She could have done so but was touched by his consideration. Lord knew she didn't get that from her own husband. "Thank you, Fallon. I appreciate it."

"Some of the flowers were crushed to pieces, milady," Fallon said, clasping his hands behind his back once the bag was secured on the table. "I took the liberty of removing them." He gave her a shy smile. "I hope that's okay."

"Yes, thank you. Very considerate."

Fallon nodded and gave her a small bow before turning to leave before stopping at the sound of his name. "Yes, milady?" he asked, turning to her.

Cateline felt a bit shy, a bit out of her element. "Can I ask you something? Well," she said with a little smirk. "Two somethings."

"Of course, milady. I'm at your disposal," Fallon said, standing at attention, handsomely beautiful face expressionless.

"What," she began, feeling very shy. "What can

I expect of tonight?"

Fallon nodded, as though he understood the entirety of what she was asking. "Well, milady," the warrior began softly. "Tonight at the dinner you can expect to be passed around from one noble to another for inspection. I'm sure you've experienced such back in France." He gave her a small smile. "I'd say it's quite clear the people approve," he added, indicating the bag filled with tributes on the table.

Cateline smiled, her heart swelling at the memory of such a wonderful day. "I hope so. I'd like to spend some time with them," she said, giving the warrior a bright smile, reflecting what she felt. "To know them."

Fallon nodded. "Can be arranged, milady."

"Wonderful. So," she said, butterflies in her stomach at her next question. "After the dinner?"

"If all goes as I expect it to with the nobles," Fallon explained. "Fergus, well…" He cleared his throat, "The prince will arrive at your chamber door tonight to claim his right as a husband." He looked away for a moment before meeting her gaze once more. "The nobles will come by on the morrow to see proof of consummation."

Cateline's stomach flipped at the thought of what activity he spoke of. Something entered her mind she'd heard of from some of her friends who had been married off. "What happens if the woman doesn't bleed?" She shrugged a shoulder. "What can be offered for proof?"

Fallon reached down to his boot and pulled out a dagger, the firelight glinting against the steel.

Cateline gasped at the sudden and unexpected move. Hand to heart, she laughed nervously. "Murder the poor woman?"

He smiled, shaking his head. "No, milady." He walked over to her and, looking her in the eye with a raised eyebrow, almost as though asking for permission, grabbed one of Cateline's hands. He pantomimed slicing her fingertip with the blade, meeting her gaze again.

"Ah," she said, nodding.

Standing as they were, her hand held in his, warm and surprisingly soft, her heart began to beat faster, nervousness sending her stomach flipping again. She didn't understand it. Needing to refocus her attention on something else, her gaze fell to the blade of the dagger still near her finger.

"You have a rose on your blade," she said, truly intrigued.

Fallon looked at the blade and smiled at her as he nodded. "Yes. My mother, before she died, used to always refer to me as her rose, the latest to bloom." The smile upon full lips was a sad one. "I was the youngest of her children," he explained.

"I'm so sorry," Cateline murmured. "How old were you when she died?"

"Just a child."

"Did she give you this?" Cateline asked.

"Yes and no." He met her gaze. "She had it forged for me, planning to give it to me when I got older, but never got the opportunity." He gave her a sad smile before lowering the blade away from her finger. "My father gave it to me later."

"That was good of him," Cateline said. "It's very beautiful, Fallon." She smiled. "I love roses. I planted an entire rose garden at my father's estate." She looked down, studying their hands for a moment, noting how pale her skin was to the deep tan of his. She also noticed that, though his hand was certainly larger than hers, it was delicate in its own way. Strong, capable, but beautiful. Kind of like the person it belonged to.

"Well," Fallon said, once again pulling her out of her thoughts. "Perhaps you can create one here as well."

She looked at him, hopeful. "Really? You think Fergus would allow that?"

Fallon waved off the idea. "Go to the king. This is still his home."

Cateline nodded, liking the idea. "All right. I'll do that."

Fallon bowed to her before tucking his dagger back into his boot and turning on his heel, headed to the door. "I shall see you later, milady."

"Yes," the princess said, letting out a long, shaky breath at the thought of where her night was headed. "See you later."

⁂

"You will wear this," Collette instructed, holding up a garment that Cateline had never seen before. "It is lighter fabric than what you wear to bed normally," the older woman said, laying the sleeping gown across the four-poster bed. "You will let your hair down, as it is an invitation, as well as something just for him."

Cateline swallowed hard and nodded. "All right."

"And," Collette continued, as though the young princess had never spoken. "When the deed is done and he has left, you are to ring this bell." She picked up the newly placed bell from the table and rang it, the shrill sound near deafening. "Marie will come in and gather your linens and bring them to me.

Understood?"

"Yes," Cateline said. "I understand." She understood that she wanted to throw up.

"Marie!" Collette bellowed.

Cateline started at the unexpected noise, already feeling on edge about the whole thing. The dinner with the nobles had been a test of her patience as it was. She'd never been touched, smiled at, talked about, or ogled so much in her entire life. She was just ready for the entire night to end.

Her attention was grabbed as Marie hurried in from her quarters and jumped to do what Collette barked at her to do, which was to get Cateline ready for the evening while the older woman put the special white linen on the bed to reflect the evidence of marriage consummation.

"*On y va?*" Marie asked, taking the gown from Collette and walking over to Cateline.

Cateline eyed the gown before finally looking away, nodding. "We shall."

The two women stepped into the boudoir where all of Cateline's perfumes and special powders and "woman things" were. The gown was hung on an iron hook as the lady-in-waiting turned to help Cateline disrobe from the many layers of her gown.

"Should I be scared?" she asked her trusted companion and servant.

Marie shrugged as she removed the top layer of the outfit. "Sex is not to be feared, *ma chérie*. It can be a wonderful experience when it's done in love."

"Yes," Cateline acknowledged. "But this is hardly that." She snorted. "Fergus barely looked at me tonight." She raised her arms as Marie needed her to do to continue undressing her. It hurt, the weight of rejection heavy in her chest. It threatened to come forth as pricks of emotions behind her eyes. Blinking several times, she said, "I think he doesn't like me."

"He is a man," Marie said, removing the jewelry her charge wore, tucking the precious pieces away in the jewelry box set upon a shelf in the small room. "Raise."

Cateline raised her arms again to allow the white gown to be put on.

"As a man," Marie continued. "He is selfish, entitled. Look at his behavior thus far, no?"

Cateline nodded. "*Oui*," she whispered. She felt so awkward and lost. Yes, she had Marie, but the entire reason for her being there was for naught.

"Give him time. Sit."

Cateline sat at the small vanity, a beautiful and elegant piece of furniture that had belonged to the queen. She sat still as Marie stood behind her and carefully unwrapped the intricate braids that comprised her hairdo for the evening.

"Do you miss Gaston?" she asked, wincing slightly as the older woman unwittingly tugged some of her hair.

"Every day," Marie said quietly. "He's been gone a long time now," she continued. "But I think about love. Is it too late for me?"

Cateline smiled at the wistfulness she heard in the other woman's voice. Despite her own situation, she wanted to believe in romance, though no doubt it was nothing more than a foolish girl's fantasy.

"I believe it's never too late," Cateline finally said. "I have to believe that."

Chapter Six

"Wake up!"

Cateline started, eyes blinking as she looked around wildly. Her gaze settled on the angry face of Collette, who stood at the side of the bed, bell in her hand. She lifted her upper body to her elbows.

"They've now come and gone," the older woman exclaimed. "Why did you not ring the bell?" She rang it for good measure, the shrill sound unpleasant first thing in the morning.

Cateline stared at it, her sleepy brain trying to catch up to what was happening and what she was being asked. Finally, she remembered. "He never came." She looked to Collette's hard gaze again. "Fergus, he never showed up." She sat up, the covers falling around her waist, just the tiniest bit of the shape of her breasts discernible in the special gown Collette had given her. "I must have fallen asleep waiting."

Collette threw her hand up in exasperation, muttering all sorts of things in Gaelic that Cateline imagined were not for a child's ears. Without another word to the princess, she slammed the bell back where it had rested and left the room.

Left alone, Cateline stared at her bedchamber door wondering what kind of storm had just blown in. It was nearly an hour until Marie was due to awaken her mistress, but clearly they were both awake after the whirlwind that was Collette.

"Are you okay?" Marie asked quietly, a yawn nearly stealing the last word.

Cateline nodded. "Yes." She ran her hand over her hair, pushing the long, curly strands out of her face. "Marie?"

"Yes, *ma chérie*?" Marie responded, running her fingers lovingly through the thick auburn strands, her motherly touch always so comforting to Cateline.

"Why am I here?" the young princess asked.

"I believe God sends us where we're most needed, Cateline," she said softly, her voice soothing to the princess. "You are here for a reason, just perhaps not to be seen so plainly."

❧ ❧ ❧ ❧

Later that morning, Cateline took breakfast on the first floor of the castle, feeling quite lonely as she sat at the long table by herself. She pushed away her plate, which had contained bread, fruit, and smoked fish. It had been quite tasty, and as she sipped some red wine, she considered what to do with her day.

"Anything more, milady?" the young serving girl asked, her words slow and the accent very off. Obviously she'd been taught a simple phrase and question in French for Cateline's benefit.

Cateline shook her head, a universal response, as well as the smile of gratitude she gave her. The serving girl nodded and bowed before gathering the used dishes and scurrying away.

"Did you enjoy the fish?"

Cateline looked up to see Fallon walking toward the table. He was dressed in his full military garb, including the double blades across his back. The young princess smiled, feeling a bit comforted at his presence. "It was good. Very good."

He nodded, stepping up to the table on the opposite side, bowing deeply in respect. "I'm so glad."

She eyed him. "Don't tell me, you went out all by your lonesome and caught it, just for breakfast?"

"With my bare hands, milady," he said, his tone and expression so staid she thought for a moment that he was serious.

It wasn't until she saw the twinkle in those deep purple eyes that Cateline smiled, almost giggled. The levity felt good. "Multitalented, I see." She returned his smile.

"Well, milady, I have been reassigned as the head of your personal guard. Please tell me what you wish to do with your day, and I'll make sure you're given what you need."

Not entirely sure what she wanted to do, she nodded. "Thank you, Fallon." She looked down into her chalice of wine for a moment before asking, "Was it Fergus who changed your assignment?"

Fallon rested a hand on the tabletop and shook his head. "The king." Clearing his throat, he asked, "How did it go last night, then?"

Cateline felt shame wash over her at the question, though she knew the warrior meant nothing by it other than curiosity, considering he'd given her advice on the event. She set her wine down and gave a little shrug. "Fergus did not arrive."

Fallon slammed a fist into the table. "What?"

Cateline was startled by the vehemence and anger. She sat back a bit in her seat, eyes wide.

Fallon took a deep breath, though it was clear he was still furious. "Please wait here, milady," he said, voice low and firm. "Think of what you'd like to do today. I shall return."

Cateline watched as the warrior rushed off, taking the stairs two at a time, his weaponry clinking against each other as he went. The princess was baffled. Where was he going? Why was he so incensed? She stayed where she was, not sure what to do. She'd been told to stay put, so she remained seated.

After perhaps ten minutes, Fallon returned. He looked angry, his face flushed and the veins in his neck standing out, but he seemed to be trying to take long, deep breaths as he neared Cateline. Hand back on the tabletop, he looked down at it for a moment before clearing his throat and looking up at the princess.

"My apologies, Your Highness," the warrior murmured.

Cateline stared at him, a bit frightened by the temper that seemed to be flowing just beneath the surface. She didn't understand what was happening, what had gotten Fallon so angry. Yes, the situation with the prince was confusing, frustrating, hurtful, and, from what she was beginning to understand, becoming dire, but she wasn't sure what that had to do with the leader of the Elite Guard.

It made her nervous. She looked away from him, not sure what to do or say. A moment of heavy, tense silence fell over the two before Fallon cleared his throat again.

"What did you wish to do today, milady?" he asked, tone lighter, friendly.

Cateline glanced over at him, tempted to simply say nothing, that she'd stay in her rooms, but she knew that was a childish attitude to take. She needed to force herself to explore her new world and her new role.

Taking a deep, centering breath, Cateline met the warrior's gaze again. "I'd like to meet some of the villagers," she said. "Talk to them, understand them." A small smile curled her lips. "Both literally and figuratively."

"If you like." Fallon's body language softened a bit, which put Cateline more at ease. "I can ask Collette to work with you, help you learn our language."

Cateline eyed him. "She scares me."

A bark of laughter burst from Fallon's lips, surprising Cateline. His grin was large and amused. "Yes," he said, chuckling. "I've known her my entire life, so I forget how intimidating she can be."

Cateline smiled, feeling shy. "Yes, well…"

"Well," Fallon said, clapping his hand. "If meeting the people is what you'd like to do, then meeting the people is what you *shall* do."

❧ ❧ ❧ ❧

It was a beautiful day, though there was a chill in the air off the sea. Cateline's dress and cloak draped across Liberté's back as she sat astride her. She'd never fancied riding sidesaddle, so was one of very few women who rode a horse in the traditional manner.

Fallon rode next to Cateline, two members of the Guard slightly back. The head of the Elite Guard and the princess's personal guard would protect her while the other two focused more on their surrounds and any threat that may try to sneak up upon them.

The wind blew through Liberté's mane, the mare so happy to be running free. Cateline smiled at the memory of her horse earlier when she and Fallon had walked into the stables. She hadn't seen her beloved horse in several days and hadn't spent any time with her in many weeks due to the events back home, the storms, and then the journey to Sursha.

As soon as the beautiful horse had seen her mistress, she'd begun to whinny and nicker, her hooves stomping in a little happy dance of reunion. There were so many times when Cateline had felt Liberté was all she had. When the two of them would go, riding free—sometimes even with Cateline's hair down and as free as Liberté's—the young noblewoman felt alive.

Now, riding with Fallon and two of his men, she could feel a small bit of that freedom return, even if she was in a bit of a new gilded cage. In the moment, however, she refused to think about that. She was outside, she was with her best friend, and she was about to meet some of the incredible people she'd only had a small glimpse of since she'd been in Sursha.

Fallon slowed his large black horse down to a more manageable gait as they entered a small village. The stone houses were set far enough apart that the owners had a small bit of land to grow crops on, mostly enough for the family that dwelled within the home. Other small buildings were clustered in the more central area of the village.

Nestled there was a granary, common stables, a place of worship, and other auxiliary buildings whose uses Cateline couldn't guess. Fallon held out a hand, indicating they should stop and dismount. Cateline pulled Liberté to a halt,

Fallon dismounted the large war horse, murmuring to him in Gaelic before walking over to Cateline. He looked up at her. "Milady?"

Cateline allowed herself to be helped down, Fallon's hands on her waist strong and sure. Being as close to him as she was when he lifted her down to the ground, she got a good, close-up look at him. Time again, no matter what word she tried to come up with to describe him, it always landed on *beautiful.*

It was unsettling to her, as it made no sense. She'd seen very handsome men in her lifetime, many who'd worked for her father. But there was something different about Fallon, and she couldn't put her finger on what it was.

Shaking herself out of her thoughts, Cateline turned away from the warrior and waited for Fallon as he instructed one of the other men to stay with the horses, the third man staying back by the tree line, watching.

"Ready, milady?" Fallon asked, walking over to her.

"Yes," she responded with a small smile. "Where should we begin?"

Fallon indicated the village with the wave of a bracer-clad arm. "Wherever you wish. You command, I follow."

Letting out a long, slow breath, Cateline nodded and looked around. She began to walk but was stopped by a small touch to her hand. She looked up to see Fallon suddenly by her side.

"Simple greeting," he said quietly. "*Dia duit.*"

She studied him, though she wasn't necessarily seeing the warrior as the words bounced around in her brain. "*Dia duit,*" she repeated softly. At his nod, she asked, "What did I say?"

"May God be with you," Fallon said then gave a little shrug. "Essentially, hello."

Cateline nodded, muttering the words under her breath to get them fully engrained in her memory. "All right," she said, nodding again. She smiled up at him. "Thank you."

Fallon shook his head. "*Go raibh maith agat.*"

Cateline glared at him. "Don't confuse me."

The warrior grinned as Cateline turned away from him, repeating the earlier phrase again. As she walked, she saw a woman beating hanging garments with a flat wooden paddle, dust erupting from every strike.

When the village woman looked up at her, Cateline smiled. "*Dia duit!*" she called out.

The woman smiled, one of her front teeth missing. She raised a hand. "*Dia duit.*"

Warmth spread throughout the princess like after a sip of fine, strong wine. It was a normal phrase, a greeting, hello, may God be with you, and the woman said it back! It felt so…normal. She had no idea what that even meant, but somehow she *felt* it.

A man walked by pushing a wheelbarrow filled with large rocks. She smiled at him and he smiled back. Two other men stood near the well at the center of town, chatting as one pulled up a bucket of water.

Initially, she was surprised that nobody was bowing as they had when she and Fergus had come through during Presentation Day, but with her wearing her cloak and no crown, she figured they didn't recognize her. She liked that. They were treating her like any other villager, though she was getting some side glances as Fallon followed several steps behind, almost as though he were trying to give her space to experience.

Farther up the way, she noticed a monastery, the

wooden cross raised high as it was mounted upon the roof of the stone building. She saw a monk in brown robes with a rope belt tied at his thick middle. He and several children were working in the graveyard in front of the building, weeding and brushing off the tall, thin headstones made of slate.

Confused, Cateline watched for a long moment, feeling a presence step up beside her.

"The orphanage, milady," Fallon explained softly. "The children often tend to the graves and the garden."

"So sad," Cateline murmured. She noticed a young girl, the same young girl she'd noticed when she and Marie were in the carriage headed up to the castle for the first time.

The girl, fifteen or sixteen, was off by herself. She was tending to a tiny plot of land in the garden where a smattering of colorful flowers bloomed next to growing vegetables. Her long, dark hair was once again in a thick braid that had slid over her shoulder as she worked.

As Cateline neared her, the girl looked up. She had coal-black eyes, a lovely girl. The princess smiled. The girl didn't return it, her face expressionless. "Beautiful," Cateline said in French, indicating the flowers. She noticed they were roses. When the girl said nothing, she pointed to the flowers and smiled bigger.

"*Grazie,*" the girl murmured.

Surprised, Cateline asked, "*Parli italiano?*"

The girl's eyes widened as she nodded. "Si."

Cateline walked over to her and knelt down. "You don't speak Gaelic?" she asked gently in the girl's language. When she got a head shake, she prodded.

"Where are your parents?"

"Dead," the girl responded. "The padre lets me work for food." She indicated the flowers and vegetables.

"You did all this?" When the girl nodded, Cateline shook her head. "Beautiful. You're a very talented gardener."

The girl smiled shyly, looking away.

"My name is Cateline," the princess said.

The young girl looked at her again. "Livia."

"It's very nice to meet you, Livia," Cateline said. She noticed that the monk was eyeing them and he looked annoyed at the disruption in the work. "I must go, but I'll be back. Okay?"

Livia nodded. "Okay."

Cateline got to her feet and walked over to Fallon, who had been watching the whole interaction. "I don't want to get her into trouble."

He nodded, looking past her at the girl and her roses.

⁂

Later that night, Cateline had, yet again, been readied for an encounter with her husband. She had seen him briefly once she'd returned with Fallon, but other than a grunted acknowledgment of her presence, he hadn't spoken to her.

She didn't like the man. She outright did not like him. She didn't understand his dislike of her, and she knew she hadn't done anything to earn his ire. She was beginning to wonder if perhaps he was just a hateful man. She wanted to grab him and shake him and say, "Listen, Fergus, I didn't ask for this, either, but here we are!"

"Here's your water, *ma chérie*," Marie said, re-entering the bedchamber with a cup of the requested refreshment drawn from the castle well.

"Thank you, Marie." She accepted the clay cup and met her friend's frank gaze. "What?"

"You have the most beautiful hair," the older woman said, reaching out and running her fingers over the long, soft curls. When her hair was down, it nearly reached her bottom. "Such a rich, dark red."

Cateline shrugged, blowing a long strand out of her face. "It gets in the way."

Marie smiled. "Do you need anything else?"

Cateline shook her head, sipping from her water. "No, thank you, Marie. Good night."

"Good night, milady," the lady-in-waiting said with a small curtsey then headed to her own room, closing the connecting solid wood door behind her.

Cateline looked around at the room, noticing that the fire was beginning to burn down. She didn't have enough logs to build it back up, so she headed to her bedchamber door. Pulling it open, she looked both ways down the hall, looking to see if one of the servant boys were around.

She heard voices, loud voices. They were coming from farther down the hall toward the king's chambers. She was about to head back into her room when she heard that one of the voices was Fallon's. She was surprised, as she'd never seen or heard him up on their floor when he wasn't attending her. She figured he likely bunked with the guards on the second floor and, since he worked for Fergus, had no real reason to be with the king.

Curious, she stepped out of her room and into

the hall dressed in the white sleeping gown with her robe over top. Taking a few steps in the direction of the king's chambers, she was surprised to hear her name—the only word she understood other than Fergus's name—as well.

As she neared, she saw that the chamber door was open. King Carthac stood his ground while Fallon paced, clearly upset. "Nil," he said, shaking his head. Fallon stopped pacing when the king cleared his throat and nodded toward Cateline.

Panic raced through her as she turned and began to hurry back the way she'd come. She heard loud footfalls on the stone floor behind her, Fallon calling her name. Worried she'd be in trouble, she hugged herself and stopped, turning to face her punishment for eavesdropping.

"I need to talk to you," he said, his expression troubled.

Cateline cleared her throat before nodding. "All right. I'm sorry. I shouldn't have been listening, I just heard raised voices and I'll never do it aga—"

"No," he said, raising a hand to stop her. "It's fine." He nodded back toward the king's chambers. "Talk?"

Cateline nodded, feeling a little better though still confused. She followed him to the Solar, closing the door behind them. It was just the three of them in the huge room. She bowed to the king before looking at them expectantly.

"The nobles are coming in the morning," Fallon began. "They've grown tired of waiting and want proof that the marriage has been consummated."

Cateline nodded. "I've waited for him."

"I know." Fallon glanced over at the king, who

was listening quietly. He looked back to Cateline. "My men found him passed out drunk in the barracks."

Cateline hugged herself tighter, not sure how to feel. "So, what will happen?" Clearly, Fergus wouldn't be coming to her that night. Yet again, the bell would go unrung, and yet again Collette would be angry with her.

"I..." Fallon cleared his throat. "I've been asked by my father to fulfill my brother's duties, to produce the proof the nobles need."

Cateline stared at him. "Your father?" she said, looking to the king. "Wait, you and Fergus are *brothers*?"

Fallon looked decidedly uncomfortable, running a hand through long, dark hair. "Fergus is my brother, yes," he murmured. "But," he said, voice stronger as he glared quickly at his father before looking back to Cateline. "I will not force you. You've had to endure enough."

"Meaning?" Cateline asked, not entirely sure what she was being offered. She thought it was that Fallon would bed her, but her brain was too shocked to fully understand.

"Meaning, it is your choice. You can say no," Fallon said.

"If I say no?" she hedged.

"Then the nobles will call the marriage null and void, and you and Liberté will be sent back home to France."

Cateline nodded, considering this. "If I say yes?"

Fallon looked deeply uncomfortable as he responded, "Then I will see you in your bedchamber in about an hour. We will...we will provide the proof needed to save your marriage and your place here in

Sursha."

"And Fergus? He'll know he wasn't with me." Cateline eyed the warrior.

Fallon smirked. "He's so drunk that he won't even remember how he got to his chambers, let alone anything else."

Cateline nodded and considered all that she'd been told. The marriage was forced, Fergus's unwanted touch would be forced—had he shown up—and now, Fallon's touch would also be forced. Well, he was trying to give her the option, though they both knew there was little she could say. But still, she respected him for his kindness and consideration.

She'd be sent home, he'd said. Home, where? France was where she'd been born, but it was no home. It was where she'd been under the constant thumb of a tyrannical father and sold to the highest bidder. Here, maybe, just maybe, she could do some good. Livia's young face came to mind. Maybe she could bring her in to work at the castle? They could garden together, perhaps.

Finally, she met the expectant gaze of the warrior who stood before her, muscled arms crossed over his well-developed chest. "I'll see you in an hour," she said softly, then turned and headed out the door.

Chapter Seven

Hands ringing, Cateline blew out a nervous breath as she waited. It had been the longest hour of her life, and she wasn't sure what to do with herself. In a funny way, it was almost as though she were waiting for the executioner, her time nearing. She was scared, anxious, and relieved it would all be over—all at the same time.

She stood before the fire, which she'd finally found a servant to restoke, her heart racing. The turning of the sandglass told her the hour promised was nearly up. Fallon seemed to be a man of his word, so if that was true, he'd arrive shortly.

Blowing out a breath, she took mental stock of her appearance. She wore the gown, yet again, given for the purpose. The normal sleeping gown she'd wear would be shapeless, a simple sack garment essentially, meant to reveal nothing and simply keep her warm through the night.

The garment she'd been given to wear had a similar shape, but the material was different. It was more filmy, a bit more revealing in how it caressed the natural curves of a woman. She felt a bit embarrassed wearing it, as her nipples had grown hard from the draftiness of a castle. Even the many tapestries that hung upon the walls of her chamber couldn't keep out every breeze.

She brought her hands up and cupped her breasts

over the material of her gown to try and warm them as her nipples were so hard and rigid it was almost painful. She experienced a bit of relief with that move and the fire before her. It was short-lived, however, as there was a knock on the door.

Cateline squeezed her eyes closed for a moment before blowing out a shaky breath and turning away from the fire's warmth, and walked to the door to open it. Sure enough, Fallon stood on the other side. He didn't have his usual weapons on him, which was strange to see. In fact, he was dressed quite casually in a basic tunic and the ever-present dark brown leather pants and boots. The braids had been let out from his hair, which was combed to a glossy shine.

Cateline spared him a quick glance before stepping back, allowing the warrior to enter. "Milord," she said softly, denoting his station.

"Fallon," the warrior said softly. "Just Fallon."

Cateline nodded. She closed the door behind him and stood there, not entirely sure what to do. She swallowed hard, her heart racing so quickly in her chest she worried it might just burst.

"Shall we sit by the fire for a moment?" he asked gently.

Relieved for some semblance of direction, Cateline nodded. "Of course."

When they got to the very warmth she'd been enjoying moments before, Fallon raised his hands. In his right was a beautiful white rose. It brought back the image of the red and white roses that Livia had been tending to earlier that day. She smiled, then noticed in his left hand was the dagger he'd shown her before, a rose etched upon the blade.

"Pick a rose," he said softly.

She looked into his eyes, noting that he still looked troubled, and wondered why. Was it her? Was he, too, repulsed by her as her own husband seemed to be? She pushed such self-defeating thoughts out of her mind and tried to focus on the moment and what it would buy her—time to be with the people and help where she could.

She took in the shiny blade of the dagger, deadly sharp. It was tempting, as it could slice her finger and sprinkle the precious crimson droplets of life upon the sheet. It would take but a few moments and it would be done.

Information filed away, she looked at the beautiful white rose, its fragrance reaching her nose. A white rose was symbolic of purity, chastity, and virginity. She took it as Fallon understood what he'd been asked to do and was offering it to her as a token of that understanding and consideration.

"I've heard that a woman's journey into her wifely duties is not often a pleasant one," Cateline said, swallowing hard again as she continued. "I have to imagine you'd be more…gentle than your brother in that endeavor. Once it's done, that first time," she clarified, forcing herself to meet Fallon's gaze. "Is it as bad the next time?"

"Well," he said, shifting somewhat uncomfortably on his feet. "In theory, yes. But," he added, giving her a small smile. "From what I understand, it depends on the man."

Cateline nodded, understanding. "So, in other words, with somebody like Fergus, it will always be something I must endure." Fallon said nothing, so Cateline let out a sigh, her fate about to be sealed. She reached out and took the white rose, twisting the stem between her fingers, careful to avoid the thorns. "I think I'd like to experience it," she said, again meeting Fallon's penetrating eyes. "At least once," she added with a smirk, considering her husband's track record.

Fallon nodded, placing the dagger on the small table that stood between the two chairs in front of the fire. Cateline noticed his gaze fall to her breasts, the nipples still hard, their rosy color visible through the filmy material. The princess felt shy, as no man had seen her in such a state. Fallon quickly looked away, his face slightly flushed, surprising Cateline. Was he embarrassed? Affected by her?

Whatever he was feeling, it gave her a bit of comfort knowing she wasn't the only one who was awkward and unsure. She cleared her throat, getting his attention back on her. "I'm not sure what I need to do," she said, feeling shy and completely inept.

Fallon glanced over at the bed, then at Cateline. "I want this to be as comfortable for you as possible," he said, gently urging her to walk over to the majestic bed.

Nodding, she set her rose down on the table, ironically, next to the bell Collette had left for her. She stood before the side of the bed, waiting for what he'd have her do next. Fallon didn't disrobe in any way, but he did grab the material of her gown as far down as he could reach and slowly pulled it up until it was bunched up in his hands at her waist, her most private parts revealed.

"I'm going to lift you, okay?" he said softly. At Cateline's nod, his grip on her tightened and, with as little ease as lifting her off her horse, he lifted her up to sit on the edge of the high bed.

Feeling unbelievably vulnerable as she sat there

half-naked, the warrior standing between her spread legs, Cateline looked up at him. She so badly wanted to pull her gown down but knew that wasn't an option. Was it too late to choose the blade? She tossed the thought out of her mind as she told herself she needed to trust him.

Not six inches separating them and Fallon standing in a most intimate position, he met Cateline's gaze, his own softening as he gave her what she took to be an encouraging smile. *It's going to be okay.*

"You're so beautiful," Fallon whispered, almost more to himself as if it wasn't meant to be said aloud.

Cateline blushed and looked away. She'd never been told those words before, certainly not by somebody she felt meant them.

"Lie back," Fallon said in that low, gentle timbre that always put Cateline at ease.

Cateline did as asked and lay back on the bed, her legs still dangling over the edge with Fallon standing between them. She looked down the length of her body as the warrior's hands, so soft and gentle, ran up along the princess's thighs, using gentle pressure to push them up and spread them farther, her heels resting on the edge of the mattress.

She could feel the cool air of the evening brush across her most private place, and it sent a bit of a chill through her whole body. She tried not to hold her breath as she waited for the pain. She waited for pain that never came. A small gasp escaped her lips as she felt a touch to a part of her that she'd never felt before.

Looking down the length of her body again, she saw Fallon standing there, one hand resting on the inside of her thigh, holding it open as the fingers of his other hand lightly trailed between the delicate folds between her legs.

As his fingers teased her, evoking wonderful feelings throughout her body, he looked up and met her gaze. To her surprise, the unusual color had darkened, almost turning black. As their gazes held, he focused his touch on one part of her sex, rubbing in small circles. The sensations that caused left her breathless, as though all the pleasure in the world that she could imagine were focused in that one small area.

Cateline could feel her body responding, her legs easing open a bit wider, almost as if in invitation of their own accord. Her head fell to the side, eyes only partially open as her eyelids felt heavy, though she was anything but sleepy.

The rustling of clothing caught her attention. She turned her head and looked back at Fallon. The hand that had been on her thigh had disappeared beneath his tunic, the thumb of his other hand still rubbing slowly upon what had become the center of Cateline's universe.

He met her gaze and smiled. "Relax," he said softly.

Cateline nodded, trusting him entirely. Her eyes slid closed again, partly in pleasure and partly in anxious anticipation of what was next. She felt a pressure against her opening, a bit of a sting as the pressure against her was pushed slightly inside. Opening her eyes, she watched Fallon, who was focused on what he was doing, his hips rocking very slowly as he eased himself inside her a bit farther with every gentle push of his hips.

Cateline gasped as the uncomfortable sting seemed to fill her entirely. She wasn't in pain, but it was a strange feeling, one that took a moment for her to absorb and relax into. The discomfort began to ease as Fallon increased the speed of the circles on the magic spot between her legs.

A long sigh escaped her lips as she began to relax again, a strange mingling of pleasure and discomfort filling her body. Fallon began a rhythm of long, slow strokes inside Cateline. The hand that had been on her thigh returned and began to caress the flesh of her hip, trailing his fingers down along her thigh before moving back up to rest on her hip again.

Cateline felt like she was lost, floating on a wave of pleasure. The gentle jostling of her body with every thrust of Fallon's hips against her, burying himself deep within, added to the sensation, as though she were floating at sea, rocked by the lapping waves.

As Cateline's breathing began to quicken, she could hear Fallon's as well. She looked up at him and saw that he was flushed, his full, beautiful lips open slightly. His hand left her sex and both arms wrapped around her thighs, pulling them wider apart as his thrusts increased, deep and quick.

Any and all thoughts of worry, anxiety or nervousness were long gone as she allowed herself to enjoy what was happening. The discomfort had subsided, though there was still a bit of an odd pressure as walls and muscles were being used that weren't accustomed to it, but all was overshadowed by the building pleasure. Like an unexpected attack in the darkness, an explosion of pleasure overtook her entire body, pulling a gasp from her throat as her back arched and head tilted back. She could hardly breathe as wave after wave washed through and over her, making her toes curl.

She heard a quiet, almost strangled sound as Fallon's hips pressed hard into Cateline, hugging the princess's thighs in almost a death grip as his head fell backward. After several moments, his chest heaving, Fallon's head fell forward, eyes closed. Cateline watched him, noting the beauty of his reaction as she assumed he, too, had felt the pleasure.

After a long moment, Fallon seemed to get himself together as he took a deep breath then let it out. His eyes opened and he met Cateline's hooded gaze, her own heart slowing to a normal cadence. He gave her a smile, reaching a hand out toward her, which she took. The short moment of connection as their hands clasped added an extra layer of closeness in that moment.

Releasing her hand, Fallon eased himself out of her, quickly turning his back as he adjusted his clothing. Cateline sat up, grimacing at the soreness. She brought her legs down and quickly covered herself as best she could with the skirt of her sleep dress. She scooted back and looked down at the wrinkled sheet where she'd been lying.

"Fallon?"

He glanced over his shoulder at her. "Hmm?"

"No blood," she said, meeting his gaze, concern in her voice.

Fallon finished up what he was doing then turned back to the bed, his clothing fully back to normal, looking as he had when he'd arrive, though notably relaxed. "Well," he said, a small smile quirking the corner of his mouth. "Guess I relaxed your body a little too much."

Dark auburn eyebrows fell. "Is that what you were doing before you…well, before?"

Fallon nodded. "Yes." He turned and walked over to the table near the fire and grabbed his dagger, holding it up as he returned to the bed. "I guess we're back to Plan B."

A loud burst of laughter escaped Cateline's lips, prompting her to slap her hand over her mouth, the burst turning into giggles. Yes, she was amused by the situation, but the need to release the pressure from months of anxiety, worry, and fear, as well as her relief now that it was all over, overwhelmed her.

"Sorry," she whispered, a smile still on her face even as it was hidden behind her hand.

Fallon grinned at her, a lightness to him that she hadn't seen before. "Quite all right, milady." He looked over the bed, his gaze resting at the center. "Milady, would you please scoot over there and lie down?"

Getting her amusement under control, Cateline did as she was asked. Lying down, she watched as Fallon climbed up onto the bed and sat next to her, though down by her legs. He pushed the covers back that were folded neatly at the end of the bed.

Meeting her gaze, he smiled shyly at her. "Forgive me, milady, but I must get a little…friendly."

After what we just did? Cateline thought but allowed him to do what he needed to do. He positioned her legs much as they had been before, bent at the knee and spread, though her feet were planted on the mattress beneath her.

As vulnerable and exposed as she felt, Cateline was surprised to feel warmth begin between her legs and spread through her belly like hot molasses. Fallon brought up his left hand, hissing softly as the sharp blade of the dagger sliced across his finger, a few beads of blood bubbling to the surface.

"I'm going to put a little bit on your gown, okay?" he said, sparing a glance up to where Cateline lay watching. At her nod, he lowered his hand, dangerously close to the part of her body that began to pulse.

Cateline was confused why her body was reacting so strongly to the mere nearness of the warrior. He'd just cut himself, was bleeding on her behalf, yet her body yearned for him to touch her. She tried to push that away as she watched. He winced slightly as he squeezed his fingertip, allowing a few drops of blood to drip down to the gown that had been shoved down beneath her bottom when she'd scooted back on the bed.

A small gasp escaped Cateline's lips when Fallon's knuckle just barely grazed her most sensitive area, a jolt went through her entire body.

"My apologies, milady," Fallon whispered, his eyes that same deep, dark purple they'd been as they'd begun the marital act earlier.

Cateline could see a vein in his neck pulsing. Her heart was beginning to race again, a deep need that she didn't understand gnawing at her. She didn't trust her voice to say anything, so she remained silent.

"All right," Fallon said, letting out a long, slow breath. "If you'll scoot back, milady, I can do this on the sheet now that I know where it's needed."

Cateline nodded, sitting up and scooting out of the way. "I'm sorry you literally had to bleed for me, Fallon," she said. "You could have cut me."

Fallon finished with the droplets on the sheet before meeting her gaze. "I've had many wounds in my life, milady, but very few as important." With those sage words, he pushed off the bed and moved away from it. "If you could, give me time to get downstairs before you ring the bell?" he asked, turning to look at Cateline, who was also climbing off the bed. "T'wouldn't be good for Collette to see me leave."

Cateline nodded, agreeing. Together, they walked to the door. "Fallon?"

"Yes, milady?" the warrior said, his usual tone, friendly yet professional, back in place.

"Thank you," Cateline said. "I was dreading this, and yes, I will still have to face him at some point, but I feel better." She gave him a small smile. "A bit more knowledge, perhaps. And," she added. "I feel my place here is more stable." She smirked. "Whatever that place may be."

Fallon held her gaze for a long moment before giving her a smile, the kind she'd seen over the last hour. "Your place can be whatever you want it to be," he said softly. He took her hand and, leaving a lingering kiss on her knuckles, met her gaze again. "You are most welcome. Good night, Cateline," he whispered, then was gone.

Chapter Eight

The door closed slowly, those beautiful blue-gray eyes staring right at the warrior before Cateline turned away, headed back into the bedchamber where Fallon had just been. When the door was fully closed, a dark head fell, forehead against the cool wood.

"What did I do?" Fallon whispered.

Blowing out a breath, the warrior lifted her head and looked down one side of the hallway, which led to the king's chambers, and then the other way, which led to the exit of the top floor of the castle. She considered letting her father know it was finished but decided she needed to leave. The princess had a duty to alert Collette that the deed was done, and it would do no good for the warrior to be seen in that moment in an area she, as head of the Elite Guard for the prince, had no business being late at night.

With catlike movements, Fallon made very little sound as she hurried down the stone stairs, lit torches tucked into nooks in the stone lighting her way through the shadows. She needed to do damage control if they were going to pull this off without suspicion.

Reaching the bedchamber, Fallon found what one of her men had warned her about a couple hours before, now relocated from the barracks to his own room. Shaking her head in disgust, she stepped through the partially open doorway, softly closing the door behind her.

Set up much like her own just down the way, the bedchamber was smaller than that of the king or queen on the fourth floor but was still much larger than the rooms servants or guards were given.

The still form lying on the floor in the middle of the room was snoring loudly, an obnoxious burst of rotten-smelling air exploding from his behind, which interrupted the snoring for just a moment.

Shaking her head, Fallon walked over to the single candle burning on the small table set near the dark, cold fireplace. She grabbed the holder by the brass handle and walked back over to the form, noting he'd thrown up all over himself. The smell met her nose before the sight met her eyes.

"Son of a…"

Fallon walked over to the bed, noting the bedding was all over the place, part of it pooled down on the floor. It had clearly been a wild night. She also noted a small clay bottle, the stopper missing, that lay on its side on the bed.

Grabbing it, Fallon brought it to her nose, sniffing. Eyebrows falling, she looked at it. "Olive oil," she murmured. She glanced back over to her brother on the floor. The fact that his pants were still on, though unlaced, indicated the olive oil hadn't been for his bedroom use, but rather whoever he'd had with him.

Walking back over to the table, she set the candle down before walking back to her brother and standing over him. She nudged his leg with the toe of her boot. "Wake up." When there was no response, she nudged him again, so tempted to just kick him. "Wake up!" She watched his belly jiggle with the movement of his body.

Fergus's snoring turned into a snort, then a cough as he choked on it. Pushing himself to a sitting position, the prince looked around, looking dazed. "What time is it?" he asked, voice rough and gravely.

"Time for you to get to bed," she said, sounding far less disgusted than she actually was. She bent down and wrapped her arms under his armpits, using her strength to pull him to his feet with a mighty grunt of exertion. "Up you go."

Fergus used his legs to help, though he was incredibly unsteady on his feet once he was upright. He leaned his considerable weight on Fallon as together they got him over to the bed. "Why was I on the floor?" he grumbled, falling away from the warrior and onto the bed once they reached it.

"I have no idea," Fallon said, dreading the task of removing her brother's boots. "Guess you were so overcome by your evening upstairs."

"Evening upstairs?" Fergus muttered, lying back on the bed as Fallon took hold of his left boot.

"Yes," Fallon responded, working on removing the footwear. She dreaded what she'd find. "You did your job, Fergus," she added, wanting to vomit herself as the boot came off and the condition of the sock indicated just how long it had been since Fergus had bathed.

Fergus stared up at him. "I didn't touch that woman," he muttered.

Fallon met his gaze then looked away, noting the white, cream-like substance that was stuck in his beard near his mouth. In a repulsed moment she wondered if the olive oil had been used as lube before or after that little explosion.

Shuddering at the mental image that brought to mind, she returned her focus to the current situation. "You did," she insisted. "The bell rang clear for all to hear." She smirked at her own unintended rhyme.

Fergus laughed, which turned into another coughing fit. "The bell rang clear for all to hear," he sang, sausage-like finger waving in the air in time with his little melody. "I bet she loved it," he groused, amused tone gone. He brought up his hands and rubbed his face.

"Does it matter?" Fallon asked, tossing the second boot to the floor. "It's done. You'll get your own castle now."

Fergus looked up at her, studying her for a long moment before saying, "You're going with me, you know."

Fallon met her brother's gaze. It hadn't been discussed what would happen beyond getting the princess to Sursha and getting her certified by the Court. Now all of that was done, or would be in the early hours of the morning to come.

The castle that had been bestowed upon Fergus, the Prince of Sursha, was on the other side of the country, more in the mountainous region. Fallon and her brothers had spent much time there when they were younger and before Ailfred had left for war and, ultimately, never returned.

"And why is that?" Fallon asked, tossing the second boot to the floor. The filthy and sweat-encrusted sock it revealed was just as disgusting as its mate. She wasn't going to touch those.

"Because," Fergus said, his eyes growing heavy. "You're my personal guard," he muttered, the last word morphing into a snore.

Fallon let out a heavy breath, running her hand through her hair, pushing the long strands out of her face. "Your personal dog, you mean."

Leaving him where he lay, she walked over to the candle and blew it out before leaving the room and closing the door behind her. She'd left the vomit for her brother's footman, Will, to clean up in the morning. After all, he was the other half of the night's mess and Fergus's lapse—again—in duty.

Fallon headed toward her own bedchamber but decided there was no way she could sleep. She needed to get out, get some fresh air and think. She turned around and made her way to the closest hallway that would lead outside and ultimately to the stables.

❧ ❧ ❧ ❧

The massive war horse had looked at her a bit confused but soon enough had them on the road, powerful hooves pounding the earth as they galloped across the moonlit countryside. Fallon's hair blew back along with Toirneach's midnight mane. Like the horse's namesake, he thundered across the land.

They headed for the forest that was part of the king's lands that surrounded the castle. Knowing the way all too well, the war horse galloped through the trees, dodging this tree, that stand, jumping the fallen log, never missing a beat.

Finally, he slowed down, Fallon patting the muscular neck of her mount, proud of his prowess. "Good boy," she said.

He brought her to the mouth of the cave, the one she and Ailfred had discovered together when she'd been about nine. At its face, it looked like a cave that went straight down to Arawn's underworld. But when they'd explored farther, they realized that it was almost like a natural protection to keep humans and animals out of the magical place it was hiding.

Toirneach left behind to graze on grasses and roam free for a while, Fallon bent down to enter the mouth of the cave, instantly disappearing from view as she jumped down the large crag that was mere feet inside. Her stomach flew up into her mouth as she fell, left hand reaching out to grab the vines she knew lined the wall there.

Getting a strong grip on one, Fallon's downward fall was stopped, slamming her into the wall, a grunt escaping her at the hit. There was an easier, and less painful, way to descend, but it took much longer and she just wanted to get there.

Making the slow climb down, her booted feet hit the mossy covering and she let go of the vine, turning right and heading back out into the warm night from the cool cavern she'd just slipped down. The area she walked into was once part of the same cave system as the small shaft she'd just left, but over time a large part of the roof had worn away through erosion from water, and the torrential rains that washed over the country had created a natural waterfall and small pool of fresh, clear water surrounded by the walls of what was left of the cave.

Behind the waterfall was a small entrance that could be reached from the forest on the other side, which was how she'd leave. The sound of the waterfall, unheard until actually in the partial cave, was loud and comforting, the water so beautiful in the moonlight that shone down through the canopy of clouds above.

She walked over to the large, flat rock she often

lay upon after bathing and reached under a small space covered by vegetation. She retrieved the leather pouch she kept there that held a bar of Castille soap, which came from Spain and was made largely from olive oil and potash.

Tossing the pouch to the rock's flat surface, Fallon grabbed her tunic from her upper back and yanked it up and over her head. Tossing it aside, she stood there, revealed to the night. From afar, she looked as though she had the torso of a man with a muscled stomach and developed pectorals to go along with well-sculpted arms.

If anyone got close enough—which she never allowed—they'd see the ruse. She wasn't a strong, capable, muscular man. She was a strong, capable, muscular woman, in the ways only a woman could be. A strong body, sure, but it was her strength of character and will that set her above the rest, using her mind for what her body wasn't biologically capable of doing in order to keep up with her men.

She unlaced her leather pants, letting them drop to gather at the tops of her boots. Only then was the true lie visible. It had begun years before when she'd begun to transform from the basic androgyny of all children to that of a developing young woman.

Her father's very talented—and loyal—armorer Colm had been a master leatherworker. Every few months until she was fully grown, and then once or twice a year thereafter, Colm would get a large piece of hide and wet it until it was malleable. It would be laid over Fallon's naked torso, contoured to the shape and size of her breasts to form little pockets for them to fit into, if pressed a bit to her body.

Once what would be the bottom layer fully dried

and hardened, more layers would be applied, each one taking on more and more shape until finally a man's torso was carved, created specifically for Fallon's age and proportions. A backplate was also added, the entire thing fitting as closely to her body as was possible, though if too much of an intimate touch was allowed, the edges could be felt.

It was a cuirass, not only to act as protection from wounds of war, but also from the wounds of hatred and fear from those who didn't understand the role she was being put into, the box created just for her.

It was a brilliant work of art and genius, but it could be hot, uncomfortable, and terribly constraining on many levels. She unlaced the cuirass, tanned to match her skin tone as closely as possible, which was tied into the leather harness that was attached to her hips. Two different phalluses had been created for her by Colm, both eerily realistic. She didn't want to know his process for that.

One phallus, which she currently wore, was used for sexual encounters. From what she'd been told by Millie, it was extremely successful in its realism, both in how it felt and how she wielded it. The second and most often used was for everyday life: a "flaccid penis" which could be maneuvered and moved like the real thing, and had a funnel inserted inside of it for urination.

Her false persona removed, Fallon sat on the rock and removed her boots and socks before pulling off her leather pants, leaving her gloriously naked and free. She stood, lifting her arms up high overhead as her head fell back, long, dark hair tickling the bare skin of her back. She felt like she could breathe.

She took in a deep lungful of air before slowly
blowing it out. The night air felt wonderful on her
skin. She looked down at herself and had to smile. It
looked as though she still wore the torso, as the flesh
of her own was pasty pale while her arms, shoulders,
face, and neck were deeply tanned.

Walking over to the water's edge, she dove in,
knowing she had clearance in depth. The water felt
absolutely exquisite on her skin, cool, crisp, and clean.
She dove down until her fingertips touched the stone
floor of the cave before arching her back and surging
to the surface, breaking through to gasp for air.

She felt amazing, a smile on her lips as she
treaded water. The pool wasn't deep, but too deep for
her to stand on the bottom. Now that she was away
from the castle, away from her brother, away from
her obligations and away from Fallon the warrior, she
could be Fallon the person.

She swam around, guided by the moon and stars
above as her mind wandered over the night's events.
She could have simply given Cateline Plan B from the
start. There never had to be a white rose, never had
to be any sort of intimate action. The naive young
woman would never have known any better. A flick of
her blade and the Court would have gotten what they
wanted and Cateline's place would have been safe.

Why? Why had she chosen the other?

From the moment she'd first seen the young
noblewoman in France, she'd been captivated. Of
course, she could never say anything, show any sort
of interest or awe, any exception of any kind.

Cateline Aubert, Princess of Sursha, was a small
woman, a small build and perhaps slightly below
average in height. She seemed so fragile, yet Fallon

had seen her inner strength from the beginning. Her eyes were a blueish gray, though more often stormy gray. She had a natural sultriness to her that Fallon was pretty sure she had absolutely no understanding or knowledge of.

Her eyes said so much, held her intelligence and a deep passion that Fallon had gotten to see a glimpse of mere hours before. She suspected it had yet to be even partially unleashed. Her hair was a rich, dark auburn, which was in stark contrast to the creaminess of her skin. When Fallon had seen her that night, her hair down and wild like a lion's mane, she'd nearly lost her ability to speak.

In her years as a warrior, the places she'd been and women she'd met and enjoyed, nobody had affected her like Cateline. She'd wanted to crawl on that bed and make love to her until the sun came up, but knew that wasn't her place. Plus, she knew the young woman would be able to feel the false torso, so she'd kept as much distance from her as she could while still completing the intimate task.

Turning to her back, Fallon used powerful legs to push her along the water as she stared up into the late-night sky, stars like tiny gems stuck into black cloth. Her mind returned to the flushed passion of Cateline's face when they were together. The little noises she made, whimpers and gasps. It made Fallon's body burn all over again.

As she turned over, swimming toward the pool's edge so she could get the soap and wash, she thought about the softness of the princess's thighs, the softness of her most private place, and how incredibly wet she got at Fallon's touch. She could hardly take that personally, she reminded herself. Cateline had never been touched with the purpose of pleasure by another before, or perhaps, even by her own hand. Why wouldn't her body react? It was a natural reaction.

And, it was at the touch of Fallon "the man." No doubt Cateline would be horrified if she ever knew the truth. Only a handful of her familiars within the castle walls had ever known her true identity, and if any outsiders had suspicions, they were not voiced nor any questions asked. The Surshan people adored their king and were fiercely protective of the royal family.

One of the reasons Fallon worked so hard to be the best of the best at what she did was so there would be no room for anyone to be unhappy with her. As long as everyone was happy, no one would start digging where they didn't belong.

But Cateline wasn't one of them, wasn't born a Surshan who'd either known Fallon or her family their entire life. She had no loyalty to the country and certainly none to Fallon. The heavy weight of obligation once again descended upon her. Fallon the warrior she must be, and Fallon the warrior she'd remain.

Chapter Nine

Fallon had fallen asleep at the waterfall after bathing, as she'd done one too many times. When she'd been riding back toward the castle, she'd seen the contingent of nobles heading there for the consummation reveal.

That had made her feel sick to her stomach on two fronts. One, it would cement that Cateline was married to Fergus, legally bound. And, two, if it were somehow disputed or the means of consummation discovered, it would mean death to both she and the princess for adultery and lying.

She'd opted to stay clear of the castle and go do some rounds in the nearby villages as well as within the shadow of the castle walls where many lived and worked for the king. Her presence would be a good thing, both for the people to feel protected and also for any who might be considering a stupid action to reconsider.

People were out and about beginning their day, gathering wood for cooking fires, filling buckets of water, and tending to their crops. The acrid smell of chimney smoke filled the chill of morning as rider and horse made their way through main streets and trails.

Fallon nodded acknowledgment to a few patrolling guards, stopping to talk with a couple as she did. Though she wasn't head of the Surshan army, she liked to get her head around any problems at their infancy. Her elite force was largely the clean-up crew for the most unpleasant of domestic and foreign situations, bloody and messy. If she could cut off the nub before it grew to a head, she preferred to.

Deciding it was time to get her own day of duties started, she sent Toirneach at a full gallop back home. No doubt her father would be making declarations that day for preparations to begin to move the prince and princess into Caislean Thiar, which essentially meant the castle in the west.

Fergus had told her she'd be going along with them, though Fallon wasn't sure how much credence to give that, the statement of a man very drunk and not entirely in his right mind. Ultimately, it would be up to the king.

Though Fallon had been assigned as personal guard for Cateline, that was before she had become official. Oftentimes an entire regiment was taken from the existing army to follow the prince to his new life, and from that crop of warriors decisions were made for personal protection.

Once inside the bailey, Fallon headed toward the stables. On the way, she noticed one of her men over by the wall. A young servant girl, who clutched a basket to her chest like a shield, looked frightened, trying to lean away from him even as he seemed to have her somewhat pinned in the corner.

Rage instantly filled Fallon. She pulled her mount to a stop before dismounting, tying off his reigns on a nearby tree. With purposeful steps and moves, she made her way over to them. As she got closer, she could see the fear in the young woman's eyes, not just her body language. Her man wasn't touching the young girl but was very much using his superior size and presence to dominate her.

When the woman looked over the soldier's shoulder at Fallon, the warrior could see the pleading in her eyes. Jaw muscles straining as she grinded her teeth together, Fallon grabbed the man by the back of his tunic and yanked him so hard away from her that he lost his footing and stumbled backward, hitting his head against the stone wall that surrounded the bailey.

It was deeply satisfying to Fallon when he looked up at her and sheer terror filled his eyes at the realization of who had caught him harassing the young woman.

"Get up," she growled. When it took the soldier longer than she liked, she grabbed him by the front of his tunic and gave him a lift, literally. He fell into her as he was yanked to his feet. Keeping a good hold on him, Fallon looked to the girl. "Are you okay?" she asked gently.

The young woman, all of sixteen, nodded. "Aye."

"Did he touch you?" When the young woman shook her head to Fallon's question, the warrior turned to look at the soldier. "Tell her. Now." She shoved him away from her so he could stand like a man to apologize.

The soldier swallowed, sparing a glance to Fallon before looking at the young woman. "I'm very sorry," he murmured. "It'll never happen again."

"If this man or *any* of my men harass you in any way, you ask for me, Fallon, and it'll be dealt with. All right?"

The young woman nodded. "Yes, sir," she whispered.

Fallon gave her a soft smile. "On your way, miss."

The young woman gave a quick curtsey then

scurried away from the situation.

Fallon turned back to the soldier, who looked like he was about to vomit. "Training field," she growled. "Now."

The man said nothing, simply took a deep breath and turned, standing tall before marching in the direction of the requested destination. Fallon watched to make sure he was following orders before she headed back to her horse. She got him to the stables and cared for before she headed to the barracks.

The men inside were just beginning to wake, other than those, like the man with the young woman, who were on early guard duty. She walked to the section where her men were, beds lined up side by side with an aisle between the rows.

She stood in the aisle. "Training field, two minutes!" With that, she left the building, headed to the practice field.

Fallon had a staunch, no exception policy with her men when it came to rape, abuse, or harassment of women. They all knew it, and they were all part of the punishment when that sacred vow they took was stepped on or broken.

Moments later, the entirety of the Elite Guard stood before her in neat, straight rows. One hundred pairs of eyes were staring straight ahead, not flinching, not looking about. The first third of the men were the best of the best, elite of the elite. Those twenty-five were those sent out on missions of absolute stealth, the Samurai of the West.

She'd chosen her best to accompany her to retrieve Cateline, and had a quiet contingent of her men snooping to find out how those *routiers* had gotten through the line of French soldiers that final night on land.

Each group had their specialty. In the very back were the deadliest archers in the country, their arrows tucked into quivers on their backs, longbows slung over their backs. Ahead of them were the spear throwers, their aim and accuracy bred into them over generations. Like the Spartans before them, their training started young and created a masterclass of warrior.

Though all of them were master swordsmen and hand-to-hand fighters, the elite of the elite were trained to be deadly without a single weapon. These men were Fallon's pride and joy, as she herself had been trained as they had, as had her beloved brother, Ailfred.

Refocusing her attention to the morning's unpleasantries, she walked to a distance of twenty yards from the first row of her men. She tossed a coiled rope to the ground, an unlit torch to the ground twenty feet away, then an unused bracer twenty feet away from that.

When the men saw that, they knew why they'd been called to gather. They began to space themselves out into a large circle, the objects tossed to the ground at the center. One man didn't move from his place in line, the man to be punished. He stood his ground, head held high, shoulders straight, and stance tall. The only sign that he was nervous in any way was the pointer finger of his left hand twitching as nervous energy raced through his body.

Fallon waited until all the men were in place and settled before speaking. Pacing at the center of the circle, her meandering path taking her around the accused. "This man," she began. "Decided it was a good idea to corner a young woman whose only crime was trying to get her morning duties done."

Fallon turned to look at the faces of her men. From the moment they'd been awarded the honor to join the Elite Guard, the importance of women had been pressed into them day in and day out—their place, their role, and respect for them. Anything less was not tolerated. Besides their warrior prowess, one of the main things that had separated the Surshans, a warring people often hired as mercenaries, from the others was how they treated humanity, especially women. They didn't beat, rape, and pillage. Anyone who did faced dire consequences.

"I came across this this morning, and that young woman, who did say he didn't touch her, looked at me with terrified, pleading eyes."

Before Fallon had even asked for what punishment their comrade deserved, a dagger was launched and landed near the coiled rope, the owner casting his vote. Next came a spear and soon enough, a volley of weapons. Fallon moved out of the way, allowing the men to speak. Finally, the last vote to be cast was her own.

Removing her dagger from her boot, Fallon flipped it around until she held the deadly sharp tip between her fingers. She sent the blade flying, end over end, until it embedded itself into the dirt, center of the coiled rope.

There were votes for all three punishments. The torch indicated a month of straight night watch in the bogs; the bracer meant the accused had to go up against Fallon in a one-on-one fight. That option, along with castration, was typically reserved for those who had raped someone, as it was a fight to the death, and many had learned that going up against the greatest warrior the Surshans had ever produced was not wise.

"With the most votes," Fallon called out. "Rope it is." She turned to the accused man who, though still stood straight and tall, had the glimmer of emotion in blue eyes. "Tomorrow at dawn," she pronounced. "You will show up at the square with this rope," she said, walking over to the object in question, grabbing it and her own dagger before walking back over to him and dropping it at his booted feet.

The men surrounding them began to pound the butts of their spears and bows, or stomped their feet as she spoke.

"Naked, you will be tied to a stake to feel the vulnerability and fear of those you are sworn to protect." She invaded his personal space, her face not two inches from his. "May the women take pity on you," she said sweetly.

By time Fallon got to the castle, the morning meal had been eaten and the day begun. She went in search of her charge. She found her sitting with the ladies of the nobility, now officially afforded the acceptance and privileges of her status.

Fallon, freshly washed up and changed into fresh clothing, stepped into the room. A dozen women sat around tables paired off or in small groups playing chess or various card games.

It didn't take long to find Cateline, as she was the youngest in the room and truly the most beautiful. She seemed to be in deep thought of her next move in the chess game she was playing, her brow wrinkled in concentration.

The room was small and cramped, often used for the ladies to knit, weave, and create other such works of textile magic. The fireplace was aglow, which helped the windows set high in the walls to light the room, and also chased away the damp chill that permeated castles year-round.

Cateline looked up from her game, as though tapped on the shoulder. She turned her head and those beautiful eyes, turned the color of ash, reflected the dancing flames in the firelight and found the warrior. A small smile curved full lips before the princess turned back to her opponent, saying something to her before she pushed away from the table and weaved her way through the small room to Fallon.

"Good morrow, milady." Fallon greeted her with the proper bow for an official princess. As she looked at the woman before her, dressed in the finery befitting of her station, her long, beautiful hair pulled up in thick braids for an elaborate updo, Fallon couldn't help but see the woman from the previous night. She had to look away for a moment and clear her throat in an attempt to clear her mind.

"Good morrow, Fallon," Cateline said. The princess looked down for a moment before looking back up, meeting Fallon's gaze. "I thought perhaps you'd left when you weren't around this morning."

"No, milady," Fallon responded, shaking her head. "I had some unexpected business to take care of this morning. My apologies."

Relief seemed to fill Cateline's eyes, that smile returning. "No need to apologize. I hope it went well, your unexpected business."

Fallon shrugged, not wanting to think about the unpleasantness. "Part of my job, I suppose."

It felt as though there was so much left unsaid between them, but Fallon knew this was certainly not the place or time to speak of it. She wondered if there ever would be. As the punishment of her men was part of her job, so was doing all that she must to keep the kingdom and its people safe. That, apparently, included making love to their future queen.

"I was told that I need to begin hiring staff for the new home," Cateline was saying, which pulled Fallon out of her thoughts. She was most grateful for that. "Later," Cateline continued. "After the ladies and I are finished here, can I talk to you about how to go about this?"

Fallon nodded. "Of course, milady. Whatever you need."

Cateline's smile grew. She gave the warrior a curtsey, her gaze never leaving Fallon's before she returned to her chess game.

"Milady," Fallon said, getting the young woman's attention. "Queen to H4," Fallon whispered with a wink, then turned and left the area.

❧❧❧❧

Fallon used her dagger to cut off a piece from the thick slab of salted bacon. "Are you wanting me to split up the Guard?" she asked before popping the piece into her mouth.

Carthac chewed on his own bit of food, heavy eyebrows drawn in thought. He took a sip from his ale before responding. "Your brother is going to need some oversight," he said. He met Fallon's gaze. "I know he has some men of his own, men that are loyal to him, and that makes me nervous."

Fallon was uncomfortable with the entire conversation but knew it was a very necessary one. "Lady Cateline asked me to help her with hiring servants for Caislean Thiar," she said. "What if," she offered, grabbing for her own cup of ale. "I helped her bring in people that could act as eyes and ears?"

The king considered her words, chewing more of his food before he nodded. "I like that. I considered sending Collette, but he detests her, and I think, like he did as a boy, he'll act out simply to defy her."

Fallon chuckled as she drank from her cup. "Agreed."

The patriarch of the family and the country studied his youngest for a long moment before asking, "How did it go last eve?"

Fallon nearly choked on the ale that she was swallowing. She couched, some of the dark liquid spit into her plate.

Carthac grinned. "I see."

Fallon glared at him. "I wasn't expecting that question." She used her forearm to wipe her mouth before responding. "It went fine. We did what needed to be done," she said, voice flat. She glanced up from her plate when there was nothing forthcoming from her father. "What? I did as you asked me to do, Daidi. As did the princess. It worked, all's well." Fallon was surprised at her own tone and just how hard she sounded. She didn't want to analyze why.

"I see," Carthac said quietly. "Well, I thank you." He sat back in his chair where the two sat in his Solar to eat the midday meal together.

A sudden burst of anger hit Fallon, taking her

by surprise. "Why?" she asked, staring at him.. "Why? Of all people for Fergus, why her?"

The king met and held Fallon's gaze for such a long moment that the dutiful warrior, understanding and respecting the hierarchy of life, finally cast her eyes to the floor. "Fallon," he said, his tone firm. "Look at me."

Reluctantly, the warrior once again met her father's gaze.

"I don't suspect they'll be married long," King Carthac said softly.

Chapter Ten

The skies were talking, a summer thunderstorm moving its way across the island. Fallon stood by, waiting for Cateline to finish her conversation with the man who ran the monastery. She'd already spoken to the young girl, Livia, who they'd discovered was a sixteen-year-old orphan. She was generally too old to live in the orphanage run by the monks, but they took pity on her and allowed her to stay in a shed on the property if she helped tend the gardens.

For whatever reason, the princess said she had felt drawn to the girl since she'd first seen her the day she arrived in the country. So, since she needed to find servants to staff the new home, Cateline wanted to speak to Livia.

After the meal with her father, Fallon had set out to find the princess and see if she was ready to talk about the hiring situation she was now faced with. She'd found her sitting alone in the room, the other ladies gone and games finished. Cateline had been staring into the flames, a look of sadness on her lovely face.

Fallon had wanted to ask after her seeming melancholy but felt it wasn't her place. Despite what had happened the night before, the beautiful intimacy they'd shared—and, dare she say, enjoyed— they weren't friends, they weren't close. That wasn't possible. They both had their place, and Fallon had to keep that well in mind.

The door to the monastery opened, and Cateline and the head monk stepped out. He bowed to her, and a smiling princess made her way down the stairs and toward Fallon, looking quite proud of herself.

"Successful mission, I take it?" the warrior asked. "Your smile is wider than the Uisci Mora, and that is the widest lake in the country."

Cateline's smile turned to one of shyness. "Yes, well…"

Fallon grinned, unable to help herself. "She accepted?"

The princess nodded. "Yes. She accepted right away, and," she added, though she was keeping her voice soft. Fallon had the distinct feeling she was fighting a burst of excitement. "Three others who wish to start over and learn a trade."

Fallon's eyebrows shot up. "How old are they?"

"Livia is the oldest at sixteen," Cateline said shyly.

Fallon raised an eyebrow. "You don't happen to be a piper, are you?" she asked, playfully reaching toward Cateline's dress, though not touching her. "You're not wearing pied clothing under that, are you?"

"You would know," Cateline murmured, an eyebrow of her own raised.

Fallon felt as though she'd been punched in the gut; a full thirty seconds passed that she was unable to speak as a wave of heat moved through her, which she was trying to put out. Also, she was stunned at the unveiled flirting. From the look on Cateline's own face, it seemed she, too, was shocked by what had just come out of her mouth.

Fallon rubbed the back of her neck, able to feel how warm the skin was. She didn't know what to say, and the sight of Cateline's mouth opening then closing only to fall open again would have been amusing had the situation not gotten so utterly awkward.

The moment was eclipsed by the opening of the monastery door again. Livia, carrying a small hessian bag over her shoulder, appeared with two children, a girl and a boy, holding hands. The younger two looked like siblings, the girl perhaps four or five, the boy around eight. The children were dirty, dressed in what amounted to rags held together by carefully placed stitches.

Fallon felt her heart fall, her emotions a mix of anger and sadness. As the trio walked toward them, she wondered how on Earth they were going to do this. But, seeing those little faces so defeated already, there was no way she could turn them away.

"I'm glad we had the forethought to bring the carriage," Fallon said, meeting Cateline's gaze. The princess seemed concerned.

"Are you sure this is all right?" Cateline asked softly before the children reached them.

Fallon nodded. "We'll make it all right," she promised.

❧ ❧ ❧ ❧

"What the hell were you thinking?" Fergus roared.

Fallon stood still, allowing her brother to throw his full and complete fit before she began to speak, knowing if she spoke too soon it would make him even angrier. Finally, after more shouts, insults, and flying objects, Fallon had the floor.

"No, I'm not an idiot, nor is Cateline," she said. "Nor will you be forced to feed someone else's unwanted 'brats,' as you call them. What I was thinking, since you asked, is saving you money."

Fergus stared her down, the two standing in the lord's chambers in the castle that would become their new home. He lifted his chin, almost as if in challenge. "Continue."

"Do you think you're actually going to have to pay those kids?" Fallon asked, feeling sick to her stomach as she forced herself to sound as heartless as her brother was. She smirked. "Hell, they'll be thrilled to do whatever you ask of them just to be given something to eat or a place to sleep that isn't in a pile of a bunch of other kids."

Fergus's shoulders relaxed as he seemed to take in what he'd been told. "So," he said, hands on hips. "Those little bastards will be grateful for the scraps I toss to them, do whatever I ask them to do?"

Fallon wanted to take her dagger out and gut him, but instead smiled. "Exactly." She reached out and touched a dust-covered table with her fingertips, drawing a little figure in the dirt. "Pretty brilliant of Cateline, actually," she murmured.

Fergus grunted. "Maybe she's not as witless as I thought."

Fallon felt her fury grow but continued to tamp it down. "Well, no doubt we can get more cheap labor to bring this place back to life." She raised her dust-covered fingertips. "While I'm here this week, I'll make sure all this gets taken care of."

"Good. I want this place perfect when I move

in," he ordered. "Right now, it's a dump."

As the prince began to leave the room, Fallon stopped him by calling his name. When he met Fallon's gaze, she asked, "Why don't you talk to Cateline? Get to know her? As much as you're playing ignorant, you speak her language."

Fergus looked at the warrior as though she'd lost her mind. "Why would I?" he asked. "Why would I lower myself to speak that filthy language when, if she had a brain, would learn Gaelic." With that, he walked past Fallon, leaving her to watch him go.

Shaking her head, Fallon looked around the chamber. The castle in the west wasn't as large as the main one where she'd grown up, but it was still imposing, still offered wonderful protection with battlements and gates and a moat and all the wonderful things, just a slightly smaller size.

One thing this castle did offer that the other one didn't, however, was a tower. The larger castle had a dungeon, as did this one, but no tower. So, on the rare occasion that a particularly important criminal needed to be housed, the tower was employed. Or, if a mischievous fifteen-year-old decided to scare the wits out of his six-year-old sister, it worked just as well.

There would be a lot of work needed to ready the place for its new inhabitants, and the small staff that lived there year-round had already begun. New staff would be arriving later the next day so they could be trained properly and help with preparations before the official move-in.

Fallon left the lord's chamber and headed to that of the lady, which would be occupied by Cateline. The bed was already there, a massive four poster with intricately carved headboard that likely took four men just to move and place. The old mattress had been infested by rats, the stuffing turned into a nest, so it had been removed and burned. Currently, a new one was being created for the princess.

The fireplace was large, an elegant stone mantel above it. It sat cold as the chimneys were being cleaned by a crew that scrambled up into them to clear away debris and bird nests so as not to send smoke or worse, fire, back into the castle.

There was a raised dais in the room by the wall that sported three large, beautiful stained-glass windows, which allowed in light from the outside in a rainbow of colors. The center window had a rose bloom as its focal point, which made Fallon smile. She'd forgotten about that, and she wondered what Cateline would think of it. It was perfect for the princess.

The raised area was in a semicircle with three stone steps that ran the entire circumference. At the top was a flat area where chairs could be situated for reading or even a small table for chess or sewing. She felt it would be a favorite spot for the new occupant.

Noting four doors in the room, Fallon checked out each one. The first and second led to Cateline's private boudoir and garderobe, respectively. The third led to the small room that was for the lady-in-waiting, which of course would continue to be Marie. Fallon wondered if perhaps Cateline might train Livia for that role as well. That position was traditionally held by young women in their teens and twenties.

The fourth door intrigued Fallon, especially once she opened it and found it led to a dark corridor. Leaving the door to the lady's chamber open for light, Fallon headed into the corridor, made of stone walls and stone floor, a narrow passageway that no more than one man at a time could pass, or perhaps two small women could squeeze their way side by side.

The walls were cool to the touch, no niches for candles or torches. The deeper Fallon went, the darker the corridor became. Finally, she reached a set of narrow stairs, which she climbed. She came to a hatch overhead. Placing her palms on it, Fallon pushed, the hatch easily lifting.

Walking up the last couple stairs, she was stunned to find herself in the room that, when the castle was first built three hundred years before, would have been where the Captain of the Guard had stayed before those accommodations had been moved into the guardhouse that had been added years later in another part of the castle. The stone walls were rounded making it a circular room as it was at the top of one of the towers.

She stepped down into the room, realizing that the flattop trunk that she'd noticed before when touring the rooms in the castle was actually a ruse; it hid a secret passage to the lady's chambers.

She walked around the small room, which had its own fireplace as well as a door at the top of a narrow, steep flight of stairs that went to the parapets that encircled the tower. There wasn't a lot of natural light in the room, but the small fireplace would take care of that and the chill.

She had to wonder what the original builders had been thinking. Why, she thought, standing at the center of the empty room, hands on hips, had a secret corridor been constructed from the rooms where the lady of the house stayed and where the Captain of the Guard lived? Perhaps to steal her away to a safe hiding place if the castle were attacked.

Fallon shook her head, intrigued. She closed the hatch, marveling at just how much it looked like a normal, wooden trunk. She walked over to the single door in the room and pulled it open. It led to the portion of the castle that was set up for the guards, including their small rooms and a communal garderobe with room for six to use it at one time.

In a way, she thought, it made sense to have a connective corridor for the military to reach the royal family, though she found it strange that it wouldn't be into a main hallway or the lord's chambers.

Heading back into the small tower room, Fallon decided she'd claim it as hers. But first, she had a little convincing to do.

⚘ ⚘ ⚘ ⚘

Her hips slapped rhythmically against the bare behind she held onto as the phallus attached to her hips was buried deep inside with her quick, hard thrusts. The woman on the receiving end, bent over the wooden plank table moaning loudly, finally cried out, her fingers gripping the edge of the table with a white-knuckled grip.

Fallon's mouth fell open as a small orgasm passed through her, but it wasn't about her, it was about Millie. She didn't stop until she knew the thirty-two-year-old widow had finished, the blond woman's hand reaching back to touch Fallon's chest in a gesture to request her to stop.

The warrior pulled out, immediately turning around to adjust her clothing, even though it wasn't necessary in front of the woman whom she'd known since the age of fourteen. That year, her father had paired her up with the pretty young woman who, at the time, had been married to one of Ailfred's best friends and fellow soldiers. In fact, they'd died together.

But, as Fallon had grown older, she'd had to learn how to pass as a warrior, which required her to take on the ruse that had ultimately become her identity. Millie had helped her learn how to act like a man in the most intimate ways, though theirs hadn't turned to a sexual relationship until after Burke and Ailfred's deaths. Their mutual grief and need for comfort had sent them across the line of friendship.

Fallon genuinely liked Millie, perhaps even loved her on some level, but mostly she trusted her. She'd been there for the warrior through everything, from the death of her brother to the first time Fallon lost one of her men. She knew Fallon's secret, though never pushed her to be her true self with her. That was just not something Fallon could risk or afford.

Once physically composed and everything was tucked away where it should be, Fallon turned back to face the woman whose breasts were still visible as she drank a cup of water in long draws. She held out the cup to Fallon, who took it.

"I needed that," Millie said, tendrils of her hair hanging down in her face, still flushed from their exertions. She tucked her breasts into her dress and fastened it before reaching for the sleeveless tunic that would go over the long-sleeved, brown dress.

Fallon nodded but said nothing as she placed the empty cup on the table. Crossing her arms over her chest, she waited until the older woman was put back together and ready to talk. Millie walked over to Fallon, giving her a peck on the cheek before heading over to the fireplace where a pot hung on the spit over the flames.

"Let me get you some stew," Millie said, glancing over her shoulder at the warrior with a questioning brow raised.

"Please," Fallon said.

"So," Millie said, scooping the fragrant slop into a wooden bowl. "We got a little distracted, but before that, you were asking about a favor."

"Yes," Fallon said, amused at her longtime friend and mentor's choice of words. Distracted. Truth was, Fallon had tried to talk to her about the situation and Millie had all but torn her dress open, making it quite clear what she wanted. Knowing Millie's voracious appetite, Fallon had come prepared for this possibility with the appropriate phallus. "Fergus is now gaining the control of the western province," she explained.

Millie looked at her, both eyebrows raised as she filled the second bowl. "I see."

"Yes. My father doesn't trust what he'll do with that sort of power." Fallon sat in one of the chairs at the table as her bowl of stew was brought over and placed in front of her. It looked hideous, but Millie had a flair with seasonings and herbs, and she knew it would taste as amazing as it smelled.

"Can't imagine why," Millie drawled, sitting down with her own bowl but not before grabbing two wooden spoons. "Your brother only nearly sank three ships because of his mouth four years ago."

Fallon smirked as she blew over the spoonful of stew she was about to put into her mouth. "Forgot about that one," she muttered. Savoring the flavors, Fallon swallowed and finally said, "I'd like to bring you in as staff." She lifted her spoon as an example.

"Cook, perhaps?"

Millie was looking down into her bowl but spared a glance up at the warrior, the wheels clearly turning behind her brown eyes. She used her spoon to play in her food for a moment before she let out a long breath, whisps of her hair blowing in the ensuing breeze. "I don't care what they said, I still think Fergus was part of that deal that went bad and got Burke and Ailfred killed." She looked Fallon in the eyes, her own filled with fire. "I'll do whatever you need me to do."

Fallon met her gaze and held it. "You'll do it?" she asked, relieved. "You'll come in and help keep an eye on him?"

"I'd poison him if you asked me to," Millie said casually before putting her spoonful of stew into her mouth.

Fallon considered her words, not entirely surprised by them. She knew the blonde hated Fergus, always had. She didn't know what she thought of Millie's supposition about the deaths of beloved their husband and brother, but she knew Millie would be loyal. In the dangerous game Fallon was entering into, that came first.

"What of this girl he's married?" Millie asked, pushing away from the table to refill the wooden cup with water from a bucket drawn from the town well. "A Frenchwomen." She glanced at Fallon. "Can she be trusted?"

Fallon looked down into the monochromatic stew. She saw Cateline's beautiful face, her eyes, even in her mind's eye, pinning Fallon to the spot. Finally, she nodded. "Yes." She looked up and looked at Millie. "Yes, she can."

Chapter Eleven

Fallon glanced over her shoulder to make sure everything was okay on the path behind her. They were taking it slower than she normally would, but she didn't want to chance Cateline getting hurt or lost. Assured all was okay, she continued leading their parade of two.

The work on the western castle had taken longer than expected so now, after just under two months, it was time for the great migration west, a journey which would begin two days hence. Knowing they were leaving the place of Fallon's birth and where she grew up, Cateline had asked what she'd miss most. Rather than tell her, the warrior decided to show her.

"Just around the bend, milady," Fallon called back. Up until the last half a mile the two horses had been allowed to run, eat up some distance, but as they'd gotten into the dense forest, Fallon brought it down to a walk. Her own mount was impatient, because if it were just them she'd still be racing through the trees, but Fallon had more to think about than just her.

Finally, the entrance in sight, Fallon pulled Toirneach to a halt, Cateline doing the same with Liberté. Fallon dismounted her war horse before heading over to the princess, reaching up to help her down. With the training Fallon had undergone, the need and ability to lift a grown man and carry him out of danger, Cateline's slight weight was so charming to her.

Hand tucked under Cateline's arms, it was the first time she'd touched her since the night the two were forced to consummate Cateline's marriage to Fergus. Several weeks ago, at times it seemed it had just happened.

Lifting her to the ground, Fallon met the gray-blue gaze that haunted her dreams. The princess's soft touch on her arms sent a little thrill through Fallon. Once her feet were on the ground, Cateline's hands fell away, which meant Fallon's had to as well. With a smile, she stepped away from her.

"Ready?" Fallon asked.

"You command, I follow," Cateline said with a smile. "Wasn't that what you said?"

Fallon grinned, remembering their first day going into the closest village to the castle. "Yes, and I imagine this is the last time I'll hear those words from my princess," she said, fist to her heart as to her duty, which was to protect the kingdom and its royal inhabitants. "Will Liberté be okay to roam free for a while, or would you prefer we tie her to a tree?"

Cateline rubbed the neck of her mare and looked from the gray to Fallon's horse. "Will yours wander?"

"Yes, milady. He comes back when I whistle for him." She smirked. "I think he enjoys the freedom for a bit."

"Well," Cateline said, patting her mount. "I think Liberté will stick with Toirneach." She met Fallon's gaze. "Let's let her wander."

Fallon nodded. "Then it shall be."

Once the horses were released, Liberté looking rather confused before she followed her tall, dark companion to frolic in the forest, Fallon and Cateline made their way toward Fallon's secret place. Fallon was still surprised at herself for bringing the princess at all.

"*La alainn ata ann,*" Cateline said casually.

Fallon stared at her as they walked, surprised. "Yes, it is a beautiful day," she agreed. She smiled at the proud grin she received. "You've been practicing."

"I have. Actually, Livia has been very helpful. She doesn't speak Gaelic fluently, but enough to give me a bit of a start," Cateline explained, softly thanking Fallon as the warrior held a low-hanging branch back out of her way.

"I'm impressed, milady." She indicated the tree nearest them, a perfectly harmless one. She asked her question in Gaelic, looking pointedly at the princess for a response.

Cateline looked from the tree to Fallon and back, tucking in a full bottom lip as her mind was clearly spinning. Finally, she looked at Fallon. "*Oui?*"

Fallon burst into laughter. "I hope not!" At Cateline's look of confusion, Fallon grinned. "I asked you if that tree was going to eat you."

Cateline blushed deeply, looking away. "Well," she said, glancing again at the tree. "Perhaps we should get going."

Amused, Fallon acquiesced and got them going again. "Milady," she said as they neared the entrance, which was at the bottom of a short but steep hill. She turned to look at Cateline, holding out her hand. "I don't want you to fall."

Cateline looked down at the proffered hand then up into Fallon's eyes. With a small smile, she accepted the hand, the skin warm and so soft. Fallon wrapped her fingers around it and held firm as she began to traverse the terrain, making sure with each step that the lady was in no danger of falling.

Reaching the bottom, they stood before the stone wall that looked like any other above-ground portion of a cave. Fallon was excited as she knew the beauty and surprise that was just beyond the small entrance. She saw the small stream that ran from just inside outward and into the ground and, though no problem for her to hop across, she didn't want Cateline's dress to get wet.

She stretched her legs wide, one booted foot on either side and turned to Cateline, reaching for her. The princess obviously understood why, as she stepped into her waiting grip. With a grunt of exertion, Fallon picked her up and lifted her up and over the water. She could feel the strain on her upper back with that one, as she wasn't in the best stance to lift a grown woman, but it was worth it.

"Good?" she asked once she set the other woman down on her feet again.

"Yes, thank you."

Fallon let her go then stepped aside, as all Cateline had to do was duck a bit to step through the entrance to see the wonder beyond. She smiled at the gasp she heard when her companion saw what was waiting for them.

Stepping inside, Fallon took in the lush greenery, blue sky overhead, and listened to the rush of the waterfall falling into the awaiting pool. Cateline walked up to the edge of the waterfall and stared up at it, a hand to her chest.

Stepping up beside her, Fallon said nothing, simply tried to take in everything through fresh eyes, seeing for the very first time what she'd seen so many times. Her special place, the only place where she felt free.

"This is magnificent," Cateline finally said, meeting Fallon's eyes. "How'd you find this place?"

"I fell down a hole," Fallon said.

"You lie," Cateline said, eyes wide.

Fallon grinned and shook her head. "I wish I were." She pointed to the way she normally entered, the small exit just barely visible in the stone wall surrounding them. "When I was a kid, my oldest brother and I decided to explore this cave we'd found," she explained. "We were all proud of ourselves. Took one step in"—she snapped her fingers—"and down I went." She indicated where they stood. "After I got over the sound of my arm cracking, I was in awe."

"I can certainly see why." Cateline hugged herself, a serene smile on her lips. She looked at Fallon. "Thank you for bringing me here. I could never have imagined this. It looks nothing like France."

"It looks nothing like Sursha, either," Fallon said. "It's sort of its own, magical place."

"Would you tell me about Ailfred?" Cateline asked softly. "I've heard you mention him a few times. Seems he was important to you."

Fallon nodded, walking over to her flat rock and lowering herself to sit. Cateline joined her, the two sitting nearly thigh to thigh. Fallon could feel the other woman's warmth and essence. It was a double-edged sword of wonderful and awful as that presence wasn't hers to enjoy.

"He was thirteen years older than me," Fallon began. "Four years older than Fergus. My father said I was his pet from the beginning." She smiled at that. "I wasn't expected. My father had his sons and they'd survived past the dangerous years. After all, Fergus was nine and Ailfred was thirteen, so…" She shrugged, "He wasn't concerned about more children."

"Were you close with your mother?" Cateline asked.

Fallon shook her head. "I have little memory of her," she said, meeting Cateline's gaze. "She died when I was but two. The mother I've known was Collette."

"Perhaps I should be nicer to her?" Cateline teased.

Fallon grinned. "She's a difficult woman to get to know, I will concede that."

"What was Ailfred like?"

"Me," Fallon said. "Well," she added. "I guess I'm like he was." She stared at the waterfall but saw him. She was always told she looked like him, though like their father and Fergus, he had darker eyes. "He was a scholar," she said softly. "He loved to learn, studied the greats." She glanced over at Cateline. "Alexander the Great, Hannibal, Caesar, Belisarius. He studied their every move, every battle, win or lose." She smiled. "He studied astrology, anything he could get his hands on."

"Like you."

Fallon nodded. "Yes." She smiled. "I used to follow him around, his little shadow. I'd tell him I had his 'history lesson,' and I'd tell him some little fact that I'd heard about that day. No doubt he already knew most of them, but he'd humor me, ooh and ahh in all the right places."

The princess smiled. "Sounds like a wonderful older brother."

"He was." Fallon was silent for a long moment, feeling the grief of his loss all over again as it washed over her. For that moment she considered what Ailfred would think of Cateline. A smile quirked her lips when she thought he'd probably have already won her away from Fergus.

"What are you smiling at?" Cateline asked. "Good memory?"

"I was just thinking, if he were still around, I think he would have really liked you." She met Cateline's gaze, but only for a moment before looking away. "I think he already would have managed to snatch you away from Fergus."

"Oh, you think that, do you?" the princess asked, eyebrows raised.

Fallon smiled shyly, sparing her a glance. "Well, Ailfred was intelligent, very handsome, an amazing fighter." She nodded at her own assessment. "A really good person."

"Well," Cateline said softly. "You said you're just like him."

Fallon nodded. "Yes. I'm proud to say, very much."

"Then I know I would have loved him," Cateline said, looking at the waterfall.

⁂

It had been a long day, the last before they were to head out in the morning to move Prince Fergus and Princess Cateline into their new home. She hadn't seen the princess since their sojourn at the waterfall the previous day. Once they'd returned in the afternoon, Fallon had to meet with her men, whom she'd been with the rest of the day.

Since her new assignment was to join Fergus on

the other side of the country, which was more than a day's ride from her current location, she had to hand off leadership to her second-in-command for the day-to-day duties, training, and handling. She trusted her men to stay the course, and she'd be around at least one day a week, more when she could, and would be in contact with her second through writing. She made sure all her men knew how to read and write; it was very unusual for a military man to be educated, but she insisted upon it.

Looking around her bedchamber, Fallon felt a bit sad. She'd slept in that room for nearly twenty-four years. Yes, she was gone often on campaigns, particularly in France when she and her men were hired out as mercenaries or for protection to the local fiefdom. But that room had been where she'd returned, laid her head, recharged for the next battle.

Hands on hips, she looked to the wall where her weapons were hung at night, to the space that was usually at the foot of her bed where her extra "male parts" were hidden. The trunk, with all of her other belongings not immediately needed, had been loaded into wagons with other such items belonging to those moving, and had left days before so that all would be ready when the incoming party arrived.

Unbuckling her sword belt, the unique design allowing her double blades to anchor upon her back gave way. She hefted their weight as she carefully lowered them to the bed, adjusting her shoulders as they were freed from their burden.

Looking at the double blades, specially made for her, their weight, size, and grips, she thought about Ailfred and how she began using the shorter blades in the first place. She thought about her brother every single day, but she rarely spoke about him. Talking about him to Cateline the day before had brought back memories that were as warm and comforting as they were cold and painful.

"Okay, Fallon," Ailfred said, his sword in his hand, the two siblings the lone figures on the training field.

He held his sword in both his hands, just like he'd shown his nine-year-old sister to do, a sister that was already referred to as Fallon only. It wasn't about a sister, a brother, girl or boy. Fallon had defied gender norms from the beginning.

She'd acted as neither, she'd acted as both, and she felt that her oldest brother taking her so completely under his wing at such a young age had kind of tipped the scales on who she'd be. Then, as she got older and it was clear that she preferred the social company of men and the romantic company of women, her fate was sealed.

"Remember how I told you," Ailfred said, encouragement in his deep voice.

Fallon looked at the sword that she held in her hands, borrowed from her brother. It was a short sword, but still heavy and felt unbalanced to her. She glanced up at him, a towering figure to her nine-year-old self, and though she knew he wouldn't hurt her, per se, he wasn't going to take it easy, either.

Noting the dagger that he'd dropped on the ground before they began their training, Fallon tucked her bottom lip in and chewed on it as she eyed him, waiting to time it just right. When Ailfred moved to swing, expecting her to parry his lunge, which she did, basically, the twenty-two-year-old man was caught off guard when she whirled around out of his reach, grabbed the dagger off the ground, and used it to slice his hand before using the short sword to knock his sword out of his hand. He was stunned from the unexpected move and superficial wound.

He stared at her with wide eyes before looking down at his bleeding hand. "What did you do that for?" he asked, his voice a mixture of shock and pride.

"Because this is too heavy," Fallon said, throwing the short sword to the ground. "This," she continued, holding up the dagger. "Is lighter and I could move really fast."

Shaking his head, Ailfred walked over to her and ruffled her hair. "Good job, Fallon," he murmured. "Good job."

That day they'd made a trip to the swordsmith's shop to outfit the precocious young warrior.

Fallon lay on her bed, head cradled in her laced fingers. She stared up at the ceiling, her brother fresh on her mind. She thought back to the day she'd found out he'd been killed. He and Burke, Millie's husband, had been sent out on a private mission. That's all she had been told—a private mission.

At seventeen, nearly eighteen years old, Fallon had lost the person who centered her most. He was her best friend, her commander in the Guard, and her mentor. He taught how to be a soldier, how to be a "man." but mostly, how to be a good person.

Ailfred had been groomed his entire life to take the throne once their father died. He was already a leader, not only among his men, but people in the country. He was beloved, every noblewoman from Sursha to Ireland to Spain wanting his hand in marriage. But, much like Fallon, he was married to his country.

She thought about her words to Cateline at the waterfall. Ailfred would have loved her, perhaps would have finally decided on a woman to settle down with, have an heir with, for sure. She could see his older brother with the beautiful young Frenchwoman. No doubt she would have fallen hard for him.

It wasn't often Fallon wondered what it would be like to have a wife, to have that one person to turn to for advice or comfort, like what she'd heard her parents were like. She had no memories, but Ailfred and Burke used to tell her about it. They were friends, they were lovers. Oftentimes her mother had spent the entire night with her husband, for no other reason than they enjoyed spending time together, if even in sleep.

What would that be like? For Fallon, she just wondered what it would be like to have somebody who knew who she was, her true self, and loved her anyway. Didn't expect her to fit into the box she'd been shoved into at such a young age.

Yes, she'd conformed to that box, that role easily as not all of it was foreign to her, but not all of it was her. She had other parts to her, too, other sides of herself. She wondered what it would be like to be with a woman sexually with only what she'd been born with, nothing strapped on or buckled in.

What would it feel like to be touched, *really* touched?

With a heavy sigh, she sat up and leaned over, blowing out the single candle she had lit in the room and lay back down, still clothed. She was too tired to care.

Chapter Twelve

It had been a long ride with a stop overnight at a nobleman's estate, but they'd finally reached Caislean Thiar on the island's opposite shore. During the last month or so, Cateline had become very close to little Laigen, who rested against her now.

The four-year-old was a beautiful little girl with long, blond hair and bright, curious blue eyes, Her eight-year-old brother Garratt was more reserved, suspicious blue eyes watching everything and everyone. The siblings had been through a lot, from what Cateline had come to understand simply from their behavior, but Laigen hadn't become jaded like her brother quite yet. Cateline hoped to stop that from happening.

The castle was smaller than the one she'd been at in her first few months in the country, but it still seemed worthy of its purpose. It was farther inland than the other, lots of wooded land surrounding once one got beyond the curtain wall and moat.

The carriage drove into the bailey, the horse's hooves echoing on the stone as they clopped their way in. Servants were waiting, some Cateline recognized, others she didn't. All their belongings had arrived ahead of time, so this was simply the welcoming committee.

"*Ma fille*," she said softly, brushing back long, golden strands with her fingers. "Time to wake up."

The little one opened her eyes, blinking several times. She looked up at Cateline, whose side she'd been leaning against, almost as if to reassure herself that the princess was still there, before looking around at the others in the carriage.

Livia and Marie were already at the castle to get things ready in the princess's chambers, which left Cateline, who shared her bench seat with Laigen, and Garratt, who sat across from them and was nearly plastered to the window, taking in every single detail of his surrounds.

A very curious boy, Cateline noticed. Observant, intelligent eyes. She considered asking Fallon if there was anything he could use the boy for. Perhaps with his troops? Give the boy a skill.

"Ready?" she asked everyone, using Gaelic.

She'd been trying to use it more and more, forcing herself to learn. Collette had compared the books that Cateline had brought with her, and books that were part of the collection at the castle. Two were the same book, one in French and the other in Gaelic so she could learn that way as well. It would be a slow process, but the process had begun.

Cateline smiled when she spotted her lady-in-waiting, who was walking toward her with Livia, who had been working closely with the older woman. Garratt hurried over to Livia, who seemed to be one of the only people, other than his sister, that he was truly close with. Laigen quickly followed, her little legs propelling her beneath the long dress she wore.

"Good trip?" Marie asked.

"It was," Cateline said with a tired smile. "Very glad it's over."

"Well, we have your chambers all set up with a

mattress newly stuffed and ready for you," Marie said as she led the princess up several flights of stairs.

The older woman tossed out bits of instruction as to what and who was on each of the three levels they passed until they reached the top floor. Cateline looked around, noting various tapestries hanging on the stone walls in hallways and the rooms they'd passed. She was glad, as it helped keep the castle warmer. With this area being more mountainous, she wondered if the temperatures were cooler than the lower areas.

"Prince Fergus is in there," Marie said, hitching her thumb in the general direction of an adjacent hallway. "And," she added, pushing open the large, squared wooden door. "This is you, madame."

Cateline felt her stomach roil a bit as she stepped into the chamber. It was quite final. She thought back to her parting words with Carthac the previous morning. *This is going to be your home, Cateline. Treat it as such. Your time has come.*

She wasn't entirely sure what he'd meant by that but was determined to heed his words. The king had been very kind to her, and she saw so much of Fallon in him. The room was smaller than what she'd stayed in over recent months, which was fine with her. It was larger than her room back in her father's home, and she loved the raised portion of the room under the beautiful windows.

Walking over to it, she climbed the few steps and found a small table there with two chairs, one draped with a warm, fur-lined blanket. On the table was a chess set. She reached out and fingered one of the carved onyx pieces.

"Fallon insisted that be placed in here," Marie

explained. "Not sure why, but we made sure it was."

Cateline smiled, thinking back to that day he'd given her advice that had won her the game. "Very sweet of him," she murmured, stroking the knight piece with a fingertip before turning away from the table to look out over the room.

She looked at it with different eyes than she had her previous chambers. She'd been a bit shy and reserved when arriving initially, as everything, from the marriage to a man she didn't know and who had seemed basically uninterested in her—a proven point by now—to the language and customs she wasn't familiar with, had been overwhelming and frightening.

Now, nearly a full season in, she needed to get stronger, though she wasn't sure how, wasn't sure what her place was, exactly. Fergus had certainly given her no lead. Honestly, she felt most days he'd be just as pleased if she fell into the moat.

Pushing thoughts of her wayward husband away, Cateline let out a long, shaky sigh. She looked at her longtime friend and companion. "I can do this," she said. "Right?" She hated the sound of her own vulnerability.

Marie gave her the soft, motherly smile that Cateline had come to cherish. "*Oui, ma chérie.* You are stronger than you give yourself credit for. So smart, such a wonderful heart." Her smile grew. "I'm not the only one here who sees you, Cateline."

✦ ✦ ✦ ✦

The great hall was a large space, long and narrow along the right side of the main floor of the castle. Massive wood timbers ran along the high ceilings and two fireplaces, one on either side, warmed and lit the space. One of the fireplaces was currently lit, which Cateline was grateful for. She could definitely tell a difference in the chill of the evening air.

She and Fergus sat at either end of one of the long tables. Easily, twenty men could comfortably be sat between them, ten on either side. A plate of food had been set before her, which she was making her way through, as was her husband. He had said nothing to her; in fact, he'd shown up several minutes after she'd sat down.

The food was quite good, despite the fact that it wasn't particularly appetizing to look at. She heard the cook's name was Millie, and though she'd seen her earlier, they hadn't officially met. She'd have to find her later to compliment her dinner.

"Good food," she said, loud enough for Fergus to hear her at the other end of the table. Her voice echoed in the cavernous space.

Fergus glanced up at her, a quick look of surprise on his face, though she wasn't sure if it was that he was surprised she dared speak to him or that she'd spoken in Gaelic. She'd never know, as the side door opened and a man entered the room, one that she'd seen at the other castle. She believed his name was Will, Fergus's footman. As such, he was responsible for the personal needs of the prince—his personal servant, as it were.

She watched Fergus light up when the man entered. He looked to be in his twenties somewhere, a close-cut beard and short, shaggy brown hair. She couldn't hear what the two men were talking about, though one or the other would let out a bark of laughter from time to time. They were obviously close, very friendly.

As she watched the interaction of the two men, it made her sad, almost wistful. She was married to Fergus, so clearly she should want that sort of bare minimum friendship with the man, but she couldn't even call him an acquaintance. She knew nothing of him, had never touched him other than the ritualistic touches during their wedding. She knew nothing of what he liked or disliked, except perhaps her.

In retrospect, it wasn't so much that this particular man didn't like her or seem to want her around, or that they seemed to be in a loveless or even friendless marriage. Sadly, that was common in arranged marriages among people of her status. What made her sad was, she was now stuck in this, trapped and, however long they were married, any possibility of finding the person who could love her, *wanted* to love her, was not an option. She could meet this person tomorrow, but it would be all for naught.

Another door opened and Fallon walked into the room. He caught Cateline's eye immediately and relief washed through her. She'd seen very little of him since preparations had begun in earnest to move the couple to their new home. Their day at the waterfall had been wonderful but fleeting in a month's time.

He immediately looked around—as he always did, she noticed—taking in his surroundings. She figured it was probably the warrior in him making sure there wasn't a threat. Cateline found it quite charming, and it made her feel safe.

His gaze swept over her, and it seemed to take him a second to register who he was seeing as he did a quick double take. Fallon gave her a quick bow of his head as he walked toward his brother, his gaze meeting and holding hers for a moment. Cateline gave him a small nod back, watching as he reached the prince.

He leaned over the table, bracing his weight on his hands as he spoke quietly to the seated man. Cateline's gaze went from Fallon across the table to Will, who stood on the opposite side of Fergus. He was looking Fallon over top to bottom.

For reasons she couldn't explain, it irritated Cateline. She looked back over to the warrior, unable to not notice the long, lean lines of his body, the muscular arms…and knowing just how strong they were. Knowing how it felt to be wrapped in them, even if for a completely innocent purpose.

He was so beautiful. Looking away, Cateline felt eyes on her. Glancing over to the footman again, she saw that he was watching her, a smirk on his face. She looked back to her meal, appetite suddenly waning.

❧❧❧❧

Cateline crawled into bed, excited to be the first to sleep upon the mattress in the huge, beautiful bed. It was definitely much cooler than it had been the previous night or the night before that, so she was grateful for the many blankets and quilts on her bed. In fact, she mused, she may even get a little too warm.

Getting settled, she thought back over her day. It had been a long one, but finally the journey was over and she was at what she should consider home. Earlier, during dinner when Fallon had entered the great hall to speak to Fergus, that had essentially been her time with her husband.

Fallon had murmured an apology to her for interrupting before he left. Not long after, Fergus had taken his plate and wine and had left with Will, leaving Cateline in the huge room to eat alone, not a single word to her before or as he left.

Cateline had spent a lifetime more or less ignored. It wasn't unusual that a girl was ignored by her father except when she became useful to him for alliances in marriage. This, of course, had been the case with her own father. He suddenly remembered he had a daughter when a suitor came calling. He simply had to decide which of three made the most sense for said suitor.

She often wondered what it would have been like had her mother survived. Would they have been close? Though Marie had certainly stepped in after her mother's death, Marie was a paid servant.

Cateline felt she and the older woman had a genuine bond and affection for each other, but she wondered what would it be like with someone who wasn't around for profit or pay. Would it be any different, or was she romanticizing it? Was what she had the best it got?

She thought about Fallon again. From the little bit of his life that he'd shared with her, it seemed they had similar childhoods. Both were the youngest of three, both had lost their mothers early. After such a profound loss, they'd been essentially pigeonholed into a box by their fathers, a box that was for the "good of the family," or in Fallon's case, the country.

So often she'd look at the warrior and catch him staring off into space, a deep sadness in his eyes. She didn't know what made him sad or look so lost, but she so often felt the same thing. Some days all she wanted was to feel found.

As though whomever was looking down from above were listening to her thoughts, her bedchamber door quietly creaked open. She didn't lift her head but saw two little figures enter the room by the light of the fireplace. She heard soft sniffles followed a quiet voice as the two figures advanced, the door closing behind them.

As they passed in front of the fire on their way to the bed, Cateline saw that it was Garratt and Laigen, the former holding the hand of the latter. She lifted her head when they reached the side of the bed. She could just barely see the little four-year-old's head above the mattress, and she had a tear-streaked face.

"She wants you," Garratt said simply.

Cateline sat up, the covers falling to her waist. She murmured softly in French, loving and comforting words to an upset little girl as she reached for her, pulling her up onto the bed. "It's okay, *ma fille*," she said, hugging the child to her. "Get scared?" she asked in Gaelic. When the little girl nodded, she hugged her closer, leaving a kiss to her head. She glanced at the boy, who looked on. "Come, Garratt," she said, patting the bed.

The boy shook his head, all pride in his face and puffed-out chest. The two had been given a room in the servants' quarters with Livia. He backed away from the bed. Cateline said nothing, not wanting to force him. Instead, she turned her attention to Laigen, who was calming down, her tears stopping.

She pulled back the covers and helped her climb under them. In that moment, pulling that little girl to her, she felt like a lioness protecting her cub. She knew she could kill anyone or anything that dare make this little one cry again.

Laigen curled up against her, her little fist curled around a handful of Cateline's sleeping gown.

As she ran her fingers through the long, blond hair of the child, Cateline saw the bedchamber door open, Garratt standing in the opening. As she watched him, he paused, looking out into the hallway beyond before he slowly backed back into the room, pushing the door closed, not a noise made.

He glanced toward the bed then hurried over to the rug in front of the fireplace. "Garratt," Cateline said softly. When the boy's head whipped around to look at her, eyes wide as though he'd been caught doing something wrong, she pointed toward the chair on the dais that had the fur-lined blanket on it.

He shook his head, again that pride in the set of his jaw. Cateline lay her head back to the pillow, settling in with her arm wrapped protectively around Laigen. She was about to fully close her eyes when she saw Garratt look over at her again. Seeming to be satisfied that she wasn't watching, he scurried over to the chair, grabbed the blanket, then scurried back to the rug.

Chapter Thirteen

She chewed on the freshly baked bread that was on her plate, along with smoked fish and fruit. She looked down the long table at the empty chair. A breakfast plate had been set out for Fergus, yet it sat untouched.

Her own appetite waning, Cateline pushed the plate away and sat back in her chair. When she'd awakened, Laigen and Garratt were gone, the blanket placed back on the chair. To her surprise, Cateline had slept amazingly well with her little bundle in bed with her and Garratt not far away.

Since the two had unexpectedly entered her home and her life, she'd become very protective of them and worried when they weren't with her. They were so young, so small, and so terribly vulnerable. But then, perhaps she was seeing herself in them, Livia as well.

One more glance down the table and Cateline felt the emotion of rejection threatening behind her eyes. She felt humiliated and abandoned. Making up her mind, she pushed her chair back from the table and grabbed her plate. She'd go seek out company with the servants.

Breakfast plate and goblet of wine in hand, she pushed through the door the servants came through when serving. She found herself in a hallway with three directions to go, no clue as to where they led.

Hearing laughter and talking voices, she followed the sound.

This castle's kitchen was not in an outbuilding as it had been in Carthac's home. The servants were sitting around a large table off to the side, eating their own breakfast. She saw the main cook, Millie, there. She was standing at the giant fireplace with hooks embedded into the stone wall to hang pots just like the one whose contents she was absently stirring with a large wooden spoon.

Other hand on her hip, the woman's blond hair was pulled up atop her head, though tendrils fell about a face that was more round. A sheen of moisture made her skin shiny, no doubt from the steam and fire surrounding her cooking duties. She was laughing with some of those sitting at the table eating, obviously involved in the conversation even as she stood apart from the others.

At the table were some faces Cateline had seen in the last day, some she hadn't. She was relieved to see Marie, feeling she'd no doubt be welcomed by her. But she also saw that her lady-in-waiting was in an involved conversation with a man who looked to be about her age, graying hair thin, a few strands falling into his eyes. She watched in surprise as Marie reached over and pushed those strands away.

She knew the man had come over with them from the other location but couldn't recall what he did. Clearly, he and Marie had become close in the months that they'd been in Sursha, judging from such an intimate gesture that was inappropriate for an unwed person. Surprised and a bit hurt that Marie hadn't trusted her enough to tell her about her new friend, Cateline turned her attention away from the older…couple?

When her presence was noticed, everything came to a screeching halt. The dozen or so people there turned away from the conversation and breakfast and took a knee, heads bowed in deference.

Millie was the first to recover. "No good?"

"Oh," Cateline said, looking down at her unfinished food. "Good," she assured in Gaelic with a small smile. "Not hungry."

The cook shrugged indifference as she took the plate and goblet and went back to her task.

Cateline decided it was best to leave the servants alone, as her presence made them obviously uncomfortable. She gave them all a nod of acknowledgment and soft wish of good morning, then turned to leave after meeting Marie's eyes for a long moment.

"Milady!"

In the hallway, headed quickly toward the stairs that would take her up, Cateline stopped, turning to see Marie hurrying after her. The older woman fell to her knees in front of the princess, taking her hands and cradling them against her cheek.

"Forgive me," Marie pleaded.

Cateline's eyes fell closed as sadness enveloped her. "Marie," she whispered. "Please stand."

The lady-in-waiting did as bade, her head lowered as she retained hold of Cateline's hands. "I should have told you," she said, her voice quiet and filled with sorrow. "I didn't expect to meet someone like Henri, and I thought you would think less of me."

"Marie." Cateline gently pulled her hands from the other woman's grasp, only to place one on the side of Marie's face to get her to look at her. "You became a widow at a very young age, and then you dedicated your life to me when I needed you most."

Marie gave her a soft smile, seeming to relax a bit. "I have loved you like you were my own."

"I know," Cateline said with a sad smile. "I wish you would have told me, not because you had to but because you wanted to."

"Oh," Marie said, eyes wide. "I wanted to," she assured with a vigorous nod. "But things here were so difficult with…" She nodded in the general direction of Fergus's bedchambers three floors above.

"Marie," Cateline murmured, giving the only mother figure she'd ever had a genuine smile. "If I've learned anything over these past months, you have to grab happiness with both hands when it comes. If Henri makes you happy, I want you to take it."

Marie looked down for a moment, then nodded. "He asked me to marry him, but I said no, didn't want you to think I was abandoning you. Which," she added quickly. "I am not."

Cateline studied her for a long moment, head slightly cocked to the side. She smiled. "God brought us Livia. You're already working with her." She pulled Marie into a warm hug. "Find your happiness, Marie," she said, the older woman returning the embrace. "You can have both," she added, giving the permission that Marie's position required. "I give you my blessing."

A small cry escaped Marie as she hugged her young charge even closer. "Thank you," she whispered.

Cateline delivered a kiss to each cheek, the two women sharing a smile of affection and mutual excitement for Marie's future. After a moment, the two parted, Marie headed back to the kitchen and Henri, and Cateline continued on her way to her bedchamber.

So many thoughts in her head, so many mixed emotions, more than she'd begun with after leaving the great hall. The position Marie held was extremely time consuming, and no doubt Marie would want to retire and switch to a different position with a new husband to be with, should she go that route. From the look in her eyes, Cateline figured it was a short amount of time and they'd be planning something special for her longtime companion.

She felt so alone as she made her way down the endless hallways and corridors made of gray stone. Cold, a little damp, and comfortless. She hugged herself, doing her best to hold her emotion back until she reached her room. There was no way in hell she was going to let that bastard see her cry, should she run into him before she reached her destination.

Relieved to be behind the heavy, solid wood door of her chambers finally, the tears fell. Cateline buried her face in her hands, the salty warmth sliding between her fingers. In that moment, she was crying for what she'd been forced into, what wasn't, and what would never be. She cried for her loneliness and for yet again feeling like she wasn't worthy of being loved. It was a heavy feeling that gripped her heart like a vise.

After several long minutes, she got herself under control. She'd let herself feel, let herself cry, let herself feel sorry for herself, but now it was time to pull herself together and figure out what she was going to do. Fact of the matter was, she was in the situation and there was nothing she could do about it. Fergus had made his feelings clear, so, due to no choice, she'd respect them and, frankly, return them.

Taking several cleansing breaths, Cateline wiped her eyes with the sleeve of her dress and looked around her bedchamber. She thought about the kids, her gaze going to her bed. Yes, she could simply put Laigen in bed with her every night and hope that Garratt would follow, but that didn't seem very realistic.

At this point, the two were officially servants, but they were so young, so small. She didn't feel they were safe down with all the other servants. She didn't know those people, and was truly worried for them.

Deciding to do something about it rather than worry, she walked in the direction of what she believed was the door to Marie's room. She wanted to see how large the space was and if there was perhaps room to put a bed in there for the siblings to share, at least until they were a bit older.

There were tapestries covering all the doors in the room, except the one in and out, to help cut back on unwanted breezes. She went to her right and to a tapestry that depicted the Gaelic goddess of fertility, Danu, as explained by Marie. She'd wondered how the French woman had known that, but now she thought she understood why. It was a strange thing for Cateline to see pagan gods and goddesses throughout the kingdom as opposed to France's Christian symbols.

Initially her Christian upbringing had recoiled somewhat, but now she found it interesting and wanted to know more. Right now, however, she just wanted to find Marie's bedchamber. Pushing aside the tapestry, she came across a door as she'd hoped and expected. However, when she pushed the door open, she didn't find herself in a small stone room but a small stone corridor.

Confused yet intrigued, she leaned in, looking

around, trying to see through the darkness, but it was complete. Chewing on her bottom lip for a moment, she went back into her bedchamber and grabbed a candle in its holder. Lighting it, she took hold of the candleholder and walked back to the tapestry, mindful not to light the heavy fabric with her flame as she passed.

The single flame sent a halo of light all around her, lighting the way along the stone walls, floor, and barrel stone ceiling. There were no doors, no passageways, no nooks for candles, just flat wall.

A set of stairs came into view, narrow and stone. At the top was a wooden door that had to be pushed upward, like a hatch. She looked up at it after she'd gone up a couple stairs, trying to decide whether she should see what was beyond or simply turn back and continue with her intended task.

Curiosity got the best of her, so she proceeded. Holding the candle in one hand, she used the other to push against the door. It took a bit of effort, but it moved, dim light seeping in a bit more as she pushed the door up enough for her to be able to see what was beyond.

The room looked to be a tower room, a bedchamber. Small but definitely efficient. There was a bed, neatly made, as well as some weapons and tools hanging from hooks embedded in the stone walls. There was a sword in its scabbard hanging from one, a battle-ax hanging from a leather strap wrapped around its handle on another.

Off to the right she could just barely make out a single chair facing something that was along the side of the room where the hatch door was. She assumed likely a fireplace. The only other thing she could see from her vantage point was a second set of stairs that led up to a regular door.

It seemed like a strange setup, but before she could contemplate that, the door opened and booted feet stepped onto the stairs. The amount of light that shone in told her the door led outside, probably a guard post. She barely had time for that to sink in when she realized the person was Fallon.

A gasp escaping her lips, she quickly lowered herself down so the hatch closed and she scurried down the stairs and back through the hallway to her chambers. Her sleeveless tunic that she wore over her long-sleeved dress fluttered out behind her in her haste to not be found out. It wasn't that she was doing anything wrong, but she had no idea why her bedchamber was connected to what she assumed was Fallon's.

Shoving the tapestry out of the way, nearly starting it on fire in the process, Cateline got the door shut, tapestry falling back into place as she blew out the candle. She waved away the acrid smoke as she walked back over to the table where she'd picked it up in the first place. Another gasp left her lips when there was a soft knock on the door she'd just retreated from.

"Come in," she called out, heart racing.

A moment later, the door squeaked open and the tapestry was pushed out of the way. Like magic, Fallon appeared. He raised a hand in greeting. "You discovered our little secret, I see."

"I'm so sorry," Cateline gushed. "I didn't know it was there, and when I saw it I just grabbed a candle and went looking to see what it was, and I saw you and I didn't know—"

"Hey," Fallon said, grinning as he walked over

to her. "Breathe." His smile grew as she did just that, taking a deep breath. "It's okay. I was going to tell you about it but hadn't had a chance as yet."

Cateline let out another breath, relieved. "I was looking for Marie's bedchamber and picked the wrong door." She gave him a shy smile. "Oops."

"Marie," he explained, a hand to her lower back as he guided her to the left. "Is behind Brigid."

"Ah, I see," Cateline said, eyebrows falling when they reached the tapestry, a woman embroidered on it. "Who's Brigid?"

Fallon, looking utterly amused, brushed back the tapestry to reveal the door she was looking for. "The daughter of the chief of the gods," he explained. "The Dagda." He met her gaze. "She was known as the goddess of smiths and childbirth, inspiration and poets."

"Busy lady," Cateline said, stepping through the door being held open for her. "*Merci.*"

"*Ta faite romhat,*" Fallon said, the appropriate response in Gaelic. They stepped into the small room, which fit a small bed and space to store clothing. "Why are we in here?"

"Well," Cateline said, hand to hip as she looked around. She felt a bit guilty about being in Marie's private space, but something needed to be done for the kids. "Last night Garratt brought Laigen in, upset and scared."

Fallon's eyebrows fell. "Who scared her?" he asked, voice low, dangerous.

Cateline almost smiled at the protectiveness she heard in his voice. "I don't think anyone did. I think she's very young and has gotten used to me. I think it was just a bit too much," she said, indicating the room around them. "New place so soon after a new situation."

He nodded. "Understandable. So, are you thinking of putting them in here? Moving Marie downstairs?"

Cateline stared up at him, surprised, as that hadn't occurred to her. Henri popped into mind. Perhaps Marie would prefer to be down with him, or at least closer to him and the rest of the servants. More freedom, more privacy.

Unaware of her internal dialogue, Fallon walked to the center of the room. "I could build them beds," he said, holding out his arms as though doing mental measurements. "Two beds wouldn't fit in here," he said, turning to look at her. "But maybe I could build stacking beds. I've seen that on ships before."

Cateline stared at him. She'd never heard of such a thing. "Stacked beds?"

"Yes," he said, walking over to Marie's bed. "Say this was the bottom one," he said, indicating it. "You build a frame that encompasses both beds, the second one about here," he explained, holding his hand at a level to show her. "Put Laigen on the bottom since she's so young and Garratt on top. A little ladder to get him there."

Cateline was so moved the tears came again, fast and hard as relief flooded her. For a moment, just a moment, she didn't feel so alone. Fallon, on the other hand, looked absolutely panicked.

He hurried over to her. "Did I say something wrong? What's happened?"

"I'm sorry," she cried, wiping at her eyes like a little girl and feeling like one, too. To her horror, the tears wouldn't stop. "Sorry," she whispered.

"It's okay," he murmured, taking her into his

arms. Cateline's eyes closed as she leaned against him, relishing the embrace. "A lot has happened in a very short time," he said, swaying them both gently. "And my brother is a very difficult person under the best of circumstances."

"He's so cold," Cateline said quietly. "Like ice." She felt Fallon nod as his cheek rested atop her head.

"He always has been." He stroked her back in soothing circles, his body so strong, so warm.

"What is this?" Cateline asked, patting the strange thing she felt that covered his back, like a hard covering.

"Um…just part of some armor I have to wear," Fallon murmured.

"How did you become assigned to him?" she asked, settling deeper into the hug.

"When he figured out I was a good fighter when I was a kid, he put me in charge of his dog," he explained, a smirk in his voice. "Honestly, I think he did that to mock me. But when I saved his hunting hound from a pack of wolves at the tender age of nine, he realized I could be useful to him. So, at eleven he put me in charge of his horse. At fourteen, I joined his private guard, then was running it by age seventeen."

Cateline smiled, easily picturing a younger Fallon, proud, stubborn. But the smile quickly fell from her lips as she pulled out of the hug, looking down at the tear stains she'd left on his tunic. "Forgive me," she said softly, wiping at the saturated material. "But you've been demoted."

Fallon met her gaze. "What do you mean?"

"You're back assigned to watch his dog again," she whispered.

Chapter Fourteen

No, no, like this," Marie said gently, the older woman an absolute expert on how best to handle the runaway mane that was Cateline's hair. Her protégé, Livia, stood with her behind the princess, who sat patiently as the two worked on her hairstyle for the day.

Laigen was playing with a doll that one of the women in the castle still had from when her daughter was younger. The child sat on the floor in front of the fireplace chatting softly to the doll. Cateline watched her, charmed.

The night before she had been proactive and sent for Garratt and Laigen, inviting them to stay with her. They'd been overjoyed, and this time, Cateline had created a little nest for Garratt, who she thought was too proud to sleep with the "girls." But she soon learned that what it was actually about was him being protective. After she'd gotten him set up, she'd seen him bring out a small dagger from the waistband of his trousers and tucked it close by if he needed it.

That had made her equal parts proud of him and sad for him, that he felt it was necessary. What had those two been through that he'd learned to do that? Fallon had stopped by early through their secret passage, which had shocked the two children speechless. He'd wanted to know if Garratt wanted to join him for breakfast, then help him build the beds.

The boy had been excited, nearly vibrating out of his skin.

Cateline was bemused as she listened to the two ladies bicker a bit over her hair, Livia insisting there was a better way while the much older and experienced Marie tried to keep her patience about her on the best way.

Her attention was taken from the two servants when a loud rapping on the door to her bedchamber rent the air. Laigen scampered away to hide behind the chair as the door was unceremoniously opened. Will stood in the hallway, beady little eyes taking in the room before him.

Angry, Cateline raised her hand to stop Marie and Livia before pushing to her feet and walking over to him, gaze never leaving his. She'd had enough of this cocky little man who should be bowing to her, not the other way around.

"Who told you to enter?" she asked.

He looked at her, eyes widening in surprise, no doubt by her tone than her words, which she knew he couldn't understand. She heard a voice behind her and realized it was Livia, translating for her. Hiding a smile of pride at the gutsy young lady, Cateline held her ground, raising her chin slightly in challenge.

"I asked you a question," Cateline said, refusing to back down from this horse's ass. Livia translated her words and his response.

"Prince Fergus wishes to speak to you," he said in response, giving her a bow, though his eyes were on her the entire time rather than the appropriate downcast of the subservient. He was going through the motions but clearly felt as the prince did in regard to Cateline. She was unworthy, and Cateline was beginning to resent it.

"Tell him I'll be in once I'm finished getting ready for the day," she said, waiting for Livia to pass the message. Then she slammed the door in his face.

Once the door was closed, Cateline felt like she was going to vomit. She was shaking, no idea where the courage—or stupidity—had come to act as such. Yes, Will might have only been a footman for Fergus, but he was the footman for the *prince*, which outranked the princess.

Bringing up a trembling hand, she touched her throat and looked at the other three females in the room with her. Laigen peeked out from behind the chair and Marie looked at Cateline with surprise—and approval. Livia, for her part, was smirking, seeming pleased with the events of the past few minutes.

Taking a deep breath, Cateline nodded. "All right," she said. "Let's finish so I can see what he wants."

The door to Fergus's bedchamber stood open and she could hear the voices of two men deeper inside the large space. She recognized Will's voice along with that of the prince. When she reached the two, she saw Fergus seated in a chair while Will leaned somewhat over him, using scissors to trim his out-of-control beard.

Fergus didn't bother to look at her when he said, "To make sure you understand my every word, I'll use your foul language to speak."

Cateline stared at him, stunned by his unabridged disrespect and disgust.

"Don't ever speak to Will like that again," Fergus

warned, sending an irritated gaze her way. "You do not throw my footman out of your rooms."

Her shock turned to downright anger at the smugness of the man standing there with the scissors and the absolute dismissive arrogance of the one seated. "I will *speak* to your servant any way I choose when he bursts into my bedchambers without permission."

Fergus looked surprised and turned to look at Will who murmured something to him in Gaelic, glaring at the princess the entire time.

"He's lying," Cateline said in Gaelic, hoping like hell she'd gotten it right. From the looks on both their faces, she had. "Yes," she admitted in French. "He did knock, but before he was invited he barged into my chambers while I was getting ready for my day. Four of us were there."

Fergus turned to the footman and murmured something to him that she couldn't hear. The servant nodded and set the scissors down before heading over to a door in the large chamber and disappearing through it. Fergus turned to her and, his tone just as firm but not as confrontational, spoke.

"Fallon assured me those brats, somebody's bastards, were simply cheap labor, not *my* problem,"

She stared at him, the floor falling out from beneath her as she suddenly felt very nauseous. How could Fallon look her in the eye and tell her she was doing right by those kids? How could he hold her and make her feel like everything was okay, when all along he saw those kids as nothing more than useful mini-servants? Perhaps she'd been a fool all along and she truly was alone in Sursha.

"I'm fine with that," he continued, unaware of

her inner turmoil and hurt. "So, my question is, why are they prancing around *my* castle with little dolls and little princess dresses? And," he added, voice stronger and sounding angry. "Why are they sleeping with *you*?"

Having to think fast, Cateline told what was essentially the truth. "Laigen is not in a princess dress, Fergus," she said reasonably. "The clothing she and Garratt arrived in was filthy, filled with holes, and we were concerned with bug eggs. As for their current sleeping arrangements, they're too young and too small to be safe down with the rest of the servants. Marie has decided to join her intended, Henri, and her room is going to the children to keep them safe until they're bigger."

He stared at her blankly. "Who's Marie?"

"My lady-in-waiting," she said, nearly shaking her head in exasperation.

"Ah, yes, right," he said, nodding. "Well, as long as those two don't become an issue and carry their weight." He turned away from her, effectively ending their discussion.

Leaving Fergus's rooms, Cateline closed the door behind her, leaning against it for a moment as she tried to pull herself together. She was hurt, angry, and confused, three emotions that seemed to be her constant companions since she'd arrived in Sursha. This time, however, she was heartbroken too.

For a moment, she considered going back to her bedchamber and gathering Marie, Livia, the kids, and Henri and heading back to France. She didn't care what her father said. She'd had enough of Fergus and his family.

Pushing away from the door, she headed back

to her own, pushing it open to hear joyous laughter. Inside the room, Livia had swept up the giggling four-year-old and was singing to her in Italian as she swung the child around overhead, Laigen's arms spread out like a bird.

Cateline stopped, watching for a long moment. No, she thought. She wasn't going to uproot those girls again, neither one of them. Steeling her jaw like her resolve, she grabbed her cloak and headed out to find a warrior for some answers.

⁂

Asking where Fallon could be found, Cateline was directed to the workshop area of the bailey where the blacksmith's shop was, the farrier, larders, and butteries, among others. It was the carpenter's workshop she sought.

Outside the stone building were stacks of cut logs, some even stripped of their bark waiting to be utilized. She loved the smell of the fresh cut oak, which permeated the air along with smells of chimney smoke and horse manure, as the stables were just down the way.

Stepping up to the shop, she was about to grab the doorknob to push the door open when she caught sight of Fallon inside. He was bent over a table, a shaping tool in his hand as he worked on whatever project lay flat. Garratt stood next to the worktable, bouncing on the balls of his feet with excitement.

Finally, Fallon blew wood dust from the project and stood erect. He lifted what he'd been working on and Cateline could see it was a fairly intricate wooden sword, just Garratt's size. His lips moved as he spoke to the boy, and though Cateline wasn't able to hear them, as the warrior held the sword out, both hands gripping the boy-sized handle, she figured he was explaining the correct technique of a warrior.

All her anger drained slowly out of her as she watched, the two inside unaware of her presence. Garratt was fully engaged in his lesson, eyes wide and bottom lip tucked in as he seemed to drink in every word.

Heart touched and even more confused, Cateline knew she couldn't interrupt, couldn't go in there waggling her finger and lobbing accusations at Fallon. She'd go to him later and talk.

⁂

Sending a note ahead to the warrior letting him know that she'd be by his room after the supper meal was served, Cateline saw light shining at the end of the tunnel extending from her bedchamber. As she got closer, she realized it was because the hatch door had been left open and the light from inside the room was shining down to guide her way.

Blowing out her candle, she set it down at the foot of the stone stairs and made her way up. Her head poking up into the room, she saw Fallon sitting in the chair, his face and the front of his body aglow from the fireplace he sat before. He was working on one of his bracers, a leather lace held between his teeth as he pulled it tightly, seeming to be doing some repair work.

"Good eve," he murmured around the lace when he spotted her. He released the lace and set the bracer aside before pushing to his feet and walking over to her.

Cateline took the hand that was held out as she climbed the remaining few stairs and stepped down into the room. She was stunned to see that she'd just climbed out of a wooden chest.

"Did you make this?" she asked.

"No, milady. That's been here a long, long time, far as I can tell," Fallon said, offering the chair he'd just vacated.

"No, you were already sitting," she said, waving off his offer.

He dragged over a small trunk that was at the end of his narrow bed and, with a smile, sat down. Cateline sat down in the chair, hands in her lap as she tried to think of how to begin the conversation as she felt expectant eyes on her. Finally, she took a deep breath and looked over at him. "I'm a bit confused by something, Fallon."

"All right," Fallon said, his total and complete focus on her. Those beautiful, piercing eyes nearly took Cateline's breath away.

Forcing herself to break the eye contact so she could catch her breath, Cateline cleared her throat. "I had a very disquieting conversation with Fergus this morning," she began. When she heard him groan deep in his throat, her gaze flicked to him. "Concerned, are you?" She felt her earlier anger returning.

Fallon shook her head. "No, I just know how unsettling he can be." He gave her a soft smile. "So sorry you had to deal with him."

Those kind, compassionate, and considerate words nearly took the growing winds out of Cateline's sails. She had to stay strong and get answers. Swallowing, she said, "He said you told him Laigen and Garratt were nothing more than cheap labor." When the words passed through her lips, she felt the anger return and had to look away from the expression of concern on his face. "He said they were bastards." She swallowed again, trying not to cry. "I thought you cared about them," she whispered.

Fallon slid off the trunk and over to her, down on one knee beside her. "Hey," he said, reaching up and gently wiping away a tear that managed to slip out with the pad of his thumb. "I did tell him that, milady," he said softly. When Cateline began to move away from him, he rested a warm hand on her thigh to still her. It was almost as though that hand had been burned, as it whipped away. "My apologies, milady," Fallon murmured.

"It's all right," Cateline replied, her heart beating a bit faster. She could still feel the slight pressure of his hand there and wished it would return. "Why would you say such a thing?" she asked, focus returned to her conversation with Fergus. "I thought you cared about the children."

"I do," Fallon said. "Very much so." An instant smile curved his lips. "But, one thing you have to understand about my brother," he explained. "If there's no benefit to him, it won't happen."

She studied him for a long moment, his face, his eyes, trying to gauge his words and weigh his sincerity. She saw nothing but honesty there. "So," she said, understanding seeping in. "You told him that so he'd allow them to stay."

Fallon nodded and grinned, a little lopsided. "Absolutely."

Cateline returned the smile, looking shyly at him. "I saw you today," she said. "You and Garratt.

The sword you made him."

Fallon looked away, but not before she caught sight of his smile. "Yes," he said, rubbing the back of his neck with his hand. "We took a little break from making the beds."

"He wants to be like you?" Cateline asked. "A warrior?"

Fallon met her gaze again, scooting back to sit on the trunk. "He says he does, but he's young." He shrugged. "I'm actually heading to the barracks in two days," he said. "Need to do some drills and training with my entire squad. I'd like to take him with me, if you're all right with that."

Panic washed over Cateline. "You're leaving?"

"Just for a fortnight," he explained.

Cateline nodded, taking a deep breath. She'd known this was coming up and was surprised by how hard it was hitting her that he'd be gone. Again, she nodded. "Yes, of course. You don't need my permission," she said with a forced smile. "You need his."

Fallon smiled. "Fair enough." He tilted his head slightly. "Why don't you come with us? I know my father would love to see you."

Cateline studied him for a long moment, mulling over the offer. "I have a strange idea, and it may not work, as," she added quickly, "I know you're there to work with your men. But, what if I talked to Marie… What if she and Henri came, too, and got married?"

Fallon chewed on his bottom lip for a moment, glancing off toward the fire. Finally, he met her gaze again. "You know, Henri has worked for my family for about as long as Marie has been with you. I think my father would really like that."

Cateline smiled, excited. "It's settled, then. Well, that is, the seed of an idea has been planted."

Fallon grinned. "You talk to Marie, and I'll send word to my father. Meanwhile," he added. "I'll finish the beds, I promise."

Cateline pointed a finger at him. "You better."

Chapter Fifteen

Though Sursha was a country filled with both those of the Christian faith and those of the Gaelic faith, Marie decided she didn't want to be affiliated with the Church anymore. Her first marriage had been Christian, and this time, she opted to go with Henri's adopted beliefs, that of the ancient Gaelic pagan faith.

It was a small ceremony, very intimate with the king, Henri's daughter and her husband, their son, and Cateline and Fallon. All of them stood in a circle around the couple and the pagan priest who was conducting the so-called Handfasting ceremony.

The couple clasped hands, the priest tying braids into a long length of rope that he wrapped around their hands as he spoke blessings over their union. Cateline watched, so filled with happiness for her longest and closest companion. She'd never seen Marie look so happy. She didn't know Henri very well, but from what she'd seen, and what she saw in that moment, he adored Marie and treated her like more of a queen than a lady-in-waiting.

She glanced past the couple to see the person standing on the opposite side of the circle from her, whose violet eyes were already on her. Their gazes met and held for a long moment before Fallon finally looked away.

Those that were closest to Henri, few knowing

Marie very well, had put together a wonderful celebration for the new couple. King Carthac had been extremely generous to offer the great hall to hold the events, as it was raining outdoors. Families from the surrounding villages had brought food, and those who could play an instrument or sing entertained.

It was a wonderful event, Cateline made to not feel like an untouchable royal but one of them, part of the community. She found Fallon with her eyes, noting he was standing in a small group of some of his men and villagers, all of them laughing, talking, eating good food, and drinking good ale.

Cateline smiled. It was good to see the warrior relaxed, enjoying himself, even as she knew that at the slightest sign of a problem or danger, that turkey leg would be tossed and one of his swords drawn. As she watched him, his gaze found hers as it did so often. He raised his cup of ale in salute, her smile growing as she gave him a low nod of deference. He grinned, then returned to his conversation.

"Milady?"

Cateline turned to see one of Fallon's men standing next to her, holding a lyre. She recognized him as the man she'd sung with as he'd played that final night of their journey in France. She smiled. "Hello."

"The bride has made a request," he explained, holding up the lyre a bit in emphasis.

Cateline found Marie, who stood with her new husband, the two looking right at her expectantly. Oh boy, Cateline thought. She knew she couldn't turn them down, so she nodded at her lady-in-waiting.

The guard stepped up onto the bench of one of the long tables, setting the instrument on the tabletop before clapping his hands loudly. Cateline stood, feeling a bit awkward as the man announced their intentions, that their "future queen" would be serenading the new couple.

She felt butterflies battering violently against her insides as she looked around. She noticed Livia toward the back of the large room standing with one of Fallon's men, the young servant apparently talking to the member of the Elite Guard.

Turning to the man who would accompany her, who had stepped down from the bench, Cateline considered what song to sing. She decided upon one that was about two swans finding each other after many seasons apart, true love. She hummed the tune for the musician, who picked at the strings of the lyre until he got the melody.

"Ready?" she asked him in Gaelic, and he nodded.

Clearing her throat, Cateline took a deep breath before she began to sing, her voice carrying easily through the cavernous room built from stone. As soon as she began to get into the song, letting the words evoke emotions from her, she forgot that she had a hundred pairs of eyes on her as everyone present stopped where they were, frozen in a moment in time as they listened.

Her gaze swept the room, but often came back to Marie and Henri. He had his arm around her waist and stood listening, smiles on both their faces. She'd never seen Marie look so serene, so content.

Her gaze drifted over to find King Carthac standing near his youngest, who was also watching her. The king looked from Cateline over to Fallon then back to the princess, who was nearly finished with her song. He had the strangest little smile on his face that she couldn't quite interpret.

She closed her eyes as the final line of the song ended in a high, held note that she wanted to make sure she got right. The note exploded out of her, her hands rising slowly from her body as she reached the top, holding it for several moments before stopping, the echo drifting around those present for a few seconds before loud applause took its place.

Eyes opening, Cateline smiled, relieved that it was over but also that she'd done well. Her gaze found Fallon's. His hands were raised over his head as he clapped enthusiastically, the smile nearly splitting his face, making her own grow.

⁂

Cateline smiled as King Carthac leaned in, giving her a kiss on the cheek, his facial hair tickling the skin there.

"Beautiful, Cateline," he said. "Truly beautiful."

She smiled, feeling pleased with herself though shy at the attention. "Thank you, Athair," she said softly.

"It's so nice to see you again," he said, offering for the princess to sit in one of the comfortable chairs in the Solar. "I know you haven't been gone long, but your absence was immediately felt."

She smiled at his words, able to hear the truth in his tone. "It's been a journey," she said, unsure what word to use of her experience in the new castle with Fergus, who had not joined them in their trek.

Before the king could respond, both their attention was garnered by giggling and the scamper of little feet. Cateline turned in time to see an excited

Laigen headed her way. Her smile was instant as the little one jumped into her lap, wrapping her arms around Cateline's neck and snuggling in.

"Did you have a good day?" the princess asked, smiling when the little girl nodded vigorously, even as she snuggled in a bit more. Cateline felt the king's gaze on her. Again, he had that strange little smile on his lips. "She played hard today," the princess said softly. "Guessing she'll sleep well tonight." She looked over at Livia, who stood nearby. "Were you going to spend some time with the others?" she asked, a conversation they'd had earlier that evening.

Livia bowed in respect to the king before turning to Cateline. "Is that still all right, milady?"

"Of course," Cateline said. "Go have some fun."

The smallest of smiles graced the young woman's face before she bowed again and turned to hurry from the room, nodding to Fallon, who passed her as he walked in.

"Sorry I'm late," Fallon said. He plopped down on one of the other available chairs, bringing up a hand to wave a few fingers at Laigen, who sleepily waved back at him.

"A wonderful day," the king said, smiling at both the adults present. "Where is Garratt?"

"He's sleeping in the barracks tonight," Fallon said with a grin. "Wanted to be a big boy, so Kellan is looking after him. Kellan promised me that if he got scared, Garratt would get a personal escort back here," he added, indicating the general area, as Cateline and Laigen would be sleeping just down the hall in Cateline's former chambers.

Cateline smiled, absently rubbing circles over Laigen's back as she snored softly, curled up in her lap.

"It's appropriate to have the little one here," the king said, reaching over a large hand and gently covering the crown of a golden head for a moment before the hand retreated. "I've made a decision, and I wanted to let the two of you know before I decree it."

Cateline said nothing, simply waited for the announcement.

"I'm going to declare Garratt and Laigen *oidhreacht*," King Carthac said.

"What?" Fallon shot forward in his chair. "You can't do that to them."

Immediately concerned, Cateline looked from one to the other, cradling the child a bit closer in her arms.

"I know you don't agree with that ancient bylaw, Fallon," the king said. "But, if I declare that with these two," he said, indicating the sleeping girl. "Nobody can compromise their lives or safety. Nobody can—"

"Make them leave," Fallon said softly, nodding.

"Exactly."

Cateline looked from one to the other. "What does this mean?" she asked, nervous, though feeling a little better as Fallon seemed to relax a bit.

The warrior looked at her, running a hand through his hair in a gesture of nervousness or irritation, the princess wasn't sure. "*Oidhreacht* is a practice done here since the beginnings of Sursha. It's essentially paid slavery."

She gasped, a hand coming to her mouth. She shook her head. "No, not for them."

Fallon raised a hand in supplication. "As the people were settling here, there was a substantial population problem. Far more men than women, so others were brought in from other countries, women largely, on slave ships. At the time, it was a more progressive form where the people were given a wage and assured a job for life."

"They were given protection by the Crown," Carthac added. "Which is why I want to declare the children."

Cateline looked down at the child in her arms, so trusting, so filled with life. She was beginning to understand, she thought. "So," she said, looking back at the king. "What would this mean for them?"

"My father will decree it," Fallon responded. "And he will gift them to you specifically. This is a horrifying situation if gifted to a bad person, which is one of the many reasons I'm against it. But it's a godsend if they're gifted to someone like you."

She met his gaze for a long moment before asking, "Fergus, he can't touch them? Make them leave?"

Fallon shook his head. "Nope." He sat back in his chair. "For all intents and purposes, they are your property."

❦ ❦ ❦ ❦

"Wait, let me pull this back," Cateline whispered, reaching past Fallon, who easily carried the little body in his arms, and pulled the covers out of the way. "All right, go ahead."

Fallon gently lowered the little form to the bed, her head on the pillow. "Her doll?" he whispered, looking around.

"Here." Cateline handed it to him, the little girl becoming nearly inseparable from the rag doll.

Fallon tucked it under one of Laigen's arms before gently bringing up the covers. "Sleep well, little one," he whispered, leaning over her and leaving a kiss to her forehead.

Cateline watched, arms crossed over her chest. She was utterly charmed by how gentle he was with Laigen. She thought he'd make an excellent father someday. Fallon backed away from the little girl and met her gaze, nodding his head toward the door.

Together, the two walked across the large space to the door, which was far enough away from the bed that they wouldn't wake Laigen by saying good night.

"You know what my father is trying to do with those two, don't you?" Fallon asked quietly, standing next to the door that led to the hallway beyond.

"No, what?" Cateline asked.

"He's trying to get himself some grandchildren," Fallon said with a grin.

"Well," Cateline said, just as quiet but amused. "Your brother certainly isn't helping with that."

Fallon's eyebrows shot up. "Would you rather he did?"

Cateline's face scrunched up in distaste. "No."

Fallon grinned at her response. He leaned his shoulder against the door, crossing powerful arms over his chest. "That song you sang tonight was really beautiful."

"Thank you," Cateline said, mirroring his position, not more than a foot of space between them. "I was scared to death. Never sang in front of that many people before."

"Your voice is so beautiful. You shouldn't hide that," he said, head tilted slightly. "Do you sing to the kids?"

Cateline gave him a shy smile. "Yes, to Laigen. I think Garratt would look at me like I've lost my mind."

Fallon grinned, nodding. "Well, I, for one, think she's a very lucky little girl."

"Oh?" Cateline asked, an eyebrow quirked. "You want to be put to sleep by French lullabies?"

"*Oui*," Fallon said.

Grinning, Cateline began to sing Laigen's favorite lullaby, very quietly. She leaned in a bit closer so Fallon could hear her without singing loud enough to wake the little girl.

"I think that would have a much different effect on me than Laigen," Fallon murmured.

"That wouldn't put you to sleep?" Cateline asked, feeling the air between them becoming heavy, her heart beginning to race in her chest.

Fallon shook his head slowly side to side. "No."

The door was suddenly yanked open, Fallon stumbling out into the hallway, barely managing to not trip over Garratt. Cateline would have been amused if not for the panicked look on the boy's face.

"What's wrong?" she asked him.

The boy said nothing, simply grabbed one of her hands and tugged, clearly wanting him to follow her. He grabbed Fallon's hand, too, tugging.

"All right," Fallon said. "We're coming."

They followed Garratt through the winding halls, the boy running, and finally, outside. The night air was cool, their breath coming in puffs as cold air rolled in off the ocean. They were led to the dark shadows between the stone buildings that housed the kitchen and the pantry.

Cateline first saw the huddled figure, then heard soft sobs. "Oh my God," she whispered, hurrying into the shadows. "Livia," she gasped, hands going to her face as she slowly lowered herself to squat next to the girl, the skirt of her dress acting as a curtain all around her lower body. "Oh, Livia."

The sixteen-year-old's face was a bloody mess, one eye completely swollen shut. Her dress was ripped and three of her fingernails were broken to the quick. Her hair was down and a mess all over her head, as though it had been pulled out of the updo it had been in earlier that evening.

"Fallon," Cateline said, a sob escaping her throat.

"I'm here," he said, moving in next to her. "Can I move you?" he asked Livia gently. "It's freezing, and we need to get you inside."

Cateline moved out of the very tight space so Fallon could get in there. Livia let out a cry of pain as Fallon carefully gathered her in his arms and lifted, cradling her against his chest.

"I'm sorry," he whispered to her. "It's okay." He looked at Cateline. "Go get the castle physician. I'll meet you in my bedchamber. I don't want Laigen to see this."

Cateline nodded, then looked down to Garratt. "Stay with Fallon and help, okay?"

The young boy nodded sagely, big eyes looking up at her.

With that, she was off to the physician's chambers.

Chapter Sixteen

Fallon stood back, so angry she was almost shaking. She knew if she spoke to the broken young woman lying on her bed, she'd come off as harsh and dangerous, and Livia didn't need that. So, she kept back and let the gentle, almost motherly nature of Cateline take over. Even though the two women were but a few years apart in age, Cateline had a way about her that was calming, comforting.

"Who did this to you, sweetheart?" Cateline asked gently.

Fallon listened as closely as she dared, leaning in a bit as Livia's voice was thin, soft. The castle physician was also asking her questions now and then as he examined her, which didn't help Fallon discern the words.

"I don't know his name," Livia said. "A soldier."

"Was it the soldier you were talking to in the hall while I was singing?" Cateline asked gently, caressing blood-tangled hair off the young woman's forehead. Livia nodded. Cateline looked up at Fallon, who stood on the opposite side of the bed. "Did you see him?" she asked.

Fallon nodded, her jaw muscles pulsing as she clenched and unclenched her jaw. "I'll return," she growled, turning to leave the room.

Her booted feet pounded down one set of stairs after another until she was outside. Long legs ate up ground as she headed to the barracks. Steam erupted from her lips and flaring nostrils every few seconds as her devastation mutated into a dangerous fury. May the gods help anyone who stepped in her path.

Once she reached the barracks, she was tempted to kick in the door but didn't want to give that bastard any notice that she was coming for him. Inside, the men were still awake, readying for bed and chatting among themselves.

Using her stealth, not making one sound, which was hard as she could hear her heart raging in her ears, she headed inside. She saw some of her men in a state of undress that wasn't pleasant for her to see, but she wasn't there on a social call.

There he was, the very same man he'd caught harassing a young lady and had punished with rope. He stood next to his bunk, about to tug his tunic over his head. Prey in her sights, Fallon made a direct line to him, grabbing him so quickly and so hard he lost his bladder, the intense smell of urine joining the sweaty smells of a barracks. Fallon shoved him up against the wall, her hand like a vise around his throat. He looked at her with wide, terrified eyes.

"Eoin," she called out to a man she'd seen in her periphery when she'd reached her target. "Grab the shackles. Now!" She pinned the bastard with her gaze. "I gave you a chance, you rotten, no-good bastard. But you couldn't leave women well enough alone, could you?"

One hand still holding him against the wall, Fallon grabbed his right hand, noting the cuts and bruises on his knuckles. It looked like one of his fingers was broken too. Looking back at him, she sneered.

"Did it hurt?" she asked. "Did it hurt busting

the face of that young woman?" She slammed his fist against his own cheek, the man crying out in pain. Her man stepped up to her, a bit cautiously, with the heavy iron shackles. "Put them on him," she said, shoving him by the throat back into the wall before stepping away to let the guard do his job. "You're under arrest," she declared. "Identity must be made," she announced to the other men. "But this man is a suspect in the brutal beating and possible rape of a sixteen-year-old girl."

A low rumble of displeasure began to ripple through the room. Fallon let the noise grow, watching as the fear grew in the man's eyes who was now her prisoner.

"You," she said to the guard who'd just shackled the filth before her. "Come with me. The rest of you," she said, eyeing every man who looked back at the trio. "To the training field. If he's identified as the man who did this…" Again, she met every pair of eyes, ending on the wide, terrified ones of the man she just knew in her gut had been responsible for Livia. "You all know what to do."

Fallon took hold of the chains that connected the two wrist shackles and yanked, nearly pulling the man off his feet as she headed out of the barracks, Eoin following along with a second guard in case their prisoner managed to escape.

Her focus like a razor's edge, Fallon led them through the castle and up to the third floor where her bedchamber was, her sheets now stained with a young woman's blood that should never have been shed. When they reached the door, Fallon rapped three times on it.

A moment later, Cateline opened the door, but

just wide enough for her to look out. When she saw that it was Fallon, she opened it a bit wider, fear in her eyes. "Did you find him?" she asked quietly.

Fallon nodded her head in the direction where Eoin stood with him. The princess gasped when she looked at him. No doubt the bloody nose he'd given himself, with Fallon's help, was upsetting to her as it looked far worse than it was.

Swallowing hard, eyes never leaving the shackled man, Cateline nodded. "That's the man I saw with her tonight."

Fallon let out a heavy breath, nodding. "I need Livia to identify him, milady," she said softly, forcing herself to calm down enough to not scare the princess or the girl.

Cateline glanced back into the room before looking to Fallon again. With a nod, she stepped away, pulling the door open with her.

Fallon walked over to the suspect and grabbed his chain again, jerking until the man followed, his mouth-breathing heavy. Fallon thought perhaps his nose was broken.

Tugging him into the room, she walked them over to the bed where Livia still lay. Fallon reached back and grabbed the man by his hair, holding his head steady. "Is this the man, Livia?" she asked gently.

The young woman looked up at him and then her face crumbled, the most horrible keening sound Fallon had ever heard renting the air. Livia curled up upon herself, the sobs coming fast and hard.

Fallon turned the man around and shoved him out of the room, sending him stumbling across the hall and into the wall across the way. A blood spot remained even as he fell backward, unable to catch himself with his hands.

She went back into the room, not wanting Livia's last vision of her that night to be with that monster. She walked over to the bed and reached down, lightly caressing her shoulder. "We got him, sweetheart," she said softly. "He'll never hurt you again. All right?"

Livia nodded. "All right," she managed.

Fallon squeezed the shoulder lightly then spared a glance at Cateline before turning to head out of the room. "Let's go," she said to Eoin, who had gotten their prisoner to his feet. They were about to head out when Cateline called Fallon's name. The warrior indicated that Eoin should continue, then turned to Cateline, who pulled the bedchamber door closed before hurrying over to Fallon.

"What will you do with him?" she asked quietly.

Fallon let out a heavy breath as she glanced down the hallway the two men had retreated down before returning her gaze to Cateline. "My men will take care of him."

"Will..." Cateline looked down at her hands, which fidgeted together for a moment before looking back up at Fallon. "Will he ever be able to hurt anyone again?"

Fallon looked deeply into the beautiful eyes of the woman who haunted her dreams, waking or sleeping. She wished Cateline didn't have to see this side of her, never wanted her to see this side of her. But she had to do what had to be done.

Clearing her throat, Fallon said softly, "This is something my men and I take very seriously. An attack like this..." She shook her head.

Cateline looked down at her hands again, nodding. "I understand."

"That's what you want," Fallon said. "Isn't it?"

"What I want isn't possible," the princess said, sadness in her voice. Finally, she looked up, meeting Fallon's gaze again. "It happened, and there's nothing I can do about that now." She took a deep breath, then quickly leaned up and left a lingering kiss on Fallon's cheek. "Avenge her," she whispered into her ear before she hurried back into the bedchamber.

Fallon stood there, still able to feel those soft lips. Shaking herself out of her stupor, she hurried after the other two men.

⁂

Just as she'd ordered, her men were standing at attention in the training field lit by the moonlight above. They stood in two perfect rows facing each other, an aisle between them for the ultimate and, most often final, walk of shame.

Eoin led their prisoner to the front of the line. Fallon walked down the aisle, explaining as she went. "You will each have one shot at him. You may use fists, pommel of your sword, end of your spear, foot, whatever. You may not use anything that will kill him. You may not cut him, stab him, spear him, stomp him, or otherwise deliver a fatal blow." She reached the end of the aisle. "That is," she added, no pleasure in her statement. "Not before everyone gets a chance."

She reached the end of the line and turned to look back up the way she'd just come, the prisoner standing at the other side. He looked terrified, and she was glad of it. Eoin was removing his shackles as she finished her speech.

"If you survive, prisoner," she said, refusing to

use his name as he was dead to her Elite Guard now. "You will be banished from our shores." She looked at all the men who still stood at attention, even as she could feel their anger building, readiness to attack. "Begin!"

Eoin shoved the prisoner into the gauntlet. Fallon watched as each man took their blow, most using fists, sending him from one man to the other just with the sheer viciousness of their hits and kicks. Often he stumbled, landing on his behind or all fours. The next man in line would yank him up by his tunic, his arm, or even his hair, only to send him flying again.

Fallon watched, part of her nauseous at such violence, so senseless, so unnecessary. Shouldn't she just have thrown him into the dungeon and let him rot there with the rats? Every time she engaged in violence, on the battlefield or like this, she felt a little bit of her humanity wilt away.

But then, she saw Livia's face, that beautiful, precious face. So young, so innocent, so deeply hurt by life already. Orphaned as a young girl and bounced from home to home until she'd ended up at the monastery where the monks had taken pity on her. That young woman had never had a break in her life, never had anyone to love her, to protect her, to give her a bed that wasn't borrowed or stolen.

Then there was Cateline. Fallon's cheek burned from that brief kiss, the softness, the closeness. She heard those whispered words again, *Avenge her.* She saw the prisoner headed her way, yet again knocked to the ground. He was bloody, and he spit out a mouthful of blood and it looked like some teeth. Stringy hair, likely from sweat and blood, hung down.

He was tugged up to his feet again where he fell

against the closest man to him, punched, then sent whirling down to the ground yet again. Finally, he reached her. One eye was swollen shut and the other cut so badly she wasn't sure he'd keep it. His nose had been broken and rebroken, and most of his teeth were missing. Dirt clung to the blood on his face, giving him the look of a filth-encrusted monster.

He tried to stand before her but kept falling to one knee. "Hold him," she said, disgust in her heart. When he was held up before her, leaning on one of the men, she met his single-eyed gaze. "You had a chance," she said. "You had the talent and spirit to be part of the greatest fighting force since the Spartans." She shook her head in sadness. "Yet, you gave in to the part of you that is nothing more than a predator, a monster, and a coward."

His head fell forward, one of the men grabbing his hair and forcing it up so he was looking at Fallon again.

"I only have one thing left for you, coward." With bared teeth, she jammed her knee as hard as she could into his crotch, sending him crumbling to the ground like a ton of bricks, curling up into the fetal position, whimpering. "Clean this up," she muttered, then walked away.

❧ ❧ ❧ ❧

The water was cold, so very cold, but she needed it against her hot skin. She gasped loudly as she splashed it onto her face, her naked body submerged to just under her breasts. Her nipples were so hard from the cool night air and cold water that she was pretty sure they could cut someone.

At some point during the struggle that night, she'd gotten hit in the forehead pretty good, the cut just above her left eye stinging and bleeding. She had no idea when it had happened, though it was likely one of the times she'd shoved him around and, in trying to catch himself which was impossible with hands shackled, he'd caught her in the head. Her adrenaline had been so intense that he could have cut off her hand and likely she wouldn't have known.

Livia's attacker would be thrown in a cell overnight, then, if he was still alive in the morning, he'd be put into a wagon and loaded into a fisherman's vessel. The fisherman would be paid to haul the exiled man off to wherever he was going to sell his wares. *If* he was still alive. If.

Brutal, she thought. Very brutal. But now, that young woman had to live the rest of her life with the memory of *his* brutality. They had to hope there wasn't a pregnancy if he'd completed a rape, which at that point she didn't know. Hopefully Livia would tell Cateline. Either way, the young woman would be haunted for life by his sheer lack of respect for a woman, another human being.

Diving beneath the water, Fallon shot across the length of the pool, feeling so free and, for a moment, clean. She wished it were that easy for her soul. How did one make that clean? Go to a priest and ask for forgiveness? To be cleansed?

She'd taken her first life at the age of twelve, nearly ten years ago. It had been in the heat of battle, but it had lit the end of a wick that she worried would someday reach the candle. How long was that wick? How much could she take, do, endure, commit? One thing that drew her to Cateline so much was her purity.

No, not purity of body but purity of soul, purity of heart.

If the Christian faith had anything right, she thought, it was angels. She was pretty sure Cateline was one. Fallon broke through the surface of the water, gasping for a purifying breath. She brought her hands up and pushed her hair out of her face. The way the princess was with Laigen and Garratt. The way she was with Livia. The way she was with Carthac. The way she was with Fallon, herself.

Why? she wondered, swimming back toward the shore. Why had her father arranged for such a woman to be with such a man as Fergus? He didn't deserve her, for one. It was a wasted marriage, and they all knew it. Surely her father had known. Yes, the future king needed to be married, needed to continue the line of succession, but then why not just use a random woman of good breeding to get an heir?

As Fallon began to wash herself with the soap she kept hidden there, she continued her line of thought. Her father clearly liked the young princess. He seemed to fully bring her in under his wing. In fact, in the short time she'd been back at the castle, he'd been talking to her about things ordinarily reserved for discussions with Fergus.

"Is he grooming her?" Fallon murmured to the night, only the cry of a distant bird-of-prey her response.

Finishing her bath, Fallon made her way back to the castle, Toirneach not happy with the surprise late-night ride. He huffed at her several times but got them back safely. Giving him an extra apple in the stable, the warrior made her way inside. She knew the castle physician would stay overnight with Livia in Fallon's bedchamber, so she headed up to Cateline's.

The room was quiet, save for the popping of the flames in the fireplace, which would keep the two occupants of the bed warm throughout the night. Fallon walked over to the bed and stood at the foot, watching for a moment.

Cateline was wrapped around the small body of Laigen, both lying on their left sides. They were deeply asleep, chests moving in sync to the breathing of slumber. Fallon was envious. She wished she knew peace like that, the true comfort of sleep's arms, sleep with no nightmares or those slain in battle come back to settle a score.

She walked over to the side of the bed where Cateline lay, watching. Her gaze traced every line of her beautiful profile, her long, curly auburn hair spread across her pillow like a flame. She yearned to touch it, to smell it.

Before she could think it through, Fallon found herself sitting on a nearby chair removing her boots. She was tired, so very tired. Weary, really. Boots removed, she looked over at the bed to see the two figures hadn't moved. Getting to her feet, Fallon walked over to the bed and, with one last chance to leave them be, slowly climbed on.

As quietly and slowly as she could, Fallon lay atop the blanket behind Cateline, slowly scooting over to her until she was loosely spooning her. Eyes closed, she inhaled the smell of that soft, auburn hair. It soothed her, and in a few moments, she fell asleep.

Chapter Seventeen

Fallon had arrived back at Caislean Thiar earlier than originally planned, just two days after the sentence for Livia's attacker was carried out. She'd been concerned of any reprisals by allies of the young soldier who ultimately succumbed to his injuries in the prison cell later that night. Cateline and her three charges departed first thing the next morning, escorted by a handpicked team of Elite Guard warriors.

Her place was with Cateline, and now Laigen and Garratt and Livia, too, to protect them all. She'd taken care of the things that her second couldn't, then left. Riding throughout the night to get back to her post. To get back to Cateline. Now, she sat in her room, staring into the flames of her fireplace. For reasons she couldn't quite put her finger on, she'd left the lid of the trunk open. Perhaps some sort of guiding light for Cateline. She needed to see her, but she didn't want to bother her. She couldn't allow her growing need for her to become something it couldn't be. Her initial instinct was that she needed the soft, comforting touch of a woman, so she'd strapped on the rigid phallus with designs to visit Millie, but thoughts of Cateline had left her ironically impotent to leave her room.

She'd reflected a lot on the things her father had done, was beginning to put in place, and had been talking to Cateline about. Fallon had a pretty good idea now why he'd chosen Cateline and not just a brood mare for a competent heir. She felt her father intended for Cateline to take over, He was perhaps grooming her to be the queen who would act as king.

She smiled, shaking her head. Pretty brilliant, honestly. Her father was a very clever man, and very quiet in his deeds. Suddenly, bam! Everything had changed and you had no idea the rules were being rewritten.

Her thoughts, unfortunately, turned from insightful back to morose. She'd been haunted by images of Livia's broken face. After she'd left with the small entourage, Fallon had spoken to the physician who told her he expected some permanent scarring about her face and perhaps a limp, as her leg had been badly twisted, he figured in her attempt to crawl away from her assailant.

The one bright spot was that it did not seem that rape had taken place, as Livia had claimed he'd tried but turned to beating her when he couldn't perform. Fallon felt she'd failed her, that sweet, yet feisty young woman.

Why hadn't she taken care of that soldier before when she'd had the chance? Yes, she'd humiliated him by ordering him tied up for the masses to throw rotten food at or hurl insults, but clearly that had done nothing but stoke his fire.

Fallon had been so lost in her own thoughts that she'd failed to hear the entrance of the woman who was currently climbing out of the faux wooden chest. She glanced over at her, almost startled by her sudden appearance.

"Hey," Cateline said softly, her second leg clearing the ledge of the trunk before walking over to where

Fallon sat.

She was dressed for bed in her long sleeping gown, her hair down and combed out in auburn curls down her back and over one shoulder. She was stunning. Standing next to Fallon's chair, she looked down at her with so much concern in her beautiful eyes. A hand came up and, with the gentlest touch, brushed over the cut and large bruise over Fallon's left eye.

"Does it hurt?" she asked softly.

Fallon's eyes closed for just a moment as the cool fingertips danced over the skin near the small wound. "A little," she said. Fallon's eyes remained closed as Cateline leaned over her, her long hair tickling the side of her face as soft lips lightly touched the cut and bruise.

"All better," Cateline whispered, lightly caressing the side of Fallon's face with her fingers before moving away.

Fallon's eyes slid open to see the princess standing before her, between where she sat and the fireplace mere feet away. Her beautiful face was completely in shadow now, though the firelight behind her created an auburn halo around her head, the sleeping gown she wore becoming transparent as the flames revealed the silhouette of the body beneath.

Fallon could see the small frame, which she'd felt in their few physical interactions. She could see a small waist and the flair of womanly hips. Against her will, her mind filled in the rest. She tried to clear the real image and those her mind was conjuring up for her, and looked up at Cateline, unsure what she was doing.

Cateline reached down and gripped Fallon's

hand that rested in her own lap, and gently moved it aside before she climbed onto the open lap, lifting her gown just enough so she could straddle Fallon's hips before letting the gown fall back into place, covering herself appropriately.

Once settled, Cateline whispered, "Come here," as she hugged Fallon's head to her chest.

Fallon's eyes once again fell closed. She wrapped her arms around the woman sitting on her lap, holding her close. She was very surprised by the move and wondered what Cateline had seen in her eyes to do it.

It seemed out of character for her. Not necessarily the need to comfort, as that was very much her nature, but to take such a step that would be seen by anyone as inappropriate for a woman with a purported man, especially when he wasn't her husband.

"When did you get back?" Cateline asked, one hand cupping the back of Fallon's neck beneath her hair while fingers of the other ran through the dark strands.

"Earlier tonight," Fallon murmured, readjusting her head to a more comfortable place against the softness that was Cateline's breasts. As quietly as she could, she inhaled the beautiful woman's scent, wanting to memorize it and lock it away for another time when she needed to feel her close. "How's Livia?"

"She's all right," Cateline said softly, the pressure atop Fallon's head making the warrior feel that the princess had rested her cheek or chin there. "I've given her some time off to heal. She's asleep with Laigen right now."

Fallon was glad to hear the good news, but her heart was so heavy. "I failed her, Cateline," she said softly.

"No, you didn't, Fallon," the princess murmured, the hand that had been at the back of Fallon's neck sliding around to the side, her thumb resting on her jaw near her right ear. "Life is about choices, and that soldier made his choice." She was quiet for a moment before adding, "You gave Livia what so few women get."

"What?" Fallon asked.

"Justice," Cateline said simply. After a moment, she continued. "I had the strangest dream the last night we were at your father's castle."

"Hmm?" Fallon murmured, so content in that moment.

"I dreamed that you were in bed with Laigen and I," Cateline whispered. "That you were behind me. Holding me." Her fingers caressed the side of Fallon's neck. "It was so real, so vivid. I was startled when you weren't there when I woke up."

A smile touched Fallon's lips for just a moment, feeling guilty about her stunt, but the longing in Cateline's voice made her feel sad. "I had to go," she said. "I didn't want you to be upset if you found me in your bed."

Cateline pulled away just enough to cup Fallon's face, urging her to look up at her. "You *were* there?"

Fallon nodded. "Yes. Livia was in my bed and I didn't want to disturb her, so…" Her words sounded hollow to her own ears. From the softening look in Cateline's eyes and her thumb lightly caressing the warrior's cheek, Fallon knew they both understood she'd been there because she'd *wanted* to be there.

Cateline touched her forehead to Fallon's, her hair falling forward to act almost like a curtain, bringing the world in to just the two of them. Fallon's heart was racing, her content from moments ago turning to a deep, profound need. Her fingers rested at Cateline's waist, itching to move.

The first touch of Cateline's lips was surreal. They were so soft, so tender, Fallon drawn to them as though by some magic pull. Softness against softness, tentative yet wanting to explore. Unable to hold herself back anymore, Fallon's hand roamed up into thick, auburn hair, enjoying the soft sigh that earned her.

Fallon's own sigh escaped at the first touch of a soft tongue against her own. Sex with Millie and one other woman in her life was one thing, but this was something different entirely. Their kissing was slow, measured, yet there was a deep passion to it, a connection of one soul to the other.

After many minutes, they were both breathing too heavily to continue. She looked into Cateline's eyes, noted her flushed face. She caressed the soft skin of her cheek and cupped her jaw. She saw the same intense desire in her eyes as she felt and no doubt reflected in her own eyes.

Hands going to cup Cateline's behind, Fallon pushed to her feet, holding the other woman snugly to her as she began to walk toward her bed. Cateline wrapped her arms around Fallon's neck, holding on.

Fallon lowered her to the bed, following so she lay on top of her, hips tucked between Cateline's thighs. She looked for any sign, any indication that she needed to stop. Quite the opposite, as Cateline wrapped her legs around Fallon's, her calves draped over the backs of Fallon's thighs.

Fallon flipped her hair to the side to get it out of the way, allowing it to fall to the side as she looked down into Cateline's face. So beautiful. She knew they could both be executed for this, but in that moment she didn't care. She'd rather die knowing what it was like to make love to the woman she knew in her heart she was falling in love with, than live a long, lonely life in the cold grip of duty.

The only thing that would make their time together better was if she could peel away the ruse and make love to Cateline as herself. But, she thought sadly, it wasn't an option, so she'd take what she could get and give her heart while in someone else's body.

Lowering her lips back to Cateline's, Fallon initiated a deep, slow kiss. Cateline's hand buried itself in Fallon's hair as they kissed, her hips beginning to rock gently against her. Fallon reached down between Cateline's legs, able to feel the immense amount of heat. She maneuvered to unlace her leather britches, their kiss continuing. As much as she'd love to take her time and explore the beautiful woman beneath her, she knew they didn't have that kind of time.

Reaching inside her pants, Fallon gripped the phallus and gently pulled its length free from the leather confines. She guided the tip to the volcanic wetness she found between Cateline's thighs. Though to her knowledge it was only Cateline's second time, Fallon was able to easily slide inside of her until their hips were tucked together.

Cateline moaned softly into the kiss as she was entered, her thighs opening wider in invitation. Fallon reached down and ran her hand along the underside of Cateline's right thigh, urging her to pull her knees up closer to her chest, allowing her an even deeper penetration.

"Fallon," Cateline whispered, eyes closed as her

head fell back against the pillows. The look on her face was pure ecstasy as the warrior began a very slow rhythm with long strokes, pulling almost all the way out before slowly pushing fully back in.

Fallon found a soft, supple throat and used her lips and tongue to explore as she continued her gentle thrusts. Her upper body weight rested on her left forearm, leaving her right hand to wander freely. As she explored Cateline's neck, her hand moved up to cup a small, firm breast through the material of the sleeping gown. She moaned in appreciation at the hard nipple.

Fallon used thumb and forefingers to roll and lightly tug on Cateline's nipple, the little whimpers that elicited exciting her beyond measure. It was taking focus and willpower to keep her movements slow, wanting to prolong Cateline's pleasure even as her body begged her to pound into her. The part of the phallus that was against Fallon's body pressed intimately against her in the very right place, rubbing and pressing with each thrust.

Cateline moaned as she arched her back a bit, offering her breast to Fallon's touch. Her hand moved from Fallon's hair down to her tunic and tugged on it. For a moment, panic flashed through Fallon like ice-cold water. Slowing down her frantic heartbeat that nearly sent her heart up into her mouth in fear, she took a deep, steadying breath as she reached for Cateline's hand, gently but firmly removing it from her tunic and placing it on the bed.

Lifting her mouth from a warm neck, she looked down into the beautiful, flushed face that looked back at her. She smiled and trailed her fingertips down along Cateline's jaw. "Not now," she said softly.

"Someday, I promise. But for now," she whispered, leaning down to leave a soft kiss on even softer lips. "Just let me love you."

Cateline nodded, returning the kiss as her hand once again slid into long, dark hair. "Love me," she murmured into the kiss before deepening it.

Fallon allowed herself to get lost in the kiss, her hips beginning to move again, though now a little faster, the thrusts a little shorter. She was so aroused it was painful, but still somehow she managed to keep her body controlled.

It didn't take long before once again they were breathing too hard to continue kissing. The need and pleasure was building. Fallon pushed up on her hands and used the power of her body to quicken her pace. She listened to Cateline's whimpers and heavy breathing, her hips moving with Fallon's, their pace seeming to urge quicker, harder thrusts.

Happy to oblige, Fallon's mouth fell open and eyes closed as her hips were finally given permission by Cateline's own need to pound into the woman beneath her, Cateline's entire body rocking with each thrust.

Cateline's moans were constant and high-pitched, growing louder with each thrust deep inside her. Fallon wanted to cry out but was afraid her voice would give her away, so kept as much vocally inside as she could. Biting her bottom lip so hard she worried she'd draw blood, she finally came with a strangled groan, a shockwave of pleasure crashing over her like the waters of a flash flood.

Cateline grabbed Fallon's shoulders with talon-like fingers as her head pushed back, throat exposed as she cried out, long and loud. When she stopped, her body seeming to have released her to the pleasure, she held on to Fallon, whimpering softly as her breasts heaved against Fallon's chest.

Fallon's hips stilled and she cradled the woman beneath her as they both calmed down. Finally, she lifted her hips just enough to pull out of Cateline before reaching down to quickly tuck away the phallus. She moved off Cateline to lie beside her, the princess bringing her legs together and adjusting her gown.

There wasn't a lot of room on the narrow bed, so Fallon remained on her side, head propped on an upturned palm as she looked down at the woman who had stolen her heart. She caressed her face, admiring her beautiful features, the softness of her skin. She ran a fingertip along a proud jaw and down the slope of her nose, making Cateline smile, which Fallon returned.

"Why are you not married?" Cateline asked.

"It was made very clear to me that I'm to remain married to my duty to my country," Fallon answered.

Cateline's eyebrows fell as her fingers instantly interlaced with Fallon's when Fallon took her hand upon the princess' stomach. "That's not fair."

"Milady," Fallon whispered. "Of anybody, you've seen just how unfair life can be."

Cateline looked up into her face, seeming to study every aspect, angle, curve, and detail. "Will you use my name?" she asked softly. "When we're alone."

Fallon met her gaze and held it for a long moment before smiling with a nod. "Of course, milady." She leaned down and murmured in her ear. "I mean, Cateline."

The younger woman smiled. "Flirt."

"Turn to your side," Fallon said, taking her hand away while Cateline did as asked, presenting her back to the warrior. That gave Fallon a moment to lace up her pants before she scooted in behind the smaller woman, pressing her body flush against her. Her eyes fell closed as she hummed in contentment at the feeling of holding the precious woman back against her. She placed her hand on Cateline's hip, pressing her own hips as tightly into the shapely behind as she could.

"Is this what you dreamed?" Fallon murmured into Cateline's ear.

Cateline let out a long, happy sigh. "Yes." After a moment, she let out a heavy, sad sigh. "I should get back." She moved away and sat up, her back to Fallon as she sat on the side of the bed. "I don't want to," she whispered, almost as if to herself.

Fallon's eyes squeezed shut, dreading the moment she knew would have to come. Letting out a cleansing breath, she moved off the bed and walked around to the other side, holding out a hand to Cateline, who took it and allowed herself to be lightly tugged to her feet.

Fallon immediately took the smaller woman into her arms, holding her close, their bodies flush. She caressed Cateline's back beneath the weight of her hair as her other hand cupped the back of her neck.

"Can I tell you something?" Cateline whispered.

"Of course," Fallon responded, resting her cheek atop the auburn head.

"This is how I thought it would be with my husband," Cateline said. "When I heard I would have to be married. I thought I'd feel like this in his arms." She let out a rueful snort. "Hoped, anyway."

"I'm sorry," Fallon murmured. In a way, she wished Cateline had felt that way with Fergus because then she wouldn't be in this hopeless predicament. In another way, she was glad she hadn't, as Fallon had gotten to touch perfection if even just for a stolen moment.

Chapter Eighteen

The two riders slowed as Fallon held up a hand, her sights on movement in the trees. Her patrol companion Gunther pulled his horse up beside her. Using hand signals, she explained why she'd stopped them. He nodded. She indicated he go left and she'd go right. The lead man of Fergus's guard nodded and directed his mount in the intended direction.

Morning patrols in the king's lands surrounding the castle was something Fallon had always taken on herself before returning to the castle to begin her daily duties. She enjoyed being out by herself, and Toirneach enjoyed it as well.

But Fergus had insisted she blend her men and practices with the men he'd brought into Caislean Thiar, and though she was the senior officer, she had to follow his orders. It was frustrating as these men— who knew where Fergus had gotten them?—weren't trained or disciplined to Fallon's standards. Now that things had settled at the castle, she was planning to bring over her best from the main barracks to help create a training regime so that the country's elite forces were all on the same page.

The movement Fallon had seen had been someone in a cloak. Not unusual, especially on a chilly late-summer morning, though it was an unusual cloak, dark blue with what looked to be gold stitching. The fact that somebody was there at all and clearly being elusive was the problem. With a click of her tongue, she directed Toirneach to go continue on, her eyes never leaving the area she'd last seen the figure.

The person popped up, saw Fallon, and took off running again. Fallon nudged her mount with a firm press of her heel against his side. Like a deer running from the hound, the cloaked figure sprinted, heavy fabric of the woolen cloak fanning out behind it. The figure zigzagged its way toward thick underbrush where prickly plants liked to live and where Fallon's horse couldn't go.

Irritated, Fallon slowed Toirneach, watching the person run. She thought it was a man by its build and size, but wasn't sure.

"He got away?" Gunther asked, pulling up beside her.

Fallon spared a glance at him before looking back to the thicket of woods. "Yes. Step up your patrols of the area," she advised, looking back to the soldier. "Day and night."

The two made their way back to the castle, Fallon putting her horse up before heading inside to the kitchen. The room was hot and steamy, food smells permeating the air. The kitchen servants hurried, getting breakfast ready for the castle but starting with Fergus and Cateline.

"I got your message this morning," the warrior said to Millie, who was pulling out a pan of freshly baked bread from the oven.

Millie glanced over at her as she hurried the hot pan to a large wood table that she used to roll dough and prepare dishes. "Good morrow," she said. "Bring me that butter, will you?"

Fallon nodded, walking over to the bowl of the creamy stuff and carrying it to the table. "Happy to fill in for Livia while she's out."

Millie snorted. "Oh, I bet," she said, glancing over at Fallon as she began to slice a loaf previously taken from the oven to cool. "Suppose you don't mind filling in for her husband either, hmm?"

The look of surprise caught Fallon's expression before she could hide it. Jaw clenching, she looked away.

"So, the rumors are true, are they?" Millie asked softly, a bit of warning in her voice.

Fallon cleared her throat, nervousness filling her. How on Earth had they been discovered so quickly? The servants always seemed to have extraordinary ears and eyes, beyond what was humanly possible. "What are people saying?" she asked just as quietly.

The cook shrugged as she performed her task. "It's just wagging tongues, mostly, but some have noticed the way the lady looks at you and think it's about time your bastard brother gets a taste of his own medicine. Some are amused, others shocked, while others still don't blame the princess at all and are in fact envious of you."

Fallon couldn't help but feel shy, a hand going to rub the back of a heated neck. It didn't help when she pictured Cateline from the night before in the grip of ecstasy once again. She glanced up at one of the few she'd ever shared the same kind of intimacy with when she spoke again.

"When did it start?" Millie asked. There was no accusation in her voice, no real emotion other than curiosity.

Fallon smirked. "That's hard to answer. Which

part?"

Millie looked at her, eyes wide and eyebrows raised. "Begin where you like, then."

Fallon stared down at the even slices of bread, unable to meet Millie's eyes. Somehow, she felt guilty. It wasn't as if Millie owned any part of her, body or heart, but she'd been there for her in so many ways through the years.

"Of our own choice, we've only been together once," Fallon murmured, glancing up at Millie to make sure she understood her meaning. When the older woman nodded, she assumed she had. She was wrong.

"Of your own choice?" Millie asked.

"The other time…" She shrugged. "Members of the Court needed their proof."

"Ah, yes." Millie sighed. "And we all know what a useless lout your brother is."

Fallon said nothing, simply smiled and looked down at the bread again.

"Does she know?" Millie asked. "About you?"

Fallon shook her head. "No."

"Is that wise, Fallon?" Millie reached for one of two wooden bowls and placed a few of the slices inside, the remaining in the other bowl. Fallon knew which was going to Fergus.

"I can't tell her, Millie," she said. "She'd hate me."

"Oh?" Millie pressed. "As opposed to this dishonesty?" She shook her head, turning back to her task of doling out globs of butter. "Do what you will, Fallon," she continued. "But God help you if you make a fool of a future queen. I don't care who your father is."

Fallon let out a heavy sigh, placing her hands on the table and leaning on it a bit, head hanging.

"Is this just about sex for her?" Millie asked. "Or, does she feel as you do?"

"I don't know," Fallon said with a sigh. "We didn't mean for this to happen, Millie." She felt a bit defensive as she knew it was wrong. "It just did."

"Fallon," Millie murmured, resting a hand over one of Fallon's. "There's nothing unusual about a king, queen, prince, or princess finding actual love while stuck in a cold, arranged marriage." She lightly squeezed, then removed her hand. "Just be careful, that's all I ask."

❧ ❧ ❧ ❧

Fallon was nervous. She stood outside of the bedchamber door, heart beating quickly in her chest. Her arms were laden with a tray that held breakfast dishes for the three souls within those rooms, Garratt having already gone to eat with the soldiers, wooden sword belted at his side.

Letting out a long, slow breath, Fallon used the toe of her boot to tap on the wooden door. A moment later, the door was pulled open and a very curious little four-year-old was looking up at her.

"Well, good morrow!" Fallon grinned down at her. "Aren't you a strong girl to get that door open all by yourself."

Rather proud of herself, so said her grin, Laigen ran back into the room, leaving the door open for Fallon to follow.

Amused, Fallon entered the bedchamber, nudging the door closed with her foot. Cateline sat in a chair, Livia behind her gathering the long, auburn hair into braids. A small shiver went through Fallon as she remembered that soft hair, how it felt on her skin, what it felt like to run her fingers through it.

She looked away so her thoughts, no doubt written all over her face, wouldn't be seen. Clearing her throat, she walked over to the table and chairs where Cateline had taken to eating her meals, setting the tray of food down.

"Good morrow, ladies," she said, turning to smile at the two.

Her gaze found Livia, who barely looked at her. The young woman seemed so shrunken within herself. A few days after the attack and the blood washed away, the bruising was extensive, especially around her jaw.

She looked to Cateline to try and get a read on how Livia was doing. The look in the princess's eyes showed concern, but the smile on her lips spoke of confidence that the girl would be okay. Fallon turned back to Livia, who refused to meet her gaze.

"How are you, child?" she asked gently.

Livia nodded. "All right, milord," she whispered.

"I want you to know, Livia," Fallon said, ever so gently using two fingers under her chin to urge her to lift her head to look at the warrior. She smiled when finally Livia met her gaze. "I just wanted to assure you, he can never hurt you again."

Her eyes widened. "Is he…"

Fallon nodded. "He is." She was surprised when the young woman fell to her knees, gripping one of Fallon's hands and kissing it.

"Oh," she breathed. "Thank you, milord! Thank you!"

"Livia," Fallon murmured. "Please stand." She

tugged lightly on the hands that gripped her own. When the young woman stood, she refused to look at Fallon, her eyes downcast. Fallon wasn't sure why. She'd never shown special deference before with her. Perhaps embarrassment? Neither necessary. "May I hug you?" she asked.

The young servant looked at her, surprise in her eyes. But, she nodded. "*Si.*"

Fallon, as gently as she could, gathered the small frame into her embrace. She knew nothing was broken but knew damn well how badly cuts and bruises hurt. Livia fell into her, her body relaxing into the warrior. Fallon cradled the back of her head against her shoulder.

"You're safe," she murmured. "You'll always be safe with us, I promise." When the young woman in her arms began to softly cry, Fallon held her a bit tighter, looking over her head at Cateline, who was watching.

After a few moments, Livia got herself under control, soft sniffles coming from her as she pulled away from Fallon. She glanced up at her, then away. "Thank you," she said, then moved over to the tray of food and began to dole it out, setting the table for Cateline to eat.

Walking over to the princess, Fallon fell to one knee before her in deference and reverence. "Milady," she said softly, glancing up into amused eyes. She took one of Cateline's hands and left a lingering kiss on the back before standing, reluctantly letting the soft hand go.

"How are you?" Cateline asked quietly, for Fallon's ears only.

The last time they'd seen each other was after

making love the night before. Fallon felt a bit nervous and, admittedly, a little needy. She wanted to be able to take the smaller woman in her arms and never let her go.

"I am well. How are you?"

"Also well, thank you," Cateline responded. "Sleep well?"

Fallon gave her a little smirk. "Like a rock."

Cateline gave her a little smile of her own, rather sensual, and it struck Fallon in the nether regions. "I'm so pleased to hear this." She walked over to the table where her chess set had been personally set up by Fallon and retrieved some documents written on parchment, handing them to the warrior. "These arrived this morning."

Shifting out of flirtation mode, Fallon took the pages and read over them, eyebrows lifting in surprise. "The official decree for Laigen and Garratt," she said unnecessarily, as the documents were titled such. "He was serious." She met Cateline's gaze and smiled brightly. "It's done. Usually it doesn't get doesn't this quickly, but Laigen and Garratt are safe."

The princess closed her eyes, her steepled fingers moving to her mouth as she seemed to take a moment of thanks. Letting out a soft breath, she met Fallon's eyes again. "Now what? Is this forever their fate? So-called paid servitude?"

Fallon shook her head. "The king can end this at any time. My father has broken this for several people over the years," she said, holding up the declaration. "As a gift or reward for bravery and such. As for your other question," she continued. "You can decide what you'd like to do," Fallon said, handing her back the pages. "The Surshan Kingdom does recognize adoption. However," she warned. "Fergus would have to agree with it, since he's your husband, and then they'd be considered *his* children."

Cateline looked over at Laigen, who was climbing on one of the chairs where Livia set up breakfast, dragging her doll by an arm. "Am I a horrible person if I say I don't want these children anywhere near Fergus?"

Fallon shook her head. "No, you're not. I think you're a brave, amazing woman with so much love to give. Laigen, Garratt, and Livia are so intensely fortunate to receive it."

"Thank you," Cateline said softly.

"Well," Fallon said, stepping back from her. "You enjoy your breakfast. I have a meeting with said husband that I have to get to."

"Wait!"

Fallon looked at Cateline, surprised by the panicked tone of her voice. "What?"

"Can you help me with something real quick?" the princess asked, turning to head toward her boudoir. "Something I can't reach."

Fallon followed her into the room only to find that everything was in perfect princess range. She quirked an eyebrow as she looked to the woman with her.

"I'm sorry," Cateline murmured, snaking her arms up around Fallon's neck. "I had to give you a proper greeting."

Fallon's eyes slid closed as she easily gave in to the kiss she received. She wrapped her arms around the smaller woman, holding her tightly against her. She longed to truly feel her against her, to know what it felt like. But for now, she relished the contact.

The kiss quickly deepened and grew passionate, Fallon urging Cateline backward until she was against the wall, the warrior's body pinning her there. Their kissing continued for a long moment until it began to slow down and the two parted, breathless.

"How do you do this to me?" Cateline whispered, fingers in Fallon's hair.

"Well," Fallon said, brushing her knuckles lightly over the softness of Cateline's face. "As I recall, you started it, milady."

Cateline smiled. "Touché."

Fallon left one more lingering kiss on soft lips before moving away from her. "I have to go."

Cateline nodded. "Will I see you…later?"

Fallon studied her for a long moment, head slightly cocked to the side. "Perhaps." She gave her a winning smile before leaving the room.

❧❧❧❧

"Good morrow, Your Highness," Fallon said, entering Fergus's bedchamber. The older sibling sat at his desk, advisers standing nearby. They all turned to look at her as she entered.

"Fallon," Fergus acknowledged. "Do come in."

Fallon walked over to the desk, bowing dutifully before her brother before sitting in one of the gathered chairs opposite the desk, the advisers following suit. "What's going on?"

"I received this," Fergus said, tossing a folded document to her.

It missed its mark, so Fallon leaned over the arm of the chair and snatched it off the floor. Sitting correctly in the chair again, she unfolded the missive and read its contents. Her eyebrows fell as a hand came up for fingers to absently run along her bottom lip. Finally, she lowered the document to her lap and looked at her brother.

"I thought you didn't want to get to the bottom of what happened," she said. "The attack on the camp while we were in France."

"Well," Fergus said, sitting back in his elaborate chair, the wood creaking slightly under his girth. "If this person says they have information, we'd be remiss to not listen, wouldn't we?"

Fallon studied him for a long moment. "It says that in a month hence, they wish to meet in Brittany to discuss this."

"They do." Fergus waved to one of his advisers, who walked over to Fallon and retrieved the parchment, handing it back to the prince. "I want you to take a squad of men and meet them."

Fallon met the gazes of the men, who all looked to her before looking back to her brother. "Do you think it's wise?" she asked. "Before knowing if this is a ruse?"

Fergus leaned slightly forward, pinning Fallon to the spot with his intense gaze. "That's for you to find out, isn't it? You're the sword of the Crown, not me."

Fallon nodded. True enough. She pushed up from her seat and bowed once more. "It'll be done."

"Fallon?" Fergus called out, Fallon stopping as she neared the door and turned to look at him. "This is a private mission," the prince said. "Keep it that way."

Fallon met and held his gaze for a long moment, a trickle of uncertainty sliding its way down her spin.

Finally, she nodded. "Aye."

⁂

Her mind whirred with everything that had happened that day. She'd met with some of her men and some of Fergus's, including Gunther. She was trying to create the perfect team in her head for this "private" mission. She felt unsettled but couldn't put her finger on why.

Entering her bedroom, her mind was a million miles away, thinking and rethinking strategy. Who would be best to join her? What sort of skills did she need to amass in her choices of soldiers to build the squad that would sail to Brittany?

Removing her weapons, she tossed them to the bed before her hands reached for her tunic, whipping it up and over her head. It, too, landed on the bed, which Fallon didn't even see. She considered who she'd meet with the following day. Perhaps a trip to the main barracks was in order?

Her fingers worked to unlace her britches so she could reach the laces to release her torso armor. Part of her wanted to speak to her father, get his council. Did he know anything of this? She looked down to make sure she unlaced the intricate system and didn't inadvertently create an ugly knot for herself, which she had done before when not paying proper attention.

Truth was, the Crown recognized that she worked for the prince and was at his disposal, not that of the king. She could get her father's advice as her father, but not as King of Sursha. One set of laces undone, Fallon moved on to the ones a bit lower that attached to the harness at her hips. She pushed her britches down a bit for easier access to those laces.

Her father, however, could offer her resources of the Crown should she need them. It might be a good idea, she thought, to at least let him know what was going on so she could access what she may—or may not—need.

Fallon let out a sigh of relief as the two plates, chest and back, loosened as the final restrictive laces were undone. She took in a deep breath, removing the hardened leather and tossing it to the bed. Eyes closed, she rubbed her torso, trying to loosen up the muscles underneath.

Her hands cupping her breasts, she stood there for a moment before her hands fell away. It was then that she heard a loud gasp. Whirling around in surprise and defensive posture, she could only stare as Cateline stood with just her head above the top edge of the chest, the rest of her body still upon the stone staircase below.

Her eyes were wide and mouth open as she stared at Fallon's breasts before they darted up to look into Fallon's face. They took in the breasts once more before Cateline was gone, scrambling back down the stairs. Horrified, Fallon hurried over to the opened chest, greeted only by the darkness below.

Chapter Nineteen

Heart racing, Cateline scurried back down the corridor, out of the light from the room above and into the soothing darkness closer to the closed door of her own bedchamber. Not pulling the door open, she stopped and leaned against the cool stone of the wall. Eyes closed, she rested her head against the wall, a hand going to her chest over her sleeping gown.

What had she just seen? A person standing there, the person she'd come to know as Fallon, a man. Treated her with the dignity and respect the way a man should treat a woman. Wore trousers, fought, was a warrior. She covered her face in confusion. Fallon made love to her like a man would a woman. Twice! But how?

She thought about what she'd seen. It was like the perfect mix of man and woman. Fallon had stood there dressed only in dark brown leather trousers, dyed such by a ground walnut shell and water mixture. Without the tunic and, now Cateline understood, the bulk of the torso—Armor? Suit?—she wore, the flair of a woman's hips and behind was noticeable, as women were shaped so differently than men.

Her bare torso was very much that of a woman with delicate collarbones and shoulder structure, even as her arms and stomach and upper back were well muscled. They weren't as large as a man's, Cateline now realized, but she'd never seen a woman with such physical capabilities.

Breasts. He...she?...had breasts. They were beautiful, Cateline had to admit. They weren't as large as Cateline's, which weren't as large as Marie's, which were quite large. When Fallon had stood there in the light of the fire, his skin had been painted an orange-gold, licked by the light of the flames. It had been almost ethereal.

Perhaps Fallon was, too. Perhaps the warrior wasn't a he or a she, but something given by the gods to keep the Earth safe. She buried her face in her hands, so confused. Gasping when she heard a noise in the corridor close to the stairs. She hurried into her own rooms.

Door safely closed and locked behind her and tapestry back in place, Cateline brought a shaking hand to her forehead. She took several deep breaths before walking over to the door that led to the children's room.

Since Marie had married Henri, the older woman now only worked two days a week, and mainly that was to help with the laundering of Cateline's, and now the children's, clothing. She'd gone into partial retirement from service, Henri fully retiring.

He'd put in so many years of service to the Crown that he'd earned a small plot of land and a home outside of the castle walls, where the two lived now. Her old room had been turned into one for Laigen and Garratt with the stacked beds Fallon had built for them. Since the incident with Livia, she'd been sharing a bed with Laigen, preferring to remain close as she healed, physically and emotionally.

As quietly as she could, she pushed open the

door to see the soft glow of the fireplace warming the stone room. Garratt was sound asleep on the top bed, one of his little bare feet sticking out from beneath the covers.

Walking over to the bed, Cateline brought the covers back over the foot, smiling at the relaxed, peaceful, handsome little face that was the boy she was beginning to see as her own son. A glance to the bottom bed showed her Laigen on her side facing the wall with Livia spooned behind her.

Assured that everyone was all right, she quietly closed the door and went to her own bed. She wasn't sure what to think, what to feel. She climbed into the bed and lay down. Unable to get the image of Fallon out of her mind, Cateline closed her eyes. She hoped she could force sleep.

❧ ❧ ❧ ❧

She was tired. Sleep had been elusive at best. Cateline sat up in bed, her head lowered and hair falling in her face. Normally she would have been up long ago, but her eyes felt like they were filled with sand and her heart filled with lead.

"Good morrow, milady," Livia said, stepping into the bedchamber with a tray loaded with breakfast dishes.

Cateline blinked a few times before focusing on the young servant. "Good morrow Livia. I'm proud of you for going out," she said with a warm smile. She'd given the young woman the time she needed before leaving the chamber, but hoped, for Livia's own emotional health, that she would sooner rather than later.

"Well," the lady-in-waiting said, walking over to the table. "Fallon came by earlier to find out what we wished to eat, but I told him you were still slumbering, milady."

The sound of his…her…Fallon's name caught Cateline's attention and brought her the rest of the way out of sleepiness. "What did sh-he say? How was he?" she asked.

Livia looked over at her, looking confused. "Fine, milady," the young woman said slowly. "As I said, he asked what you wanted for breakfast, then bowed and left when I told him you were still sleeping." She shrugged. "He looked tired, but as always, milady."

Cateline nodded, pushing the covers off her so she could slide off the bed. She padded over to the table, looking down at the assortment of bread, fruit, and ham that lay on the plate. A small flask of watered-down wine—per her request—had been added to the tray as well.

"Thank you, Livia," she said, scooting out a chair to sit down.

Livia gave her a slight curtsey then scurried off to take care of Cateline's bed, making it to perfection just as Marie had taught her. Left alone at the table, Cateline grabbed a piece of bread and smeared some butter on it, enjoying the tastes as she ate in silence. Her mind somersaulted over everything.

She'd had strange dreams with the sleep she had gotten. Some, she was embarrassed to remember, were very erotic. She could see Fallon's breasts in her mind's eye and had a vague memory of touching them in one of her dreams. She'd never seen a woman's breasts before that didn't belong to Marie. As a young girl, Marie had occasionally bathed with her to not only help her, but also save on time as they were heading out on a trip with Cateline's father.

During her very short relationship with Sophie, she'd never seen any part of her body, though the irony wasn't lost on her that she likely would have the very night Fallon and the others had arrived at her father's estate.

She wondered if—

"Milady?"

Cateline's head jerked up at the voice that had haunted her all night. Her eyes were wide with surprise as she stared at Fallon, who stood a few feet away. The warrior looked sheepish, and Livia was right: tired. And, to Cateline's surprise, a bit timid.

"Yes, Fallon?" she responded, the walls of her heart slamming upward at the very sight of the person who had caused her so much confusion and hurt.

Fallon seemed a bit taken aback by her tone, clearing his throat before proceeding. "I need to go into the village just beyond the gates to visit the cobbler there, and I'd like to take Garratt with me. If he's to march with us, as you know, he enjoys spending time with the soldiers, I'd prefer to get him some boots for the occasion."

"You don't need to ask my permission for that, Fallon," she bit out.

Fallon clasped his hands behind his back and straightened a bit, irritation in his expression. "Yes, milady," he said, voice low and curt, "Legally, I do."

Feeling stupid, Cateline looked away. *Right. Legalities.* Looking back in his general direction, she nodded. "That's fine," she said softly.

He bowed deeply then turned to leave.

"Fallon,' she said, the warrior turning back to

look at her.

For just a moment, Cateline saw a profound sadness in the deep, soulful eyes that had so captured her from the start. Just as quickly, it was gone, the eyes staring back at her now guarded. She had no idea how to ask what she wanted to ask. How to put into words what so plagued her.

"I don't know what…" She stammered, frustrated at her cowardice. "You. I don't know—"

"My mother gave birth to three children," Fallon said quietly. "Two of which were sons." With that, the warrior turned and briskly left the bedchamber, leaving Cateline to look after her. "And," Fallon said, once she'd reached the door. She turned and looked at Cateline, the sadness back in her eyes. "I'm sorry I frightened you, milady," she said, emotion in her voice. With that, she was gone.

❧ ❧ ❧ ❧

The castle physician had recommended Livia rest at times during the day to continue healing. So, after the midday meal, Cateline left her to do so, leaving her bedchamber so it would be quiet. Laigen was napping with her, as she'd had a busy morning of playing and her daily lessons. Cateline was determined the young one would know how to read and write.

She decided she wanted to get out and wander around the castle, stretch her legs. She felt antsy and restless, and she didn't quite have an understanding of why. She felt lonely yet could be surrounded by any number of people at any moment, should she seek them out.

This was different, she realized as she walked

the halls. It wasn't a loneliness or want of company, it was deeper inside. Her heart felt lonely. She felt like something was missing but couldn't put her finger on what. She felt empty. She had the strangest feeling that, if only she looked to her left, she'd see another walking with her, the shadow of her soul.

Doing her best to shake such dark, morose thoughts, Cateline turned down another long, dim hallway and reached a fork in her road; she could go straight, turn left, or turn right. She was in a part of the castle she'd not been in before, so wasn't sure where she was. She'd been so deep in thought, she'd gotten herself lost.

Standing at the intersection, she looked down both ways, left and right, and saw that they were twin hallways, long, both ending in doors. Straight ahead ended in a wall. About to turn right, she stopped, glancing straight ahead again as she thought she heard something.

Taking a few steps, she heard it again. A moan? As quietly as she could, she neared a small alcove about a third of the way down the hallway. It was a recessed doorway, the door partially open.

Cateline's eyes nearly popped out of their sockets when she saw what was happening inside that room. There were three men, all naked but only one of them on the bed. That man was Gunther, Fergus's main man in his guard. He lay there on his back. His erect penis was being stroked by the hand and mouth of the man who stood next to the bed, bent over it. That man was Will, and something was being done to him that Cateline had no idea could be done to a man, or anyone, for that matter.

A man stood behind him, meaty hands gripping

his hips as he thrust his penis inside Will's anus, much the way a man would inside a woman's vagina. What stunned her even more than what was being done, or that Will seemed to be very much enjoying it, was that it was Fergus lazily thrusting behind him.

Fergus's head was back and his eyes were closed, clearly lost in the pleasure of what he was doing. A particularly good spot must have been hit as Will stopped his ministrations to Gunther and turned his head, rapture on his face. He opened his eyes and looked right at Cateline. He gave her a little smirk before returning his attention back to his task.

Not sure whether to be shocked, disgusted, or intrigued, Cateline knew she needed to be gone. She hurried away as quickly as she could, randomly selecting her route, which ended with a door at the end. She pulled it open and flung herself inside, hoping against hope that she hadn't been heard by the other two.

Taking a deep breath, she turned around and found herself in yet another hallway, unlit wall-mounted torches every ten feet or so, leading to a narrow staircase that spiraled upward. Curious, she took the stairs, bracing her hand on the cool stone as it corkscrewed its way up. Finally, she reached a wooden door ribbed by iron. It had a small square part of it that looked like it could be opened.

Curious, she grabbed the iron ring used to pull the door open. Inside was another tower room, like Fallon's, though smaller. There was no fireplace in this room, however. A single, very narrow bed was on one side, the mattress thing, worn. Iron rings were mounted to the wall above the bed. A small wooden table with one chair was placed near the one window, no more than an arrow slit.

It was cold, damp, and sent a chill down her spine, though not all from the cold. The energy in the room was heavy and dark. It occurred to her what it was—a place for criminals. The tower. Shivering, she quickly hurried from it and down the stairs. She longed to be back in her own bedchamber with the fireplace playing chess with Livia or curled up reading.

She hurried down the torch-lined hall, intending to retrace her steps and find her way back when she heard voices. She stopped, hand on the wall as she listened.

"You're so lucky, Millie," a woman was saying, the two servants hurrying by. "Fallon can use his sword on me any time." The cook and the speaking woman giggled as they hurried by, not seeing Cateline who stood frozen, watching as they hurried past.

The princess stood there, unable to breathe for a moment. A wave of jealousy rushed through her in a tidal wave that took her by surprise. Her mind was spinning, images in her head of Fallon having sex with the cook. An attractive woman, she supposed, older than herself by a dozen years, she'd guess. When? How? Why?

She pushed away from the wall, her mind in a fog as she headed back the way she'd originally come. When did this happen? How often? Did Fallon love her? Did she love Fallon? With all she'd learned, such betrayal on all sides, she just wanted to curl up into a ball and cry. Now perhaps she understood why her own husband didn't want anything to do with her. He was already getting his needs met by his footman and Gunther.

"My God," she whispered, burying her face in

her hands for a moment as she walked.

She had no idea men did that with each other. But then, the little bit she'd done with Sophie, with want to do more, why wouldn't they? She was confused, though. And Millie. Did she know Fallon was a woman? Had she and Fallon made love since Fallon and Cateline had? Anger flared through her. Perhaps the nights she didn't see Fallon, which were most, it was because she was with Millie. Was she talking sweet to her, too? Peppering her with kisses and stroking her body?

Feeling the emotion building, the tears stinging the backs of her eyes, Cateline found a recessed doorway and pressed her back against the arched wall, slowly sliding down until her behind hit the floor. Knees pulled to her chest, she allowed the tears to come fast and hard, streaming through her fingers as her hands covered her face.

She'd never felt so alone in all her life, and considering what her life has been, especially in the last many months, that was saying a lot. Lowering her hands, she wiped them on her dress before wrapping her arms around her shins and resting her chin on her knees. Tears continued to silently fall down her cheeks as she stared straight ahead. She didn't see the plain stone that comprised the archway, but different aspects of her life.

So much of her life she'd felt ignored, an obligation. Now, she felt utterly used. She thought about Fallon's sweetness, his—*her*, she corrected in her mind—gentleness, compassion, and the way she looked at her. She looked at Cateline like she was the only woman on Earth. The only woman in Sursha. The only woman in the castle. Clearly, Cateline thought with a snort, that wasn't true.

She considered Millie and something occurred to her. When Cateline had to start thinking about hiring staff for the home she'd share with Fergus, Fallon had offered to help. She'd brought in a few people, including Millie. She'd insisted on Millie, in fact.

"I am such a fool," she whispered.

The door was pulled open right next to her and Cateline looked up, finding herself looking into the face of Millie. She quickly looked away and scrambled to her feet. She felt embarrassed and angry, all at the same time.

Turning her back to the cook, she quickly tried to wipe her tears away with the sleeves of her dress, stopping and growing stiff when she felt a gentle hand on her shoulder.

"Milady," Millie said gently. "What's wrong?"

"Absolutely nothing you can help me with," Cateline bit out before her brain could even filter her words.

The cook moved around until she was standing in front of the younger princess, her eyebrows drawn in concern. She looked into Cateline's face, a hand coming up to brush a few tendrils of hair that had fallen out of Cateline's updo.

"You heard us talking, didn't you?" she said softly, a statement more than a question.

Stubbornly, Cateline refused to answer. Instead, she looked away, unable to look at the woman any longer. All she could do was envision Fallon having sex with her, using "his sword," just like he'd done with her.

"I think we need to talk, milady," Millie said,

bringing Cateline back from her bitter thoughts. "Will you come with me?" she asked. "Was on my way out to pick some vegetables for dinner," she explained, indicating the large, empty basket she carried.

Cateline looked from the basket to the woman holding it. She wanted to curse her and run back to her bedchamber to hide beneath the covers like Laigen after a bad dream. Instead, she nodded.

"Yes."

Chapter Twenty

Millie took Cateline down a narrow hallway that led to an outside door, which Cateline had no idea existed. But then again, she didn't know the area of the castle that she'd managed to wander into at all. The door was peculiar: much shorter than usual and very narrow.

The two women had to take a moment to get through it. Millie explained it was to stop any invaders from easily breaching the castle should they get on the premises. A soldier, in bulky armor and weapons, would struggle to get inside without making noise or getting stuck.

Once outside, Cateline took a long, deep breath. It felt good to have the sun on her face and to be around the lush vegetation of a substantial garden, row upon row of carrots, potatoes, turnips, beats, and many others. She did notice, also, that many of the vegetables had not been picked in time and had rotted.

"Why so much waste?" she asked, deeply bothered.

"Yes," Millie said, nodding as she looked around. "We have to make sure we have enough for the household."

Cateline looked at her, surprised. "There's a large enough garden here for two households," she said. "Why is this not being shared?"

"We've not been given permission to, milady,"

Millie said simply.

"That's going to change," the princess said, resolved. "Right now. This extra food will see its way to the orphanages, disabled, anyone who needs it. Am I understood?"

Millie looked at her, a little smile curving her lips. "Yes, milady. I understand very well."

Cateline nodded, forcing herself to calm down. "Thank you," she said. "Back when I was still in France, I used to have a rose garden that I tended."

"Come with me, milady," Millie said, setting her basket down and walking toward the end of the building. Cateline followed.

The vegetable garden extended quite some bit, but there was much land beyond that nothing was being done with. It was overgrown and could easily be turned into a wonderful rose garden, replete with pathways, benches, perhaps a fountain. Cateline looked on, imagining so much as her eyes widened and mouth fell open a bit.

Feeling eyes on her, she turned to see the cook watching her, a look of amusement on her face. "Can this be used to create something?" she asked.

"Oh, yes, milady," Millie said with a smile. "I know your lady Livia rather enjoys the art of growing. I'd say it would be good for the both of you. And little Laigen." She shrugged nonchalantly. "Don't know that Fallon is all that good at gardening, but I know," she added, pinning Cateline to the spot with her gaze. "That she'd do anything you asked of her."

Cateline stared at her for a long moment. Was she the only one that hadn't known, then? "So, you know?" she said softly. "Does everyone?"

Millie indicated that the princess should follow

as she headed back to the main garden and her basket. As she began to pick vegetables, she spoke. "No," she said easily, plucking some carrots and examining them before placing them in the basket.

"What all do you need?" Cateline asked, indicating the surrounding vegetables.

"A bit of everything, if you don't mind." Once the princess began to help, the cook continued. "I've known Fallon since she was around eight years old or so. She was a little spitfire even then."

Cateline smiled, easily able to envision that. She placed a few carrots into Millie's basket as she listened.

"She followed Ailfred around like a little shadow. Collette tried desperately to get her to do the things a royal princess should do, but she wanted nothing to do with it." She smiled, seeming lost in memory. "Finally, I think the king just gave up, realizing that he had an asset in allowing Fallon to be who she wanted to be."

"A soldier?" Cateline asked.

Millie shrugged. "That," she hedged. "But to not focus on her gender." Her mood seemed to become more serious, a bit darker. "You see," she added quietly, as if for Cateline's ears only. "It was quite obvious early on that Fergus would never amount to much of anything. From what my late husband Burke said, he was lazy and uninspired from the time he was a boy."

"Clearly, not much has changed," Cateline said, looking at a nice, large potato that she'd just dug. Deciding it was worthy, she added it to the basket.

"I have a theory, milady," Millie said sagely, "And it's one that could get me tossed into the dungeon."

Intrigued, Cateline looked at her. "I assure you,

I won't allow that to happen."

"I appreciate that, Your Highness," the cook murmured. "One thing you'll find about King Carthac is he's very smart, very strategic." She smirked. "Don't ever play him in chess, I assure you." She chuckled. "Ailfred is the only person I've seen beat him there."

Cateline smiled, remembering Fallon's own prowess in winning moves. "Must run in the family."

"Who do you think taught them?" Millie asked with a raised eyebrow. "Anyway, you were handpicked by the king, milady," she said. "I don't know if you realize that. Yes, that's often the case, but it's not usually about the specific woman, but what she can bring regarding influence in name or money." She shook her head. "These things had no bearing in your case."

"Then, what?" Cateline asked, so badly wanting to understand her purpose. "To run in Fergus's stead?"

Millie shook her head. She walked over to Cateline, taking her hands in her own. "You were picked as a mate for Fallon, not Fergus," she said, shaking her head to emphasize her point. "That got you in the door of the country in a legal, accepted way."

Cateline's eyebrows fell as she slowly shook her head. "I don't understand. Fergus is the legal heir of the throne."

"Indeed," Millie muttered, continuing her task again.

Cateline was quiet for a long moment, absorbing all that she'd been told. "How did you and Fallon..." She couldn't even make herself finish the sentence. She was seeing enough in her head.

"To answer that, we have to go back several

years," Millie explained. "It was easy to let Fallon do what she wanted to do as a child, as one child looks like the next unless you put 'em in a dress or breeches. But, as she began to get older, mature, a very clear problem was emerging."

Cateline nodded, thinking back to those breasts and the glorious woman's body that she'd seen. "Yes, that would be an issue." She cleared her throat, "Is that when—"

"No," Millie said. "I was a very happily married woman, milady. Things didn't happen between us, the handful of times that they did, due to my draw to her feminine qualities. She was someone trusted, a trusted friend, who could give a lonely, grieving widow what her dead husband no longer could. And, Fallon could learn."

"Learn to what?" Cateline asked bitterly. "Learn to deceive?"

Millie crossed her arms over her chest, challenge in her eyes. "What did you do when Fallon told you?"

"She didn't," Cateline spat. "I walked in on her."

"And let me guess," the cook pushed. "You embraced her and asked questions and got all the facts."

"No, of course not!" Cateline gasped. "I was shocked!"

"Then, is it little wonder she chooses to deceive rather than be rejected?" Millie said softly.

❧❧❧❧

With a basket filled with fresh vegetables, bread, cheese, and wine, Cateline headed back to her bedchamber. A troubling start to her day had ended up quite enjoyable. She'd very much found Millie entertaining, intelligent, and deeply loyal to Fallon and her family. Her love story with Burke had been as heartwarming as it had been heartbreaking that the soldier had been killed with Ailfred.

She felt that Millie could be a friend, certainly an ally, which made the princess feel better. She'd given her insight into Fallon, and certainly a lot to think about. As she headed to the stairs which would take her to the third floor, something caught the corner of her eye.

Stopping her ascent, she glanced down over the railing, which overlooked the great hall. A figure was hurrying through the massive space, the dark blue cloak they wore floating out around them in their haste. She couldn't see anything of the person, their hood pulled low, but something about them made her uneasy.

As though they felt they were being watched, the figure stopped and turned to look her way. Cateline stepped back to hide behind a massive stone pillar which extended from the floor of the great hall to the ceiling of the second floor.

Holding her breath, she waited a moment, then peeked out around the pillar. The figure was gone. Releasing her breath slowly, she hurried up the stairs. In her bedchamber, she was happy to see Livia was sitting with Laigen and Garratt, who was excitedly regaling them with his adventures with Fallon the past day.

"And, look!" he crowed, holding up a miniature, but very real, sword. He saw Cateline enter and ran over to her. "Cata!" he exclaimed, using the name both children had begun calling her. "Look!"

Cateline shifted the basket to her left hand as

she took the sword that he proudly handed her. "My goodness!" she said, happy for her excited charge but also very concerned that a boy so young would possess a real sword that could do real damage. "Where did you get this, Garratt?" she asked.

"Fallon," Garratt said, all proud smiles. "It was the very one he was given when he was my age. I can be a warrior like him too!"

Cateline reached down and ran her fingers lovingly through shaggy brown hair. "You can be whatever you wish, Garratt," she said softly. "I'll make sure of that."

"With Fallon?" he asked, so innocent as he looked up at her with wide, blue eyes.

She smiled and nodded. "Of course."

"Fallon got something for you, Laigen, and Livia, Cata!" Sword in one hand, he grabbed hers with the other and tugged her toward the table where they ate meals.

Sure enough, stacked upon the table were a pair of little leather shoes for Laigen, a new cloak for Livia, and a beautiful gold ring for Cateline. It was a torc ring, bands of gold twisted together made up the ring, which was not a full circle, but rather ended a very small distance apart in two knots. It was very beautiful in its simplicity. The princess slid the ring onto the ring finger of her right hand where it fit perfectly. She stared at it for a long moment before looking up when Garratt called her name.

"Fallon left this for you, Cata," he said, handing her a folded note.

Taking it, Cateline looked at the ring again, heavy on her finger, before opening the note:

Milady,

I left tonight to work with the men at the main barracks. I should be gone a week. Don't fret, I have somebody to be there in my stead. You'll be safe.

Regards,
Fallon

At the bottom of the note was written:

I hope it doesn't upset or offend you that I'm giving you this ring. I've been meaning to for a while now. It belonged to my mother, her favorite next to her wedding ring, which she was buried with. My mother was a strong, loving woman who loved her people and her children. It seemed fitting that you should have it.

She smiled, looking at the ring again. It meant even more to her to wear it, as she knew what Fallon's mother had meant to her, though she'd lost her so young. It also made her sad. The note said Fallon had been wanting to give her the ring for some time, which meant before the events of the previous night, before Fallon thought she'd been completely rejected, as Millie had said. But then again, that was essentially exactly what Cateline had done.

※ ※ ※ ※

Fallon had been gone for three days. Sure enough, a guard named Daniel had taken her place. He was quiet, studious, and malleable to whatever Cateline wanted or needed to do beyond the castle walls. Laigen wasn't sure what to make of him, and Garratt was downright defiant, as Daniel wasn't Fallon. He was upset that he hadn't been allowed to go with his hero back to the main barracks.

Everything was quiet as Cateline sat in front of the fire. She couldn't sleep, feeling Fallon's absence acutely. Her thumb reached under her right hand to caress the ring on her fourth finger, a habit she'd noticed she'd begun to do when she was missing the warrior, which was a good deal of the time.

Glancing over her shoulder to the tapestry that she knew covered the doorway that would lead to Fallon's room, she chewed her bottom lip, pondering. She knew she should just go to bed and try to fall asleep. After all, tomorrow she and Livia were going to begin organizing the harvesting and gathering of extra vegetables the castle did not need to take to surrounding villages for the people to use in their own homes.

Pushing up from the chair, still caressing the ring, she lit a candle. Cateline walked over to the tapestry and pushed it aside. She entered the dark corridor, a halo of candlelight illuminating the smooth stones all around, lighting the way.

Though she hadn't expected to see light at the end of the tunnel, it made her sad that, indeed, she didn't. The trek, which had become very familiar to her by this point, was made quickly. She mounted the steps, noting the hatch door was closed. For a moment she considered just turning around and heading back to her own space, her own world. But something told her to continue.

Placing her palm on the door, she pushed, the wood creaking upward. Stepping up the remainder of the stairs and down into the room proper, Cateline looked around. As usual, it was neat and as spotless as life in a drafty castle could be.

The bed was made to perfection, everything hung or tucked away in its place. Nothing left lying around, even the small fireplace swept clean. Turning to the bed, Cateline set her candle and holder down on the small table that was in the room and walked over to it. She didn't dare disrupt the perfection of the smooth, tight tuck of the blanket over the mattress, but did brush her fingers over it.

She thought back to the incredible moments they'd spent on that bed. Their first time together, her first time at all, had been out of necessity, nothing more. Fergus's refusal to be a husband had forced the Crown's hand. For Cateline, she'd just been grateful that it had not only been a nonviolent or painful experience, but a surprisingly pleasant one, pleasurable, even.

But, the night in Fallon's room, on her bed, that had been mutual want, mutual need. One could argue that it was born of a deep loneliness within them, considering the boxes they'd both been forced into in their lives, but Cateline knew it was more than that.

She looked at the trunk that was set at the foot of the bed. She was curious. She knew so little of the person underneath the leather, the armor, the weapons, the *man*. Who was the woman? Who was the real Fallon?

Hoping perhaps the trunk would give her some insight, even as she felt guilty for snooping, the princess knelt down in front of the thigh-high trunk. Inside, she found folded clothing and towels and some toiletries. Something hidden beneath those items, however, made Cateline's breath catch.

It was all connected in a bit of a leather spiderweb of straps that attached to an appendage, the shape giving very little doubt what Fallon used it for. Standing, Cateline held the phallus against her hips by the straps, looking down at it as it protruded from her body.

It was made of leather like the straps but was the definite shape and size of what she'd seen of a man's penis in etchings and drawings in books. Also from its size, she had a suspicion that it had been what Fallon had used with her. Part of her was unsettled by it, and part of her, admittedly, was intrigued.

Setting the contraption aside, she saw aged parchment beneath. Carefully, she brought them up, realizing it was several letters written between Carthac and a woman named Roishin. She wondered if that was Fallon's mother.

Lowering herself to sit on the floor, Cateline began to read. The words spoken between man and future wife were filled with longing and love. Though some of the words Cateline couldn't quite make out in the language gap that still existed, but she was able to work out much of it in context. It would seem the young bride-to-be was born and raised in Dublin, Ireland.

Much like Cateline being French, it seemed the marriage between Roishin and Carthac was to bring Sursha and Ireland closer together as allies. Sadly, Cateline and Fergus were not a love story in the making, but at least it got her to the country that she was beginning to fall in love with. It brought her to Laigen and Garratt. It brought her to Fallon.

Chapter Twenty-one

Fallon met her father's gaze, the look on his face that of surprise. Finally, the king said, "You cannot go."

"What do you mean, 'I cannot go'?" she asked. "Fergus gives me my orders and he's the prince."

"And, I am the king!" Carthac's words reverberated off the walls of the Solar as he turned away from his youngest, hand reaching out to rest upon the top of an ornate chair. "You don't understand, Fallon."

"No, Daidi, I don't understand. I can't look weak to Fergus, you know that. I can't go to him and say, 'Sorry, Brother, Daidi said I can't go.'"

Carthac nodded. He let out a long breath before turning to face his daughter. "He's setting you up," he said simply. "Whomever he's sending you to meet knows nothing of who attacked your camp that night."

Fallon blinked a couple times. "How do you know?"

"Because I sent the *routiers* to attack your camp," the king said, gaze strong and steady as he looked at Fallon.

Fallon stepped back, a hand flying out to brace herself on a table. "What? Were you trying to kill the princess?" she asked, stunned. When her father slowly shook his head, Fallon asked, "Me?" Again, the slow shake of the head. Thinking she understood, Fallon looked away, her hand combing through her hair as she tried to reconcile what she'd just been told and what had been insinuated.

"I love your brother, Fallon. But," he added with a heavy sigh. "I love the people of this country more. Not more than Fergus, but more than his selfishness. More than his instinct to destroy. He would absolutely destroy this country and everything in it, Fallon. And he'd destroy Cateline."

"Then why did you sentence her to be married to that monster?" Fallon demanded, whirling around to face her father. "Why? Why would you do that to her?"

"Because she wasn't meant for Fergus!" Carthac boomed.

Again, Fallon could only blink.

"I never had any intention of Fergus *ever* sitting on that throne," Carthac said, pointing in the general direction of the throne room just off the great hall. "He's not qualified, he's not willing, he's not safe."

Fallon took this in, nodding, as she knew her father spoke the truth. "So," she asked, calming a bit. "You intend for Cateline to take the throne in his stead, then? As queen?"

"No," Carthac said, shaking his head. "Well," he amended. "As queen, yes, but at the side of her partner. Her husband."

That hit Fallon in the heart. She cleared her throat and turned away again. She couldn't bear to hear anymore, to know who her father had in mind. "I see," she said softly. But then again, it wasn't as though it mattered. Clearly Cateline had no interest in Fallon the woman. The look in her eyes that night and avoidance after made that crystal clear.

"No, you don't see," Carthac said. "What are

our bylaws regarding the death of a male in the royal line?"

Fallon turned back to him, confused. "There are many bylaws, Daidi. There are—"

"What must become of the widow of a man who is in line for the throne?" the king asked.

"She must marry an unmarried brother or close relative," Fallon said automatically, not considering what she was saying until it hit her. "Wait, are you saying…"

"That's exactly what I'm saying." Carthac walked over to her, placing large hands on her shoulders. "You *must* return from this asinine errand Fergus is sending you on." Heavy eyebrows were drawn in concern, the lines in the older man's face seeming to be deeper than usual. "Your country depends on it."

"But," Fallon said, shaking her head. "You tried. Fergus barricaded himself in his tent that night, heavily guarded by my men. He lives."

The smile that slowly spread across Carthac's face was downright chilling. "I have a backup plan." He walked over to a small gold chest he always kept near his bed. He opened it and fished something out. Closing the box, he walked back over to Fallon, a jeweled medallion resting in his palm, the gold chain dangling off his fingers. "Go to Brittany."

Fallon met his intense gaze, a bit surprised by her father's reversal about her upcoming trip. She took the medallion, noting it was heavy. It was a large stone, transparent though a strange mixture of purple and orangish-gold running through it. The skull-shaped stone had a gold snake coiled around it.

"Wear it," the king ordered.

❧ ❧ ❧ ❧

Wrapped in a fur-lined cloak, Fallon stood on her flat rock and looked over the pond. It bubbled and curled in on itself as fresh rainwater fell over the edge above into the waterfall. She wrapped her cloak around her a bit tighter. The autumn was soon upon them, and the rushing water before her made it colder in the little canyon of her secret place.

She considered the conversation she'd had with her father the previous day. None of it sat well with her, and she'd been stunned to find out what his plan had been all along. As she stood there on that rock, she thought about her years with Fergus as her brother, a lifetime of mockery, snide comments, demands, and commands.

She thought back to the story she often told, had even told Cateline. Once it was clear Fallon had natural talent and athleticism with weapons and such, she'd been assigned to Fergus's dog. What she usually didn't say was that the dog had been a vicious beast and had torn apart more than one of the other hunting hounds.

Fergus had "assigned" her to dog duty in order to see what would happen. Would the brute tear apart his kid sister? What entertainment it would be! To his shock, Fallon had managed to whisper to the dog's soul, calm him, and, eventually, befriend him. Part of what had made the dog so vicious had been Fergus's own abuse of the animal, Fallon had realized. Her kindness had turned a snarling, drooling death sentence into a lap dog.

Fallon brought her left arm out from beneath the cloak, turning it over and looking at the three parallel claw scars that ran along the underside. Now mostly just faded white lines, the trio ran from her wrist nearly to her elbow. That day had been harrowing at best, nearly deadly at worst.

It had been after that Fergus had realized Fallon was useful, and he'd taken her talents seriously. She'd become his little puppet ever after, leading to where she stood now. All this time, she'd seen it as her honor and her duty. Now, something had changed. She felt like a fool. Fourteen years wasted on a man who literally didn't care if she lived or died. Only twenty-three years old, more than half of her life had been spent at his feet.

Fallon's father was not an impulsive man or leader. He was methodical, smart, strategic, and did his level best to look at every situation from all sides. Many times, Fallon had been in the room when major decisions were discussed and made. She knew how he thought and how he weighed each decision.

Initially she'd been horrified to learn that Fergus had essentially been set up. It hadn't worked as planned, but the plan was for his own son to be murdered that night. Paid mercenaries. The irony was thick. Sursha had kept its independence from the larger countries of Europe because of their fierceness. They had the best fighting force in the western hemisphere. A sword for hire had been their origin, and still largely was. Mercenaries.

It now made sense how those assassins had gotten past Cateline's father's men who had been camped in the larger perimeter in the woods. They'd allowed the paid *routiers* to waltz on by, given the nod ahead of time. This made Fallon wonder if Cateline's father had been in on it too. Was that part of the dowry?

Turning away from the water, which she knew could very well be the last time she saw it, she headed out, whistling for Toirneach as she did. She needed to get back to her brother to button up details, as she would be leaving with her chosen squad in three days' time. She needed to organize the men left behind and resituate them in the castle, as some posts would be open as those men were going with her.

She stood waiting, watching as her horse trotted through the trees toward her. "Take your time, big boy," she muttered. "Got all the time in the world."

When the war horse finally reached her, Fallon mounted and, with the nudge of her heel and click of her tongue, got them on the road. They had a long ride ahead. She planned to ask for permission to say goodbye to the kids and Livia before she left. Despite her father's plans for Cateline to be forced into yet another marriage, this time with Fallon, Fallon wanted some time to think about it.

Perhaps it would be best if she never returned from Brittany, then Cateline, a most capable woman, could go on as queen on her own. Millie had warned her that she needed to just be honest with the princess. Would it have made a difference? Fallon would never know. What she *did* know was that her time with Cateline, however brief it had been, was over.

Fallon rode hard, her hair blowing back behind her, her cloak more like a cape riding the wind as they pushed onward. She needed the cold, icy winds blowing in her face to keep hot, bitter tears at bay. She was angry. She was hurt. She was heartbroken.

She thought of the ring she'd given Cateline. That ring had been her father's first token of love to a young Irish princess, she'd been told. He'd been in love the moment he'd seen the beautiful brunette. She'd had several suitors, but she'd said it had been that ring that had sealed her decision for her.

Carthac often said he'd never remarried after the death of Roishin because she'd already given him heirs, and he didn't want any more children to cause infighting. Fallon, however, knew that wasn't true. He'd been gutted when she'd died.

Fallon had very few memories of those days, but one winter her mother had fallen sick. She remembered her father holding her mother, pressing a cloth to her face as she coughed violently. One morning, Fallon wasn't allowed into her mother's bedchamber, held back by Ailfred. She'd heard the most awful howling from inside. She'd never heard pain and loss like that, before or since. There were nights it crept into dreams.

She did, however, understand the emptiness that went along with the loss. She'd felt it again the night she'd seen the horrified look in Cateline's eyes. The moment the princess had ducked out of view, Fallon's soul had been ripped, the younger woman taking part of it with her.

※ ※ ※ ※

Fallon looked over everything, ticking items off in her head as she surveyed the packed wagon. Finally, she looked to the driver and three guards that would be accompanying it to the harbor to load in the ship for the following day's leave.

Nodding, she turned to the expectant soldier. "Nicely done, Eoin," she said, slapping him on the shoulder. "You boys have safe travels, and I'll see you shipside tomorrow."

The soldier let out an audible breath of relief then smiled, bowing before turning back to the wagon and his comrades as Fallon turned away from him.

Jogging up the stairs to the side door of the structure, Fallon re-entered the castle and made her way to the top floor and Fergus's bedchamber. She raised her hand and rapped loudly on the closed door. After a long moment, it was pulled open, Will standing on the other side.

"Will," Fallon greeted. "Fergus asked to speak to me before I left."

Will nodded and pulled the door open a bit more, stepping aside so the warrior could enter. "He's had a headache today, but I know he's been anxious to speak to you."

"About time," Fergus grunted, glaring at Fallon as she walked over to where he sat at his desk, a stack of parchment before him. "I asked for you to be here yesterday."

"Yes, well, I was on the road yesterday," Fallon responded flatly. "My horse can only go so fast."

Bushy eyebrows raised. "Getting a little big for your britches, aren't you?"

Fallon stared down at the seated man. After everything she'd learned over the last week, she felt differently about her brother. She had the feeling that, one way or the other, this would be the last if not one of the last times she ever had to deal with him. Her days of deference to him were over.

"I have things I need to do to carry out your little mission, Fergus," she said. "What do you need?"

Fergus sat back in his chair, gaze locked on Fallon. Will hurried in with a silver cup filled with fragrant warm spiced wine. "This will help my head?" Fergus asked the footman.

"Aye," Will said. "That's what the castle physician suggested. As well as better sleep."

Fergus nodded and grabbed the cup handle with a meaty hand. He took a sip before setting the cup aside, eyes never leaving Fallon. "Everything ready to go?"

"It is," Fallon said. "Just checked on things, making sure we're all packed and ready. The wagon is heading out here shortly, and myself and the rest of the men will leave on the morrow."

"Good. Gunther told me he, too, is ready. Do you think you can trust him?" Fergus asked, taking another sip of the wine.

Fallon wanted to say, *No, he's an idiot,* but simply nodded. "I think he'll get the job done."

"Excellent." Fergus sat back in the chair and eyed Fallon for a moment. "I saw the brat, the boy, running around with your old sword at his hip."

Fallon's jaw muscles worked for a moment. She wanted to pull her boot dagger and slit his throat at the way he spoke of Garratt, but took a deep breath mentally before nodding. "I gave it to him."

"Why?" Fergus asked, disgust in his voice.

"Because he wants to be a warrior," Fallon responded coolly. "I figured I'd let him run around with it for now, get used to its weight." She shrugged. "See if it's still something he's interested in after a while, or if it's simply the fantasies of a boy learning who he is."

"Well," Fergus said, holding the silver cup to his chest with one hand as he waved off Fallon with the other. "Hope he has no visions of fighting in *my* army someday."

Fallon ignored the snarky comment and gave Fergus a bow. "I'll see you when I return, Your Highness."

Fergus nodded as he took another drink, dismissing the warrior. Barely stopping herself from shaking her head in irritation, Fallon left the large chamber and, after taking a deep, steadying breath, walked to Cateline's door. She'd been told the princess was in chamber so figured it was a good time to say her goodbyes.

Knocking on the door, she waited. After a moment, it opened, Livia just barely visible behind it. Fallon's smile was instant as she saw the young woman was healing well, much of the bruising on her face fading, the swelling all but gone. Her smile grew even more at the small grin upon the servant's lips because it reached her eyes as well.

"Good eve, Livia," Fallon said.

Livia curtsied and stepped aside, allowing Fallon to enter. Garratt and Cateline were seated on the dais at the chess table while Laigen was in her usual place by the fire playing. The princess glanced over at Fallon as she entered, Livia softly closing the door behind her.

"Good eve," Fallon said. "I'm leaving tomorrow at dawn for a bit and wanted to say goodbye." She looked down at her hands, which fidgeted uncharacteristically. "I hope that's all right." It was only the second time she'd seen Cateline since everything had happened, though she'd been by two other times, the princess absent.

"Of course it's all right," Cateline said, pushing back from the table and standing. She looked at Fallon for a moment, almost as though she weren't sure what to do. "Where are you going?"

"The prince needs me to do something for him," Fallon said cryptically.

"Can I go?" Garratt asked, jetting across the space from the chess table, which he nearly knocked over in his haste to get to the warrior.

Fallon met him with hands on shoulders in order not to get bowled over. "No, Garratt," she said with a smile, not wanting the would-be warrior to see the concern in her eyes for what she was about to go do. "Not this time. I'm not going to be training or playing war games." She tousled his hair. "This time it's for real."

"Do you need my sword?" Garratt asked quietly, his hand already on the grip of the sheathed blade.

Fallon smiled at him, so proud of the bravery and chivalry he already possessed. "No, *mac*," she murmured, surprising herself when the Gaelic word for son tumbled from her lips. She knelt down to his height when she saw the disappointment flash through his eyes. "Tell you what," she offered. "I need you to hold on to it. You see, even though Daniel will be around to protect Cata, your sister, and Livia, they'll still need you to be here for them." She placed her hand over his on the grip of the sword. "Always at the ready. Can you do that for me?"

Garratt nodded sagely, seeming to understand the importance of the assignment. "Aye."

"Good boy." Fallon ruffled his hair again before getting to her feet. "Milady!" she crowed as Laigen threw herself into her arms, Fallon catching her and lifting her high overhead.

The little girl giggled, wrapping her arms

around Fallon's neck when the warrior brought her back down and hugged her to her.

After a tight squeeze, Fallon rested the child on her hip and looked into the pretty little face. "How's my girl?"

"Good," Laigen said, playing with the neckline of Fallon's tunic. "Why are you going away?" she asked, face scrunched up in consternation. That made Fallon smile, charmed by the little one.

"I have to," Fallon said gently. "I have to do my job. Just like your job is to be cute." She reached up and lightly tapped Laigen's nose. "A job you do well."

The little girl grinned. "You come back to us?" she asked, bright blue eyes filled with hope.

Fallon smiled and left a kiss on her forehead. "Everything will be okay," she murmured, not wanting to make promises she couldn't keep.

She set the girl on her feet, pleased to see she was wearing the new shoes she'd had made for her. She hadn't taken the girl to get fitted, as she wanted the shoes to be a little big so she could grow into them. She didn't do the same activity as Garratt, who needed a good, snug, comfortable fit for his training.

Glancing up, she saw that Cateline still stood back on the dais, her hands clasped in front of her. Fallon turned to Livia, who stood nearby. "You, young lady," she said, pointing at the young woman who had become such a fixture in their world just as quickly as the children had. "Take care of yourself and take care of your lady," she added, meaning Cateline.

"I will." Livia studied Fallon for a long moment, to the point of making the warrior feel a bit uncomfortable. "You take care of yourself," she said softly, yet sternly. "Trust in this," she added, pointing in the general direction of Fallon's heart, even as she didn't make physical contact with her chest.

After a long moment, Fallon nodded. "I shall try." She gave a sad smile to the young woman, then took her in a one-armed hug. Releasing her, she stepped over to the dais, keeping her distance, as that seemed to be what the princess wanted and she would respect that. "Milady." She was surprised to see that Cateline was wearing her mother's ring. At one time it would have pleased her greatly, but in that moment, it left her feeling sad.

"Please be safe," Cateline murmured, looking down at Fallon. Despite their height difference, the height of the dais gave Cateline the advantage in that moment. Somehow, Fallon thought, it was appropriate, considering how low she felt.

"I'll do my best," was all she was willing to say. An uncomfortable silence fell between them, and it was tearing a bit more of Fallon's soul away, so she decided it was time to take her leave. With a low bow of deference to Cateline's position, she turned to leave.

"Fallon?"

The warrior stopped, surprised to hear the note of panic in Cateline's voice. She stopped and glanced over her shoulder at the woman who still stood on the dais but had taken a step forward. She held Cateline's gaze for a long moment, no words spoken between them. She felt so much uncertainty coming from the younger woman, and she was just not in the right head space to read between the lines.

Saying nothing, she turned away and left the bedchamber.

Chapter Twenty-two

Fallon was forced to sit on a wooden bench, the room she was in was dark, only the buttery light of a lantern lighting the scene. Four men were around her, two of them holding the thrashing warrior while a third tied her up. The fourth stood back, a burlap sack in his hands.

The man who was tying her up shoved a rag into her mouth, silencing her protests into muffled cries. He moved out of the way as the man with the sack moved in, tugging it roughly over Fallon's head, the third man moving in again to fasten the sack in place with a rope tied around Fallon's neck.

Out of the shadows and into the circle of light stepped Fergus. He held Fallon's own dagger in his hand. He tossed it up into the air, the blade flipping around so it landed once again in his palm with a soft plop. He sauntered over to the detained warrior, continuing to lazily toss the deadly sharp weapon into the air, catching it every time.

Without warning, Fergus took the dagger by the handle and shoved the blade as hard as he could into Fallon's chest, all the way to the hilt.

"No!" Cateline shot up in bed, wrestling with the blankets to get them off her, mistaking them for the dream villain.

She looked around with wide eyes, and slowly

her world came into focus. She was in her bed in her own bedchamber. It was still dark out and very cold. She started as she heard voices, but then realized they were from far below. They were men shouting to each other, directions and responses.

Climbing out of bed, Cateline hurried over to a window and looked down. She saw the men and horses gathered and knew it was Fallon's men, ready to leave.

"No," she muttered, grabbing her cloak and slipping her feet into slippers before hurrying from the room.

She hurried, chest heaving as she felt the desperate need to get to Fallon before it was too late. She nearly fell down the stairs but caught herself and kept going. Opting to use the shortcut through the garden, the princess passed through the small door and out into the early morning. The cold air made her gasp as it pulled the very breath from her lungs, and the breath she was finally able to take came out in white puffs of steam.

She saw the group beginning to move, her heart in her throat. "Fallon!"

The lead horse kept moving, even as the rider glanced back over her shoulder. She muttered something unheard by Cateline to the others before turning her horse around and heading in the princess's direction, even as the other men continued. Pulling Toirneach to a step a few feet away, Fallon looked down at her.

"You can't go," Cateline said, shaking her head as she met the warrior's gaze.

"Milady," Fallon responded, "I have to."

Cateline bridged the gap between them, placing her hand on Fallon's leg. "You can't. I had the most horrible dream. You can't go."

Fallon glanced off toward the men who were leaving before looking back to Cateline. She swung her leg over the massive horse's back before her boots hit the ground. "Cateline," she said softly. "I have to. I won't lie, this is likely to be pretty dangerous, but I can't not follow an order. Even from Fergus." She ran a hand through her hair. "What was your dream?"

"They tied you up," Cateline said, reaching out and adjusting Fallon's cloak, which was about to fall off one shoulder. "They put a bag over your head and…" She had to swallow back her rising emotion at the vivid image she could still see. "Fergus killed you."

Fallon stared at her for a long time before looking away. "I'll be safe," she murmured.

Realizing that nothing she said would cut through Fallon's stubborn stance toward her obligation and duty, Cateline nodded. She wanted to cry. "I need you to come back," she said softly.

"Don't worry," Fallon said flatly. "There are plenty of people in there to protect you and the kids."

Stung by the flippant words, Cateline looked into the guarded purple gaze. She shook her head. "No." Unable to stop herself, she cupped Fallon's face. As she looked at her, she wondered how on Earth she'd ever thought she was anything other than the beautiful, strong woman that she was. "I need you to come back to *me*," she whispered. Her hand moved from Fallon's face to cup the back of her neck and pull her head down.

The touch of her lips, which were a bit cold and stiff from the morning freeze, pressed against Cateline's. Within moments, the kiss was deepening. Fallon wrapped her arms around Cateline, pulling her close. Though they'd kissed before, to Cateline it felt like the first time, as this time, there were no lies between them, just honesty, honest need, honest emotions.

As the kiss came to a soft end, she cupped Fallon's cheek again and looked into her eyes. "I love you," she whispered.

Fallon held Cateline's face in her hands, leaving a lingering kiss on her lips before murmuring against them, "I love you too." She hugged the smaller woman to her, almost painfully tight.

Cateline clung to her, such a horrible foreboding feeling in her heart. One last kiss, then Fallon pulled away and climbed back atop Toirneach's back. She looked down at Cateline for a long moment, as though memorizing her face, before with a cry to the horse, she jetted off into the pre-dawn darkness.

The princess watched, silent tears falling down her cheeks, cold against her heated skin. She watched until she was out of sight, even no longer able to hear the horse's hooves. With a heavy sigh, Cateline turned around, only to nearly walk right into Will. He was staring at her.

Hand to chest, Cateline took a step back, meeting his gaze. "You frightened me," she muttered.

His smile was slow, and certainly unsettling. "My apologies, Your Highness," he said, issuing a slow, almost mocking bow.

"Get out of my way," Cateline said, frightened, but doing her best not to show it.

The footman stepped aside, sending his arm out in invitation to pass. As she clutched her cloak closer around her body and hurried by him, he called out to her. "We're not so very different, you and I. Princess," he added.

She glanced at him over her shoulder. "We are nothing alike, Will," she hissed, then hurried back to the castle.

⁕⁕⁕⁕

"*Beannacht leat!*" the old woman said, grabbing Cateline's hand with her free hand, the other holding the bag of vegetables she'd just been given. "*Beannacht leat!*"

Cateline smiled at her, nodding. As the old woman shuffled away from the wagon filled with the excess food from the garden, the princess turned to Millie, who worked by her side. She'd been hearing that all morning but had no idea what it meant.

"She was blessing you," Millie explained, filling more bags for Cateline to hand out.

"Well," the younger woman muttered. "As much as I've been blessed today, you'd think I'd have good luck for the rest of my life." She met Millie's amused gaze.

"It's a good thing you're doing for these people, milady," Millie said, eyeing the princess as she worked.

"Call me by my name when we're alone, Millie," Cateline said with a welcoming smile. It had felt good to have somebody to talk to over the past couple weeks since Fallon had been gone. Despite their admission of love to each other before she'd left, Cateline felt deeply unsettled by her absence. That feeling of foreboding hadn't eased.

Millie nodded. "I can do that. Cateline."

After the events of yet another food drive they'd delivered on for the villagers, Cateline headed upstairs to her bedchamber. She was tired and considering taking a little nap before Livia returned with the children. The three of them had been doing their morning studies. It had been a wonderful distraction for Garratt, who was almost as heartbroken as Cateline herself was.

Stepping into the room, she walked in and tugged the tie to her cloak. It would be nice to take it off, as she'd been wearing it for hours, and relax. She was grateful that a servant had already been in and started a fire in the fireplace, the room warming up nicely. As the colder temperatures were coming upon them, she understood why Fallon had been insistent on so many tapestries covering the stone walls.

She whirled around when she heard footfalls on the stone floor and saw Fergus wander in. The big man looked around, touching this and touching that. He was pale, and she was surprised at the weight he'd lost. They didn't spend any time together, and if she saw him, it was because he demanded her presence in his chambers to complain about something.

"Fergus," she said, letting him know she knew he was there, even as he picked up one of her many books and looked at it.

"Where is your wench?" he asked, flipping through the pages. "I hear she's good with herbs."

Anger quickly flashed through Cateline, but she managed to keep it down. She hated watching him finger her beloved books. For that matter, she hated having him in her space at all. To her memory, it was the only time in their ill-fated marriage that he had been.

"Livia," she said, emphasizing the young woman's name. "Is not here at the moment. What do you need with her?"

Fergus looked at her finally. The dark hair of his beard was in stark contrast with the pallor of his face. His eyes were bloodshot. "Seems I've caught the flu," he said. "The worthless castle physician can't seem to find anything to make me feel better, so I want that young servant to see what she can do."

"I will tell her, and I'm sure she'll be happy to see what she can do," Cateline said, hugging herself. "I will, however," she added firmly. "Not let you punish her if she can't."

Fergus smirked, tossing the book back to the table before turning to leave the room, leaving a shaken Cateline behind.

⁂

"How do you know what you're looking for?" Cateline asked, carrying the basket Livia had handed her as the two women searched through the forest in the Crown's lands.

Livia grinned, shaking her head. "I don't know. Guess just a mixture of what I've been taught and gut instinct." She stopped them and made her way through the thick vegetation toward the trunk of a large tree.

Cateline watched as her lady-in-waiting bent down and plucked a few more flowers to add to her previous finds. She held the basket out for the girl once she rejoined the princess. "What will you do with these?"

"I'll put them in some water," Livia explained, leading them off again. "Boil it down so he can drink it." She met Cateline's gaze. "Drink it at night, then again in the morning."

"What will it do?" Cateline asked, looking into the basket, noting the different types of flowers, plants, and leaves that had been gathered thus far.

"Should help with any chest congestion," Livia responded. "Should help him sleep and just overall feel better."

Impressed, Cateline followed, not sure where her charge would take them next. She was startled when suddenly there was a hand on her shoulder to stop her progress. She pulled herself out of her thoughts that had begun to wander to see why Livia had stopped them. Then she heard it as well.

The voices of two men speaking quietly to each other. The two women moved as quietly as they could toward the voices, hiding behind some trees when they saw the two figures sitting at the base of a tree, one man leaning back against the other. The two held hands at the front man's belly.

The scene was sweet, yet very surprising. What surprised Cateline the most was the man in back was Will. Her eyes widened as her hand went to her mouth. She bit her tongue so as not to say anything and listened, Livia standing nearby.

"Seventeen years today," the man in front said. He had shaggy blond hair and was dressed like a common villager. He looked to be around Will's same age, his beard a bit scruffy. "Seventeen years today we said 'I love you.'"

Will smiled, nodding as his cheek rested against the other man's head. "We were just kids," he added. "But, I knew." He let out a long sigh. "How have we done this so long, Aaron?"

The blond man nodded. "I hate that we have to do this," he said, defeat in his voice. "Maybe Fergus would bring me into the castle as a servant of some sort? Put me in the blacksmith's shop?"

Will shook his head. "That bastard would never let us be together," Will said, voice bitter. Cateline was stunned to hear it. Not only the situation of the men, but Will's true feelings about Fergus. Clearly, they had a sexual relationship, but she thought they were close.

"Maybe Princess Cateline could bring me in?" Aaron offered, though the hope was thin in his voice. "I've heard she's a nice lady, feeding the poor and everything."

Will was silent for a long moment, staring off into space. Finally, he said, "She deserves better than she's gotten. She's a good woman."

Again, shocked, Cateline could only stare at them. She felt a tap on her shoulder and looked over to see Livia nodding with her head back toward the way they'd come. Cateline gave one final look at the two men, who she felt deserved their privacy, and the two women left the area as quietly as they could.

❧ ❧ ❧ ❧

"My goodness," Millie said from where she stood at the fireplace, banking the fire. "You're up and at 'em early, Cateline."

"Yes," Cateline agreed, walking over to the pot on the stove. She looked inside and took in the fragrance of stew. It was a very cold morning, and she was happy about something so hearty and warm for breakfast. "Livia and I went out to gather some herbs and such to see if it can help Fergus feel better," she explained.

Millie rolled her eyes and shook her head as she turned back to her task. "Lout isn't worth the bother," she muttered.

Cateline smiled, agreeing completely but saying nothing. Her mind was on what she'd witnessed with Will and Aaron, two men clearly in love. From what had been said, they had been for a very long time. "Millie?" she said, a question forming in her mind.

"Hmm?"

"Do you know much about *oidhreacht*?" she asked.

Millie glanced at her again, eyebrows drawn. "What do you want to know?"

"Can they get married? Have love, a family?"

"Well, sure," Millie said, finished with the fireplace and walking over to the oven for her ever-present baking bread, which made the entire room smell amazing. "But there are limitations."

"Which are?" Cateline asked, walking over to one of the two trays that were set out on the table. A main plate sat on both, both with fruit already placed on them. She went to snatch a blackberry, but her hand was slapped. She looked up in surprise at Millie.

"No," the cook said. "This is for Fergus." She pointed at the other one. "That one is for you." Millie turned away like nothing and went back to her work with the bread. "They cannot live outside of the castle walls," she explained, responding to the previously asked question. "So, they can only marry or court those who are essentially in the same circumstances they themselves are."

"Wow," Cateline murmured, tossing a blueberry into her mouth from the designated plate. "Very sad."

"Why?" Millie asked, a smirk on her lips. "Got

your eye on somebody?"

Cateline grinned and shook her head. "No. My eyes are fixed, thank you."

"Oh?" Millie's eyebrows raised. "Are they, now?"

Cateline nodded, then said, "I'm worried about her, Millie." She let out a heavy sigh, then met the cook's gaze. "I had a terrible dream before she left."

"I can understand that, Cateline. I can. But I'll tell you this," Millie added, a finger up for emphasis. "If anyone can take care of herself, it's Fallon. She's smart, she's quick, she knows what she's doing."

"I hope so." For reasons she'd never really understand, she looked at Millie, pinned her to the spot with her gaze so the older woman knew she was serious. "If anything ever happens to me, Millie," she whispered. "Promise me you'll get Livia, Laigen, and Garratt out of here."

Millie nodded sagely. "Of course. What are you worried about?"

"I don't know." Cateline looked around, hugging herself. Though they were alone in the kitchen, she felt eyes on her. "I just don't know."

Chapter Twenty-three

The crew dropped anchor, the ship they'd taken a shallow bottom so they could get in closer to shore, as there was no harbor where they'd landed. Before they'd left, Gunther had given her the map that had apparently come with the letter, and it had told them to land where they currently were.

"It'll be nightfall soon," she called out to the men that were coming ashore with her. "Let's make quick work of this so we can set up camp."

The nearly two-day trip had been uneventful, though there had been a tension in the air that Fallon had felt acutely. The men she'd chosen were blissfully unaware of anything other than a basic mission, though she had been sure to tell them to keep their guard up at all times. The men Gunther had chosen were stiff and ill at ease.

Though Fallon was the top commander of the Elite Guard, Fergus had insisted Gunther be given equal say in this mission, including the men be split down the middle between her picks and his. She'd been infuriated by it but had no choice but to comply. Things had been made a bit more complicated with the way things had gone with Cateline the morning of deployment.

She'd made up her mind that she wasn't coming back from Brittany. Chances were, whatever Fergus had set up for her would take care of that, but if by chance it didn't, she was going to sacrifice herself for the greater good of Sursha. That decision was largely, if not solely, because she believed that Cateline did not want her after stumbling upon her secret.

The thought of spending a lifetime married to somebody that was disgusted by her or repulsed by her very core was something she couldn't face. For once, an opponent the great warrior Fallon couldn't bear to face. Now, everything had changed by three little words. She could still hear those words coming from Cateline's sweet lips, their meaning felt in her heart and in her soul.

Now, as she made her way down the plank and stepped into the ankle-deep ocean, her mind refocused on the assignment ahead: survive. Cateline had made one request, and she intended to fulfill it.

The shore before them was rocky, cliffs off to the left and heavily wooded area to the right. Fallon took it all in, looking for anything or anyone that was out of place or could be a danger to her and her men.

She was also looking for a good place to camp for the night. It was getting too late to make their way through the forest to the village the map pointed them toward, which indicated it was a day's hike. They'd opted to not take the horses as the terrain was more conducive for a horse breaking a leg than making anything easier or faster for them.

"Thoughts?" Gunther asked, stepping up beside her.

Surprised the often-arrogant soldier asked, Fallon said, "I think we should camp just inside the tree line."

"We'll be sitting ducks," he said, looking over at her as they stepped out of the water finally and onto dry land.

"Just inside," Fallon explained. "We have a bit of protection from the weather, but we have the cliffs in that direction and the woods in that direction." She indicated both sides. "With the sea or cliffs at our backs, all we have to pay attention to are the woods. If we go far in, yes, we'd lose the wind," she said, the cold sea breeze whipping her hair and cloak around. "But then we'd be surrounded by plenty of hiding places for the enemy. They could close in, and we'd never even know it."

Grudgingly, Gunther nodded but said nothing.

"Eoin," Fallon called out, turning back to see the men still making their way to shore. "You take one man to go gather firewood. Shea, take one man and go get dinner. The rest of you, Gunther, and I will set up camp."

The groups split up and the men splashed to shore then beyond to fill their assigned task, dropping the packs of materials and foods they wore on the beach before heading off into the woods, weapons drawn for those on the hunt.

The six remaining grabbed the dropped packs and headed toward the trees, Fallon's gaze everywhere at once, looking for both danger and accommodations. They spotted a natural clearing just inside the tree line, exactly where she'd wanted to break for camp. Others must have found it a good place as well, as a rough circle of rocks had been gathered with ash inside.

"Let's camp here," Fallon said, visually measuring the area to make sure all ten of them would have enough space for their bedrolls, a few campfires, and their gear. Nodding, she said again, "Yeah, let's camp here."

Fallon decided where she wanted to camp and dropped her pack as well as the other two she was carrying. She bent over to unbuckle hers, the heavy medallion her father had given her tumbling out from under her tunic, dangling from its chain.

"What's that?" Gunther asked, nodding at the necklace.

Fallon stood, cupping her hand around it and dropping it back out of sight. "A gift."

He smirked. "Protection?"

She raised an eyebrow. "Why would I need protection?" she challenged.

"Well, I don't know. The great warrior, right?"

She stopped what she was doing and studied him. "Do you want to find out?" She opened her arms, indicating their surrounds. "Do you really feel the need to have a pissing contest here in a foreign country on a mission?"

He glared at her and turned away, focusing on his task, Fallon going back to her own. Her unease was growing. She had a gut feeling that Gunther wasn't brave enough to start a fight outright with her, so he was picking, trying to goad her into swinging first, a justified attack on his part to his men and the Surshans.

Silly, silly man, she thought. Women were just naturally more intuitive than men, in her experience, but also her entire life she'd had to be better, faster, smarter, and listen to her inner quiet, since most men could outmuscle her just by the sheer virtue of their physical makeup.

Fallon had found that listening to her inner quiet was a better weapon than any blade, kick, or hit. When she stilled her thoughts, shut out the noise of the world, even that of her opponent, her senses flourished.

She knew how close somebody was to her, she could feel the slightest bit of air move with the drawing of a sword.

She could hear the ground crunch under the turning toe of the boot as someone was moving toward her. She could smell sweat, smell the fear, and she could hear his heartbeat. She knew instinctively how far away he was and how quickly she needed to move or strike. She didn't understand it, but she took full advantage of it. It had kept her alive.

❧ ❧ ❧ ❧

Later that night, after the sun had gone down, the ten of them had arranged their bedrolls around two fires, five per fire, each sleeping facing away from the fire and each with a weapon at the ready. Fallon's blades were sheathed on the ground by her side, her boot dagger still in place. A good warrior never *ever* took off their boots while in the field.

The boys had done well with dinner, and the entire squad fed on wild turkey. Fallon was lying there, head raised on her pack as she chewed on a leg, enjoying the pretty darn good flavors Eoin had managed to get into the meat.

She stared up between the tops of the trees into the night sky. Above the haze of the campfires, she could see the stars twinkling in the velvet black that was the night sky. She thought about where they were and what little she knew of the Bretons. They were a spiritual people, but spiritual in a different way. They had deep roots in mysticism, casting spells and, as a very private people, many outsiders were, rightfully or wrongly, afraid of them.

Lying there, chewing lazily on her food, Fallon's gaze fell from the sky to the trees beyond the ring of light made by their campfires. The dark was so utterly complete, not even the shapes of the trees could be made out. As a lifelong warrior, well-trained and well-disciplined, it was rare for Fallon to feel fear or ill at ease. But for some reason, as she lay there, she felt both.

Glancing to her left, she saw Gunther a few feet away on his bedroll. He lay in a similar position to her, minus the turkey leg. One hand rested on the grip of his sword, the other on his stomach. His eyes were closed and he seemed relaxed as he dozed. To her right, one of Gunther's men sat up on his own bedroll, playing dice with the man to his right.

Nibbling the last little bit of meat off the turkey leg, Fallon tossed the bone behind her into the fire, listening to the crackle and pop as the fire licked the little bit of grease from the meat away before everything settled down again, as did Fallon. Pulling up the fur that she was bundled under, she let out a long, heavy sigh. She wanted to try to get at least a couple hours of sleep.

As her body relaxed, so did her mind, thoughts drifting far away from Brittany and back to Sursha. It wasn't hard to bring the image of Cateline, Laigen, and Garratt into focus—even Livia as part of that family picture. Though the young woman was technically a servant and Cateline's lady-in-waiting, both royal members seemed to have taken her under their respective wings as a younger sister.

Her focus zeroed in on Cateline. A smile came

to Fallon's lips as that beautiful face filled her mind's eye. Full lips, gentle sway of womanly hips as she walked. She looked into those eyes, so expressive, so filled with love...and passion.

"Fallon," Cateline whispered.

The warrior relished in the sound of her name from the lips of the woman she loved, the woman who straddled her hips. Fallon nuzzled the soft flesh of Cateline's neck as gentle fingers ran through her hair. She could feel the smooth warmth of Cateline's back against her fingertips as she ran them down along the length of her spine, fingers spreading out on the hips of the woman in her lap.

Cateline's head fell to the side as Fallon's mouth explored, teeth and tongue licking and nipping at the flesh she encountered along the way. She thought Cateline was so beautiful, so soft and sensuous.

"Fallon?" Cateline whispered.

"Yes, my love?" Fallon murmured against her throat.

"Fallon, open your eyes."

"No."

"Open your eyes, love. Open your eyes..."

Fallon's eyes popped open only to focus on the deadly sharp point of a sword aimed directly at her throat. Shoving the remnants of sleep and her dream off like a blanket, she propelled her leg up, a hard kick sending the sword flying across the embers that had once been the campfire.

The man standing over her looked on in surprise, only to find himself flying backward as she used both powerful legs to plant her boots in his gut with a forceful kick. Without waiting to see where he'd land, she was on her feet, hands sweeping down to grab her swords at the same time. She whirled around to face the rest of the men, shaking her blades free of their sheathes in one fluid movement.

She saw one of Gunther's men pinned to a tree, the sword she'd kicked buried in his stomach. One hand rested lifelessly on the grip as his head hung limply forward. The other sleeping men had been awakened by the sudden drama. Heads were lifting, men jumping to their feet when they spotted Fallon in her fighting stance or the dead man on the tree.

Fallon spotted Gunther standing nearby. For just a moment he looked stunned, but then he shook himself out of it. He held a burlap sack in one hand and a length of rope in the other. A cold chill coursed through Fallon as Cateline's panicked words came back to her.

She glared at Gunther, watching his every move. "What are those for?" she asked casually, though her stance was anything but casual. Every muscle was taught, every fiber of her being ready to do what it took to keep herself and any on the side of the Crown safe.

"Why don't you come over here and find out?" he said, a sneer deforming the normally handsome face, his calm, deferential demeanor to his superior officer long gone. In its place was a man that studied at the altar of Fergus of Sursha. It was disgusting to Fallon, and a shame.

Curious what he'd do, she took a small step toward him, satisfied when he took a slight one backward. That told her that he wasn't entirely secure with the situation and hadn't prepared for the contingency of his plan going awry.

About to play with her prey further, Fallon sensed the movement of somebody behind her. She focused on it, even as she never looked away from Gunther. The man made the mistake of releasing a battle cry before making his assault. For just a moment Fallon mentally rolled her eyes, thinking he was definitely not one of hers. One of the first things she drilled into her men was to attack in silence; it was part of what made them so successful at what they did.

With a snarl and lightning speed, Fallon whirled around and swung one blade, slicing the would-be attacker's throat. He stood there for a moment, a stunned look on his face with his dagger still held high in the air before he collapsed, blood shooting out of his destroyed jugular.

No time to marvel or weep, like a tornado Fallon was over by Gunther, the second blade slicing through the burlap sack and rope he still held, the bottom half of both items falling harmlessly to the ground. Using the knuckles of the hand wrapped around the first sword, she punched him in the throat. It wasn't enough force to crush his windpipe, but it was intended to knock him into submission.

Gunther fell to his knees, gasping for air as he gripped his throat, eyes bulging. Fallon turned from him and looked to see the fifth and final man on Gunther's squad staring at her with wide, terrified eyes. Two dead and two out of commission.

"Next?" she growled.

He dropped his sword and raised his hands in surrender, shaking his head vigorously. Fallon was finally able to relax, standing to her full height and walking over to her sword sheath belt. "Eoin, go check to see how Jude is and bring him back to camp," she ordered, nodding toward the trees and the direction of the man she'd kicked. "Shea and Taber, tie these two up," she said, indicating Gunther and the man who had surrendered.

As the men jumped to fulfill her orders, Fallon walked away from camp for a moment, toward the sea. She was shaken by what had happened, even as she'd expected it on some level. She'd hoped, perhaps, that maybe she'd been wrong, that her father had been wrong, that Cateline had been wrong. They hadn't been.

Now, here they were, the group of them just off the beach on foreign soil, sent there by Fergus. Yet again, he was trying to kill her. He hadn't tried that in a while, so she was out of practice on how to handle it or how to feel. Since the only thing she'd really ever cared about was her job and protecting the Surshan people, she'd been able to shake off such things much easier, as her life was all about sacrifice anyway.

Since meeting Cateline and falling in love with her, everything had changed. Everything. Now, she had something to live for, *someone*, and she would never take that for granted again. She turned when she heard someone walking up beside her, the man making noise on purpose, she could tell, so as to not lose his head, literally.

"Sir?" Eoin said, stepping up beside her. "The man in the woods is dead. Looks like he hit a tree and broke his neck."

Fallon nodded with a heavy sigh. The news didn't leave her with joy or make her feel like the big warrior. The entire situation was unnecessary, life lost for no reason other than a petty little man's threatened ego.

"Gather the bodies in camp," she instructed quietly. "We'll take them with us and dump them in the sea." As traitors, they would not be allowed burial in their homeland in any case. "I'm not leaving their carcasses behind for the Bretons to deal with."

Eoin bowed in acknowledgment. "And the other two?"

"I'll be there in a minute," Fallon said, meeting his gaze. "I'll interrogate Gunther. Make sure he's ready."

"Yes, sir." Eoin turned away but stopped, turning back to her. "You have blood on your face, sir." With that, he left her at the shore's edge.

She took a couple steps until the ocean washed into the toes of her boots. She squatted down and cupped her hands in the cold water to wash the blood off. Now, able to feel the stickiness of it on her cheek and jaw, it made her feel like an animal. She splashed the area with the water to rewet the substance before using her fingers to wipe it away. When she went to gather more water in her hands, she noticed that the medallion had come out from under her tunic during the fight, and it, too, had some blood on it.

She bent down low enough so the large serpent-surrounded stone was dipped in the water, her thumb rubbing over the carved surface of the skull. It was when she sat back up on her haunches that she began to hear it.

Looking over her shoulder, Fallon surveyed the land behind her. Her men seemed to hear it too, as she saw a couple of them begin to look around. It started out very soft, almost like a low buzz. She turned to fully face the land, eyes scanning the woods then the cliffs, no idea where it was coming from. It began to get louder, and as it did, she realized that it wasn't a buzz, per se, but more of a ghostly hum. It was eerie and deeply unsettling.

"What is that?" one of the men called out from camp.

Fallon shook her head, even as she didn't verbally answer. The hum grew louder still, and it sounded more human as it got louder. Like, the voices of many people, humming in unison. Something caught her eye to the left. Looking up, she saw light begin to appear atop the cliffs, many, many little lights. Then, they began to appear in the woods, their golden hue interrupted by tree trunks and branches, but the light managed to peek around, each one creating a glittering tapestry of dancing gold.

"What on Earth?" Fallon whispered.

Chapter Twenty-four

I think it sounds like a wonderful thing," Cateline said with a smile. "I will approve the festival and hope to get an invitation."

The old farmer blushed deeply, his hand nearly crushing the hat it held as his fingers began to fidget nervously. He knelt before the stairs to the dais where Cateline sat upon the throne chair in the great hall. It was the custom for those coming before the ruler of the principality.

The man nodded vigorously as he pushed up, groaning as his knees popped at the task. He stayed bowed as he backed away from the dais before he was escorted out and Cateline had a few moments before her next case.

She reached up and straightened the heavy princess crown she wore, as she was dealing with official business. It was a smaller version of the one she'd worn during her presentation to the people, but it was still uncomfortable.

"Next, Your Highness," Fergus's main adviser announced, standing not far from Cateline's chair. "Sean O'Clery. He claims his neighbor stole his chickens."

Cateline nodded, understanding. She readjusted in her ornate, oversized chair and waited as the doors were opened by guards and a figure appeared in the doorway. He looked like an average villager, no better and no worse than any other. He looked to be in his late twenties, skin tanned from working hard outdoors.

As he neared her, his eyebrows drew. "Who are you?" he asked.

As his fell, Cateline's shot up. "Who do you think?"

"I don't much care," he retorted, standing at the bottom of the five stairs leading up to where she sat. He had the audacity to raise a foot, resting it casually on the first step.

Her gaze fell to such a disrespectful action before they trailed back up his body to his face.

"I don't much care," he said again. "Go get Prince Fergus. I don't deal with women."

Cateline's conditioning and training her entire life nearly had her apologizing to him for the inconvenience of her inferior gender. But then, something kicked in. She thought about Fallon and all that she'd achieved, including the respect of men, all while wearing an invisible dress.

She sat up straighter, steel in her spine and fire in her belly. "And," she drawled. "By the looks of you, I'm guessing women don't deal with you, either."

Laughter erupted in the room, echoing off the stone walls of the cavernous space. The man looked around, embarrassment on his face as he looked at the advisers and servants present. He glared back up at Cateline but said nothing.

Tilting her head slightly, she studied him, bemused. Pushing up from the chair, she slowly made her way down the stairs toward him. "My husband is currently unavailable," she said. "Today, I'm taking care of business." She reached the stair that put her above him, sure to look down her nose at him. She brought up her hands and, with a light tug, removed the large, gaudy wedding ring she wore and held it out to him. "However," she said lightly. "If you think you can do it better."

He looked at the ring, then up at her with a mixed expression of disgust and shock.

"No?" she asked in mock surprise. Her own expression fell from mockery to disdain. "Didn't think so. Get on your knees and show some respect."

She didn't even have to turn back and look as she made her way back to the chair—she heard him kneel. A slow smile spread across her lips.

꙳꙳꙳꙳

After her judicial duties had been completed, Cateline was able to hand the crown off to the most trusted servant in the castle, his sole job handling such valuable items, cleaning them and keeping them safe and accounted for.

The morning had run into the afternoon as cases had been terribly backed up. Fergus was getting worse by the day and hadn't been in any shape to leave his bedchamber, let alone serve in his capacity as prince and ruler of their portion of the country. Worried about a revolt from frustration, his advisers had gone to Cateline out of desperation, as only she or the king had authority to hear and judge cases.

She was tired but hungry, as she'd missed lunch. She headed to the kitchen, intending to grab some fruit before heading upstairs. A few of the kitchen staff were there, beginning to prepare the upcoming dinner, but Millie wasn't among them. Will, however, was.

Ever since she'd seen him in the woods with Aaron, she'd gotten a better sense of who he really was, as well as a better understanding of why he acted the way he did. The morning Fallon had left, when Will had told her that he and Cateline weren't so very different, he hadn't been wrong.

It was untrue to call them friends, but they were no longer enemies. She smiled at him as he turned to see who had entered. "Good morrow, Will."

He nodded at her as he poured some wine into a cup. "Milady," he greeted her. "Would you like some?" he asked, holding up the jug.

"Please."

Without a word, he reached up and grabbed a cup from the shelf nearest him. He filled it and handed it to her. "He's gotten some sleep today," he said conversationally.

"That's good." Cateline grabbed an apple from the basket and filled a small bowl with berries. "I'm wondering if we should call in Carthac." She met his gaze. "What do you think?"

Will let out a long, heavy sigh before shaking his head. "He won't let me. I asked him."

"Not surprising," she muttered. She studied the man and saw how tired he looked. Exhausted, really. "Will," she said, turning to him. "You look dead on your feet. I'll take over for a bit. Why don't you get some sleep?"

He ran a hand through his hair, sighing heavily again. Shaking his head, he looked at her. "I shouldn't, milady. He's my responsi—"

"And, according to the law, he's my husband," she interrupted. "Is this going to him?" she asked, indicating the wine. At his nod, she took the cup from him, then grabbed his arm and turned him toward the door. "Go."

He sent a grateful smile over his shoulder and headed out. Left alone, she grabbed a tray and loaded her fruit and the two cups of wine, then made her way upstairs. Fergus's room smelled of vomit and diarrhea. It was revolting. From what she'd heard, Will and the other servants had tried to keep up with Fergus's stomach sickness, but it wasn't always possible, especially since he was often too weak to make it to the garderobe.

The figure in the bed was breathing slowly and evenly as she walked in. She set the tray down on a nearby table, not sure she'd be able to eat her fruit while there. She already felt a bit nauseous as it was from the smell and condition of the bed linens and his sleeping gown.

She hurried from the room and stopped the first servant she came to, insisting that person grab a few others to come to the room and change the prince into a fresh gown and do some cleaning.

"Yes, milady," the younger servant said.

"Thank you very much," Cateline said.

The young woman looked at her in surprise for a moment before, with a curtsy, she scurried off to do Cateline's bidding.

Going back into Fergus's bedchamber, she walked over to the fireplace to ensure it was burning strong. It was a bitterly cold day as storms were coming in off the ocean.

"Why do you thank them?" was muttered behind her in a low, gruff voice, followed by coughing.

Glancing over her shoulder, she saw that Fergus was awake and looking at her. "Why wouldn't I?"

Satisfied with the state of the fire, she walked over to the table where she'd left the tray and carried it closer to the bed.

"Because they're servants," he said, as though that explained it all.

"They're still human," she said quietly, taking the cup of wine that Will had poured for him. "Here. Would you like some? Will poured this for you."

Fergus looked from the proffered silver cup to Cateline. "Where is he?"

"I sent him to go get some sleep. He looked dead on his feet." When he didn't move to take the cup, she lowered it and rested it in her lap as she sat in the chair next to the bed. "Guessing he was here all night with you."

Fergus studied her for a long moment, a small smirk on his gaunt, pale face. "You're jealous of him," he finally said.

Eyebrow quirked as she sipped from her own wine, Cateline met his gaze. "Why would I be?"

"Because I don't love you," he said simply.

It was her turn to smirk. "I don't love you either."

He stared at her for a long moment, almost looking surprised, but then he looked away, a small chuckle leaving his lips. He said nothing more, and a handful of servants hurried into the room, separating into groups that began to scrub the place down while others moved to Fergus and the bed.

Cateline stood from the chair and moved to stand near the fire, getting out of the way. She watched the efficiency of the servants as they made quick work of their tasks. In less than fifteen minutes, they had Fergus changed and cleaned up and the room smelling as fresh and clean as circumstances would allow.

"Thank you all very much," she said as they quickly bowed and hurried from the room like a little tornado of clean. Left alone again, Cateline went back to her chair. "Are you hungry?" she asked, indicating the bowl of fruit she'd prepared for herself.

He shook his head and looked away as he got settled into a clean bed with clean bedclothes.

"Feel a little better?" she asked, popping a berry into her mouth. "Cleaned up."

He shrugged, his eyes still closed, though obviously awake. "Just waiting to throw up again."

"Can I get you anything, Fergus?" she asked. "Are you cold? Hot?"

He said nothing, but his face began to scrunch up as his stomach began to gurgle and make horrible sounds. Cateline nearly threw her bowl of fruit aside as she grabbed the bucket that had been left by one of the servants in case he got sick again.

Moving to the bed, she sat beside him, helping him to sit up as he began to retch. She wrapped her arm across his upper back to brace him as she set the bucket in his lap. It was astonishing to her how much weight he'd lost. She figured easily a hundred pounds had gone in the past weeks.

"It's okay," she whispered, running her fingers through his hair, which was damp from sweat. She didn't know what was wrong but could almost feel the life force leaving the man's body as he leaned against her.

He retched a few more times, but nothing came out. Fergus's head fell, a keening sound coming from him. His body shook as he began to cry. Cateline hugged him to her. She knew he was an awful, awful man, but nobody deserved such a horrible fate.

"I'm so miserable," he whispered through his tears.

"I'm so sorry, Fergus," she said, rubbing his back through the sweat-soaked material of the fresh sleep shirt they'd put on him.

His body stilled, almost as if suddenly frozen. "Sorry?" he asked, voice low and hard.

Cateline was confused by the sudden change in him. She pulled away a bit, her hand still resting on his back. She studied his profile as he stared straight ahead. She looked to see what he was looking at, but there was nothing more than the fireplace, so she returned her gaze to him. When he did look at her, it chilled Cateline's blood.

"You're sorry?" he asked again.

"Yes," she said, beginning to feel uncomfortable. "I hate seeing you so sick—"

"You did this to me!"

Stunned, Cateline flew off the bed. His face was beet read, the veins sticking up in his neck and forehead. His eyes were pure rage and hate. He swept his arm across his lap, sending the wooden bucket flying toward her. She just barely managed to move out of the way, even as the projectile brushed across the skirt of her dress and slammed into the wall, smashing into several pieces.

"You did this!" he raged again, crawling toward the edge of the bed. "Guards!"

"What are you doing?" she asked, backing away from him as he neared the edge of the bed. "Fergus—"

"Guards!" he bellowed again, sliding his legs out from under the many blankets on the bed.

Three castle guards ran into the room, swords drawn as they looked for the enemy. Two more ran in, out of breath. "What is it, milord?" one of them asked. "What's wrong?"

"Arrest her!" Fergus said, feet hitting the floor, though he nearly collapsed as he tried to stand. He braced himself on the bed. "Arrest that witch! She's killing me!"

The guards all turned to Cateline, whose heart stopped at the outrageous claim. She shook her head as the guards looked at each other, then to Cateline, walking toward her. "No," she said. "No, I've done nothing wrong."

"Milady," the guard said softly. "Give me your hands."

Panic was setting in as she looked into his face. Though his words were kind, his expression was firm. He had a job to do. She shook her head. "But I've done nothing wrong," she said again, tears pricking the backs of her eyes.

Another guard stepped up behind her and grabbed her wrists in a tight grip, bringing them together as the first guard brought out a pair of shackles from a pouch worn on his sword belt. He met her gaze briefly before he applied the heavy iron bracelets one at a time.

They were incredibly loose on her small wrists, and they both knew he hadn't put them on as tightly as he could have. The look he gave her after said, *Please don't fight me. I don't want to hurt you.*

She looked over at Fergus, who had fallen to the floor. Two of the guards had hurried over to him to help him up. He looked out of it, confused, which gave her the smallest bit of hope that he'd come to his senses and not let this happen. But, it had already been set in motion, and Cateline was led out of the room.

"Fergus!" she yelled. "Don't let them do this! You know I did nothing to you."

"Throw away the key!" Fergus yelled back, his words garbled and nearly unintelligible.

Cateline was quiet even as tears streamed down her cheeks. She was scared, she was humiliated, and she was confused. As their little parade made its way down the flights of stairs, servants stopped in their tracks and watched, most looking utterly shocked. Cateline couldn't bring herself to look at them.

Reaching the main floor of the castle, she expected to go down one more flight of stairs to the dungeon. Instead, she was taken toward the area of the small door they used to go to the garden. For a moment, hope sprung upon her. Maybe they were going to take her outside, out of the view of the servants who may be loyal to Fergus and let her go, maybe send her to Carthac?

Fresh tears, hot and bitter, fell when they walked past that hallway and toward the one that would lead to the tower. She saw Will step out from an arched doorway. She met his gaze, her eyes pleading with him to do something. He turned away, walking back into the room from which he'd come.

She couldn't stop the sobs from beginning as they led her up the stairs to that lonely single door. It was opened for her, the lead guard standing aside as he waited for her to enter on her own. At the threshold of the room, she turned and looked at him.

"Please," she whispered. "Don't do this."

With tears in his own eyes, the guard pushed the heavy wooden door closed, the latch clicking home, followed by the sound of the key in the lock.

Chapter Twenty-five

Voices. She heard voices, men. They were speaking in a language she didn't understand, though the more she listened, she could pick out words here and there as the language was close enough to French to grab context. They were identifying who was dead and who was alive.

With great effort, Fallon forced her eyelids to open. They felt heavy, her eyes tearing as they burned. She lay there and relaxed for a moment, able to hear the surf not far away. She tried to think of the last thing she remembered. The noise. The eerie humming noise. As suddenly as it had started, it had stopped. Following that, the lights they'd seen had begun to pummel the beach.

The sound of breaking glass had been all around them, men diving for cover so as not to get pelted. The little dancing fire inside turned into rancid-smelling smoke once the glass broke, making them cough and choke. Fallon had finally collapsed due the release of whatever was inside the one that landed near her feet.

Opening her eyes again, she looked around as best she could, able to feel the ebb and flow of the ocean tickle the top of her head. Tilting her head back, she gasped when she saw that their ship was on fire. She went to sit up when she felt a hand on her shoulder.

Turning her head back again, she saw a man

kneeling in front of her. His head was largely shaved with full facial hair. He was dressed much like Fallon and her warriors, just slight differences of accessibility to materials and plants for dyes.

Fallon met his gaze, blinking several times as her eyes continued to water. The man's eyes fell to Fallon's neckline before they widened. He looked into Fallon's eyes for a long moment before he stood, hurrying over to another warrior. The two spoke, the man who had been at Fallon's side pointing over at her.

Pushing herself to a sitting position, Fallon nearly fell back down. She was so dizzy, her head pounding. Some of her men were throwing up and gasping for air, even though the smoke had cleared out.

Wanting to draw one of her blades but too weak to even try, Fallon watched as the man walked back over to her, the second man in tow. The first man pointed down at her. "Ankou," he said.

The second man nodded, then muttered, "We must take him to Enori." The other man nodded in agreement as they looked back to Fallon, who lost her battle to fight the darkness creeping in once more.

❧ ❧ ❧ ❧

When Fallon came to again, she was cold. She was lying on a hard surface, which sent a chill throughout her entire body. She began to shiver.

"My apologies," a soft female voice said in accented Gaelic.

Fallon looked to her right to see a figure several feet from her. She was sitting on a stool carved from stone with parchment and quill placed on a natural tabletop etched into the stone wall from years of erosion. Candles were lit sporadically around the small cave.

The slight figure wore a dark blue cloak with gold stitching, or so it looked in the candlelight. Fallon studied it for a moment, trying to remember where she'd seen a cloak like that before. Her brain was foggy still.

The woman stood from the stool and turned toward Fallon, her face nothing but darkness in the deep shadows of the hood. She walked over to a niche in the wall where a cot was tucked away and gathered a wool blanket.

"Can you sit up?" she asked.

Fallon focused on her body, making sure all her parts were in attendance. Finally, she managed to gather the muscles necessary to sit up. When she did, she realized she had been lying on a flat slab of rock. She now understood why she was so cold. She was definitely grateful as the strange woman placed the blanket around her shoulders, Fallon pulling it close around herself.

"Who are you?" she asked. "Why am I here?"

The woman brought her hands up and brushed her hood back, revealing a beautiful face that looked to be perhaps around her age or a bit older. Her blond hair was cut very short, which took Fallon by surprise. She'd never seen a woman with short hair before.

"I am Enori," she said simply. "Head Priestess of the Order of Ankou."

There was that word again, Fallon thought. "What is Ankou? The men out there called me that."

The woman shook her head. "No." She reached inside the blanket, Fallon jerking away from her at the invasion of her touch. Enori either didn't notice or didn't care as she took the medallion between her fingers and brought it into view, the chain still around Fallon's neck. "This is what they were talking about," she explained, intense blue eyes looking into the warrior's. "Where did you get this?"

"My father gave it to me," Fallon said, feeling a bit defensive for reasons she didn't understand.

"And, who is that?" the priestess asked.

"The King of Sursha."

"When?" she demanded, suspicion in her eyes.

"Just before I left for Brittany," Fallon answered, beginning to get annoyed.

"Your mother," Enori said, her voice growing soft and entire demeanor changing from suspicious and slightly on edge to awestruck. "Was Roishin," she said, a statement, not a question.

"Aye," Fallon said with a slow nod. Who was this woman? Her mother was rarely ever mentioned in her own country, let alone in a foreign one. She'd been gone a long time. "Who are you?"

The woman smiled, releasing the medallion, allowing it to lightly fall back to rest against Fallon's chest. "I am Enori," she said again, as though that explained everything. "And you," she added. "Are she." The woman in the cloak turned and walked away from her and toward a bottle that was on the rock table.

Fallon looked at her, stunned that this woman, this *stranger* knew. "She, who?"

"She," Enori said, glancing over her shoulder, hand on the bottle. "Who would be king." She reached up to a shelf made of stone and took down a cup made of gold. Pouring some of the contents of the bottle into the cup, she set the bottle down and turned to face Fallon again. "Your mother's birthright was stolen from her," she explained. "That medallion belonged to her."

Fallon shook her head. "I'm so confused."

"Your mother was born here," Enori said. "Her line of the Order of Ankou."

"What is Ankou?" Fallon asked, slowly lowering herself down off the cold slab to stand, though she needed to lean against the hard surface to steady herself.

"Not a what," Enori said, walking over to her and handing her the cup before wrapping her hands around Fallon's arm to help her to the stool she had abandoned earlier. Once Fallon was seated, the priestess sat at a second stool at the other end of the table. "A who. Ankou is our God of the Underworld, God of Death."

Fallon stared at her, setting the cup down on the table. "What?" She shook her head. "No. My mother was not a dark woman."

Dark blond eyebrows raised. "Dark?" She cocked her head somewhat to the side. "Death is not dark, Fallon."

"How do you know my name?"

"I know everything about you. Who you are, what you are to be. Why Carthac asked us to help him."

It hit her. "It was you I saw in the woods that day, wasn't it?"

"Not me," Enori said with a smile. "But someone I sent, yes. Upon your father's request to help Ankou in his quest to make things right."

"I don't understand," Fallon said. "Make things

right, how?"

"Roishin was to take the throne here," Enori explained patiently. "But she was taken from this country as a girl and raised in Ireland as nothing more than the daughter of a nobleman, eventually sent off to marry Carthac."

"I had no idea she was born here," Fallon said softly.

"Only your father knows, now that she's gone. And," she added. "Your father knows that you were chosen to wear the crown. So often the gods work their magic in the background to make things happen. Such as," she said with a broad smile. "Your father being wise enough to recognize your mother's spirit within Cateline."

Fallon slowly shook her head. "How do you know all this?"

The woman gave her a cryptic smile. "Ankou."

"Of course," she muttered. "So, now what?"

"Now," Enori said. "We need to get you home. You and those who survived are free to leave, except the one called Gunther." She pushed up from the stool. "He brought corruption and murder to our shores." She made her way over to where Fallon sat, the warrior still weak. "The dead, we'll give to Ankou to sort."

"My men and I can't get home," Fallon said, using the table to help stabilize her as she, too, stood, looking down at the shorter woman. "You burned our ship."

Enori smiled, reaching down and grabbing the golden cup. She held it out to Fallon. "Don't worry," she said. "We'll get you home. Now, drink. It'll ease the effects."

Fallon took the cup and looked down into its contents. It was brown liquid, her nose wrinkling a bit at the smell. But, knowing the potency of whatever was in those bottles thrown, she didn't question.

❧❧❧❧

Fallon had never been so glad to see the shores of Sursha in all her life. As the gate fell to allow the Breton ship to pull into the harbor, all of the surviving men with her, including the crew who jumped ship and swam to shore when the barrage of those glass bottles had started, she smiled. She looked forward to seeing Cateline, *needed* to see her.

The Surshan crew gathered on deck to disembark as the ship made a smooth glide in, the Bretons yelling directions to each other as the ship crew did what needed to happen for a successful closure to the voyage.

The gangplank launched, Fallon bowed her gratitude to the Bretons, then hurried down to the docks and Surshan land. After some finagling, the group was able to get a ride to the castle. The men that were based at the main barracks would just stay the night at Caislean Thiar. They'd set out in the morning on their own horses.

Stepping into the castle, she greeted a few people but immediately noticed that something wasn't right. Servants weren't around as they usually were, many of the halls and stairs empty. Neither fireplace in the great hall had been lit. There was an eerie silence and stillness to the place that made her uneasy.

Quickening her steps, she bypassed her room and hurried to Cateline's. The door was open, which made her heart stop. It was never open. She cautiously walked inside to see everything where it should be, though the fireplace was cold, as was the room itself. Clearly there hadn't been a fire burning for some hours, at least.

Heart racing, she hurried to the kids' room only to see that it too, was empty, fireplace cold. But even worse, there were no clothes, no toys or books that usually littered the small room. Nothing belonging to the children remained.

Panic setting in, Fallon slammed out of the room and into the main hall at a dead run to Fergus's bedchamber. She didn't bother to knock, simply kicked in the door, drawing one of her blades as she entered. She marched to the where Fergus lay, Will at his bedside, though the footman had popped up from the chair next to the bed, eyes wide at Fallon's dramatic entrance.

"Where is she?" she growled, grabbing her brother by the sweat-soaked front of his sleeping gown and yanking his upper body up off the bed. Fallon was stunned at how, seemingly overnight, he'd aged fifty years. His hair was gray, cheeks gaunt, and eyes dead. "Tell me or I swear by Ankou, I'll kill you myself."

Fergus, whose head bobbed a bit, focused on her. A small smile broke out on chapped lips along with a wheezy laugh. "I'm dying, you fool," he said, voice whispery. "Do it."

"Where is she, Fergus?" Fallon asked, voice low and dangerous. Her entire body felt like it was filled with ice as fear gripped every fiber of her being. "What did you do?"

"Dead," he said, followed by a creepy little giggle.

Rage like she'd never felt rushed through her. She grabbed him by his hair and yanked his head back, exposing his throat. She raised her sword.

"No!"

With what tiny bit of self-control she had, Fallon looked to see Will standing next to her, his hand on her upper chest. She looked at him, her face screwing up into a mask of rage. "Do not touch me."

Will pulled his hand back as though he'd been burned. "No," he said again, voice softer. He reached into a pocket in his trousers and brought up a small, dark blue pouch. It was the same color of dark blue as Enori's cloak. A gold cord cinched it together. "Allow me," he said, gently tugging open the pouch. He met Fallon's gaze. "The final dose. I was going to do it tonight so he'd be gone by morning, but now is just as good."

Fallon stared at him, shocked.

"Hold his mouth open, if you wouldn't mind?" Will continued, voice calm and matter-of-fact.

Fallon said nothing, simply dropped her sword to the bed and used that hand to take a tight grip of her brother's face, squeezing until his lips were forced open. Fergus was too weak to fight them, but the hatred in his eyes lived on as he stared up at Fallon.

Will reached his forefinger and thumb into the pouch and brought out a fine, white powder. He looked at Fergus with absolute disgust before he forced the powder into his mouth. "It's supposed to be diluted with liquid. Supposed to be less painful," he explained casually. "However," he added, pinching the last that was in the pouch into Fergus's mouth. "I don't care anymore."

Fallon released her brother, who fell back to the

bed helplessly. She grabbed her sword and re-sheathed it, never taking her eyes off him. It didn't take long, as the prince's body began to jerk, his face becoming the picture of pain.

She moved off the bed as he began to contort, grunts and gasps escaping his lips as he began to foam at the mouth. His hands raised, as if of their own accord, fingers slowly curling into claws as he began to gag. His eyes were open wide, staring up at the ceiling with fear. His body jerked several times, involuntary movements as all noises stopped from him other than a long, guttural gurgle as more foam spewed from his lips.

Fallon stood next to the bed and watched. As she watched the life drain out of him, she thought back to a lifetime of abuse at his hands. The loss of her own identity largely due to him, wanting to please him, prove herself to him as worthy. The loss of her beloved brother Ailfred, and Millie's loss of Burke. What he'd tried to do to Fallon in the last days, what amounted to an assassination attempt. And, she thought, her rage threatening to return, whatever he'd done to Cateline.

Finally, a long, breathy sigh, the last breath to leave his body as Fergus stilled, his gaze fixed. "It's over," Will said softly. "I'm free."

Fallon looked at him, the servant meeting his gaze. "Why did you do this?"

"Your father came to me," Will explained, looking back down at the dead man on the bed. "Said he'd release me from three generations of *oidhreacht* if I did this." A small smirk curled his lips. "I didn't blink an eye. Agreed immediately. So," he continued, meeting Fallon's gaze again. "The man with the blue cloak came, never knew his name. He gave this to me." He held up the empty pouch. "Told me how to use it, how much, what to expect, then he disappeared. Never saw him again."

Fallon didn't know what to say, so said nothing for a long moment. Finally, she said, "Thank you."

Will nodded. "Come on, Fallon," he said. "I'll take you to her."

Chapter Twenty-six

S he could see the fear in his eyes as she stormed up to him as he stood guard at the bottom of the stairs. She swung, sending him sprawling with one punch. Feet wide in aggression, she reached her hand down to him. "Keys. Now."

A small line of blood dribbling from the corner of his mouth, the soldier nodded and rolled over onto his right hip as he reached behind his left for his key ring.

Fallon snatched it from him, the long, iron keys heavy in her hand. "How could you do that to her?" she murmured, before turning and bolting up the stairs to the locked door at the top.

Not sure which key to try, she began with one on the ring and kept going until one finally slipped into the lock. It turned with a loud *click*, then she was able to open the door. Inside the small tower room, which was bitterly cold, lay a figure on the so-called bed, curled up. A threadbare blanket was wrapped around the figure, just the barest bit of auburn curls visible.

"Oh no," Fallon whispered, her words coming out in puffs of steam it was so cold in the room. She hurried over to the figure, falling to her knees next to the bed. "Cateline?" she whispered. "Cateline, please wake up."

"Oh God," Will murmured from the open door.

Fallon looked over at him, tears beginning to well in her eyes. "Go to her bedchamber," she said, voice shaky with rising emotion. "Get a fire started."

He nodded, then hurried from the room.

"Love," she said, reaching a hand into the blanket and feeling around for her hand. When she found it, the skin was cold to the touch. A tear rolled down her cheek as she searched with fingertips to find her wrist. When she found it, Fallon nearly held her breath as she tried to find a heartbeat. "Please," she whispered, feeling desperate. A whimper escaped her lips when she felt a pulse, as weak as it was. "Let's get you out of here, my love."

Fallon gently gathered the smaller woman toward her chest, using powerful thighs to push to her feet with the extra weight in her arms. She looked down into Cateline's face, which was pale, her eyes closed. Her lips were blue.

"I'm so sorry I wasn't here," she murmured, leaning down and leaving a soft kiss to a chilled forehead.

She'd never forgive herself if Cateline didn't make it. Pushing that thought out of her head and steeling her spine that the princess *would* make it, she carefully eased through the open doorway so as not to hit any part of Cateline against it or the wall, then made her way down the stairs as quickly as she could.

It seemed to take a lifetime, but finally she reached the bedchamber. Will was there and the bedding had been pulled down for Cateline. He was working on loading logs into the large fireplace. Deciding she couldn't wait for him to finish, Fallon set her precious cargo on the bed and quickly went about undressing her down to her chemise.

She was going to leave her in that bottom layer,

but opted to remove that as well. She knew from her years in the field that, when a person was in a state of hypothermia, often skin-on-skin was the best thing for the person.

She removed the thin gown, then gathered Cateline in her arms again and placed her on the bed so that she could lay her head down on the pillow and cover her up. That done, Fallon began with her own clothing, whipping her tunic off over her head then getting started on her trousers. By time she'd removed all the leather bits and stood completely naked beside the bed, she felt eyes on her.

Looking over at the fireplace, she saw Will staring at her, wide-eyed and mouth hanging open. She lifted an eyebrow. "Fire?"

Shaking himself out of his shock, Will turned back to his task.

Fallon quickly climbed into the bed as gingerly as she could, pulling Cateline on top of her, the smaller woman's head resting against Fallon's upper chest. She made sure Cateline could breathe, then pulled the covers up over Cateline's back, tucking them in. It was shocking just how cold Cateline's skin was against the warmth of Fallon's.

Wrapping her arms around the smaller woman, Fallon rested her check against the top of an auburn crown. She could feel Cateline's breasts pressed against her, just below her own. As she smoothed her hands over the softness of Cateline's naked back, Fallon couldn't help but think of how cruel it was that when they were finally able to be naked together, it was because Fallon was trying to save her life.

"Will?" she asked quietly when the servant was heading for the door, the fire burning and popping.

She could already feel the warmth heading their way. He stopped and looked at her. "Where are Livia and the kids?" she asked, terrified for the answer.

"The day he did this," Will said, nodding toward the still figure lying upon Fallon's body. "I grabbed them and took them to Millie. Told her to get them out of here."

Fallon held his gaze for a long moment, wanting him to know her gratitude. Finally, she gave him a small smile. He nodded, seeming to understand, then turned and left the bedchamber, closing the door softly behind him.

She returned her focus completely to the woman in her arms, holding her as tightly as she could, continuing to stroke her back, trying to rub warmth and life back into her. "Come back to me, Cateline," she whispered. "Please, come back to me." She used Cateline's own words against her, leaving a kiss on her head. "Please, please."

Fallon's eyes squeezed shut in relief when she heard a soft whimper from the woman atop her. She hugged her closer, relishing the feel of soft skin that was slowly beginning to warm and become more pliant. She'd hold her as long as it took. Cateline's shallow breathing began to grow deeper, a bit more even

"Keep coming," Fallon whispered. "Breathe, baby."

Cateline began to shiver, which was a good sign. Her body was coming back, trying to jump start her own body heat again.

Fallon wanted to cry, she was so relieved. She rubbed Cateline's back, shoulders, her arms, reached down to massage her behind, anything she could reach to help with the blood flow. She left another kiss to Cateline's head when she heard her teeth begin to chatter.

"You'll warm up, love," she whispered. "It's okay."

"S-s-s-o-o c-c-old."

"I know. I've got you."

It took several minutes, but finally Cateline's body began to calm, the shivering slowing and finally stopping. Her breathing was even and more normal. Finally, Cateline's body moved, controlled movement instead of involuntarily shivering. She slowly lifted her upper body, resting on her forearms. Most of her long, tangled hair fell over one shoulder as she looked down at Fallon.

The warrior looked up at her, noting how glassy the blue-gray eyes were. "Good morrow, milady," she whispered, a smile curling her lips.

Cateline didn't say anything for a moment, as she still seemed a bit confused. "Fallon," she said at length, as though her brain was finally catching up with everything. "You're alive."

"I am," Fallon said, nodding. She brought her hand up and cupped the gloriously warm cheek of the beautiful woman who looked down at her. "I made it. And, so did you."

As if it all hit her at once, Cateline began to cry, really cry. Fallon held her as Cateline buried her face in Fallon's neck. The warrior stroked her back, her hair, murmured words of comfort to her.

The tears eventually slowed down, Cateline's breath warm against Fallon's neck as she sniffled, but calm. Her hand had come up and rested against the opposite side of Fallon's neck, her thumb on her jaw.

"I'm sorry," she murmured, her voice sounding

sleepy.

"Don't you dare apologize," Fallon said, hugging Cateline to her. "It's been a very long, hard few days."

Cateline nodded. "I was so scared," she mumbled, almost unintelligibly.

Fallon smiled. "Let's sleep."

Cateline nodded again, murmuring something before her breathing became deep and even.

❧❧❧❧

Fallon's eyes opened and she found herself looking at curly, auburn hair. She was spooned up behind her, the back of Cateline's body pressed as closely to Fallon's front as was possible. Clearly, in her sleep she was still trying to protect her princess. She pulled her even closer, wanting to melt into her.

The warrior had never in her life, except perhaps in missing memories as a baby, been naked in front of another person, and certainly not *with* another person. Even on the farthest battlefields, she'd found a way to keep her distance from her men.

The previous night had been a necessity, born of life or death. And now, the morning after, it felt like the most natural thing in the world to be with Cateline in this fashion. They'd both fallen asleep with Cateline lying atop her, but at some point in the night they'd changed positions.

She'd never slept as well as she had with Cateline in her arms. The sense of calm and peace that filled her took her away from her usual nightmares of battles won and lost, lives saved and taken. Instead, it had been a deep, soul-recharging sleep. She'd have to be careful or she'd get addicted and wouldn't be able to sleep without her.

As though she'd heard Fallon's thoughts, Cateline covered the forearm that was draped over her stomach with her hand. Fallon smiled. "It wasn't a dream?" Cateline murmured sleepily.

That precious sound made Fallon's smile grow. "No," she responded. "No dream."

Cateline's hand roamed down Fallon's forearm until she reached her hand, lacing their fingers. "Why am I naked?" she whispered.

"Because when I found you yesterday, you were suffering from hypothermia," Fallon explained. "Being skin-to-skin was the quickest way for me to warm you."

"Likely story," Cateline murmured, teasing in her voice. "I truly thought I was dreaming again when I woke up." She was quiet for a moment before continuing. "In that horrible little room, I'd try to sleep to pass the time, but it was so cold."

Fallon's eyes squeezed tightly shut for a moment as her emotions threatened to rise. She took several deep breaths before saying, "Someday I pray you can forgive me for not being there to protect you, Cateline."

"There's nothing to forgive, Fallon," Cateline said, releasing Fallon's hand and trailing her fingertips over Fallon's forearm, unknowingly sending delicious little thrills throughout the warrior.

"What happened?" Fallon asked softly, trying to take her mind off the sensations Cateline was causing.

"I sent Will off to go take a nap. He looked awful, so tired. I think he'd been with Fergus pretty much night and day. So, he agreed. I went in and tried to take care of Fergus, got him cleaned up." She let out a sigh and shrugged the shoulder that wasn't pressed to the mattress. "Just tried to be there for him. Like a flame blown out, he switched. Blamed me for making him sick and called the guard on me."

"I'm so sorry," Fallon whispered, leaving a kiss on Cateline's shoulder. "He can never hurt you again."

Cateline pulled away from her enough to turn on her back, her expression that of surprise. "Is he dead?"

Fallon nodded. "Yes." She brushed her fingers along Cateline's cheek. She used that hand to cup that cheek before leaning over and, after a slight hesitation, placed her lips lightly against Cateline's. She was relieved when Cateline buried her fingers in Fallon's hair and drew her closer, their kiss deepening.

As much as Fallon wanted to stay, she knew she had things she had to do, such as deal with Fergus's body and her father. Plans had to be made, as well as announcements. One more lingering kiss on soft lips, and she backed away.

"I have to go," she said softly, brushing some of Cateline's hair back from her beautiful face. "I'll send up breakfast and a bath for you, okay?" she offered, knowing the princess had had neither during her captivity.

Cateline nodded, cupping Fallon's cheek again. "Will I see you again today?"

Fallon smiled, leaning into the touch. "Of course." One final kiss, and she climbed out of bed.

❧ ❧ ❧ ❧

Fallon was quiet as she stood there, waiting to see what he would say. She'd been surprised, and relieved, when her father had shown up late in the morning. Knowing when the final dose was to be given to Fergus, he'd left the previous night with a small entourage to be there for the fallout. When he'd spotted Fallon, alive and well, the warrior had received a hug from her father like she'd never gotten before.

In that moment, she wasn't a pawn, wasn't a prop, wasn't even an heir. She'd been a daughter. Now, they stood in Fergus's bedroom, looking at his body, which lay where it had fallen. Will had returned to the room and doused the fire and removed the tapestries from the windows to allow the bedchamber to fall to freezing temperatures. Just like Cateline's tower room, Fallon mused. It had preserved the body, so they had time to plan.

"Everybody knew he was sick," Fallon said. "It was the quiet whispers of the castle."

Carthac nodded, stroking his beard. "Well, I think we should just stick with that." He met Fallon's gaze. "He was sick, died from it. Give him the proper burial per his status."

"Doesn't it make you angry to think that he'll be buried with Ailfred and Mamai?" Fallon asked dryly.

Carthac sighed and nodded. "Yes, but we don't have a choice, Fallon. You know that. And," he added. "You need to speak with Cateline."

"About what?"

"The announcement will have to be made soon that the two of you are now officially betrothed by the bylaws of Sursha."

Fallon nodded, hiding her smile as an entire company of butterflies was just set free in her belly. "I can do that."

"The two of you will need to get with your

advisers and begin to set up for the wedding," Carthac said. "You'll need to start backing away from military service as well."

Fallon's eyebrows fell. "Why?"

The king looked at her with a little smirk upon his lips. "Now, we can't very well have the future king killed in battle, can we?"

Fallon met his gaze, those butterflies going crazy again. It nearly took her breath away at the realization of just how much her life had changed the moment Fergus had taken his last breath. "Yes, sir," she said softly.

❧❧❧❧

The carriage pulled up in front of the small house that Fallon knew so well. The guard who was driving stayed put while the warrior dismounted her horse and, with long, sure strides, made her way to the door. She hadn't even reached it when the door flew open and Garratt and Laigen flew out at her.

Falling to one knee, she caught Laigen, who wrapped her arms around her neck so tightly Fallon could barely breathe. Garratt was just as excited, Fallon's childhood sword belted at his waist.

"You two ready to go home?" she asked, looking up into tearful faces. She looked past Garratt to see Livia making her way slowly toward them. She looked unsure. Leaving a kiss to Laigen's forehead, Fallon stood up and walked around the children to the young woman. "She's missed you," she said softly, holding out her arms. Livia walked into the hug, leaning into Fallon, who wrapped her arms around her.

"I thought we'd been left again," she whispered

into the hug.

Fallon rested her cheek atop the dark head. "No, Livia. We'll explain what happened later. Just know that Fergus was an evil man who can never hurt us again."

Livia nodded. "All right." She pulled away, looking down at the ground for a moment before she looked up at Fallon. "Are we going home?" she asked softly. "For real?"

Fallon nodded. "Forever."

Chapter Twenty-seven

Cateline cradled a sleeping Laigen against her chest as she sat near the fire. Garratt, the big, bad warrior-in-the-making was curled up in the twin chair to the one Cateline and Laigen occupied. He was fast asleep, cradling his sword almost like Laigen did her rag doll.

"Checkmate," Fallon said.

A little growl of frustration left Livia's lips. "How on Earth am I ever supposed to beat you?"

Cateline glanced over at the two, amused. "I still can't either, Livia," she said softly, not wanting to wake the children.

Fallon grinned at her before looking back to Livia and the board. "Look how well you did," she said, indicating her two pieces that had been taken during the game.

"Two whole pieces," Livia groused.

"As compared to none every other game we've played," Fallon pointed out. "Don't focus on what you lost," she said wisely. "Focus on what you gained."

Livia looked down at the board, then at Fallon and nodded. "All right. I'll try."

"Excellent game, Livia," Fallon said. "I think we should all get some sleep." She glanced over at Cateline and Laigen, Cateline meeting her gaze. "Looks like those two already got a head start."

Cateline left a kiss on the top of a blond head as

she nodded. Holding the girl tight, Cateline got to her feet so she could carry her to bed in the bedroom she shared with her brother. Livia had decided she needed to go back to her own room down in the servants' quarters. In her words, "Time to be a grown-up."

Fallon had surprised her earlier that day with the arrival of the children, and Cateline had literally been in tears. Now that Fergus and the fear of his actions were gone, she wanted to make Laigen and Garratt her own. She already loved them as if they were. And, she thought as she watched Fallon gather Garratt, that little boy adored Fallon. He shadowed her every move, wanted to be just like her. It was endearing.

"*Merci*," Cateline whispered as Livia opened the door to the kids' room for them to pass.

Cateline gently lay her precious bundle into her bed, a fire already built in the fireplace an hour before to warm up the space. Laigen whined a little bit as she was tucked in but never woke up.

"Good night, little one," Cateline whispered, leaving a kiss to her forehead.

"*Mamai*," the girl murmured.

Cateline looked up at Fallon, who was looking at her with wide eyes.

"I think that was for you," Fallon whispered. "Why wouldn't she think of you as her mother?"

Blinking back tears, Cateline moved out of the way so Fallon could heft her heavier bundle to the top bed. Garratt was awake enough to help, crawling onto his bed and immediately falling back to sleep.

Cateline reached up and tucked in the boy and kissed him as well, with the help of standing on the bottom step to the ladder. Children safe and secured, Fallon and Cateline left the room, Livia closing the door softly behind them.

Back in Cateline's bedchamber, Fallon looked at Livia. "Want me to walk you to her room?"

Livia chewed on her bottom lip for a moment before looking up at her, nodding. "Please?"

Fallon smiled at her before looking at Cateline. "I'll be right back to say good night."

Cateline nodded. She gave Livia a tight squeeze. "I really missed you," she said into the hug. She cupped Livia's cheek affectionately. "Thank you so much for taking care of Garratt and Laigen these last few days." She sighed. "Been such a nightmare. You're an amazing older sister to them, Livia."

It was almost as though the sunshine had come through the clouds, the young woman's smile was so bright. "Really?"

"You're part of our family now," Fallon said, moving to stand just behind Cateline.

Livia looked down as though trying to gather her emotions. Her hands fidgeted together before finally she nodded, looking up at both of them. "I like that," she said softly. "All I ever wanted." She smiled shyly.

Cateline hugged her again, a symbol to the young orphan that her days of being alone were over. She left a kiss on her cheek before Livia, her entire countenance bright and happy, departed with Fallon.

Left alone, Cateline took in a deep breath, feeling so much heaviness leaving her. Since marrying Fergus, it had been the most difficult time of her life, while also being the most amazing time of her life. The rejection of her husband had been so painful, yet there had been a strange relief that she hadn't had to be with him, please him.

She went to her boudoir and stripped out of her

clothing to change into her sleeping gown. She had no idea what was to come now that Fergus was dead. She was of confused mind and heart. She was glad he was gone, no longer an anchor around her neck. But what now? She knew Fallon loved her and knew Carthac liked her, but again, what now?

She walked out into the main chamber, ready for bed. She was combing out the tangles from the updo her hair had been in that day. She hummed softly to herself as she stood in front of the fire, looking into the flames. So beautiful. She was grateful for the warmth. She'd never known cold like she had in that tower room, and now she was deeply afraid of being cold like that again.

Her days in that room weren't days she wanted to think about. She'd screamed and pleaded with the guards until her voice had become raw. Then, all she could do was curl up and cry, pray that some way, somehow, Fergus would change his mind or one of the guards would dare defy him, though she knew it would have been at their own peril. No doubt, in the state of mind he'd been in that day, he would have had them executed.

She hugged herself as she thought about it, easily able to envision it. Her morose thoughts were interrupted by a soft knock on her door. She called out for the person to enter, and a moment later, Fallon stepped inside, closing the door behind her.

"Is she okay?" Cateline asked.

Fallon nodded, walking over to her. "I think she'll be okay. It's a big step for her to try being in her own room again after everything." They stood there in somewhat awkward silence for a moment, which was unusual for them, until Fallon gave her a shy smile.

"Well, I said I'd come back to say good night, So..." She shrugged bashfully. "Good night."

Cateline smiled, finding the woman standing before her adorable. She reached out and tugged playfully on Fallon's tunic. "Actually, um, well, I was wondering if maybe..." Feeling quite bashful herself, she looked up into Fallon's face. "Would you stay?" She felt silly asking, but the thought of not having Fallon there, her arms around her, it left her feeling cold and sad.

Fallon studied her for a long moment, then smiled. "All right. Let me go to my room and change into sleep clothes."

Cateline nodded, relieved. "Of course."

Fallon took the private corridor between their rooms, once again leaving Cateline alone. She made sure the fire was burning well and blew out all the other candles that had been lit for their earlier evening activities. That done, she went to the bed, pulling down the heavy blankets. Climbing under and getting settled, she waited.

She felt nervous, almost like a bride on her wedding night all over again. It was silly, as her intention wasn't for them to make love. She didn't know what Fallon wanted, and she certainly didn't want to make any assumptions. She just knew she wanted her close. She'd come so close to losing her once, and somehow, some way, she'd make sure that never happened again.

She heard the door open, and then the tapestry was pushed aside for her to enter the bedchamber. Fallon was dressed in a basic sleep shirt, her hair combed to a shine. Cateline turned to her side, watching as the other woman walked over to the bed.

She'd never seen her in anything other than usual warrior garb of one sort or other. That is, other than her brief views of her glorious naked body.

Somehow, seeing her in that long, white gown took away the intimidation factor from the fierce warrior and brought her back down to Earth, as any other person. The thought made Cateline smile, even as she admired just how beautiful Fallon really was. She was almost painfully beautiful, in a way.

"What?" Fallon asked as she climbed beneath the covers.

Cateline shook her head. "Just admiring you, that's all."

Fallon raised an eyebrow. "Oh?" She scooted over toward Cateline, leaving six inches or so between them. She mirrored the younger woman's position. "Then, I guess we have something in common."

Cateline grinned. "I like the sound of that." Her smile fell from her lips as she said in all seriousness, "You're okay with staying here, right? I don't want you to feel like you have to, Fallon. Out of obligation."

Fallon shook her head as she rested it on an upturned palm, her elbow planted in her pillow. "No obligation," she said. "I want to be here."

"Can I ask you something?" At Fallon's nod, she said, "What happened in Brittany? I was so scared you weren't coming back. My dream..." A shiver passed through her. "It was so real."

"You weren't that far off in your dream," Fallon said. "Honestly, if you hadn't told me about it, I might have missed what was about to happen."

Cateline blinked a few times, unsure what to say. "What?"

"The bag, the rope..." Fallon gave her a sad-looking smile. "It was all there."

Cateline didn't know what to say. An internal battle waged within. Shock at the prophetic nature her dream seemed to have, but also getting a better sense of what Fallon was put through. "I'm so sorry."

Fallon shook her head. "Don't be. You saved my life." She lightly cupped Cateline's face before her hand dropped back to the bed in the space between them. "From what I understand thus far, Fergus sent Gunther to do his dirty work, wanted me gone. Only one of Gunther's men returned with us. I need to interrogate him tomorrow to find out what the full plan was. I didn't have time today."

"Why would Fergus do that to you?" Cateline asked, covering Fallon's hand with her own. Fallon instantly wrapped her fingers around Cateline's.

"I think he felt threatened by me somehow," Fallon explained. She looked off, past the top of Cateline's head, as though in memory. "I've been thinking about him a lot lately. My relationship with him." Her gaze fell back to Cateline's. "I think I mistook his abuse as him trusting me to be able to handle anything, any situation thrown at me." She smirked. "Now I realize, *he* was the one often throwing them at me."

"Why do you think he put you in charge of me?" Cateline asked, something she'd always wondered.

"Honestly?" Fallon asked. At the princess's nod, she continued. "Two reasons. I think he knew that I'd do anything I could to keep you safe so he could do what our father expected in order for him to take the throne." She smirked. "A throne he didn't want, mind you. But, also, I think he wanted to torment me."

"Torment you?" Cateline asked. "How?"

Fallon looked downright shy as she responded. She cleared her throat and said, "Because he knew I have a weakness for beautiful women. And, um, well." She gave Cateline a lopsided grin. "They don't get any more beautiful than you."

Cateline smiled, touched, as she knew that Fallon meant those words. She leaned forward, placing a lingering kiss on soft lips. "Thank you for that," she whispered.

Fallon nodded as Cateline moved back to her original spot. "It's true. I think he knew it would be hard, knowing I'd be attracted to you but couldn't have you."

Cateline studied her for a long moment, saddened by what Fallon must have gone through in the entire, sordid affair. "Why wouldn't you able to have me?"

"Well," Fallon drawled. "For starters, you were married to my brother. But, also, though you may not have known this, I was a woman. Case closed, as far as I understood." She cleared her throat again. "Which brings me to something I need to talk to you about."

"All right," Cateline said slowly, a little nervous.

"Sursha has an ancient bylaw that states that when the male member of the royal family dies for any reason, his widow must marry an unmarried male member of the royal family, beginning with brothers but extending out beyond if a brother isn't available."

Cateline studied her for a long moment, brain turning. "So, Fergus is dead." Fallon nodded. "The country believes you are a man, Fergus's younger brother." Again, Fallon nodded. "And you're not married." Fallon shook her head. "So, by the ancient bylaws, you have to marry me, then?" Cateline pushed

Fallon to lie on her back and moved atop her. She whipped her hair to one side and looked down at the woman looking up at her, uncertainty in those unique and beautiful eyes. "Fallon?" she whispered, brushing the backs of her fingers down along a proud jaw. "I'd marry you right this very minute if I could."

"Even though I'm a woman?" Fallon asked, genuine fear in her voice.

Cateline hated herself in that moment for how she'd reacted when she saw Fallon that night. She turned her hand around, brushing dark hair away from the beautiful face. "You really confused me when I first saw you," she explained. "I was so utterly attracted to you that first night at my father's home."

Fallon's eyebrows drew. "Why were you confused?"

"Because I thought you were a man," she said simply. "I've never been attracted to a man before."

Fallon looked surprised. "No?"

Cateline shook her head. "No. There were always handsome soldiers or nobles that came and went, but they never interested me. It was usually the lady on their arm who caught my attention." She smiled.

"But," Fallon said, surprise turning to confusion. "You were so upset that night, when you saw me topless. You didn't even speak to me unless you had to."

"I'm so sorry," Cateline whispered, her hand once again coming to rest on her jaw. "I was shocked. I was angry that you hadn't told me." She shrugged a shoulder. "I felt duped, like a fool."

"You weren't disgusted?" Fallon asked, almost sounding like a little girl, afraid to hear the answer.

"No," Cateline said emphatically. "You're

absolutely beautiful, Fallon. In fact, I felt foolish for ever believing you *were* a man. Since the night I first met you, the only word that made sense was beautiful. Not handsome, not manly, beautiful." She shook her head. "I didn't understand why." She left a small kiss on Fallon's lips. "Now I know."

"Have you ever been with a woman?" Fallon asked softly as Cateline pulled away from the kiss.

"No," Cateline responded. "A few sappy letters and some kissing, but that's all. Have...you? As a woman?"

Fallon shook her head. "No."

Cateline looked down at her, studied her face, her features, her eyes, and her magnificent lips. She tucked some dark hair behind an ear before meeting those eyes with her own. "Fallon?"

"Hmm?"

"Ask me," Cateline whispered.

Fallon looked deeply into her eyes, her hand cupping the side of Cateline's head. "Would you marry me?" she asked softly.

Cateline smiled, big, bright, and full of happiness. "With all my heart, yes." She initiated a slow, exploratory kiss with Fallon, caressing her face and neck the entire time. She couldn't touch her enough. It almost felt like touching her for the first time. She broke the kiss and lifted her head. "I want to make love to you, Fallon," she whispered. "Can I?"

"I don't...I didn't bring..."

Cateline smiled, shaking her head. "I don't care about that. All I want is you. The *real* you."

Chapter Twenty-eight

Cateline found herself being pushed to her back, and she went willingly. Fallon lay next to her, her hand running down the side of Cateline's face, along her neck. She lowered her lips to Cateline's, teasing her with her tongue on her bottom lip before she was granted entrance. Cateline sighed into the kiss, her hand burying itself in thick, dark hair.

She had no idea what she was doing or how two women made love, but Cateline did know that she wanted to be touched, wanted to touch Fallon. As they continued to kiss, she reached down as far as she could on Fallon's sleeping gown, tugging on the material to try to communicate what she wanted.

Fallon pulled away, looking into Cateline's gaze. The warrior looked a bit anxious for a moment, but then took a deep breath and pulled fully away. Cateline watched as she pulled the gown up to her knees before rising to them and pulling the garment up and over her head. Fallon shook her head so long, dark hair fell back into place as she tossed the gown over the side of the bed.

Cateline sat up, riveted by what she was looking at. She'd seen Fallon briefly the night the warrior's secret was revealed, and then briefly again when Fallon had gotten out of bed the morning after her rescue. Now, to sit there and be able to truly study her, unabashedly, she was struck speechless.

Moving over to Fallon, Cateline also rose to her knees. She studied the breasts before her, so beautiful. They were perfectly shaped, the nipples dark rose and rigid. Her fingers itched to touch them. She brought her hands up and tentatively cupped them. They were so soft, and though she had breasts of her own, they were strange to her, strange to touch them on another woman.

Looking up into Fallon's face, Cateline saw that those violet eyes were hooded, lips slightly parted. She longed to kiss those lips again, so she did, her hands continuing to gently fondle the gift they held. Fallon returned the kiss, deepening it. She reached down and gathered the material of Cateline's sleep gown until it was above her waist and then pulled away long enough to pull it over her head and toss it aside before she resumed the kiss.

Cateline could feel the warmth of the fire against her naked skin and the gentleness of Fallon's hands on her back and shoulders until they were finally in her hair, holding them together as she kissed her.

Cateline was urged to lie back down, which she did, Fallon following. Wanting Fallon as close as possible, she spread her legs, welcoming the warrior to lie between them. They both sighed into the kiss at the feel of full-body contact. Fallon's breasts were soft against her own, her warmth spreading through Cateline to her very soul.

She relished the feeling of having the woman she loved with all her heart against her, nothing between them, no clothing, no lies. Just love. She ran her fingers up over delicate collarbones, then down over strong shoulders and powerful biceps. It was amazing how much of a contradiction in terms Fallon was in every way. A strong warrior, capable and powerful, yet sensitive, loving, and deeply caring.

Fallon ran her hand down Cateline's thigh, urging her to raise it higher, which she did, the other one following. This move opened Cateline's most sensitive area more to Fallon, sending a white-hot bolt of sensation lancing through her. From the look on Fallon's face, she must have felt it too.

The warrior adjusted her hips slightly, sending another jolt of pleasure through Cateline, who couldn't help but release a soft moan. Fallon looked into her eyes as she began to move her hips slowly, rubbing that incredibly sensitive spot against Cateline's.

When they'd been together before, Fallon using her attachable phallus, it had felt wonderful, it had been intimate, but this was something different altogether. It was intimate, yes, it felt amazing, absolutely yes, but now she knew that it was Fallon's body, her flesh, her *womanhood* that was touching her, caressing her, and eliciting such incredible sensations from her body.

Fallon raised herself to her hands, leaving plenty of room for Cateline's hands to cup her breasts as the warrior continued her slow, lazy thrusts against her. Fallon's eyes fell closed as she groaned when Cateline tugged lightly at her nipples. She had no idea what she was doing, so was trying to go with her instincts and with what she'd fantasized about many times before in her most private moments.

Cateline's eyes closed as the pleasure began to build. Both she and Fallon were breathing hard, little whimpers escaping Cateline's lips beyond her control. It felt amazing, a different kind of pleasure from that when Fallon was inside her. This was more intense, more focused, and it nearly took her breath away.

After a few more thrusts, the pleasure got to be too much and Cateline's body exploded in release. She moved her hands from Fallon's breasts to her shoulders, gripping them with talon-like fingers as she gasped, her back arching. It wasn't long before Fallon cried out, her head falling forward as she pressed her hips into Cateline's as hard as she could, grinding against her for a moment until, with another soft gasp, she stilled.

Lowering herself to the woman beneath her, Fallon buried her face into Cateline's neck, her rapid breathing hot against Cateline's flesh. The younger woman held her tight, eyes closed as she tried to get her own breathing under control.

Fallon finally lifted her head and looked down at Cateline, a look of tranquil calm on her beautiful face. She left a soft kiss on Cateline's lips before she moved to her neck again.

"I love you," Fallon murmured into her ear before tracing her tongue down the side of Cateline's neck and then to her throat.

Cateline's head fell back and to the side. "I love you too," she whispered, her fingers finding Fallon's hair. To her surprise, her body was already beginning to heat up again as very talented lips and tongue explored her collarbones and upper chest. Finally, a nipple was taken into the warm, wet depths of Fallon's mouth.

The princess released a long, languid moan at the new sensations that washed through her. Fallon's hand cupped the other breast as her mouth continued on the first. Cateline could feel Fallon's stomach press against her, putting pressure where she needed it. She began to move her hips, pressure building again with her arousal.

"Nope," Fallon murmured, taking a swipe at the second nipple with her tongue before leaving a kiss to the breast and looking up at Cateline. "Not like that."

Confused, Cateline watched as Fallon moved downward toward where she ached the most. She wasn't sure what Fallon was going to do until a passage from one of Sophie's letters from so long ago popped into mind: *I want my tongue in your most sweetest place.* She hadn't understood it at the time, but now it made sense, and her body burned as Fallon's intent became clear.

Her eyes fell closed and mouth open at the first touch of Fallon's tongue between her legs. It was a strange sensation, but deeply erotic. Her hips began to move with the long, slow licks, then she groaned again when that special spot was sucked into Fallon's mouth, her tongue caressing it at the same time. She was lost in ecstasy, her mind scattered, thoughts nonexistent except for that incredibly demanding tongue.

Cateline felt strong arms wrap around her spread thighs and hold them down as Fallon's mouth devoured her, relentlessly. Her body began to buck at the unceasing pleasure, but Fallon's strong hold kept her pinned until, with a loud cry, she came a second time, even stronger than the first not even ten minutes before.

Gasping for air, Cateline's fingers dug into Fallon's hair, her body loose from its earthly tether. She felt lightheaded and, for just a moment, everything went dark. When she came to, Fallon was kissing her way back up her body and cradled her in a loving embrace.

"I've got you," Fallon murmured, moving to her

back and pulling Cateline with her until her head was resting upon the warrior's shoulder.

It took several moments for Cateline's body to calm down, her sex pulsing and blood racing. As she got her wits about her again, she snuggled in even closer, her arm moving over Fallon's stomach, hand cupping her side. Fallon's fingers ran through auburn hair as they lay there in contended silence for a bit. Finally, Fallon spoke.

"I never thought I'd get to know what love felt like."

Cateline said nothing, sensing she had more to say. Instead, she left a kiss on Fallon's neck to let her know she was listening.

"I remember when Burke and Millie met and fell in love. They were pretty young, fifteen, sixteen, something like that. God, he loved her," she whispered. "Millie turned Burke, a large man full of piss and vinegar, into a pussycat."

Cateline smiled at that. All she knew was that she was forever indebted to Millie for taking in and caring for the children when everything happened. "How did they meet?"

"Millie was working in the kitchens, helping to cook for the men in Ailfred and Burke's unit. I was young, but I would watch them, wanting that for myself someday."

"Did you ever try?" Cateline asked. "Ever court anyone?"

"No. Never." Fallon rested her cheek against Cateline's forehead. "After my brother was killed, and Burke, watching what Millie went through." She was silent for a moment, though Cateline could feel the sadness coming from her. She left another kiss on her neck and began to caress her stomach with her fingertips. "Plus, I had my own hurt from both Ailfred and Burke's deaths. I think a part of me just shut down. The part that loved, or could love. I put everything into my service."

Cateline lifted her head, resting it in an upturned palm. She looked down into Fallon's face. "I know about Millie," she said softly, no longer upset about their previous relationship. Millie had proven time and again to be a worthy, trusted friend to them both. "Was there ever anyone else?"

Fallon met her gaze. "Just one. Once. We were over in Spain doing some work for the king, and upon our arrival, we were offered...company."

Cateline felt the small sting of jealousy, but then remembered she was the one who had asked. And, she was the one in bed with Fallon, not a random, faceless woman in Spain. "Did you enjoy it? Your time with Millie or the Spanish woman?"

Fallon shrugged a shoulder. "Millie I care about, as you know. But with both women, it was nothing more than physical release."

"You never loved Millie?" Cateline asked, not entirely sure why she was probing.

Fallon shook her head. "Not like that, not romantically. And," she added, looking deeply into Cateline's eyes. "Not like I love you. I've never loved anyone the way I love you."

Cateline smiled, able to see the truth in her eyes at those words. She knew she wasn't just saying it to make her feel better after hearing about the women the warrior had been intimate with.

"I love you with all my heart," Cateline murmured as she leaned down, initiating a slow kiss.

A small sigh left her when she realized that what she was tasting on Fallon's tongue was her own desire.

As the kiss deepened, curious fingers began to roam Fallon's torso, reveling in the softness of her skin. Her hand once again found a breast and cupped it, her thumb rolling the nipple into rigidity. Fallon sighed into the kiss, arching her back a bit, which pressed her breast farther into Cateline's hand.

Though Fallon had much more sexual experience than the princess did, this was her first time with a woman *as* a woman. From what she'd gathered in their conversations and Fergus's cruelty over her lifetime, this was a scary prospect for Fallon, and Cateline had a huge responsibility to show her that she was wanted, desired, and loved for who she was, not for who she'd been forced to portray to an entire nation.

Leaving Fallon's mouth, Cateline explored, very much wanting to taste her soft flesh. She wasn't quite ready to do what Fallon had just done, didn't trust herself yet, but she wanted to make her feel good.

Tucking her hair behind an ear, Cateline bent down over Fallon's chest, taking a tentative swipe with her tongue on her nipple, enjoying the long sigh she got in response. Figuring she was doing it right, she ran her tongue around the puckered flesh. As she focused on the breast, her hand wandered down a muscular stomach and down lower still.

Cateline hummed happily into her task as her fingers came into contact with the immense wetness between Fallon's legs. From her previous two experiences with the warrior, she'd come to understand that wetness was from the arousal and desire. Fallon's thighs spread apart for her, one of them moving to rest over Cateline's own legs.

Using her tongue to flick the nipple over and over again before sucking it into her mouth, Cateline ran her fingers through the saturated folds, feeling the terrain that made Fallon a woman.

She thought back to the first night they made love, when they had to consummate her marriage to Fergus. What a sweet blessing that had been, and neither of them had realized it at the time. She remembered how it had felt as Fallon had used her fingers to stroke her, to get her ready for penetration. It had felt wonderful, and so she focused on doing the same for Fallon now.

Her fingertips came into contact with a nub that was hard and slick, and when she touched it, a long groan erupted from Fallon's throat. She figured that must be the amazing pleasure spot on a woman that she had felt herself, so she focused on it.

"Does that feel good?" she murmured, leaving Fallon's breast to look down into her face.

Fallon nodded. "Yes," she gasped. Her eyes were closed and her lips were parted.

Cateline watched her as her fingers worked over that special spot, trying to read Fallon's reactions to see if she needed to speed up, slow down, what happened if she went from rubbing side to side to small circles at the very tip of the nub. Fallon seemed to react more fiercely when her two fingertips rubbed quickly side to side.

From her increased breathing and the copious amount of wetness, Cateline sensed she was close. Her forearm burned with the unusual exertion, but she didn't care. She'd do it all night if that's what Fallon needed. All night wasn't what she needed now, as Fallon's hips bucked and her head flew back into the pillow. She bared her teeth and growled out her release, Cateline's fingers covered in thick, warm fluid as she came. Cateline groaned in appreciation and sympathy. She pressed down on that nub until Fallon weakly batted her fingers away, her breasts heaving as she panted.

Watching Fallon's desire in that moment was one of the most beautiful things Cateline had ever seen. She returned the favor from before and gathered Fallon into her embrace, raining kisses down on her face, whispering words of love

Cateline's eyes opened, though she wasn't sure why. It was still dark out and it was very cold. She lay on her stomach, Fallon not far away, sound asleep on her side with her back to the princess. Looking around the room, she realized the fire had burned down, neither she nor Fallon stoking it before falling asleep after yet another round of lovemaking.

As quietly as she could, she scooted toward the edge of the mattress, her lower regions letting her know just how unappreciative they were of the extreme workout they'd received hours before. Her bare feet hit the massive rug spread out beneath the bed. She found her sleeping gown and slipped it over her body before padding over to the fireplace.

It didn't take long to get it started again, the warm glow comforting. She stood there for a long moment, staring into the flames. She couldn't keep the small smile off her lips. She was happy, truly happy, for the first time in her life. She and Fallon had a lot to discuss and certainly a lot to get to know about each other, but she knew in her heart of hearts that Fallon was absolutely the one meant for her. They were connected in a way she'd only dreamed about.

Turning, she looked at the sleeping figure in her bed and knew it wasn't a dream, but the way her life was to go. As happy as she was, more important to her was the fact that Fallon would be loved and happy. She intended to spend her life making sure Fallon knew she was cherished and to try to give all that Fallon had so selflessly given her entire life thus far.

She walked to the bedroom the kids shared and checked on them. They were both still sound asleep. She'd been worried that they'd awaken them, as they hadn't exactly been quiet while making love, but the walls were three feet thick and the doors several inches thick, so apparently they hadn't been overheard.

Stoking the fire in their small fireplace, Cateline checked on each kid, satisfied that they were comfortable and sleeping peacefully. She looked into their precious faces for a long moment, wondering where their parents were. Why had they ended up in an orphanage? Likely, she'd never know, and at this point, it didn't matter. They were hers. Hers and Fallon's.

Now that the threat of Fergus was gone, she intended to talk to Carthac about ending their *oidhreacht* and make them recognized officially by the Crown as their legal children. The following day would be the procession for Fergus's body which, from what she understood, had already been boiled down to his bones. Those would be interred into the family crypt beneath the church on the castle grounds.

Though the current royal family was not Christian, previous generations had subscribed to the religion, so the church was built and the crypt was established. Cateline would be glad when it was all over.

Chapter Twenty-nine

Let's see here," Carthac said, looking Fallon over from top to bottom. He brought up large hands and swept away unseen lint from Fallon's shoulders. Finally, he smiled at her. "You look wonderful."

Fallon took a long, deep breath. "Thank you, Daidi." She wore a brand-new tunic made specifically for the day. It was bright white, and a red silk sash was worn from left shoulder to right hip. Red, the color of Sursha. The leather pants she wore were black, a very rare color to wear as it was difficult to find ingredients used to make such dyes.

Carthac walked over to the ornate desk in his Solar and took hold of the ceremonial sword that Fallon would wear, as opposed to the double blades on her back. He gently slid the long, gleaming blade into the sheath already attached to her sword belt. "I can't even begin to tell you how proud I am of you," he said. "You've always exceeded my greatest expectations of you, Fallon. But I've come to understand I misjudged the situation terribly."

She studied him, confused. "Meaning?"

"Well," the older man said with a shrug, he, too, dressed in his finery as king. "I thought Ailfred would be the best choice. Yes," he conceded. "He was the oldest boy, and unfortunately, so goes our laws. But the truth is, he never wanted the throne. Yes, he would have taken it, stepped up, but he loved what he did."

Fallon gave him a sad smile. "He did. He loved the fight, the strategy of outwitting an enemy."

"The female adoration," Carthac added with a quirked eyebrow.

Fallon's smile grew into a grin. "Definitely."

"But," Carthac said with a sad sigh, stepping back and looking Fallon over again. "He never wanted to be tied down to a wife and family, nor the throne." He looked at Fallon, a troubled expression deepening the lines of his face. "How was I so terribly wrong?"

"Daidi," Fallon said gently. "Ailfred was a hero to all of us. We all expected him to take us into the next generation of rule. You groomed him from the time he was a boy, from what I've been told. Nobody failed here."

"No," Carthac said, "I failed *you*. I had to lose both my sons to find out that my daughter was the right man for the job all along."

Fallon smirked at the little joke but was deeply touched. "Thank you, Daidi," she murmured.

"Are you nervous?"

Fallon nodded, blowing out a breath. "Very."

"Don't be. To be a good husband, as it were, be loving, listen to her, give her what she needs. Be fair, be just, and be honest." He smiled. "All the things you already do and are." He walked away from the warrior and back to the same desk, picking up a couple documents. "I wanted to tell you this before the ceremony, after which I intend to make the announcement. Feel free to tell your bride-to-be."

Fallon accepted the documents and read them. She looked up at her father, eyes wide. "You not only canceled their *oidhreacht*, but you've officially recognized them as our children?" she asked, shock in her voice.

Carthac nodded. "Yes. To the two of you, to me, and soon enough, to the entirety of the world. Garratt and Laigen are official and legal members of our royal family."

Fallon had no words, so simply took her father in a tight, one-armed hug, the precious documents tucked protectively in her other hand. "Thank you."

Carthac returned the hug, patting her heartily on the back. "Come now," he said, a bit of emotion in his voice. "Let's go get you married."

❧ ❧ ❧ ❧

Fallon had been surprised to see Enori, dressed in ceremonial robes of her Order, ready to perform the marriage rites. She smiled at Fallon with that little twinkle in her eye that Fallon remembered from her time in Brittany. It was a bit unnerving, as Enori always looked like she had something up the large sleeves of her robe.

In her hands were two long pieces of ribbon. Her blue eyes met Fallon's gaze before she turned and looked straight ahead, which made Fallon look too. They were in the church, but it wasn't going to be a Christian ceremony.

There was a large audience in the nave, and from what she'd been told, a massive audience outside. A large part of the population had shown up for the ceremony and to witness the marriage of Fallon and the woman who had become beloved to pretty much anybody with a heartbeat in the country.

Her programs of using the extra food to hold

festivals and food banks had been a massive hit and was now countrywide in all regions. It had also expanded into clothing, toys, tools—anything people had to spare to help their neighbors. Though it had spread across the nation, it was all done in Cateline's name. She'd been their princess for less than a year, but she was already raised as a saint by many.

Cateline's father and a small contingent had traveled from Les Trois-Moutiers for the wedding, as well as meetings with Carthac and Fallon to deal with some business. It would be strange for Fallon to sit across from the baron, now as his "son-in-law," but in many ways, also his equal.

Also, Fallon knew that it was quite probable he'd been in on the plan to kill Fergus after the marriage to his daughter. Fallon couldn't even wrap her mind around arranging or agreeing to something like that if it were Laigen or Livia, knowing they could get hurt or killed in the melee.

For now, she refocused her attention, as she needed all her wits because Cateline was being escorted up the aisle by her father. Fallon could hardly take a breath as she looked at the beautiful woman who would be her wife in mere moments. The princess wore a beautiful gown of blue, which no doubt made her eyes, usually more gray, blue to reflect the color. The gown was made of fine silks with ribbons and jewels. Fallon thought perhaps it had been Cateline's mother's, as it looked of another time.

The veil she wore covered the face that Fallon craved to see. As they neared, Fallon's heart nearly beat out of her chest. Her palms were sweaty and her ears were ringing. She barely heard the music announcing the bride's entrance. She took several deep breaths as finally, her soul, her heart, her future reached her.

Once Cateline was standing in front of her, she could see the smile on her lips through the material of the veil, a smile she returned. In that moment, it was just them, not hundreds upon hundreds of pairs of eyes on them.

"Thank you to all who are gathered here," Enori called out in her accented Gaelic, her voice echoing loud and clear in the cavernous stone structure. "We are here to honor Fallon and Cateline, beloved to you all." She turned to the two before her. "Fallon," she said, handing the warrior one end of one of the ribbons. "Cateline," she said, handing the princess one end of the other. They each held one end, Fallon in her right hand, Cateline, her left. "Now," the priestess instructed. "Clasp your free hand together."

Fallon reached her hand out and Cateline placed her smaller one in it. Fallon smiled, loving the feel of her soft skin. She could feel Cateline's eyes on her, even if she wasn't able to see them all that clearly at the moment. She was so soft, so amazing. Just the nearness of her made everything okay.

Enori began to chant in her language. With Fallon and Cateline both speaking and understanding French, they were able to pick out enough of what she said to know they were to begin wrapping the ribbon around their joined hands, first one lap by Fallon, then one by Cateline.

When the ribbon had been halfway wound around their joint hands, Enori reached over and gently lifted the veil to reveal Cateline's beautiful face.

"I lift the veil between your old and your new life, for you both," the priestess said. "Cateline, look into Fallon's eyes. See your future. Fallon, look into

Cateline's eyes. See *your* future."

Fallon studied her eyes, the color, which sure enough, was a more vivid blue. There was so much light and life in them, so much love. She'd never known anybody who had so much to give, even as she'd been given so little. Fallon's father had been more of a loving, guiding figure to her in the months she'd been in Sursha than Cateline's father had been in more than twenty years of life.

And now, they had Garratt and Laigen, a family. Livia was part of their family and had asked to become more than a lady-in-waiting. She wanted to learn how things worked, learn about the politics, and perhaps someday speak for the family abroad.

"Now," Enori said. "Your hands are completely bound, as are your hearts and souls." She placed her hands on the four hands that were literally bound together by the full lengths of the two pieces of ribbon. "You've already vowed to each other your love and bond," she continued. "With your hearts, silent words the verbal can never repeat." She raised her hands, long sleeves falling away from her arms, Enori looked to the ceiling many feet above. "By the love and grace of Ankou, I pronounce you partners in life and partners beyond death. Fallon, kiss your bride."

Fallon smiled at the very idea of it. It would be the first time she'd ever entertained a romantic move toward a woman in public out of fear, despite the facade. But, in that moment, the audience who watched her every move mattered not. Only Cateline mattered.

The lips that Fallon was becoming to know and need were as soft as ever, pliant under her ministrations. Their kiss wasn't chaste, but it wasn't filled with the passion that Fallon knew would come later, as it had earlier that morning before the sun rose.

The thunderous applause separated them, Fallon grinning down at her bride, who was already doing the same. Enori unwound their hands and they exchanged their rings. It was unusual for men to wear a wedding ring, but the heart of a woman that beat in Fallon's chest wanted something to denote what she was so incredibly proud of.

Cateline's ring was gold with a sapphire and emerald set in a Claddagh. Fallon's ring was what was known as a Gimmel ring, thin bands of gold intertwined, ending with a much smaller Claddagh with a small emerald and a small sapphire to echo Cateline's ring.

Fallon looked down at the beautiful ring on her finger and smiled. Yes, she thought. This was what she'd been waiting for.

⚜ ⚜ ⚜ ⚜

The great hall was filled with laughter and music, food and wine. Anyone and everyone was invited, from nobleman to peasant. Cateline insisted on it. Fallon had never seen anything like it, and thought it was amazing. There was plenty of muscle around to keep any problems down, but there were very few to be had.

Fallon and Cateline stood together as an unending line of well-wishers stopped by to chat with them, kiss Cateline's knuckles, or shake Fallon's hand. Fallon was surprised to see Will and another man step up to them. She hadn't seen Will since he'd helped them remove Fergus's body and he'd been officially released from his bonds.

"Congratulations to you both," Will said, a genuine smile on his face. In fact, Fallon couldn't recall ever seeing the man look happy, but that night he looked relaxed, happy, and at peace. He leaned in and kissed Cateline's cheek, whispering something in her ear that Fallon couldn't understand.

"And you as well," she said softly, cupping his cheek. The two seemed to share a moment, which Fallon didn't understand. "You must be Aaron," the princess said, turning to the man standing with Will.

The man bowed deeply in reverence and kissed her knuckles. "Aye, milady." He looked to both Fallon and Cateline. "Congratulations to you. May you live and love long."

"Thank you," Fallon said, accepting the man's hand with a smile. He turned to Will, curious to find out the story from Cateline later, and was surprised when Will leaned in and hugged her.

"Keep her," Will said into her ear. "She's a gem."

Fallon nodded. "My absolute intention."

The two men walked away, leaving Fallon to look to Cateline. "I'll tell you later," the princess murmured.

"You are beautiful," a woman's voice said, suddenly before them.

Fallon turned to see Enori. She stood before Cateline, taking her hands in her own. The priestess's eyes were very focused on Cateline, as though reading her very soul. "I was very much looking forward to meeting you in person."

Cateline seemed riveted by the blond woman, much as Fallon had been when she'd first met her. "Thank you," she said. "Thank you for marrying us."

Enori smiled. "It was my pleasure, Princess." She held onto Cateline's hands as she opened her arms, looking Cateline over in the beautiful dress she wore. "You wear Roishin's dress well," she said softly. "It was good to have Fallon's mother involved."

Cateline stared at her. "How did you know?"

Enori said nothing in response, simply smiled. She looked to both of them. "I have a gift for you." Reaching up into the large sleeves of her robe, she withdrew a single red rose. Handing it to Cateline, she spoke, her words aimed at both of them. "Tonight is the night of your joining," she began. "Love well and true. At the summer solstice, your family of four will grow to five for you." She leaned in and left a kiss upon Cateline's cheek and then Fallon's, then walked away.

Fallon watched her go, seeming to nearly vanish within the crowd. She turned and looked to Cateline, who twisted the rose stem in her fingers. Their gazes met, then looked to where the woman had last stood.

☙☙☙☙

Eyes hooded, Fallon watched as Cateline's hips gracefully rolled astride her own, the phallus attached to Fallon buried deep inside her. The warrior glided her hands up Cateline's sides to cup her breasts, thumbs rubbing over her nipples to add to her pleasure.

Cateline's head fell back, exposing the irresistible column of her throat. Sitting up, Fallon's hands cupped a gorgeous behind, encouraging Cateline's movements as her mouth found that throat. She moaned into her task, loving the taste of Cateline's flesh.

The princess moaned as she buried her hands

in Fallon's hair, soft whimpers from her lips making Fallon want to take control. Nipping at her neck, she whispered into Cateline's ear. "Lie back, my love…"

Cateline did as asked, leaning back on the bed, her head toward the foot. Fallon followed, setting herself between her spread thighs. She reached down and guided the phallus, already slick with Cateline's desire, back inside of her, making the woman beneath her moan deep in her throat as she reached for Fallon.

Fallon initiated a short but passionate kiss before she raised herself to her hands and began to use the power of her lower body to thrust quick and deep inside her wife, married for a month. Nearly every night had been filled with unimaginable pleasures, even if it was just cuddles and kisses.

Cateline's hands grabbed Fallon's behind in a tight grip, her cries of growing pleasure constant with Fallon's ruthless thrusts, skin slapping against skin. Finally, she cried out, long and hard, nails digging into Fallon's flesh. Fallon's own release came swiftly. She slammed her hips into Cateline one final time, grinding into her to milk the last of the pleasure.

Spent, she pulled out and flopped over onto her back. Her chest heaved as she tried to catch her breath, her body pulsing with aftershocks. She smiled and turned her head to look at Cateline when her hand was taken in the softness of the smaller one.

"When do I get to wear that?" Cateline asked, an eyebrow arched in question.

"You want to?" Fallon asked.

"*Oui*," she said with a grin. She turned to her side, moving their clasped hands to rest on Fallon's stomach. "I want to know what it's like to be inside you." She rested her temple against a fist, looking down at Fallon, who met her gaze.

"I'd like that, I think," the warrior said. "And, I guess considering how many times we've made love, I figure it's about time we 'officially' and 'fully' consummate our marriage."

Cateline grinned. "Now you're thinking like a good wife," she said, reaching down and playfully tugging on the phallus that jutted up from Fallon's hips.

"You know," Fallon said, changing the subject a bit, but her wife had made her think of it. "Garratt called me Daidi the other day."

"How does that make you feel?" Cateline asked, releasing the phallus and scooting in closer to Fallon, resting her head on her shoulder as Fallon wrapped her in her arm. Both children had begun to call the princess Mamai.

"At first it was strange, as I'm not his father," Fallon said quietly, running her fingers through long, auburn hair. "But then I thought about it, and it made sense. Obviously, he and Laigen don't know, they're too young to understand and keep it secret. But," she added, thinking about what she was feeling, what she'd felt that day. "I don't know. Somehow, it really felt good. Garratt can be so reserved and somewhat detached. He'd been through so much before they came to us."

"I know," Cateline agreed. "They amaze me every day, how loving they are when they have absolutely no reason to be."

"Me too," Fallon said softly. "So, if he sees me as his Daidi, I'm honored."

"I think it's wonderful," Cateline whispered, bringing up her hand to caress Fallon's face. "They really love you, and so do I." She leaned down and left a soft kiss on waiting lips.

"I love you, too," Fallon murmured into the kiss.

"So, the night we got married Enori told us to love well and true," She trailed her fingers down the side of Fallon's neck and along a prominent collarbone. "Do you think we've done that?"

Little shivers trailed along with Cateline's teasing touch. "Oh, I think so, and multiple times a day." She grinned. "Are you pregnant yet?"

Cateline chuckled low in her throat, which shot right down between Fallon's legs. "Not for lack of trying."

Fallon pushed her wife to her back and followed suit. "Practice, practice, practice," she murmured against her lips.

Epilogue

Milady!" Fallon called out, tapping the heavy iron head of the hammer against her palm as she stood the appropriate amount of feet from the target.

"Yes, milord?" Cateline responded from her place of privilege beneath the shaded structure built specifically for the ladies to watch the summer solstice games.

"Do I get special favors from Her Highness should I win?" she asked.

"Well, now," Cateline responded, teasing in her voice. "I suppose that all depends on the thrust of your hammer."

A burst of laughter erupted among the other competitors, one slapping Fallon on the back as she grinned. "Then I shall aim to please, milady." More lascivious laughter followed her remark before Fallon grew serious and focused on her target.

Taking the wooden handle in both hands, Fallon lifted her hands above her head, eyeing the bullseye as she aimed the head of the hammer at the target, pulled it back, aimed it, and pulled it back again before letting it fly with a grunt of exertion.

The blacksmith's hammer—donated for the games by the local shops from surrounding villages—flew end over end until it hit the tree stump with a solid *crack*, the hammer head stuck in the hole created by the force of impact.

Fallon grinned, cheers going up around her. She glanced over at her wife, who gave her a look of *not bad* before looking away, only to give her the side-eye. Fallon would never understand how that woman could make her burn without even touching her.

Her turn spent, Fallon stepped off the field to let the next competitor try his lot. She walked over to where the ladies sat and chatted, watching the men, to get the drink that Cateline was holding for her.

"Proper thrust, milady?" she asked softly in French, for her wife's ears only.

"I suppose we'll see later," the princess purred, handing Fallon her ale. "Won't we?"

Fallon grinned as she sipped from her ale. Her gaze turned to the right, over by the tree line where Garratt had been playing with some of the other boys in the village where the games were being hosted.

She went to turn away, satisfied that they were safe and having fun when she saw the look on Garratt's face as he turned in her direction. For all his bravado as a "warrior-in-the-making," he was a very sensitive little boy, deeply caring.

Call it her instinct as a parent or as a warrior, Fallon handed the ale back to Cateline and, without a word, bolted off in his direction. Vaguely she heard people reacting to her taking off at a sprint, but she ignored them.

Reaching the kids, she could see just how panicked Garratt really was. "What's wrong?" she asked. None of the children had to say anything as she heard it. At first she thought it was a hurt animal, but as she gently nudged the children away, just in case, she stepped farther into the trees and, reaching out cautiously, pushed aside some foliage.

"Oh my," she whispered. "Garratt?" she called out, never taking her eyes off it.

"Sir?" she heard him call back.

"Tell Eoin to take his men and surround the forest and search for any person in the vicinity."

"Sir!"

Knowing her orders would be followed, Fallon slowly knelt down and gathered the tiny bundle in her arms. The cries and flailing little fist that had managed to escape its wrappings made Fallon all the more watchful as she stood, scanning the trees for any kind of movement, animal or human. Nothing.

She held the bundle close to her chest as she made her way out of the forest and into the bright June sun. She was surprised to see a group of women headed her way, Millie one of them. She hurried up to Fallon and peeled the blanket down, looking into the upset little face.

"This child is a newborn," she said, looking at Fallon's concerned face.

Fallon looked past the women to see Cateline hurrying to them. She felt better, almost as though Cateline would know what to do.

"Let me see," the princess said softly, most of those present for the festival and games surrounding them now. Fallon handed the baby over to her wife. "My goodness," she whispered. "This is a new baby, Fallon."

Fallon nodded, looking around again, looking into every face that had gathered. Was there a guilty conscience among them? Was a man quickly looking away, not wanting to support the new baby his wife had just given birth to? Perhaps a desperate woman?

She saw nothing but concern and curiosity.

It was then, looking back to the baby in Cateline's arms, that she noticed what the baby was wrapped in. A blanket, dark blue with gold stitching. Cateline looked up and met her gaze.

"What?" the princess asked. "Do you think they'll find who left it?"

Fallon shook her head. "No," she said. "There's nobody to find."

※.※.※.※

"I don't understand this, Fallon," Cateline said, looking down at the tiny baby in her arms.

A local woman who was nursing her own baby offered to help with the unexpected bundle until they could find a wet nurse. The little girl had been fed, bathed, and changed into a fresh cloth diaper, and swaddled in the blanket she'd been found in.

"I know," Fallon said, walking over to her. She stood behind her wife and wrapped her arms around her waist. She rested her chin on Cateline's shoulder to look down into the sleeping face. "She's so tiny," she whispered. "There's not a lot to understand, my love. Remember what Enori said on our wedding day?"

"I do," Cateline said, leaning back into Fallon. "And, today is the solstice, but it doesn't make sense. Somebody had to give birth to her."

"When I was there," Fallon explained softly, reaching around to just barely touch the soft skin of a teeny tiny nose. "I saw that the Order of Ankou is something I don't understand. My entire life has been spent on the battlefield and they did things I'd never seen before. They're..." She wasn't entirely sure what to say. "Magical."

Cateline moved away and turned to face her, cradling the baby tighter to her. "What if her mother is out there somewhere, missing her baby, Fallon?" Cateline asked, her eyes troubled. "I'd never forgive myself for causing that kind of pain."

"I know, my love," Fallon said gently, giving her a smile. "But I feel it in my gut. I don't know how, I don't know why, but she was intended for us. To raise her as our own." She looked over at Garratt and Laigen, who were sitting on the floor together in front of the fireplace playing. Garratt was so gentle and patient with his younger sister. "You guys want a baby sister?" she asked them.

Both kids scrambled to their feet and hurried over to them. It was almost as though they'd been waiting for permission. Cateline sat down in a chair, the older children standing on either side of her.

"What will we name her?" Garratt asked, looking from Cateline to Fallon.

Fallon, who stood just beyond the chair, met Cateline's gaze, shrugging a shoulder. "I don't know why I feel the need to say this, and you can certainly disagree, but I think—"

"Roishin?" Cateline asked.

Fallon nodded. "Yes."

Cateline looked down at the sleeping babe, then at Laigen, at Garratt, then up to Fallon. "We are now five," she said softly.

"As promised," Fallon murmured. She watched as Garratt walked over to her, reaching up and taking her hand in his. "Hey, what's up?" she asked.

"I'll protect her," he said. "I'll protect all of you."

Fallon smiled, taking her hand from his as she

wrapped her arm protectively around his narrow shoulders. "You and me, little man," she said. "We'll keep her safe."

Cateline looked up at Fallon's eyes, their gazes holding for a long moment before the princess looked back down to her bundle, Laigen's head resting against her Mamai's shoulder.

This was it, Fallon thought. What she'd always dreamed of while at her waterfall or asleep in her bed, all alone. Now, wide awake, she knew dreams did come true.

About the Author

Kim has spent her life in Colorado and can't imagine living anywhere else. She's been writing since she was 9 and stumbled into her first book being published in her mid-20s. She's worked in the film industry as a writer, director and producer, but now enjoys the quiet, happy life of a professional author. She can be reached on Facebook and on her website at, www. kimpritekel.com

IF YOU LIKED THIS BOOK...

Share a review with your friends or post a review on your favorite site like Amazon, Goodreads, Barnes and Noble, or anywhere you purchased the book. Or perhaps share a posting on your social media sites and help spread the word.

Join the Sapphire Newsletter and keep up with all your favorite authors.

Did we mention you get a free book for joining our team?

sign-up at - www.sapphirebooks.com

Check out Kim's other book

Zero Ward - ISBN - 978-1-943353-19-4

Danny Felts grew up in the heart of the Midwest on a dairy farm, expected to follow in her mother's footsteps and marry a farmer and become a mother. Danny had other ideas. As World War II heats up, she makes a decision that will change her life forever as she becomes a lie, serving with the Seabees in the Navy as Daniel Felts.

Kate Adams is about to graduate high school in her prestigious and elite San Diego neighborhood when she's dragged to the USO for a dance with friends and servicemen. There, she meets the person that will catch her eye and her heart, only for jealousy and vengeance to tear her apart.

Are Danny and Kate strong enough to win the battle within and fight for their love?

Connection - ISBN - 978-1-939062-24-6

Julie Wilson lives a charmed life as a beloved teacher and aunt in the small town of Woodland. Close to her brother and guardian of two adorable Yorkies, she loves her life, the only negative being ex-boyfriend, Ray who can't seem to understand the phrase, "We're done." Believing that's her only problem, Julie has no idea what hell awaits her during a normal summer afternoon.

Remmy Foster is the quirky, friendly drifter who has never found roots after a difficult childhood, as well as the difficulties her very special gift brings into her life. Though she may call it exploring, the truth is she's running from ghosts that haunt her every step.

After a chance meeting with Julie while hitchhiking, Remmy will be thrown head first into darkness she could never have foreseen, regardless of her abilities. As the clock ticks, life and death is on her shoulders to make the right connection.

Warning - Some scenes may be too intense for some readers.

1049 Club - ISBN - 978-1-939062-97-0

Almost two hundred souls, one plane, six survivors, endless heartbreak.

When flight 1049, headed from Buffalo, NY to Italy falls from the sky, a firestorm of drama, pain, angst and sorrow ensues. Can an author, a business owner, a teenager, good ol' boy, veterinarian and ruthless lawyer survive? Better yet, can those left behind?

1049 Club is a story of survival, love, deep regret and miracles. Can the living make peace with the presumed dead? Can the presumed dead make peace with the lives and loves they thought they had before?

Blinded – ISBN – 978-1-943353-53-8

After a horrible explosion sends local television news

reporter, Burton Blinde reeling both physically and emotionally, she walks away from her life and the dream job she was about to start at a major news network.

For six long years she hides out in a small mountain town, working at the local library, though is haunted by the life she had, including mysterious messages and gifts she was receiving before her life was turned upside down, a veritable bread crumb trail leading to the unknown.

Unable to resist, Burton begins to follow the clues, which will lead her into the darkest places of human nature that she may not be able to return from.

Damaged - ISBN - 978-1-939062-45-1

Family. A group of people you are related to by blood or love.

Nora Schaeffer has come home to her family after twenty years working around the world as a photographer for National Geographic. She's welcomed into the open arms of her father and siblings.

Family. A group of people who support you, lift you up when you fall.

Shannon, the youngest of the four Schaeffer siblings, has vanished, leaving her five-year-old daughter, Bella, terrified and alone. To help find Shannon, Nora has no choice but to turn to the dark-haired specter who has haunted her for twenty years. Along the way, she finds her own long-dead heart and uncovers chilling family secrets beyond imagination.

Family. A group of people who will stick together to hide the rotten soul at its core at any cost.

Who will live? Who will die? Who will be the most damaged? And who will learn to love again?

The Gift - ISBN - 978-1-948232-47-0

The dead do speak. You just have to listen. Homicide Detective Catania "Nia" d'Giovanni is the only daughter in a large Italian family of six children. The backbone—a position not applied for nor wanted—she continues to create new glue to hold the dysfunctional group together. For Nia, family time feels more like herding cats than spending time with her brothers and feisty, aging parents.

Her heart has always been in her career with the Pueblo Police Department, especially since it will never be okay with her very Catholic mother to openly give her heart to any woman, until she meets a secretive waitress who has her at, Can I take your order?

And then it begins…

Three murders that are so gruesome, so horrible, they rock the small town to its core. Nia and her partner Oscar are left to piece together a deadly puzzle to find the key to unlock the monster they hunt.

Or, are they the hunted?

As they dissect the murder scenes where not one shred of evidence is left behind, more bodies begin to show up, each cleaner than the last, the shadowy specter that is the killer vanishing without a trace, making the woman Nia loves disappear right along with it.

When there is no evidence to follow, Nia must trust her instincts…or, is she being guided?

The Plan – ISBN – 978-1-948232-43-2

As the dark days of the Dust Bowl came to an end, the midsection of the United States tried to rebuild and revitalize. In the small, dusty farming town of, Brooke View, Colorado, teenager, Eleanor Landry and her mother were dealing with her father, a self-appointment fire and brimstone preacher to his congregation of two. A plan to survive.

As the dark era of the robber baron comes to an end, giants of industry and innovation emerged with fabulous fortunes manifested in the mansions that dotted the landscape across the country. Lysette Landon, the teen daughter of the wealthiest family in Brooke View, was everything a good, proper girl of privilege should be. Only problem was, she wasn't dreaming of finding a young man to raise a family with. A plan to be free.

One look, one touch, all plans are off.

Secrets deeper and darker than the grave would bring Eleanor and Lysette together, their families connected by a web of lies and broken promises. A plan to escape.

Be careful because, life has other plans...

The Traveler Book One: The Hunted - ISBN - 978-1-948232-91-3

A story so epic one book can't contain it.BOOK ONE:

1977: In the era between flower power and the yuppie, Sonia Lucas is a young wife and mother, just starting out in life. Without warning, a strange presence and dark force enters her life, clouds building...

1917: ...and a storm brewing as the world reeled from the horrific events of World War I just before it was ravaged by a Spanish flu epidemic that would kill millions. Sephora Lloyd is a 16 year old girl lost in the responsibilities of an adult world helping to support herself and her mother. A beautiful young nun-in-training enters her life, bringing love and hope with her. That is, until a force bigger than either of them threatens everything Sephora holds dear.

Four women - three deaths - two words - one house
THE HUNTED

The Traveler Book Two: The Hunter - ISBN - 978-1-948232-93-7

A story so epic one book can't contain it. BOOK TWO:

1890: In the dying days of the Old West, Sally Little runs her booming brothel with the passion and tenacity the business of sex requires. Savvy and indulgent, there's one itch Sally can't let herself scratch. Afraid of hurting the woman she loves, she instead unleashes...

Present Day: ...her renovation crew and fixer upper TV show on a dilapidated mansion that has known nothing but death since a murder there in 1977. Samantha Leyton sees ratings gold in bringing the sagging old house to life, but instead she discovers only she has the power to unlock the mystery that hunted four women across time, leaving death and destruction in its wake. Can she release her sisters who came before her and finally be granted the gift of love that is stronger than any evil?

Four women - Three deaths - two words - one house
THE HUNTER

Finding Faith - ISBN - 978-1-952270-16-1

Faith Fitzgerald thought that if she got an education and became a high-powered attorney in Manhattan, maybe—just maybe—she'd gain the attention and respect of her absentee father. Considering he was the only parent she had left after her mother's suicide when Faith was just a child, she thought that's what it would take.

She was wrong.

What she dreamed would be glamorous and satisfying turned out to be grueling and thankless. Since she wasn't willing to play the game between the sheets, she was forced to stay in the cubicle jungle doing all the heavy lifting while the men got the credit and the rewards.

Deciding she is done, Faith packs up and, with the flip of the bird to the rearview mirror, leaves New York and heads home to Colorado. She has nothing there: no job, nowhere to live, no relationship with her father. Truth is, she barely has a relationship with herself.

On the drive home, she finds herself in Wynter, a tiny mountain town at the foot of the Rockies. Looking more like it belongs in a made-for-TV Christmas movie than on the map, Faith is utterly enchanted. When she tries her luck and buys a raffle ticket at Pop's, Wynter's charming café, her prize is far more than meets the eye—or the heart.

Enter Wyatt, a feisty, sexy southerner and waitress at Pop's, who just happens to be married to a local sheriff's deputy. All is not as it appears with the All-American boy and his Georgia peach.

A colorful cast of unforgettable and charming characters will teach the jaded attorney that sometimes to find yourself all you have to do is go back to the basics...and have a little Faith.

Taking Liberty - ISBN- 978-1-952270-24-6

A victim of a massive corporate downsize, Liberty Faulkner suddenly finds herself without a job, without a home, and without a plan. Though certainly not part of her vision, Libby decides that the familiar is the safest path back to her life goals. In this case, the devil she knows is home: the tiny mountain town of Wynter, Colorado, a close-knit place where everybody knows everybody and everybody's business. Seems like the perfect place for the twenty-five-year-old to start over and figure out who she is without being noticed…not.

Sergeant Grace Montez escaped her dead-end job and toxic relationship in New Mexico and moved to Wynter to help build their police department from scratch. Now an established figurehead in the community, she's got her professional life dialed in and even mentors new recruits on the force. After a challenging childhood and lifetime of abandonment and disappointment, Grace hasn't been interested in another relationship—especially because no one has caught her eye since a certain quirky college student who used to make her caramel macchiato at the local coffee shop moved away three years ago.

Now that quirky college student has returned as the beautiful, mature woman Libby has become. Can Grace keep her distance, or will she finally take liberties with what is being offered?

Justice Won - ISBN - 978-1-952270-36-9

In 1890, seventeen-year-old Justice Kilkoyne and her mother, Ninny, are one bad decision away from living on the streets of Azrael, Pennsylvania. Ninny's propensity for the bottle has left Justice to play the adult, her androgynous good looks helping her pass as a young man to gain employment and keep them—if just barely—above water.

Determined to find a better life for them, Justice saves every penny to get them on a train headed west to the sunshine of California. Before they can leave, the bigotry of one shopkeeper sends Justice on the run, chased by the police for a crime she didn't commit and straight into the unwitting arms of a stunning young prostitute, who, after an unexpected connection, becomes Justice's Angel.

The day arrives to leave Pennsylvania for good. As Justice and Ninny get settled, they're surprised by the appearance of Angel, also wanting to start anew. When the trip is violently interrupted in Colorado, Angel just may be lost to Justice forever.

Can Justice find a new life when she makes her way to the fledgling mining town of Wynter, Colorado? Can her heart ever be whole again?

Curtain Call - ISBN - 978-1-952270-42-0

What do you do when you come from a long line of dancers that spans the globe and generations, yet you can't tell your right foot from your left? You fall in love with a dancer, of course!

Gray Rickman is an awkward seventeen-year-old when she first sets eyes on Christian Scott at the dance studio/theater Gray's parents own and run in Denver, Colorado.

Though only a handful of years older than Gray, Christian carries herself with poise and wisdom far beyond her years. A woman of few words, she speaks volumes with her body.

Before Gray even really knows what her type is, Christian stars in endless daydreams and even fulfills a couple of her fantasies before vanishing out of thin air, leaving Gray in an empty bed with nothing but bittersweet memories and broken dreams.

With no choice but to move on, Gray attempts love, even moving with her college girlfriend to New York City to pursue a career in journalism. But her standard has been set, the bar way too high for any other woman to reach or clear. It's an unexpected encounter in an obvious place when Gray sets eyes on her dancer again. Will the bright lights of Broadway illuminate the way back to the woman of her dreams? Or will they blind her to any other possibility of happiness?

Break a leg, Gray. The Great White Way calls.

Encore Performance - ISBN - 978-1-952270-52-9

Grey Rickman, a journalist for The New York Times, is offered the opportunity of a lifetime and a huge boost to her career—ghostwriting a memoir for one of the world's most beloved actors. She is deeply in love with her girlfriend, dancer Christian Scott, and her world couldn't be better.

Christian, though proud of Grey and all that she's accomplished, is facing her own career dilemma. All she's ever wanted to do is perform and create, her body her kinetic canvas. But, in one of the few industries where youth matters above all else, her time is coming to make decisions that no woman in her mid-thirties should have to make: is it time to retire?

As the career of one begins to explode into the stratosphere and the other's implodes after a career-ending injury that makes any retirement discussion irrelevant, Grey and Christian begin to drift apart. Changing priorities and newly built walls lead to fears and accusations, further tearing at the fabric of the love they've worked years to create.

Will cooler heads prevail to warm up the hearts of the deeply passionate couple in time to create a new dream for their second act?

Swann Song - ISBN - 978-1-952270-63-5

Christine Swann is a world-famous singer/songwriter and lesbian icon, known for her edgy style and heart-pounding songs. Gorgeous, rich and miserable. Her music has always been her life, her escape from an unimaginable childhood, and choices no thirteen-year-old should have to make.

Now, pushing thirty, she wants out. From all of it.

Willow Bowman lives in the farmhouse her beloved grandmother left her, with her husband. A pediatric nurse and small-town girl, she relishes in the safety of her marriage that keeps difficult questions at bay and keeps her life quiet and peaceful, because that makes sense to her.

Until one night when Willow is driving home and is

about to cross the old, rickety Dittman Bridge not far from the farmhouse, and she sees a figure jump off into the cold waters below.

The moment she jumps in and pulls the woman dressed in leather pants out, both their lives change forever.

Keeping Hope - ISBN - 978-1-952270-78-9

Twenty-four-year-old Hope DeSilva has been released from a three-year stint in a Georgia prison. After returning to her family property in a tiny Georgia town, she decides she's had enough of the poverty, violence, and profound family dysfunction. It's time to get out on her own. She buys a $400 car and heads to find work out west.

After the car breaks down in Colorado, she's given a ride into a mountain town called Wynter where she runs into brash, aggressive police officer Samantha Gains, who has not one ounce of patience or sympathy for a felon in her black-and-white world of right or wrong, good or bad.

But, running from her own family trauma and inexplicably bewitched by the young newcomer Hope, Samantha begins to realize that maybe her strict worldview isn't as simple as it seems. When a freak accident brings the two women together, it will take both of them letting go of their pasts to truly move on.

Take another trip to Wynter and revisit old friends as they work their magic to help Hope and Samantha find their footing—and ultimately bring them home.

Other Sapphire books from Sapphire Authors

The Serenity Nearby – ISBN – 978-1-952270-65-9

Veronica Hockmeier's relationship with her girlfriend/ PhD supervisor is on the rocks. A graduate student has died by suicide in her English Department. And her eating disorder has returned with a vengeance. All Veronica wants to do is get out of town for a weekend, and when her paper is accepted at an academic conference on Emily Dickinson, in Dickinson's hometown of Amherst, Massachusetts, Veronica takes this as a good sign.

On the way there, she is greeted with calamity after calamity: an accident on the road, a person from her past, and what appears to be the ghost of a graduate student in her hotel room. When a friendly hotel worker named Bo Wu shows her some kindness, Veronica can't help but fall for the tall woman with a winning smile—even if she does have a creepy collection of items dead patrons have left behind.

When Veronica's passport goes missing and another body turns up at the hotel, she becomes trapped in a nightmare she can't escape from—not without Bo's help.

Thundering Pines – ISBN – 978-1-952270-58-1

Returning to her hometown was the last thing Brianna Goodwin wanted to do. She and her mom had left Flower Hills under a cloud of secrecy and shame when she was ten years old. Her life is different now. She has a high-powered career, a beautiful girlfriend, and a trendy life in Chicago.

Upon her estranged father's death, she reluctantly agrees to attend the reading of his will. It should be simple—settle his estate and return to her life in the city—but nothing has ever been simple when it comes to Donald Goodwin.

Dani Thorton, the down-to-earth manager of Thundering Pines, is confused when she's asked to attend the reading of the will of her longtime employer. She fears that her simple, although secluded life will be interrupted by the stylish daughter who breezes into town.

When a bombshell is revealed at the meeting, two women seemingly so different are thrust together. Maybe they'll discover they have more in common than they think.

Diva – ISBN – 978-1-952270-10-9

What if…you were offered a part-time job as the personal assistant to someone you have idolized for years? Meg Ellis has just completed the school year as a nurse in the Santa Fe school system. It isn't her first choice of profession, but a medical problem derailed her musical career years ago. The breakup of a bad relationship is still painful. The loving support from her close-knit family and good friends has buoyed her spirits, but longing still lurks below the surface. She can't forget the intoxicating allure of the beautiful diva who haunts her dreams.

Nicole Bernard is a rising star in the world of opera, adored by fans around the globe. When Meg learns that Nicole is headlining a new production at the renowned New Mexico outdoor pavilion—and then is asked to accept a job offer to be her personal assistant—she is beside herself. After a short time learning the routine and reining in her hormones, Meg discovers that Nicole's family will be visiting for the opening. Her responsibility to the charismatic singer immediately becomes more difficult when Nicole's young husband Mario shows up and threatens the comfortable rapport between Meg and the prima donna.

The two women brace for a roller-coaster interlude composed by fate. Will the warm days and cool nights, the breathtaking scenery, and the romance of the music create summer love? A heartbreaking game? Or something very special?